C000205748

'A love   ┌ ┘┘┴
with a touch of Peaky Blinders.'
SE Moorhead, Author of Witness X

'A thoroughly enjoyable debut.'
Catherine Fearns, Author of the Reprobation Series

'A truly British and Irish thriller.'
Readers' Favourite, Reviewer

'I was hooked from the first chapter.'
Readers' Favourite, Reviewer

JACK BYRNE was born and raised in Speke, Liverpool to an Irish immigrant father and grandparents. *Under the Bridge* is his debut novel and follows reporter Anne and student Vinny around Merseyside, as they become involved in a story of unions, crime, and police corruption after human remains are discovered at a construction site.

Follow Jack on Twitter @Jackbyrnewriter
And find him on www.jackbyrne.home.blog

UNDER THE BRIDGE

A LIVERPOOL MYSTERY

JACK BYRNE

Northodox Press Ltd
Maiden Greve, Malton,
North Yorkshire, YO17 7BE

This edition 2021

1
First published in Great Britain by
Northodox Press Ltd 2020

ISBN: 978-1-8383430-0-2

This book is set in Bembo Std

For Agnes, Rita and Peter;
Vinny McInerney, Tommy Healey,
and Bob Pennington

2004

Chapter One

Michael

The bone poked out of the mud and into Michael's life.

'Whoa, stop, stop!' Michael, the site caretaker, waved his hands above his head and shouted over the grinding diesel engine.

The digger emptied its load on a growing mound of damp earth, a strip of blue tarpaulin hanging from its scoop. The bone disappeared, reburied immediately. But Michael knew he had seen it and started digging through the soil, his fingernails becoming clogged and his hands cold as he dug deeper.

'What's up?' The driver killed the engine and climbed down from the cab.

'I saw a bone.' Michael was determined to find it now.

The drizzle came in waves, sweeping in from the Mersey and across the building site, leaving dew drops on everything it touched.

The foreman shouted, 'Why you stop?'

'Paddy 'ere reckons he saw summat,' said the JCB driver.

'Michael, what you see? Why you stopping job?' Istvan turned to the driver. 'Get back on machine.'

Michael's fingers dug through the congealing mud to reveal a hard, brown shape. 'Here it is.'

'Fucking dog bone. Get back to work.'

Michael ignored him and pulled the earth aside to reveal a

long shaft. 'This is no dog bone - this is a man's.' He looked round as other workers gathered. 'Check the trench to see what else we got down there,' he said.

'Who you think you are, CSI? You are caretaker - get back in shed.'

The driver joined Michael. He grabbed a shovel and jumped down into the shallow trench. 'Here, this is where it come from.'

He scraped away the soil as a growing band of workers watched.

Istvan was losing control of the situation. Flashes of blue appeared in the ground, and the driver bent and tugged at the plastic sheeting. Another worker joined him, and they began to prise free the plastic, pulling and tearing it.

'Careful there.' Istvan leaned forward, now as intent as everyone else.

The site was quiet as work stopped, and people gathered around. There was something there, wrapped in plastic sheeting. 'That's enough, back to work, everyone,' Istvan ordered in vain.

'Go on, lads,' Michael urged.

He wanted to see what was there. If it was human, Christ. This was Raglan Street - he knew this street. This is where the builders' yard was back in the day.

The two men in the trench climbed out. Leaning back in, they wiped away the loose soil and got a grip of the tarpaulin from each side and heaved. There was a ripping sound, and both men fell backwards as a cloud of soil exploded into the air, a mud-covered skull in its midst.

'Bingo,' shouted Michael.

Chapter Two

Vinny

Vinny reached for his phone. *Bollocks. Twenty minutes to get there.* He couldn't afford to be late, not today. Today, everything holding him back would end. A son he never saw, an average history degree, and part-time work in a crappy shoe shop, all of which had reduced his finances and his reserves of optimism to zero. His clothes were laid out: ironed jeans and a smart polo shirt. Not over-formal. He wasn't a geek. He had debated a collar and tie but rejected it. He was dressed and out in ten.

Panic and hope were two butterflies that fluttered round in Vinny's stomach as he cycled along the busy streets of Liverpool, rehearsing his lines in this audition for life. He dodged and weaved through the mid-morning traffic. Sweating, he pushed himself up the wide spare avenues of Toxteth until he reached the narrow, crowded streets around the University. He had done his preparation; he knew his arguments. He didn't want to mess this up. The building he was heading for wasn't among the lifeless concrete structures or the new steel and glass blocks. As he flew along the pavement of Hope Street, he could see his destination - the glorious red brick creation poking out behind the modern funnel-shaped Catholic cathedral.

He dismounted, patted down his wavy brown hair, and smoothed out his jeans. As he was bending to lock his bike to the street barrier, a tall, dark-skinned woman approached him.

'Can I give you a flyer?' Her accent was broad, rich, and not local.

Vinny looked into her bright eyes. She wore a multi-coloured band around the black hair that topped her slim face and sharp features.

'Sure.' He took the leaflet.

'Do you work for the University?' She was advancing, clipboard in hand.

'No.' He didn't want to get into a discussion.

'A student?'

She was persistent, he would give her that.

'No. Look. Sorry, but I've got to get inside.' He was moving away from her as he said this.

'The student union supports us,' she declared.

'I have to go.'

He didn't wait for a reply. He scanned the leaflet as he edged his way through other campaigners and took the three steps into the building. *Justice for Cleaners.* He did something he would never have done if Anne were with him. He scrunched up the leaflet and tossed it in a waste bin just inside the double doors. He checked his phone. *Bang on time.*

Vinny walked through the high arched main entrance into a wide atrium and felt the cool air on his face. The contrast between the busy street outside and the cathedral-like interior was immediate. *Wow*, he thought, *this is where I belong*. He looked up to the richly decorated ceiling rectangles of deep blue with red and gold borders. The wide-open space below had a polished floor, and blood-red ceramic tiles covered the walls up to the first-floor level. Not an easy place to clean, he realised, thinking of the "Justice for Cleaners" woman. A heavy balustrade ran round a first-floor gallery supported by columns dressed in the same deep red tiles. He scanned the room list of plastic letters and numbers on a brass stand. He found her. *Dr A Sheehan, room 4B.*

The brass nameplate shone yellow-gold with age. Tiny, almost invisible swirls indicated years of assiduous polishing. Vinny knocked lightly and waited before inching the door open. The heavy oak door swung too easily on its hinges, opening faster than he'd intended.

The first thing he saw was a crucifix. The body hung heavily with arms outstretched, sinews and muscles strained, a crown of thorns with sharp points sticking out at the world or embedded in the skull of the drooping head. Rivulets of deep red blood were streaking down the pained, angular face. *Fuck*, Vinny thought.

'Yes?' someone from within called out.

He opened the door wider. 'Sorry, Sheehan? Professor Sheehan?'

The woman behind the oak desk looked busy, distant, turning away from the computer screen to face him. 'Yes?' she said again.

'Vinny, Vincent Connolly. I have an appointment.'

'Ah, come in, Mr Connolly.' She checked her wristwatch and smiled.

Entering the room, he closed the door behind him and made his way over the carpeted floor to the chair facing the broad oak desk.

'I'm sorry, forgive me. I get so carried away at times. Is it Vincent?' she asked, pushing her glasses high on her head - they balanced precariously on her bunched-up hair.

'Yes. It's Vincent.'

He hoped the formality would equate with gravitas. He took a deep breath to try and settle himself, and sat upright, leaning slightly forward.

'So, Vincent.' She started looking through papers on her desk. 'How can I help you?'

'I raised the idea of investigating Irish immigration to the UK after the Second World War. I have the emails here.' He rifled through his bag.

'Ah, yes, that Mr Vincent Connolly. No need...' With a wave of the hand, she released him from his search. 'I remember.' She smiled, leaning back in her chair, her arms resting on the black leather.

On the shelf behind her head, he could see a number of her titles, including her most celebrated work, *The Making of Modern Identity – A History of Liverpool.*

Doctor Sheehan's voice was soft and melodic. He couldn't quite work out the accent. 'Go on. I'm listening.'

Vinny took a breath and launched into his practised spiel. 'There is a wealth of material available from the 1840s and '50s on the effects and consequences of the famine and mass emigration from Ireland. There has, however, been very little research on the scale and impact of changes since then. Everything seems to stop around World War Two. Some of the largest changes in the structure of Liverpool have been since that period: the slum clearances, the building of new housing developments on the edge of the city. This was all happening when there was a shortage of labour. This shortage was partly filled by returning troops, but it also required an influx of Irish workers.'

'Okay, that's a fair point, and although I think some people are beginning to look into this, you are correct; it's an under-researched area. Can I ask what your interest in this is? Are you Irish?'

Vinny allowed himself to relax back against the chair. 'No personal interest,' he said. 'I just think it's an area rich in potential. It's a period when a lot was going on. The city was changing, not only geographically, but culturally. It's also when the Scouse identity was being developed.'

'Connolly is an Irish name, isn't it?' she asked.

'I guess so, but I was born here,' Vinny said.

'So, you are English, Irish, and Scouse?' she asked.

Vinny thought for a moment. He had never heard it put that way before. 'Does it matter?' he asked.

'Not to me,' she replied. 'But you may find it does to you.'

Chapter Three

Anne

Anne was hunched over her keyboard, entering website subscriber details into the advertising database. A simple software fix would automatically transfer this information, but someone thought it was more useful to have a journalism graduate input the data one line at a time. She looked over the open-plan office at her colleagues, who were working hard to produce a daily city newspaper in an industry that was dying on its feet. Everyone knew sales were declining every year, and yet, here they were, like Canute trying to turn back the tide.

'Anne!' The shout came from her immediate boss, Anthony.

She was quick to respond, rising from her desk.

'Here, have a look.' Anthony was well into his forties with a receding hairline and pot-belly; he would be perfect in a chart showing the seven ages of man, just before the figure of the hunched and bald old man with a walking stick. She scanned the copy that he shoved at her.

PRESS RELEASE

Merseyside Police Press Statement. 10.06.2004
Merseyside Police were informed of what appeared to be human remains discovered during building work in Liverpool 19.
Scene of Crime Officers and forensic experts have recovered

the remains that are believed to be an adult male. They were discovered early on Monday morning and have been removed to the Merseyside Police Laboratory for further inspection.

Police are working with the construction company and the local community in an attempt to establish the identity of the individual concerned.

Further details will be announced in due course.

'Where's L19?' Like most city dwellers, Anne knew her area and the centre. Apart from this, the rest of the city had been largely unknown to her until she'd joined *The Chronicle*.

'You should know that - part of your extensive knowledge of your home city.' He grinned.

She liked Anthony and knew he liked her. 'Aha...actually, I think I do know. It's Garston.'

'Are you sure?' His swivel chair was not only swivelling but also swaying from side to side; he smiled.

'Yeah. I've been transcribing these addresses into the database all morning.' She tried not to sound too frustrated.

'You see...God's plan in all its glory...and what's the date today?'

'The 12th, isn't it?' She always had the feeling he was toying with her.

'That's right, and what happens on the 12th of July?'

Anne's face scrunched. 'Oh, bloody hell, it's the Orange Lodge.' She was mad at herself. How could he respect her if she didn't show initiative?

'Bingo. The celebration of all things Protestant and orange. Primarily William of Orange - '

'Who defeated King James in the Battle of the Boyne in 1690,' Anne added.

Anthony finished the verbal ping-pong. 'And proved beyond doubt the superiority of the men in bowler hats over the bog-trotting Irish

Catholics. We've got Phil down at Lime Street station taking photos. Can you go and get some quotes and details?'

'Phil?'

'Phil the cot, the photographer.' Anthony was smiling.

She knew he was waiting for her to ask.

'Yeah. Yeah, I'm on it.' Anne ignored the nickname.

'And do you fancy this one?' he asked, pointing to the press release in her hand.

Her heart jumped a little in excitement. 'Really?'

'Yeah, sort yourself out, get down there and see what you can find out. A hundred and fifty words for tomorrow's edition.'

'You got it.' Smiling, she turned to her desk, stopped, and asked, 'Phil the cot?'

'I knew you couldn't resist. He's got five kids.'

'Oh. Hilarious,' Anne declared.

It was a thirty-minute drive, and Anne wanted time to look around. Getting through town was easy enough. She could go along the dock road toward the south of the city. She knew the area vaguely: it was near the new airport, where they had built the out-of-town shopping park. Garston and Speke had always been places she drove through on the way out of Liverpool - always on the way to somewhere else, but never a destination in themselves. At least, not until they moved John Lennon Airport terminal and built the shopping village.

She drove past the terraced streets of the Dingle, down through the leafier and more affluent Aigburth, with its cricket ground and fake Tudor buildings, and beyond to Garston. A new bypass that skirted what was called "The Village" had been completed in the '90s. On the bypass, traffic sped by without a sideways glance at the once thriving centre of Garston. She turned onto St Mary's Road and drove into the village. A lot of the shop fronts were boarded up, streets of terraced houses running off each side. Halfway, she was shocked to see a burnt-out building. At the bottom, she turned right under the railway bridge.

Anne always knew when she was outside Liverpool 8. She was more aware. Her senses heightened, always the feeling of going back in time. Her unease increased as she drove under the bridge. She carried straight on past the red brownstone of St Michaels. A rail line ran along to her right, and she could see the embankment through the gaps in the demolished buildings. She noticed a taxi office and chip shop, the only two surviving businesses in the row of around ten buildings. An advertising hoarding between two derelict buildings announced, *"Speke Garston Partnership. Investing in our future."*

Not sure where to go next, Anne realised she was facing the docks. All this was new to her, though at school, she had been teased she had "come off the banana boats."

She parked at the kerb and walked up to the metal gates. She could see through the chain-link fencing on the right-hand side. The docks looked deserted, the grey-brown water still and murky. Old cranes and winches dotted the concrete sides. Behind them were rail tracks and metal sheds. Looking out beyond the dockside, she could see the river. It was weird for her; she knew her father had come through this dock, or one just like it further up the Mersey. It must have been strange for him entering the city - a spectre of greys and browns, metal and concrete, after the lush greens and blues of the Caribbean.

She walked along, and a few minutes later, she reached the main entrance of the site on Banks Road where a sign indicated the office. Anne lifted the unlocked padlock, released the latch, and pushed the makeshift door. It swung heavily, scratching against the ground inside. A small hut, like a garden shed, stood just inside on her left. Straight ahead, she saw a mound of earth and a couple of diggers, their arms and claws resting and their cabs empty. Over in the far corner stood a white tent with police tape stretched over metal rails stuck in the ground.

Anne slipped slightly. She looked down, realisation growing that a body had decomposed in the mud, which was now sticking to her shoes.

She poked her head into the shed on her left. The man inside looked over his newspaper.

'Hi. I'm looking for the foreman.' She checked the phone in her hand. 'Stan Fogel?'

The voice carried a familiar Irish lilt. 'I know who he is, but who wants him?' he asked as he folded his newspaper.

'Tell him it's Anne McCarthy from *The Chronicle*.'

He had a face like a prune, all shriveled up. 'Oh, right. Yeah, sure.' His facial lines decreased. 'It'll be about the bones, will it?'

'The bones?'

'Oh aye, nothing else going on here. We have to get the okay from the police before we can start again. Not too happy he isn't, yer man there. Come in,' he said. 'You've to sign in.'

Anne signed her name in the logbook, finishing with the time and date: 9.32am, 12th July 2004. Her eyes scanned the notices and warnings on the wall. 'Does all that apply to me?'

'Fraid so, love. But we've got a hi-vis and hat here. No boots, though.'

'Seriously? Boots?' she asked.

'Hold on. I'll get Stan on the radio.' He peered over the counter as he spoke through the radio crackle. 'He'll be over in a few minutes. He's on a call. McCarthy…Irish, is it?'

'Yeah, in a roundabout way. Let's say Irish via Barbados.' She smiled.

'Oh, well, it sounds warmer than Irish via Wicklow.'

Anne liked him. 'So, about these bones, then?' She pulled her notebook out of her bag. Her main fear was getting an important fact wrong. It was something that kept her awake at night.

'I'm sure the boss will want to tell you all about that,' he said, before carrying on. 'It was on Monday, the day before last. The cops have been and gone now. Didn't get anything else, just the bones. They had a couple of guys in the white suits and that, searching through the muck. But they gave up after a couple of hours. It was me that found them.'

Anne tried to look impressed. 'You found the bones?'

'Oh, aye. They were all brown and broken like, wrapped in plastic. Well, some were broke. But them scoops on those diggers are not too delicate, if you know what I mean?'

'Yeah, of course. Did you hear anyone say anything about the cause of death?'

'Oh, no.' He looked shocked. 'They wouldn't tell me a thing like that.'

He looked at the ceiling as if deep in thought for a minute and then said, 'Although I don't suppose the big fuckin' hole in the head would have done him any good.'

Anne's heart skipped a beat. 'Him? You said, "him"?'

'Yeah, well, I saw him coming out, didn't I? I knew it was a man from the off.'

'How did you know?' It was a stupid question, and she knew it.

'Ow, he was an ugly fucker all right. Those big eye holes and half his teeth missing.'

'So, it was a skeleton, not a corpse?' She tried to clarify.

'Yeah, like I said - bones - but such an ugly skull. I'm telling ya must've been a bloke. Came flying through the air, it did.'

She didn't understand his last comment and assumed she'd misheard.

'That's me.' Anne handed him her card.

He handled it with care before opening his jacket and putting it in the chest pocket of his shirt.

'And you are?' she asked.

A voice from behind her broke in. 'You don't want to know him, believe me.' It was a strong voice with a guttural accent.

Spinning around, she held out her hand. 'Anne McCarthy, *Liverpool Chronicle*.'

He ignored her hand.

The caretaker shook his paper open in a clear sign of disapproval.

'Stan? Are you Stan Fogel?' Anne asked.

'Istvan, Istvan Fogel.'

He didn't seem upset by the mispronunciation. Anne thought he was probably used to it. 'Sorry. I was told it was Stan.'

'No problem, all the time, it happens.' He nodded in the other man's direction.

Istvan indicated for her to follow. Once outside the hut, he turned to face her. He was well-built, with a rugged face, stubble, and thick eyebrows turning to grey. He wore heavy boots, jeans, a bomber jacket, and - seeming out of place - a collar and tie.

'Sorry for the old man. Just two years left, then...' He made a downward motion with his thumb.

A look of concern crossed Anne's face.

Istvan saw her reaction. 'No, I mean he's sixty-eight - he'll be retiring…not dying.'

Anne smiled, embarrassed. 'Oh, right.'

'Sorry, I can't tell anything. The police have told me not to be speaking.'

'We got a report about a body.' Anne corrected herself. 'A skeleton. Found here?' She left the question hanging in the silence a moment before she continued. 'Look, I'm not stupid. I can see the police tape; the site is empty. Come on, it doesn't take a genius to work out something is going on.'

'I'm sorry, I must say nothing. The police, you know.'

'That means the bones must be fairly recent, not from antiquity…'

'Not from where?'

'Not ancient. They must be modern. The bones,' Anne said.

'I don't know.' He produced a card. 'Here, talk to him.'

The card held the details of a Detective Sergeant David Cooper, Merseyside Police.

'Okay. Thanks.'

'Sorry, but I need ask you to leave.' He put his head back in the shed. 'Mike, you make sure the lady leaves.'

He gave her a shrug, turned, and walked off toward a Portakabin directly behind the shed.

'Look on the bright side,' said Mike, appearing next to her.

'And what's that?' asked Anne.

'You won't be needing those boots now, will ya?' His broad smile showed missing teeth.

Anne slipped her notebook back into her bag and walked to the badly hung gate, opening it. She stepped outside. Michael turned, about to head back.

'Mike, isn't it?' she asked.

He turned round. 'It is. Michael. M-I-C-H-A-E-L, in case you want to write it down.'

She didn't make a note of it. 'Would you let a young woman buy you a pint?'

Michael smiled. 'Ooh, now, that's an idea.'

Chapter Four

Vinny

After his meeting, Vinny walked his bike into town, not trusting himself to negotiate the traffic when his head was full of ideas. A smile broke his look of concentration as he punched the air with an audible, 'Yes!' A woman in her fifties, who was approaching him on the pavement, glowered at him.

His phone vibrated in his pocket. He pulled it out to read the text message from Anne: *Wer r u? In Vs.*

He couldn't wait to tell Anne. Jumping on his bike, he took Brownlow Hill straight down. At the crossroads with Renshaw Street was the statue known locally as Dicky Lewis, a classical nude figure above the main doors of Lewis's, Liverpool's version of Harrods department store. Instead of heading down Ranelagh Street, which would be his normal route, he turned right and cycled along the pavement, past the Adelphi Hotel. This once-grand, now somewhat dilapidated Portland stone structure was built to house first-class passengers on the White Star Line, with liners such as the *RMS Titanic* and *HMHS Britannic*, both of which came to tragic ends.

Vinny heard music and some commotion coming from the direction of Lime Street train station. As he got closer, he could see the flashes of orange and hear the beat of drums. *Shit, it must be the 12th.*

Various Orange Lodge bands had organised themselves

on the steps of Lime Street station and were pounding out their tunes. He felt a chill as he manoeuvred his bike across the busy road. Liverpool was home to The Orange Order in the UK, and the Protestant Party had local councillors right up to the mid-1970s. After the invasion of Iraq, the rest of the country might have moved on in its religious conflict with the burgeoning Christian-Islam divide. In Liverpool, a more traditional Catholic-Protestant divide, though not as deep as it had once been, was never far from the surface. A few people smiled and clapped in appreciation of the music. Parade members in sashes and uniforms streamed from all directions. Loyal Orange Order Lodges from all over Liverpool met to board their train to Southport for the annual July 12th parade. Vinny saw commuters coming out of the station and changing route to avoid close contact with the marchers.

Vinny cycled down through the gyratory, a long, curved bus stop that led down from St George's Hall. At the bottom, he turned right and went through Mathew Street, home to the Cavern and The Beatles, and left into the commercial part of the city.

The Vaults was just behind India Buildings. At one time, it was a cellar, maybe even a wine vault. It had an arched, brick-built ceiling spanning around five metres. Vinny locked his bike to the cast-iron gate at the head of the steps. It didn't matter what time of the day or night it was, it always felt right being there. It was cosy, and it felt like "pub time," as if it had its mooring in the space-time continuum - a place that never closed, with the constant sound of pool balls clicking and crap music.

Anne was nursing a half-pint, sitting opposite the door. He was pleased to see her. Vinny was constantly surprised he had a friend as pretty as Anne, with her shoulder-length black hair usually worn up, olive skin, and big grey-green eyes. When Anne dressed, she did her best to look smart, but somehow, she never quite managed it. Today, she wore black trousers and a white shirt topped with a grey-pink flecked jumper. She was in her mid-twenties, but her clear complexion made her look younger. She was his first female friend in a while. He was estranged from Helen and their son Charlie. It wasn't painful but there was deep knowledge that one day he would have to fix it.

'Hey.' Anne smiled, her fingers tapping to the music.

Vinny crossed the bar, his feet sticking to the carpet. The jukebox was playing a '70s ballad.

'Who's that?' He gave her a chance to display her knowledge.

She rolled her eyes. 'Elkie Brooks, Pearl's a Singer.'

'Christ, you know some shit, don't you?'

'What do you mean, "shit"? This is a classic.' She smiled.

'Did you see the Lodge in town?' he asked.

'They've been arriving all morning. I've just got back from Lime Street. We've got a photographer going along with them.'

'What were you doing there?'

'Just background, a few quotes.' She read from her notebook. '"It's a family day out," said Margaret from Tuebrook. "A lovely tradition" - that's from Angela, Park Road.'

'I'm surprised no one said, "It's a celebration of community,"' Vinny added sarcastically.

'Well, now you mention it…I keep forgetting you're Catholic.'

'No, get it right,' he said, sitting down. 'Brought up as one, but it doesn't mean anything to me now.'

'Anyway, I don't mind it. The Lodge, I mean.' Anne was finishing her drink. 'I remember seeing the parade march through Toxteth, lots of noise and colour.'

'Me neither, though there is something odd about it.' Vinny knew the history but had never connected it to himself.

'What do you mean?'

'You get them celebrating their victory, rubbing people's noses in it, but what about the other side?'

'Your side?'

'No, not mine. I didn't mean that. I meant the losers.'

'Yeah, exactly.' She smiled. 'Your side…Anyway, you having a pint?' Anne started to get up.

Vinny held his hand up, palm facing her. 'Yeah, but I'm buying.'

She sat back down. 'What's the occasion?'

'I'll tell you when I'm back. Another of those?'

'If you're buying. A pint,' Anne said.

Vinny returned with two pints of lager.

'What's the celebration?' Anne asked, taking off her short black jacket and unwinding the keffiyeh from around her neck.

'I think I've gone and swung a Master's place at Uni.' Vinny was smiling.

'Where?' Anne looked surprised. 'Liverpool?'

'The first "Red Brick University."'

'Where's that?' Anne asked.

'The building I just had my meeting in. The Victoria Building. It really is amazing.'

'Wow, well done.'

'Yeah. I have to work out the details and do a proposal, but as long as I don't mess that part up, then, yeah, I should be in.'

'How and when did this happen?' She lifted her pint and began ripping pieces off her beer mat.

'This morning. I've been emailing Angela Sheehan at the Uni for a while.'

'*The* Professor Sheehan? The one who has done all the stuff on Liverpool?'

'Yeah, the same.'

'And you know her?'

'Long story, but she's kind of the "go-to" person in academia on Liverpool. She's led this whole urban heritage renaissance. Well, if not led, at least given it intellectual coherence.'

'Okay, you're losing me now.' Anne smiled.

'She's built this whole thing, turning Liverpool's history into a marketable commodity. To be fair, it's worked. Liverpool is all about The Beatles and Football.'

'So, it's all good, then?'

'I don't know. There's this perception of Liverpool as a melting pot of cultures.'

'Actually, that's quite funny.'

'How?' he asked.

'Well, a melting pot of cultures, producing a stew. Duh - Scouse being the stew.'

'Yeah, I get it. A bit lame, but yeah, 'lobscouse' was the Scandinavian name for the stew sailors ate.'

'Yup.' Anne looked proud of herself. 'Anyway, I don't see what the problem is.'

'Nah, I'll be happy to get this place, a bursary for living expenses, Ph.D., become a professor. Pack in my shitty job, get married, and have a couple of middle-class kids called Nigel and Sarah and die completely bored and unfulfilled, but smug.' His sarcasm carried him through the guilt he felt for an unacknowledged son.

'And ride a unicorn to work every day until it gets hit by a double-decker bus, of course, and the road is covered with unicorn blood and guts.'

Anne collected up the bits from her beer mat into a tidy pile.

'Yeah, something like that,' Vinny said.

'But anyway, well done getting the place. Just promise me you'll let yourself do it.'

'What do you mean?' Vinny gave her a quizzical look.

'Don't sabotage yourself. You can be your own worst enemy sometimes. You get all miserable and down. You know you can talk to me if you need to.' She paused. 'Sorry, didn't mean to piss on your parade.'

Vinny waved his hand. 'Whatever.'

She tried to lighten the tone again, 'But, I'm really chuffed about it.'

Vinny moved his stool back a little and crossed his legs. She thought he would fuck it up, that's what she meant.

'And here's me thinking I had all the news.' Anne changed the subject.

'What's up, then?'

'Well, you know, I've been moaning about cats up trees and sports days.'

'Yeah, and centenarian parties,' Vinny said.

'Tell me about it! If I never see another telegram from the Queen…Anyway, finally got to do something that might be interesting.'

'What?'

'It's in Garston,' Anne said. 'They're building some new houses, and a digger pulled up some bones.'

'Human?'

'Apparently.'

'How do you know?'

'I was down there this morning. The police have already issued a statement. My boss says I can look into it.'

'So, you finally get your own story?'

'Yeah, possibly. Who knows how it will turn out, but it might be good. At least I've finally got something real.' She leaned over the table. 'But, the thing is, the caretaker - a guy called Michael - said the skull had a hole in it.'

'I can see it now, on the bookshelves: Anne McCarthy, *True Crime: The Liverpool Mystery.*'

Anne smiled. 'Must admit, it has a good ring to it.'

Vinny's brow furrowed. 'Did you say Garston?'

'Yeah.'

'Whereabouts, exactly?' Vinny asked.

'Off Banks Road. There's a new housing development. Why? Do you know it?'

'Under the Bridge,' said Vinny.

'Hang on, I thought you were from Speke?'

'I am, but all my family came through Garston.'

'Oh, I didn't know that.'

'Not exactly Mudmen. But yeah, under the bridge.'

'What?' Anne looked confused. 'Wait, wait -' She interrupted herself. 'Do you know it?' The opening bars of a new song had just started.

'Shit, I should, I mean, I do.' He sang along with the rhythm, 'Da-da dada dada...da-da dada dada.'

'Blockhead,' said Anne.

Vinny laughed. 'Yeah, of course. Ian Dury.'

Anne was smiling. He enjoyed the sparkle in her eyes. 'And...' they announced together, 'The Blockheads!'

'Jeez, do they have nothing after 1980 in here?' Vinny asked.

'You know what, they don't. That's partly why I come here.' Anne checked her phone.

'What time are you due back?'

'After this,' Anne said, raising her glass. 'But first, what was that *Under the Bridge*, and the...what was it, *Mudman?*'

Vinny put his drink down. 'If you go down through Garston Village, not over the bypass, but through the old, actual village, St Mary's Road -'

'Yeah.' Anne was trying to follow a mental map.

'You turn right at the bottom of the hill, go under the railway bridge.'

'Yeah, I'm with you.'

'Well, it's just that anywhere that side of Garston behind the docks is called "Under the Bridge."'

'Window Lane? It was along there.'

'Anyone born and brought up round there supposed to be called Mudmen. Probably 'cos the river goes out and everything down there is full of mud.'

'"Death of a Mudman." That could be my headline.' She smiled.

'Or book title?'

'Let's not get ahead of ourselves, eh?'

'If it ever does get printed, you owe me a pint for the headline. And…maybe it was a woman?'

'Well, I'm told the skull was so ugly it must've been a man.'

'I didn't know you could have pretty skulls.'

'Me neither.' She took a long drink of her pint. 'I'd better be going. Do you want to finish this?'

'Does a bear shit in the woods?' Vinny asked.

'Okay, look, since you're the local, can you do me a favour?'

'Depends.'

'I promised to buy the old guy from the site a pint. Can you be my chaperone?'

'Chaperone or shotgun?'

'He's harmless.' Anne was collecting her things. 'I've got to go. I'll text you later.'

Vinny watched her leave. Then he moved to sit in the seat she had just left. It felt like things were finally going right.

Chapter Five

Vinny

Anne was surprised; after driving through Garston village, past the old terminal, there was nothing. On one side, the airport runway was set back from the road; all she could see was the steel fence, and on the other side, demolished or closed factories. There was a faded sign for The Metal Box on a huge empty site. It was a sign of the times - the factory was closed, but there was a poster for a Westlife tribute band in the social club.

Her phone buzzed, and she pulled it out of the bag on the seat next to her. It was her mum. She decided to call back later.

Anne turned right off Speke Boulevard. She had done her homework, read the Wiki links. If she carried on through the lights, she would be outside of Liverpool in minutes. Ahead, about a mile, was Ford's Halewood Plant. The wide Western Avenue with neat ex-council semis on either side of the road surprised her. There was little sign of the poverty she was expecting. She had seen areas far worse in her travels around Liverpool. Circling the new shopping development, she quickly found the police station.

Squat and quiet, it sat on a corner. Parking opposite, Anne approached the double doors. She pulled the handle, but the door was locked. She pressed the buzzer, and, looking up, smiled into the camera. The door sprung open, and she entered. A counter-to-ceiling, toughened glass screen separated her from the uniformed officer behind it.

'Good morning,' she offered.

The officer rifled through paperwork in front of him, ignoring her for the moment. Anne stepped back a little from the counter. She wasn't sure if he was rude or if she hadn't been assertive enough. He lifted his head. 'How can I help you?'

'Anne. Anne McCarthy.' She placed her card in the stainless-steel drawer in the centre of the counter. He pulled the drawer to his side of the screen and examined it. She felt a flutter of nerves as he checked her card and then looked her over.

'I'm here to see Detective Sergeant David Cooper,' she said with a smile.

'Okay, one minute.' He nodded and retreated through the door behind him.

She was alone in the reception area. She scanned the notices of neighbourhood watch schemes and home protection. The place gave her the chills.

A door to her left opened, and a plainclothes officer stepped out. Holding the door with one hand, he extended the other. 'DS Dave Cooper.'

Anne shook his hand. She could feel his strength and the weakness of her own grip. She guessed he was in his early thirties. He was well-built without being muscular and had a friendly face. The big smile was not what she had expected. His body language and expression were open. She began to relax a little.

'Please.' He indicated for her to enter the side room.

She edged past him and took a seat. The room was bare. Four plastic chairs surrounded a worn, scratched, and graffitied plastic-topped table. She noticed it was bolted to the floor.

'So, Anne, nice to meet you. What can we do for you?'

He was doing his best to charm her, and she was surprised by her reaction - it was working.

She quickly pulled out her notebook.

'It's about the discovery of human remains in Garston.' She was trying to sound formal and confident.

He held up a hand. 'Look, I'm happy to tell you what we know, but do me a favour?' He nodded toward the notebook. 'I'll give you a run-down, and then if you like, we can make things official.'

Anne nodded, not sure what else to do, and closed the notepad.

'Okay, this is just for you.' He smiled.

Anne stopped a smile of her own forming.

He continued. 'I assume you've seen the press release? I can get a copy for you if you'd like?'

'No, it's okay, thanks. I have that. I was looking for background or any lines of inquiry you have?'

'Pretty straightforward, really. There are procedures for situations like this. We kind of follow the playbook, if you know what I mean.'

'Yeah, of course, I was just wondering if you could shed a bit of light on it.' She paused. 'Do you have any idea how long we are talking about?' She kept the question about the condition of the skull to herself for now.

'Well, it's not recent - that we do know. We are waiting for a full report, but to be honest, from the state of the remains, we are talking decades, not just years.'

'Okay, that's a start, I guess. Decades, but not centuries?' she asked.

'Yeah, according to the forensic guys, they can tell by the rate of decomposition - no flesh, for example - but there were some material remains, which would indicate it is what we would call modern.'

'You mean the plastic?' she asked.

He looked surprised. 'That wasn't in the press release.' His tone made it sound like a question.

'That's correct,' Anne said.

'So, can I ask how you know?' He looked troubled.

'I'm a reporter.' She felt good saying it.

'Okay, well.' He looked at her card again. 'Anne, I'm impressed.'

'So modern and male?' she asked. She was trying to sound clinical and precise.

'Yeah, definitely. Male, adult male.'

'Any age on that? Are we talking twenty, forty, sixty?'

'Good question. Like I say, we will know more later, but from what I've heard, adult but not yet middle-aged.'

'Cause of death?'

'That is still under investigation.'

Anne noticed a tightening of the muscles around his mouth and neck. 'So, were there any signs of injury that might have caused death?'

'I'm afraid I have given you all we can at the moment.' DS Cooper's tone had changed.

Anne felt the shift in the dynamic and pressed ahead. 'So, if I were to report that eyewitnesses had seen significant damage to the skull?' She held his gaze and could see his discomfort growing.

'Is that what you are reporting?' he asked, eyes widening.

'At the moment, no.'

'That's good. We should be working together on this.'

She felt nervous but was enjoying the sense of control. 'What can you tell me?'

'This is not official, but blunt force trauma to the skull.'

Her eyes narrowed. 'That information hasn't been released yet, has it?'

'Like I said, this is just for you.' He smiled and held her gaze.

A little embarrassed, she diverted her gaze to the closed notebook on the table.

'We need time to make inquiries, and we haven't finished the forensic pathology yet.'

Raising her eyes again, she asked. 'So, what happens now?'

'We go through the motions, 'misper' reports, a press appeal, not much more we can do except wait for the report.' There was a pause before DS Cooper continued. 'You're new, aren't you?'

'What do you mean?' she asked.

'Well, in the past, I dealt with an older guy - bit of a pain in the arse, to tell you the truth.'

'Yeah, well, let's just say he's humouring me.' She changed the subject. 'So how come you've got it, not someone in Garston?'

'There's nothing in Garston anymore. They've got a part-time station in Heald Street, but that will be gone soon. We get all the Garston stuff now.' He looked at her. 'The thing is, the police couldn't leave Speke, even with us here - it's like the Wild West. There are 25,000 people in Speke. No jobs, no real facilities, even the pubs are going one by one.'

'Why?' Anne asked.

DS Cooper shrugged. 'Who knows. There's fuck all here. Running a pub in this place, you've got to be on your toes, keep in with a few families, turn a blind eye. It's just not worth it. If the punters don't get them, we do, or the council. We get them for allowing dealing or running an unruly house. It's not their fault, but in truth, it just makes it worse.' He shook his head. 'Hiding to nothing, really.'

'What's this, a social conscience?' Anne smiled, warming to him again.

'I dunno. I do my job, lock 'em up when we catch 'em, but it's everywhere. Most people here are the same as anywhere. There's a few nasty bastards right enough, excuse my language. But what can you do? No MOT or insurance on the car, fiddling the meters, insurance scams, credit cards - keeps us busy, but it's useless. The funny thing is that the real villains police themselves. We're lucky to get near it these days.'

'Wasn't there a shooting recently?' Anne asked.

'Not one, love, fairly regular…not just kids either, although there is that. Everyone knows who's who, no secret who's doing what, but we can't get near them.' DS Cooper shuddered. 'Anyway, this isn't helping you, is it?'

'I don't know. It's all background. And yes, it is helpful.'

'Here.' He peeled off his card. 'If you need more.'

Anne slipped the card and notebook into her bag. DS Cooper stood to open the door.

'Thanks for your time.' Anne extended her hand.

DS Cooper held it slightly longer than necessary. It wasn't an unpleasant feeling for her. When she glanced back, he had waited, watching until she exited through the main doors.

Outside the police station, it was eerily quiet. There was no traffic, no people on the street. Just the faint echo of music drifting through the still evening air from the pub over the road. Anne let out a breath and crossed the empty street, feeling like a reporter.

Chapter Six

Vinny

He was seized by panic, frozen to the spot. The siren was getting closer. His hands were sticky with blood. His fingers clogged together around the handle of the hammer that swung heavily in his hand. The chill evening air swirled around his head. He tried to lift his feet, but they were connected to the ground, immovable. In the half-light, he could see nothing but shapes, moving shapes. He felt as much as heard the moan reverberating through his body, a deep wail, competing with the ever-closer noise of the siren... then... light.

The sound was intermittent but persistent. Vinny heard the car horn. He grabbed his jacket and phone and went to the window to check. It was Anne. She smiled and waved at him to hurry.

'What kept you?' Anne asked as he opened the door and climbed in.

'I dozed off. You could have texted.'

'Easier to beep.'

'Not for the neighbours,' he said, buckling his seatbelt.

She pulled out into the street, moved up the gears, slowed, and turned into Catharine Street. As they moved through the lights into Princes Avenue, Vinny asked, 'Remember the pub, the Alex?'

'Yeah, I knew it. Can't say I ever went in, though.'

'It's a crime what they've done round here.'

'What are you on about?'

'The pubs and clubs, especially the clubs: The Nigerian, The Casablanca, The Gladray, The Silver Sands, the Yoruba, Stanley House…I could go on.'

'Yeah, and what's your point?'

'They're all gone, all of 'em. There used to be clubs all over here. They shut the whole lot down in the '90s, one by one they disappeared.'

'All right, there is such a thing as progress, you know.' Anne paused for a minute, concentrating on getting through the junction. 'Look, can we just do what I need now, much as I sympathise with your…obsession…depression.'

'It's got nothing to do with depression. It's true.' He played with the heating controls.

'All right, sorry. Can you leave that?'

'Has this thing got air con?'

'No, stop pressing things.' She changed the subject. 'We're going to The Dealers - do you know it?'

'Yeah, I know it.' He folded his arms.

Partway down St Mary's Road, The Dealers Arms had a grey classical exterior. Decades of petrol fumes from the once busy road had eaten into the fabric of the building, leaving a dark, oily residue on the brick surface.

Vinny and Anne entered. The furniture looked straight out of the 1950s. The carpet was soft underfoot, and the smell of stale tobacco hung in the air. The comfortable bar had two drinkers at the end near the door. Two men were a few feet apart, leaning on the bar, eyes straight ahead. As Vinny passed, he heard a deep mumbling exchanged between the two, but he didn't catch the words or the meaning, if there were any.

The barmaid appeared through an arched gap behind the bar between the snug and the long bar.

Anne volunteered. 'I'll get these.'

Vinny found a table. The shiny leather seat and wooden arm rest felt good - old, but good. The whole place had the feel of a time left behind.

Anne arrived at the table, managing three drinks: two pints, and an orange juice. 'Nice lady,' she said, putting the drinks down. 'She said Michael would be in soon. He usually stops in on his way home for a pint.'

'That his, then?' Vinny nodded to the dark pint next to his lager.

'Yeah, a half-and-half. Landlady told me. What is a half-and-half?'

'Half bitter and half mild,' Vinny answered.

'What a concoction.' Anne lifted her own lager. 'Have you been in here before?'

'Yeah, once or twice, nothing special. It's always been an old man's pub. Well, all the time I've known it.'

Radio City, the local commercial station, was playing in the background. The DJ tried to build interest in a competition. Vinny was half-listening.

'I went to see the police yesterday,' Anne said.

She had his full attention now.

'What did you do that for?' he asked.

'All this - the bones, Garston.' She opened her hands in a sign of exasperation. 'What do you think?'

'Dunno? And did you discover anything?' Vinny asked.

Anne smiled. 'A rather fetching DS Cooper, if you must know.'

'Oh, come on! You're kidding, right? No, don't tell me you've got the hots for a copper.'

'Calm down, will you…Jesus!'

'Ay up, looks like your current boyfriend is here.'

Anne pretended to scowl, then turned. Michael made his way over to the table. He looked tired and scruffy in his work gear. Wisps of silver hair strayed out from beneath his cap. When he sat, he stamped his boots, giving off a small cloud of dust. There was a shout from behind the bar. 'Michael, what've I told you? It's bad enough you coming here from work, but don't bring the pigging site with you.'

'Yeah, sorry, doll, won't happen again.' Michael waved. 'She's got a gob on, doesn't like people coming in this side in their workies.'

'I don't blame her,' said Vinny.

'Who's he, then?' Michael pointed at Vinny. 'Your chaperone.'

'You're flattering yerself,' Vinny snarked.

'Okay, now, boys,' Anne interjected. 'Let's keep it civil. Shall we move to the other room?'

'No, Molly'll be fine as long as you keep putting money over the bar.' Michael looked at Vinny.

'Sorry. Michael, this is Vinny, a friend of mine. He's from round here.' Anne made the introduction.

'Is that right, is it lad?'

'Yeah.' Vinny shrugged. 'Many moons ago.'

Michael lifted his pint. 'This for me, then?'

'Yeah, cheers.' Anne clinked glasses.

She nodded to Vinny, who raised his. 'Yeah, cheers, mate.'

'Any news from the site?' asked Anne.

'Starting work again sometime next week. The police gave the all-clear.'

'Oh, right, your boss must be happy, then.'

'Yeah, right one, he is.'

'So, Michael,' Anne asked, 'what would have been there before the site?'

'A street like all the others. They're getting rid of the old terraces, putting up these new ones.'

'Nothing else, just terraced houses?' asked Anne.

'The site covers a couple of old streets. There could have been an old bomb site that was never built on. It's going back a while. So, where you from, lad?' Michael nodded toward Vinny.

'Living in town now.'

'She said you were local?' Michael nodded toward Anne.

'Like I said, many moons ago. My mum's in Speke.'

'What's the name? I might've known your family.'

'Connolly,' said Vinny.

Michael lifted his pint. There was a pause before he responded. 'Well, not an uncommon name.' He extended a hand. 'Good to meet you.'

Vinny accepted his hand. Anne looked at Michael.

'Looks like we'll be back in business soon.' Michael turned the conversation back to Anne.

'Yeah, you've already said,' Anne replied.

'So, I have.'

'So, Mike, you've been in Garston a while?'

'Michael, it is, and yeah, come over when I was a lad.'

'To Garston?'

'Yeah, straight off the boat at the bottom of King Street.'

'When would that have been, then?' Vinny asked.

'The fifties, I guess. Long time ago now.'

'You've seen some changes,' Vinny said.

'Oh, back in the day, Garston was a busy place. You had the docks, the tannery, the bobbin, and the match works, plus you had all the stuff down the road: car factories, railways. Sure, there was money to made here right enough.'

'Easy life, then,' said Vinny.

'You're kidding, aren't you? It was good enough with your mates, and if you stuck to the right pubs, but otherwise, it could be dodgy, no mistake.'

'How?' asked Anne.

'It was a hard place, people knocking lumps out of each other. If you were in the village Friday, Saturday nights, you'd to have your wits about you, so you did. Boys would come down from The Dingle. There were dances in the swimming baths, and then you had the Protestant-Catholic stuff. It was all going on,' said Michael.

'In the sixties?' Anne asked.

'Well, yeah, but going back before that.'

'Did you work in the factories?' Vinny asked.

'Ended up in Standards for a while.'

Vinny tried to delve deeper. 'What brought you over here?'

'A long story, lad.' Michael shifted in his seat. 'But everyone was doing it. There was work here, ya see, after the war. Who do ya think built all your motorways and houses? You must be Irish yerself? With a name like Connolly.'

Vinny shook his head. 'Born here, so English.'

'I see.' Michael took a drink.

Vinny straightened up. 'What do you mean, "I see"? See what?'

'He didn't mean anything,' Anne said.

'She's right, lad. Now, why doesn't this nice lady get us another pint,' Michael suggested.

'I'm on it.' Anne stood up as Michael drained his glass.

Vinny joined her at the bar.

'Really? You're gonna listen to this old pisshead?'

Anne ordered the drinks, then turned to Vinny. 'You need to get a grip of yourself, mate.'

'What do you mean?'

'Well, you go on about history and all that, but here we've got a guy who has lived in this area for decades. He has got stories to tell, and you're bloody moaning. You can be so cynical, sarcastic.'

'Because it's bollocks, that's why. He doesn't know anything.'

'What you mean is it won't impress your University mates. Not philosophical enough.'

Vinny pulled a face. 'Funny,' he said, and walked back to the table, but Anne's words had hit home.

'So, what has she found out?' Michael asked as Vinny settled himself back at the table.

'About the old skeleton?'

Nothing yet, as far as I know.' Vinny shrugged.

'And has she been to the police?'

'She was there yesterday.'

'Any news from that side?' Michael probed.

'Not that I know of.'

Anne arrived at the table, balancing the three drinks. 'You two okay?'

Michael changed the subject. 'And what do you do? Vincent, is it?'

'I work in a shop in town, nothing very exciting.'

'Are you working tomorrow?' Anne asked.

'I was supposed to be, but Robbie cancelled it. So I'll try and get some Uni work done.'

'Why has he cancelled?'

'You know Robbie. Maybe he's got some student hottie he prefers to the oldest shoe shop worker in town.'

'He's not that bad, is he?' Anne asked.

'No, it's not just him. They can cancel your hours and call you in any time they like. It's crazy.'

'You don't know when you're working, no regular hours, like?' Michael asked.

'There's supposed to be, but they are always changing them.' Vinny took a drink of his lager.

'Casual, day labourers. On the lump, we used to call it. No contract, cash-in-hand. It was all over on the buildings 'til the unions got in and sorted them out.'

'We've got contracts, zero hours.'

'How can you have a contract that is no hours? That doesn't make sense. Sounds like the bad old days coming back round.'

'Yeah, that's true, but don't be modest now,' Anne teased. 'Tell him what else.'

'Yeah, okay, and I'm also doing some research at the University.'

'Sounds very grand.'

'Actually, it's about the influx of Irish after the war.' He paused, then added, 'And identity, I guess.'

'Oh, so you might be studying me, as it were?'

'I'm not sure about that.' Vinny's eyes narrowed.

'So, you won't be interested in my story?'

'I am,' Anne offered.

'And how about you, young Vincent? Would you be interested? True, it is, as well.'

'Sure, go on then.' Vinny sat back.

'Well, I had a mate. His name was Pat, short for Patrick, but Pat was his name. Pat or Paddy. Now, all the jobs we had, the English fellas only ever called us Paddy. Paddy this, and Paddy that. Maybe the odd time "The Mick." Well, the foreman says, "Right, Paddy, we'll have you over here," and Pat says, "I didn't realise you knew me? Did you know my mother or father?"

'The foreman's looking confused. He says, "Look, just do what I tell you, will you, Paddy." Paddy says, "Sure I will, but how do you know my name?" The foreman says, "What's your name?" And Paddy says, "My name's Paddy." "Oh, right," the foreman says, looking even more confused. And Paddy asks, "Do you know my mate here, Mick, too?"'

Michael laughed, but neither Anne nor Vinny joined him.

'Is that why you spelled out your name?' Anne asked.

Michael said, 'Back home, they would say Mihail. Here, it's enough to get Mick.'

Michael turned as the pub door swung open, and new voices exploded into the room. A man and a woman came in, arm-in-arm, holding onto each other. Michael raised his hand in greeting.

'You know them?' Anne asked.

'Yeah. Yoyo is one of ours.'

'Yoyo?' Anne asked.

'I dunno his real name. Bollos, or something, Yoyo to us.'

The man, whose real name was Balasz, waved back. A minute later, he walked over to the table. 'Mike, when work again?'

Michael nodded. 'Soon. Hopefully next week, mate.'

Balasz smiled and gave Michael the thumbs-up. 'Need the money.'

'You found anything else?' Michael asked.

Balasz shrugged. 'It's all shit, waiting outside B&Q, men come along, we take you and you.'

'Sounds like the pen. Used to be outside the docks,' said Michael.

'Some days, okay, but mostly, not. Heavy work, shitty money. Some days nothing.'

'Well, fingers crossed for next week, eh.' Michael tried to sound encouraging.

Balasz shook his hand again and went to join his friend.

Vinny nodded at the departing figure. 'I know I shouldn't ask, but why YoYo?'

'It means good in their Polish lingo.'

'You mean Jol?' Vinny questioned.

'If you say so, mate. He told me it means good. That's all we could get out of him, ask him to do anything, and he would be like, "yo, yo." Or again, again.' Michael laughed. 'Right old game it is, and they used to say they couldn't understand us,' Michael said.

'It's not Polish; it's Hungarian. Igen is yes, and Jol means good,' Vinny explained to Anne.

'Listen to Marco Polo here. I'll take your word for it.'

Anne interrupted before Vinny took the bait. 'Anyway, what were you two on about? You looked deep in conversation.'

'The old days,' Vinny chipped in.

'I'm surprised your dad didn't tell you all this if you're from round here.'

'Nah, he wasn't around.'

'Sorry to hear that, son.'

'Don't be. I'm fine.'

At that moment, there was a shout from the bar. They turned

just in time to see Balasz's friend vomit, except "vomit" wouldn't describe the force with which the contents of her stomach were projected on and over the bar.

Various forms of 'eeew' and 'arrrgh' resounded. Balasz's face drained of colour. He stood wide-eyed and open-mouthed for a few seconds, before transforming into a whirlwind of activity. Balasz grabbed towels off the bar and began frantically wiping and consequently spreading the vomit, pushing out ever-wider circles of semi-liquid gunge.

'Jesus,' Michael said.

One of the two guys who had been mumbling their way through the last two pints stopped mumbling and clearly said, 'Dirty bitch.'

Balasz apologised as he spread the vomit.

Michael put his head down, then lifted his pint. 'Think that's it for me.'

'Are you going?' Anne asked.

'Sorry, love, but there's no point staying here now.'

A second later, the landlady appeared. She looked stunned, unable to respond adequately to the sight that greeted her.

'Out, out!' she shouted. The second "out" was half screamed, as she pointed to the door.

Balasz's friend was doubled up, clutching her mouth and stomach at the same time.

'Go on - out! - you heard her. Why don't you go back where you come from?' The second mumbler opened up.

The first man grabbed Balasz by the shoulder and pulled him toward the door.

'Go on, fuck off, you dirty bastards.'

Anne raised her voice. 'Hey, there's no need for that.'

Michael downed his pint and stood. He went over and pushed aside the mumbler, saying to Balasz, 'Come on, mate. Time to call it a night.'

Balasz, who was still carrying the wet towels with sick dripping off them, placed them on the bar. He guided his friend towards the door. Michael was behind him. The landlady disappeared again.

The two mumblers started to push and shove the whole group towards the door. 'Go on out, fuck off. We don't want you here.'

Anne took a drink, then collected her things and moved towards the group. Vinny remained seated, watching as events unfolded.

'Go on, out.'

The whole group pressed up against the door. Michael went out first, closely followed by Balasz, who held the door for his friend. One of the mumblers kicked out at Balasz. Anne stepped forward and gave the kicker a strong shove with both hands. He flew forward, banged his head on the door frame, and fell through. He landed half in and half out of the pub. Michael reached in from outside and dragged him out by the scruff of his neck. Vinny reached the group as Anne shouted, 'Michael, don't!'

She followed the scrum out the door, and Vinny joined her outside. Michael dragged the kicker along the ground. Balasz and his friend looked on, shocked.

'Apologise, you twat.' Michael spat at him.

Vinny saw the second guy on his way out. Anne noticed, too. She grabbed the door handle and held the door shut.

'Apologise,' Michael said again.

The whole group watched. Anne struggled to hold the door closed. She looked away from the face on the other side of the glass shouting at her.

'Apologise.'

'Fuck off, you bastard,' the guy responded.

Michael released his grip on him and stepped back just enough to send a full kick into his face. When the kick landed, Vinny jumped back, shocked. The force of the kick sent the man's head up and back, and he arched backwards before collapsing to the ground.

There was a flashing blue light as a police van rounded the corner from Heald Street. After he had delivered the kick, Michael turned and walked off down the road. The second mumbler pulled at the door, and Anne let go and jumped away. With a screech, the police transit van mounted the kerb. Officers jumped out from the front and back; in seconds, four officers were on the pavement.

Vinny froze as Michael walked away down the street.

'It was him, him and his mates,' the guy coming out of the pub shouted, pointing at Vinny.

The guy on the floor struggled to his feet, moans gurgled out from his bloody face. Two cops grabbed Vinny, pushing him towards the back of the van. As they did so, the second guy tried to land a punch on Vinny. Another copper grabbed him from behind and pushed him towards the van too. Attracted by the commotion and the flashing lights, drinkers came out from the other side of the bar to see what was going on. The fourth copper urged people back into the pub with arms outstretched. He started pushing people away, including Balasz and his friend.

'Come on now, the show's over, get back to your drinks.'

Vinny was shoved into the back of the police van, and the second guy was pushed in after him. The van doors closed, and the final copper moved to the front passenger door and climbed in.

Anne was left stranded. Michael had disappeared down the street. His victim was propped against the wall with drip mats held against his face to staunch the flow of blood. Anne fumbled for her car keys and raced to her car. She looked over her shoulder and saw the police van pulling off.

She got in her car and started the engine. The blue lights made it easy to follow, down through the village, over the railway bridge, on past the old airport. Anne knew where the police van was going.

'Back so soon?' DS Cooper said when he saw Anne. 'I guess you couldn't keep away.'

Though tired and anxious, Anne couldn't help the edge of excitement she felt. She hoped it didn't show in her face. They were speaking over the reception counter in Speke police station, where she had spent the past hour waiting for news of Vinny.

She sat in one of the plastic chairs against the wall facing the counter. It had been a long and fairly useless day. She hadn't uncovered any new information. This wasn't how she imagined herself as an investigative reporter, hanging around a police station after midnight, waiting for her best friend to be bailed, released, or locked up. She didn't know which, yet. She felt like a complete amateur - or worse, a fraud, and she was embarrassed in front of Dave Cooper.

DS Cooper came out. 'Well, he's lucky.'

Anne stood. 'What does that mean?'

'He's being cautioned as we speak. The desk sergeant was going to keep him 'til the morning, but if you're here, you can take him with you.'

'Thanks.' Anne smiled weakly. 'No charges, then?'

'No, it's not worth our time. Handbags at dawn stuff. They brought them in just to stop the thing developing, get everyone off the street.' After a short pause, he said, 'Can I ask what you were doing there? I'm guessing it's not your usual choice for a night out.'

Anne replied, 'Would you believe, looking for information?' She paused before saying, 'Does that sound stupid?'

'Depends, who from?'

'A guy I met at the building site, Michael Byrne.'

DS Cooper paused for a minute. 'Old guy? Was he involved in this?'

'I couldn't really see. I didn't get out the pub 'til it was all over,'

Anne lied, not sure if she was protecting Michael or her story.

'Is he from Garston, the old fella?'

'Yeah,' Anne half-mumbled.

'What happened to that determined, pushy reporter who was in here this morning? Difficult day?' he asked.

'Something like that.' Anne looked away, feeling out of her depth and useless.

'Well anyway, if it's the same guy I'm thinking of, then yeah, I know him, and you should be a bit careful.'

'Careful, why?'

'He might be an old-timer, but he's no fool. And, I would guess, he still has connections.'

'Connections to who?'

'Let's just say, I think you're getting in over your head. You should leave this stuff to us. It's our job, remember.'

Anne was too tired to answer.

'Look, if you want me to keep you up to speed, how about meeting for a drink?'

'That didn't exactly go well tonight, did it?' Anne managed a half-smile.

'Promise I won't get you arrested. But you have to promise to let us do our job.'

Before she could answer, Vinny appeared through the side door, accompanied by a uniformed officer. Vinny was pale, tired, and shaken.

'You've got my number,' Anne said to DS Cooper as she turned toward Vinny.

The uniformed officer buzzed the door, and Vinny and Anne stepped out into the night.

'What a crazy old bastard that Michael is. Come, let's get out of here. I don't like Speke.' Vinny said.

★★★

Michael slumped on his sofa, alone. The TV was on, but he wasn't really watching. His head nodded forward as he dropped into sleep.

1955

Chapter Seven

Michael

Michael turned the truck into King Street. The night was dark and wet, and the headlights bounced off the cobbles. Once on King Street, he slowed, his eyes straining to see through the dark and the rain to Garston dock gates at the end of the street. It wasn't far, no more than three or four hundred yards. Terraced houses ran the length of the street on the left, doors closed against the weather with the warmth of electric lights breaking through the curtained windows. On the right, the buildings were less regular, and at least three different pubs were interspersed along the road, casting a glow through large windows, signs flapping in the wind.

Shite. They were outside. He could just about see the shape of a group of men huddled at the side of the gates. He drove slowly. *Fast or slow?* He wasn't sure what to do. He thought there would be no one there. He hoped the gatekeepers were keeping their eyes open.

He passed the second pub on his right, The Kings Arms. Despite the wind and rain, two men were talking outside. *Okay, steady*, he thought, *keep calm*. One of the men pointed at his truck. Michael kept his eyes firmly on the road ahead. The light from the pubs was reflected on the wet cobbles, a shimmering effect that for a second looked like hot coals.

The men started walking alongside the vehicle. 'Hey, you!'

one shouted.

Michael heard the shout but ignored it. A bang on the door reverberated through the cab.

He pressed his foot on the pedal, and his speed increased. He could see the men running alongside. He passed the final pub in the row, and the street opened up a little. There was a gap in the housing, and a new row of terraces ran at forty-five degrees, ending just before the gates. Two heavy gates broke up the solid brick wall of more than a man's height. The gates looked no easier prospect than driving into the wall itself.

Fuck...this is it.

Michael floored the pedal. The tyres slipped on the wet road, then gained traction, and his speed increased rapidly. He left the men behind now, and as he sped forward, he could see the group by the gates. He pressed hard on the horn. The road ahead was full of moving bodies. Twenty feet away, men spread themselves across the road. The gates were still firmly closed. He pressed the horn again this time, keeping his hand firmly down.

Shiiiite.

With horn blaring, his speed picked up, and he couldn't have stopped if he wanted to. He half-closed his eyes. He didn't want to see - he was hurtling toward both the men and the gate. At the last moment, the men dived and jumped clear. He expected to hit the gate, but it swung free, flying backwards. Two coppers were pulling it open from the inside. He swept in the opening, the left corner of his cab catching the edge of the gate. One of the coppers went flying backwards.

He was in the yard. He slammed his brakes on and came to a screeching halt. He had made it.

Seconds later, his door was yanked open, and a striker reached in, trying to pull him out.

More coppers came running around his truck from the left, truncheons drawn. More of the men from outside had run through the open gate after him. He looked at the face of the man pulling him out of the cab.

'You bastard!' the man shouted, clutching at his jacket.

There was a dull thud as a baton whacked the man's head; his cap stayed on, but blood trickled down from under it as he was dragged backwards, still shouting at Michael, 'Bastard!'

Michael turned his ignition and lights off and jumped out onto the wet, slimy cobbles. The police were pushing the strikers back out of the gate. Beyond them, he could see more men coming out of the pub and running towards the gates. The air was thick with shouts and threats. The gate was slammed shut and bars lowered to secure it.

Walking over to the brick-built gate and tally house, he was pulled around sharply by a hand on his shoulder. A fist whacked into the side of his head. He stumbled sideways and slipped on the cobbles, crashing to the ground. 'Fuck.'

'Don't you ever try anything like that again.' A sergeant was standing over him. He looked as if in two minds whether to continue the beating but decided against it. Turning to walk away, he spat out, 'Fucking idiot, you could have killed someone.'

Michael was lying on his side now, his trousers and jacket soaked from where he'd landed among puddles on the ground. His head was banging, aching. He ran his hand over the side of his face, but he could feel no blood. He staggered to his feet and followed the sergeant through the door into the gatehouse.

The sergeant was taking off the cape he wore over his uniform, shaking the rain off. He hung it on a free-standing rack. Michael stood just inside the doorway. The air was warm and clammy, the light harsh from an uncovered bulb hanging from the ceiling. Smoke from the open coal fire on his right sent shimmering stains through the air. A large wooden counter stood to his left. Ahead, stacking trolleys were parked against the wall. On the wall in front was a large notice board full of handwritten notices. The central feature was the front page of the Manchester Guardian for Wednesday the 6th of April, 1955.

Prime Minister Churchill Resigns

Foreign Secretary Eden to become PM

The newspaper cutting was yellowing and looked about six months old. The rest were warnings and instructions to the dockers who would pass through here at the start and end of each shift.

Michael approached the counter sheepishly. The sergeant opened a large register, slapping down the cover as he did so. 'Right, bollocks. Do you want to explain yourself?'

Two other coppers came in behind Michael. 'It's locked again, Sarge, and they're all out.'

'Right, lad. What have you got to say for yourself?' the sergeant asked.

'I got a bit of cargo, for the Esmerelda. She's due in tomorrow.' Michael delivered his line as practised.

'Oh, have you now, and what gives you the right to come barging in here, breaking those fellas' strike?' The sergeant nodded toward the dock gate. 'And putting my men at risk?'

'I was sent by Mr Power.'

'Oh, and that's it, is it? The fuckin high and mighty Jack Power says so, does he?'

Michael didn't know what to say.

'Cat got your tongue, has it, little gobshite?' The sergeant sneered as he continued. 'Between the commie bastards out there and you fuckin' Paddies, I don't know what's worse. Scum of the fuckin earth, you are - you know that? Do you?'

One of the coppers behind him dug into Michael's back with his truncheon. 'Shall we turf him out Sarge, let them have 'im?'

'That would be proper fuckin' justice now, wouldn't it, eh?' the sergeant said. 'What do you reckon to that? Shall we let those men have you for breakfast?'

Michael started, 'Mr Power said Sergeant Barlow-'

The sergeant swung his open palm, swiftly slapping him across the face. 'Enough outta you.'

He turned his attention to the register, his finger moving slowly down the left-hand column and stopped.

His cheek stinging, Michael straightened, and although it was upside down, he could see the entry.

'11.09.1955 Stalybridge Dock M.V. Esmeralda Flagged Eire 139.6 ft by 23 ft out of Arklow. Tonnage 244 gross, 124 net. 330 dwt.'

'Put him in shed number three,' the sergeant said. 'With the lumber, truck 'n' all. Get the box off. Wait 'til just before light, then send this toe-rag on his way. If he's lucky, they will have given up for the night outside. If not, tough shit.'

Michael reversed slowly, the rain making it difficult to see anything. He parked in a dockside shed, and one of the coppers guided him back.

'Right, right, that'll do,' the copper said.

Michael stopped, turned the engine off, and jumped out of the cab. He unhitched the tailgate, allowing it to fall, then jumped onto the back. The wooden crate had iron handles on either side, and Michael dragged it toward the edge. 'Here, give us a hand, will ya. I can't get down by meself.'

The copper moved over, reached up, and grabbed the handle on the other side, and they began to heave the box, Michael pushing and the copper pulling.

'Jesus, what have you got in there?'

'Not my business,' said Michael.

The sun was up when Michael parked the truck. Facing him was the Palatine, a corner public house. Instead of going through the double doors at the front of the pub, he walked around the building through the alleyway to the backyard. Passing through the piles of crates and empty beer kegs, he rapped on the glass of the back door. Mrs Power, a thick-set woman, opened the door. Her hair was covered by a faded patterned scarf knotted on top, and she wore a pinnie over a floral-patterned dress with short sleeves, exposing her thick arms. 'Come on, get in here,' she instructed.

A gruff, rasping voice rang out behind her. 'Shut that door, will ya, mother.'

Two men sat on either side of the table. The older one, Jack, had short dark hair swept back with Brilliantine. Thin, sharp features dominated his face. 'Any trouble?' he asked.

'You know they've got a strike on?' Michael replied.

The younger man, Charlie, chipped in, 'Yeah, the guys are all het up about it.'

Jack asked, 'But you got through?'

Mike shrugged. 'Yeah.'

'Okay, come on in, then. Do him a tea, will you, mother?'

The woman collected a cup from a hook on the sidewall. Although old and heavy-set, she moved with ease around the small kitchen, reaching out for the cup with one hand, while the other picked up a pot from the stove. Michael edged past her.

'What the fuck's up with them now?' Jack asked.

'Will you cut the language,' Mrs Power said, breaking her usual silence.

Jack uttered the only apology Michael would ever hear from him. 'Sorry, Ma.'

'Recognition,' Charlie offered.

'Recog what?'

'Recognition,' Charlie repeated.

'What's that when it's at home?'

'It's the Blue Union, isn't it,' Charlie explained.

Jack looked directly at Michael. 'Never mind all that. Was the parcel delivered?'

Michael nodded his thanks as a cup of tea was placed in front of him. 'Yeah, it was.'

'Okay, get yerself some brekkie,' Jack said. 'Then have a kip. Well done, lad.'

Michael woke in the late afternoon the next day. The room was cold and gloomy. No fire had been set, and the curtains were closed. He pulled the blanket tighter around his clothed body. Closing his eyes, the snug feel of the cover took him back to the shared bed in Wicklow. Huddled with his brother Jim was the place he had felt most secure, being next to the smell and heat of another living, breathing body. Almost as soon as he remembered this feeling, the shock of its opposite came crashing through his consciousness - cold, dark, pushed and pulled about in swirling waters. Deeper and deeper he went, his chest hurting, almost bursting, his eyes straining, arms pulling at the water trying to drive himself lower and lower. The line for crab baskets had snagged, and it was his job to get down there and free it.

Unsettled by the images, Michael roused himself. Sitting upright, he lifted the corner of the threadbare curtain. *It must be about seven*, he thought. He could see the glow of the setting sun disappearing behind the roof of the hospital. He stood, letting the curtain fall back into place. Picking up his heavy coat, he slid his feet into his boots. His throat was dry now, and awake, he felt the chill of the unheated room. He listened, but couldn't hear anything from the landing outside, which was a good sign.

Michael went down the stairs into the kitchen. The warmth from the range reached out across the room.

'Any chance of a cuppa?' he asked.

'Sit yourself down, lad.'

When her son Jack was around, she rarely spoke. Michael didn't recognise the accent immediately. Or rather, he knew it was Irish, and from the country. It had a warmth and a drawl that city accents didn't have time for.

'Thanks, Mrs Power.'

'You've not been over long?' She swung the knife expertly, chopping vegetables for a stew.

'Couple of days,' Michael replied.

'What brought you?' she asked.

'Aah, you know.'

'I do indeed, lad. You won't be the first fella passing through these doors. And Wicklow, was it? And how old will you be?' she asked, throwing him a look.

'It was. Nineteen.'

'We're Rathnew ourselves. There's plenty round here from town and county.' She paused as if in thought. 'Well, I'm sure your ma will be praying for you.'

'Is Jack about?'

'No, lad. He's off doing his devilment, I'd be sure of that.'

Mrs Power turned away from her chopping, and, wiping her hands on a tea towel that was tucked in the waist of her pinnie, she sat down heavily. She finished wiping her hands, and slowly smoothed out the tea towel in front of her, precisely folding it lengthwise in half before threading it back through the ties that held her pinafore.

'You seem like a good lad, and God knows it's hard to find a crust, we all know that, and whatever it was that made you leave your folks and your home, you don't need to do this here, lad.'

'Do what, Mrs Power?' Michael asked.

'God forgive you, son, you might be green, but you're no cabbage. I'm doing for your ma what I wish someone did for my lad. There's real work here, son. Go on and do yerself a favour. At nineteen now you should be making a man of yerself.'

Michael gulped his tea. Mrs Power stood, turned her back to Michael, and resumed chopping vegetables. It was a hint for him to leave. He walked through from the back kitchen, opening the door that led behind the bar. The barman was cleaning glasses, drying them off and stacking them below the counter. Michael looked around. There was a piano on the left, its lid closed. The tiled floor was swept and clean. The room was airy and open, a large space that seemed too large with the few early evening drinkers. The smoke trails from cigarettes and pipes rose as from funnels on a busy river. Friday and Saturday the place paid the rent; during the week it paid the barman.

Jack was in a corner, sitting centre stage surrounded by younger men. A few of the other tables were populated with working men, caps and thick coats set against the miserable autumn weather.

Jack waved Michael over. 'Come on, lad, over here. Give the man a pint, will you.' He directed the latter to the barman who immediately pulled a dark frothy pint. Glass in hand, Michael walked over to the table.

'Move over, give the lad a seat.' Jack motioned to the other men. 'Okay, everyone. This here is Michael.' And for Michael's benefit, 'And here we've got Charlie, Joe, and Paddy.'

The men gave various nods and winks of acknowledgment.

'Michael's one of our own, and so you welcome him and treat him as a brother.' Jack raised his drink.

'To Michael.' The men raised their glasses.

It was Michael's turn to nod and smile. After this ceremonial welcome, he was largely forgotten as attention turned to Jack, who was the centre of this particular vortex, pulling the swirling streams of conversations towards himself.

Jack turned to Michael once again. 'Did you have any trouble from the coppers?'

'The sergeant didn't seem too happy,' he replied.

'That greedy bastard is paid well enough to keep his eyes closed and his fuckin' mouth shut. I can see he left his mark on you, boy.'

Michael raised his hand to his face. 'It's nothing.'

'Should've clocked the bastard,' Charlie suggested.

'He could've,' Jack explained with pride. 'Our boy here, our new boy, just out of the "Joy", aren't you, son?'

Michael looked uncomfortable.

'How long did you get?' Charlie asked.

'Twelve months,' Michael replied, taking a draft of beer and hoping Jack would change the subject.

'Twelve months in Dublin's finest Mountjoy jail. Assault and battery. But wait, that's not it.' Jack slapped the table. 'Who was it, son, go on, tell 'em, who did you batter?'

'Nah.'

'Come on.' Charlie nudged him.

'Don't be shy, lad,' Jack said. 'We're all family here. It was only the Guards, eh, lad?'

'It's right.' Michael nodded. He didn't want to celebrate his time inside.

'As I heard it now, two of them from Wicklow town tried to cart him off, and he sent them packing. It took four of them sent down from Dublin. Came and got him, isn't that right, lad?'

'Yeah, it's right.'

As they were celebrating this story, the door to the street on their left opened. A slim round-faced man with short jet-black hair marched in. Three men followed a few feet behind him. When he reached the table, one of the men behind him tried to pull him back by the arm. He shrugged him off.

'It's ok, Tommy.'

The man stood in front of the table and looked directly at Jack. 'You must be Mr Power.'

The group around the table went quiet, and all faces turned toward the stranger.

'Who wants to know?' Jack asked.

'Pennington, Bob Pennington.'

Jack half-smiled. 'Pennington, what kind of name is that?'

'What matters,' he replied, 'is that I am here on behalf of the National Amalgamation of Stevedores and Dockers.'

'The Blue Union,' Charlie chipped in.

'Okay, Mr Blue Union, what do you want, marching into my pub like this?'

'You had a truck break our line last night, into the dock.'

Jack pushed his shoulders back and his chest out, and stretched his arms behind his head. 'So what?'

Kevin, standing behind Pennington, pointed at Michael. 'It was him, Bob. He was driving. I saw him clear as day.'

Michael remained still. His face, although motionless, started to redden.

Pennington continued. 'Look, we've got no argument with you, Mr Power. We saw the truck outside, and it looks like this young lad was the driver.'

Jack lowered his arms, and his face sharpened as he replied, 'For the second time, so what?'

Bob took a step back. 'Mr Power, I know you are a big man in this area, and I respect you for that. But you should consider that hundreds of Garston dockworkers are now on strike, with solidarity strikes happening by many of the sixteen thousand Liverpool and Birkenhead dockers. We want the right to be organised by the union of our choice.'

Jack pulled a face as if bored.

Bob spoke, his voice remaining calm and clear, the volume rising imperceptibly, but enough so that all faces in the bar were now turned towards him. 'We have defeated the National Dock and Labour Board before today, and we have defeated Prime Minister Eden and his government.'

The men behind him murmured their approval.

'No doubt.' Bob looked round the pub. 'Many of the men here have fathers and brothers who rely on the docks to put food on the table for their families.'

The men around Jack were mostly looking down into their drinks, at the table, or anywhere except Jack. Although he was still speaking to Jack, Bob turned round to address the room.

'And make no mistake, we will win this strike.'

Jack was quiet.

Turning to face Jack, Pennington concluded, 'Finally, Mr Power, I know you want to stay a friend of the working men of Garston. So, I will expect no more midnight runs through the docks while our strike is in progress.' He kept Jack's gaze for a few seconds, turned around, and, with his supporters, left the bar as quickly as he had entered.

There was a stunned silence until Jack announced, 'Okay, the show is over. Barman, give these working men of Garston another pint on me.'

This order was greeted with relieved claps and cheers.

In a quieter voice, Jack spoke to his table. 'What kind of Protestant bastard name is Pennington?'

Chapter Eight

Tommy

Tommy was relieved to be leaving the Palatine. The five men, including Pennington, turned right and walked down towards the bridge. If they turned left, they would head out towards the leafier and more comfortable streets of Allerton and Mossley Hill, places Tommy rarely visited. Reaching the bottom of the street, they were in the centre of Garston Village. The name harked back to a time before industrialisation, when a lively brook came down from the hills of Woolton, running through the village, powering the old mill and emptying into the Mersey.

Bob led the men along the same route downhill. They continued straight ahead under the railway bridge. On the left was the church of St Michael. Behind the church were the huge circular grey storage tanks of the gasworks and at the end of King St, Garston docks.

Under the Bridge was Tommy's home turf. It was a triangle, an island. On one side: the docks, with the river Mersey curving inland. The railway tracks met the river north of the docks with hundreds of miles of tracks behind them. To the south, Liverpool airport and runway ran from the river to meet the train tracks forming the third leg of the triangle. Inside this space, closely packed terraced streets housed thousands of workers' families for the surrounding industry, the bobbin factory, the match works, the brickworks, the tannery, and the docks themselves.

'What do you think, Bob?' Tommy wasn't sure it had been a good idea to challenge Jack Power so publicly.

The men walked closely together, huddled under caps and coats in protection from the slanting rain that was blowing in off the river.

'We've done what we could. It's up to him, now.'

'We could go to the coppers,' Kevin said.

Tommy struggled to hear through the wind and rain. 'We can go to mine for a cuppa, my mam will be in bed by now.'

The group walked on until they reached Raglan Street.

'Aren't you worried?' Tommy asked, fitting his key into the latch.

Tommy lived alone with his ageing mother. His father, a merchant seaman, had died in the last weeks of the war in a support ship serving the Normandy landings.

'I'm always worried,' Bob said, smiling. 'Come on, let's get the kettle on.'

Tommy, a squat, well-built man, had been on the docks on and off since he was fourteen. He had offered the living room in Raglan Street to Bob after he had heard him speak at an outdoor meeting. There had been an appeal for accommodation for Bob while he worked on behalf of the Blue Union. Tommy was quick to volunteer his mum's parlour.

He remembered listening to Bob's speech that day - how it had opened up the world for him. He was no longer just "under the bridge," where local men spent most of their lives working twelve-hour shifts on the docks or the railway, a few pints on a Friday or Saturday night in a local pub. These dark, narrow streets were all they knew of the world. Tommy's world had always been broader. It had been brought to life by the stories of his dad: voyages to Cape Town, the West Indies, and America. He heard about the adventures of a seaman in dock sides in the Panama Canal, the coast of Africa, and the world over.

When Bob spoke about the world, it was different. It wasn't the wonders of the towns and cities, the harbours, dolphins, and whales. He spoke about the solidarity between people - longshoremen from America, who refused to unload ships from Garston or London when strikes were on. He talked about Tom Mann and Liverpool's own James Larkin, men who had forged the unions on these very docks.

'Get the kettle on, Tom.'

'All right, but shhhh.' He raised his finger to his lips. 'Come through here and keep the noise down.' He led them through the living room and into the back kitchen. 'Do you think he will do anything?' Tommy asked as they arranged themselves around the kitchen table.

'I'm not worried about him.' Bob sat at the simple wooden table while Tommy filled the kettle and placed it on the gas ring. Kevin and John pulled the chairs out from beneath the table. The kitchen was cold. The window above the sink had two cracked panes. One of the squares of glass in the back door was missing and had been replaced by an ill-fitting piece of wood.

'Here, I'll put the burner on.' Tommy wheeled a brown square heater into the room. He turned a lever then threaded a lit match through the opening. The blue flame flashed up, and the smell of paraffin filled the room. Tommy returned to the kettle.

'But you are worried?' asked John.

'We've got to make sure we're solid,' Bob Pennington explained. 'We can't have men in Salford, Birkenhead or Liverpool strike if we can't keep things together here.'

'We should go to the police,' Kevin volunteered. 'Those guys are always up to no good.'

'Half the time the coppers are in on it,' said John.

'Then we go into town, not just the local mob, tell the officers,' Kevin said.

'No. What for? Do you think the police would be on our side?

John's right,' Tommy said.

'These guys could be running guns or anything. You know they're all Paddies,' Kev answered.

'What's wrong with that?' asked Tommy, feeling insulted. 'Running guns?'

'No, Paddies being Irish,' Tommy declared.

'I don't mean Irish like you. I mean, you never know, IRA and all that bollocks. It wouldn't be the first time through Garston.'

There was a brief silence. Tommy placed the metal teapot in the centre and covered it with a woollen cosy. He grabbed cups hanging from hooks under the sideboard and placed them round the table. There was no sugar, but he put a quarter-full bottle of sterilised milk in the middle. 'Go easy on the milk,' he asked.

'No one's going to the police. We have to sort this out ourselves,' said Bob.

'I'm not standing by if I think those bastards are running guns through here.' Kevin looked determined.

'No one is asking you to. We can close this down. Who loads the ships?'

'We do,' John answered.

'Exactly, and who checks the loads?'

'We do, or the checkers, anyway,' said John.

'So, anything that looks dodgy, you report it to your union steward. The Powers can only move things if everyone looks the other way. We use our brains.' Bob was tapping the side of his head.

'I don't know.' Kevin folded his arms across his chest.

'We're talking about building a fighting union, one that can protect us all. We've just been up there to warn the guy off. We can't expect the police or anyone else to fight our battles. Anything we do, we have to do it ourselves,' said Bob.

'All right, I've said my piece. I'm off. Are you coming, John?' Kevin's chair scraped the floor as he stood.

'Yeah,' John drained his tea. 'See you tomorrow,' he said, following Kevin out the door.

Tommy waited until he heard the front door close. 'You think Kev will be okay?' he asked.

'I hope so, but he's right. We have to be careful - more than anything else, this can split us down the middle,' Bob answered.

'It's all good,' Tommy insisted. 'When we came out, it didn't matter who was white, who was blue, Protestant or Catholic. It was everyone together.'

'Okay, that's fine for now, but it's not just the Transport and General full-timer we have to worry about - there's the Orange lot as well. The last thing we need is someone talking to the coppers.'

Tommy sat with his teacup in hand. 'It was a great feeling yesterday. You know what it's like.' He paused. 'It's a long hard day out there, so anything that shakes it up is a relief.'

'We need more than that. We need a strategy,' said Bob.

'I know, but that feeling. Can't beat it. Men everywhere moving mountains of cargo. Sometimes it seems like there's no end to it. Then, you feel the air change.' Tommy's eyes lit up. 'A buzz of excitement, someone comes running along: "We're going out," "everyone out." I didn't know why or what was wrong. All I knew, we all knew, was that it must be important. But it's also saying, "fuck it." Men grabbed their coats, coming down the gangplanks, climbing out of cranes. All headed to the gates. The change in people's mood, laughing and joking, calling out to see who knew what. Then outside the gates, at the "Nook" - '

'Look, don't get me wrong. I understand you.' Bob interrupted his flow. 'That's the feeling we all get when we stand up for ourselves. But that doesn't last. These men have families, kids to feed and houses to heat. We have to replace that feeling with organisation. We have to show that we can win, that things get better because we act together.'

'I'm with you, Bob,' said Tommy.

'I know you are.' Bob drained his tea. 'Come on, let's get some kip. We've got a lot to sort out in the morning.'

'It wasn't that we didn't care, leaving the job like that. It's weird. It's kind of the opposite. We knew we would be able to decide something. We would be men, not cart horses, or donkeys to load and unload, but here we could have our say,' Tommy said.

'Come on, sleep.'

Tommy turned down the paraffin burner and watched the flame flicker and die.

Tommy woke to the sound of hammering on the front door. It was dark and cold. The banging continued. Tommy shook himself and rose stiffly. He opened the curtain over the front window, looking down into the street. No light came in. He pulled on his shirt and trousers and descended the linoleum-covered stairs. Bob was shrugging off the blanket he had used to cover himself in the armchair as Tommy reached the bottom. They met at the front door. Tommy flicked on the light switch, anxiety on his face, and opened the door.

'Mister Evans wants to see Pennington.' A slight boy stood there, not more than ten years old, wrapped up against the cold in an oversized overcoat. His cap was pulled down over his ears, a tuft of greasy hair sticking out from under it. 'He has to come now, Mr Evans said.'

'Tell Mr Evans to go - '

'No, it's okay, Tom.'

Bob addressed the boy. 'Tell him I'm on my way.'

The boy turned and his footsteps rang out as his heavy boots clopped away.

'Come on, get your boots and coat on.' Bob had been sleeping in both and was ready to go.

As they walked to the docks, Tommy remembered the last days of the open pen - dog eat dog. They competed for work. Foremen came out and picked who would get work that morning or afternoon. He remembered hanging round all day in the hope of someone coming out for extra men. Of the 20,000 to 25,000 dockers who stood for work each day across the northern ports, 16,000 to 17,000 would be "put on" for a day's work. Tommy would be ignored along with other youngsters and the older men whose health was failing. Pushing and shoving, men were debased in the struggle to survive. The common practice of buying the foreman a pint at the weekend in the hope of securing the next week's work was despised, but still existed. But things had changed now. Men were allocated work or paid a minimum attendance fee, and Tommy knew it was because of the union. Registration as a dockworker required a union card, a white T&G card.

While some still gloried in the hard-drinking, fighting, and strong-man image, dockers were changing. With no father to hand down wisdom or life's lessons, Tommy was given an old copy of *The Ragged-Trousered Philanthropists*, promising to pass it on when he'd finished. Stories of past dockers - Harry Constable and Liverpool's own James Larkin - were told and retold, and Tommy loved them because it was a way for him to be someone. After the slaughter of the war, there was a renewed determination to achieve a country worth the sacrifice.

One story stood out for Tommy and represented the new mood among dockworkers. Harry Constable was a union man in London, and, after leading unofficial walkouts in support of Canadian seamen, refusing to unload ships manned by strike-breaking scabs, he was sacked by management and threatened with discipline by the union. Bob told Tommy this story, and Tommy passed it on. Thousands of dockers demanded his reinstatement, and, in fear, management offered him the pick of the jobs on the docks that day. When the foreman came out to the pen and listed the highest-paying work, offering the choice places to Constable, he replied, 'What is the worst job you've got today?'

After being told, he said, 'That's the job I'm doing.' The men crowded round waiting for work cheered. Solidarity had replaced selfishness.

In Garston, dockers were refused registration when they presented the blue NASD card. This had led to the walkout and strike the day before. Bob and Tommy walked up to the dock gates. A copper stood on either side of the gate.

'We are here to see Mr Evans,' Tommy said.

'I know who you are,' the copper replied, not to Tommy, but staring at Bob. Nevertheless, he swung the gate open.

As they walked through the gate, Tommy could see the boy through the glass of the tally house door. They walked on, darkness covering the dock. In the dim light, a few figures could be seen moving about on the decks of the ships. The caws of the seagulls ripped through the silence, sounding like screams of anger to Tommy.

The office light was on at the end of the dock. Up an external wooden staircase, the dock manager's office glowed above the brick warehouse. Bob entered first. A coal fire roared, and the room was warmer than any house Tommy had known.

The Manager, Mr Evans, was a lean, sharp man, all elbows and knees. 'I'm not going to beat about the bush. We need the port working today. We will have ships backed up the river if I can't turn this thing around.'

Bob and Tommy were both standing. Tommy stood in front of the coal fire, and he lifted his coat, allowing the heat from the fire directly up his back.

Bob was closer to the manager's desk. 'John Hughes, Dave Kelly, Simon Calder - these men reported for work yesterday and were refused.'

'Okay, okay, I know. Calder and Hughes can come back, but Kelly is a communist, he's a troublemaker,' Mr Evans said.

Bob responded, 'Calder, Hughes, and Kelly are registered

dockers, and have the right to join a union of their choice. We met with boys from Birkenhead, Salford, and Hull last night,' he lied, 'and we telephoned Millwall, Wapping and Stepney. Unless you want ship owners across the country on your back, you know what you have to do.'

'Don't you talk to me about owners. Don't you think I know what's going on?' Evans spat out.

Tommy noticed the manager fighting to control his growing anger.

'Okay, look, they can report for work - even Kelly - they can work. You call off the strike. But I'm warning you, we will meet with the Transport and General this morning. They want to see the back of you too. Tread carefully, Mr Pennington. No one likes an outsider stirring things up.'

'We will want a short meeting on the Nook this morning to ratify the return to work, but the men will be here,' said Bob.

'Have your meeting, but know this: this isn't over, not by a long shot,' warned Mr Evans.

As they walked back to the dock gates, Tommy veered off to the side. He put his head inside the door of the gatehouse. 'Hey, kid.' He gave the boy a halfpenny coin. 'Go knock people up, spread the word. The dock is open again.'

The boy took the coin and was off, reaching the gates before Bob and Tommy.

Outside the gates, Bob turned to Tommy. 'I'll do Hughes and Calder.'

'Great, I'll go see Dave Kelly.'

Tommy turned to walk away, as happy as he had been in a long time.

'And tell them noon on the Nook.'

Tommy smiled. 'Got it.'

When he turned for the last time, Tommy saw Bob waiting outside the dock gates. Although it was cold, the sun had burned off the mist that drifted in off the river. The gates were open. The coppers would regularly stop and search dockers on their way out, but not today.

★★★

'You're early,' Bob said as Kevin and Tommy reached him.

'You've never seen the foremen so quiet,' Kevin replied.

'Okay, come on.' Bob led them across the cobbles.

'I think you should address the meeting,' Bob encouraged Tommy.

'Me? Why me? You're the union rep.'

'I can do it,' Kevin volunteered.

'Thanks, Kev, but I think it's Tommy's time.'

Tommy felt his stare.

'You work with these men. They know you. They trust you more.'

'I'm not sure.' Tommy was both nervous and excited. He wanted to, but was afraid of messing up.

'You'll be fine. Just say what happened, and what we need next.'

A black Austin A30 was heading down King Street. Instead of driving through the dock gates, it veered right, and in a few seconds, it was within feet of them.

'Who's this?' Tommy asked and then gave his own reply. 'Oh shit.'

First out of the car was Michael, then Paddy Connolly got out from the driver's side. Only after this were Charlie and Jack Power able to get out of the two-door vehicle.

Jack placed himself directly in front of Bob and was the first to speak. 'Bob, isn't it? Isn't that what you said your name was?'

The four men stood directly in front of Bob, Tommy, and Kevin.

'It is.'

'Well, listen, Bob, I don't know who you think you are, but I don't appreciate someone coming into my pub and telling me what to do.'

Tommy knew Jack had a reputation for violence. In fact, he knew all four did. He tried to intervene.

'Mr Power - '

Jack cut him off. 'No one's talking to you.'

Paddy Connolly reached out and pushed Tommy back. Kevin took a step back, leaving Bob facing the four men. Jack turned back to Bob. 'Do you box, Bob?' Not waiting for an answer, he said, 'I box.'

Jack leaned into Bob's face.

Bob tried to take a step back but felt a hand behind him, keeping him in place. Charlie had swung round and extended his arm.

'I just want you to know something. I am going to fuck you,' said Jack.

Tommy could see behind Jack, and men began to stream out of the gate. The laughing and joking stopped as they realised what was happening, and silently, they began to surround the group. Ten, then twenty. Jack backed off a step from Bob. Charlie let his arm drop. All the while, more and more dockers surrounded them. Jack started backing away and said under his breath, audibly and directed at Bob, 'I don't warn people twice.'

Jack, Michael, Paddy, and Charlie edged their way out of the crowd. Relieved, Tommy shouted, 'Okay, guys, let's get on with it.'

Tommy moved to the raised ground near the wall. 'First, as you all know - otherwise, we wouldn't be in there today - we won!'

There was clapping and cheering.

'John, Dave, and Simon are back at work.'

There was more clapping and cheering. These men were singled out, slapped on the back, their hands shaken in congratulations.

Tommy could see the black car reversing and turning around as he spoke. 'We have one thing to do, but before that, I want to thank all of you brothers. All of you, whatever union you are in. Your solidarity has pushed management back on its heels. Today we have shown that we will not allow them to decide who gets to earn a living or who doesn't, just like they can't decide who has the right to speak in our name. It is your strength that has won today. Because this was such a clear victory, we didn't want to wait and stop you from earning any longer than needed, so we put the word out this morning, but now, can we please have a show of hands for all that agree to this return to work.'

Hands shot up and were waved in the air.

'Thank you, brothers. One last thing, with your permission, I would like to ask Bob Pennington to say a few words.'

Bob, who was standing next to Tommy at this point, cleared his throat. 'Can we have a vote of thanks for Tommy here. He has shown himself to be a fighter for you men of Garston.'

After a further round of claps and cheers, Bob continued. 'You know, what you have done here, what we have done as working men - and I don't just mean today, but in docks up and down this country, especially in the docks - is near on miraculous. I'm sure many of you remember the days when dockers were the most selfish, most individualistic, out-for-themselves workers anywhere. Back then, dockers fought, not the bosses, but each other for the pittance they would give us. Now, look at you, whatever union, whatever trade. A worker is a worker and is one of us. You have made the slogan "an injury to one is an injury to all" not a dream, a hope or an aspiration, but a reality. If this can happen among dockers, with people like you leading our class, just think about what is possible. There is nothing at any time or in any place that we can't achieve. Our fight is not with the T&G, not with other union members. We stand together, and when we stand together as workers, there is no bully in this country, no bullying owner, no criminal, no copper, no government that can beat us.'

The men cheered and clapped for the final time that morning, and, as the crowd broke up, Tommy, like the men all around him, felt elated.

Above the departing heads, he could just about see the black Austin A30 containing Jack, Charlie, Paddy, and Michael disappear under the bridge.

Tommy knew they had won this battle but remained at war.

Chapter Nine

Paddy

Paddy took it all in. Michael came with a big story. A year in Mountjoy was no mean thing. Jack made sure everyone knew. Paddy didn't need telling. He knew Michael's history by looking him in the eye. The windows to the soul, people call them, but to Paddy, the window to the balls on a man. He saw more in Michael's eyes. He had a spark. He saw that from the off.

Michael came to Garston recommended from Aiden, some big bollocks in Wicklow, and those boys stuck together. Never mind when Paddy came over from Tipp, he did it on his own. No fucker to hold his hand or shine a light showing him the way. No. Paddy Connolly was his own man, made his own way. He would have to keep his eye on this new fella.

Jack, Charlie, and Paddy were in the back room of the pub.

'I want you to pay a visit,' Jack said. 'There's a hauler in Aigburth, has a couple of trucks run in and out of the docks regular. His office man is in the Dingle, let him know we would be pleased if he kept us in the know with interesting shipments coming and going.'

'What will I tell him?' Paddy asked. He was always one for keeping his eyes and ears open.

'Don't you worry yourself with that,' said Jack. 'Charlie knows what's what.'

Paddy didn't respond, but he knew what was going on.

Because he wasn't a Wicklow man, they would never trust him properly. Jack was so secretive. *If he could have men in blindfolds and do the job, he would*, thought Paddy. "Close to the chest" had nothing on him. Paddy usually found out most things, not everything, but most. You can't stop a fella yapping when he's having a few jars. It just comes out naturally.

Charlie drove. He rarely let Paddy drive, though he was keen to do it. Paddy liked the Austin. It was the first car he'd been in. Back home, it would be trucks or being pulled by a tractor. After skipping from home, he caught a ride with a truck on the Waterford-Wicklow road. Before leaving, he got into one of his rages at the Father in the schoolhouse. Pure bastard, Paddy thought he was. He tried to cane Paddy one time too many. Paddy broke the cane over his head. He enjoyed his wailing too. He'd had enough of being fiddled with by the Fathers at Clonmel. He wasn't hanging round for any more.

They followed the Dingle man to his yard and waited while he opened the gates and his office.

'Are ya set?' Charlie asked.

Stupid question, thought Paddy. 'I've been set me whole life,' he said.

'We've to frighten the man if he's not cooperating,' said Charlie.

'I'm with ya.'

With no one else there, it seemed like the perfect chance. Charlie went in first, Paddy straight after. The guy sat at his desk, shuffling papers around. It wasn't a big office, so Paddy and Charlie were kind of filling it. The man didn't look too comfortable.

'Can I help you, men?'

'Ya can,' said Charlie. 'We want to see your shipping lists from Garston.'

'Excuse me,' he said, looking surprised.

'Maybe I should say that another way. Mr Power is interested in your loads,' Charlie said.

Paddy thought that was a good way of explaining things, kind of making a point. The man wasn't looking surprised now, more like a dog had just eaten his breakfast. 'Look. I don't want any trouble,' he said.

'Then best you give us what we come for,' Charlie replied.

'Okay, look, leave it with me. I know Mr Power. You tell him I said I will contact him. He can be sure of it.' He straightened his pencil and notepad beside his phone.

Charlie looked at Paddy. Paddy guessed that wasn't the right answer, so he edged round the man's desk, slowly, so as not to get him agitated. But the guy got a bit het up anyway, and he leaned back in his chair. Paddy hadn't planned what he was going to do. When the man put his hands up in defence, Paddy thought, *Thank you very much*.

Paddy grabbed the middle finger of the guy's left hand and bent it back. The man moaned. Paddy knew they didn't want any bother, so did it quick. Bent it back until he felt the bone snap. He couldn't really hear it, but he knew right enough when it happened. Paddy could feel the top part come free. But he did it quick, to cut down on the noise. After it snapped, the guy was whimpering, not so much noise.

'That's great then,' Charlie said. 'We will be waiting.'

Charlie left, and Paddy followed him. 'Did you see what I did?'

'Of course I did. You broke his finger,' said Charlie.

'No. Not that. I did his left hand, so he could still write. There's an awful lot of paperwork in sorting out those shipments.'

'Yeah, nice one.'

Paddy hoped Charlie would tell Jack. That's the kind of forward-thinking he was developing. Thinking some way down the road.

Even before he'd broken the cane over the brother's head, Paddy knew he was okay with violence. It wasn't that he liked it. He didn't enjoy doing it. It was that he knew he could do it, and it didn't bother him.

He learned that with violence, you had to do it enough so that whoever you were doing it to wouldn't come back at you because they knew they would have to stop you for good, and nothing was ever worth that much to them. So, you can't mess about with it. You have to be level-headed with it, not hot-headed or in a rage.

Paddy learned that.

2004

Chapter Ten

Anne

Anne enjoyed her studio flat, her own front door and bathroom, not forgetting the comfortable, warm bed. If she had these things, she was a long way down the road to happiness. The double mattress on the floor had progressed to a double mattress on two pallets. The slight elevation in height from her student days was somehow important to her.

Anne had written her article the previous evening, remembering her catechism of the five W's for news reporting. She cut and excised any extraneous language, removing any tone or implication of mood; it was pure reportage. Satisfied that it fulfilled her professional obligations, and profoundly aware that those restrictions were constraining and frustrating, it was ready.

As a professional writer, she wasn't free to write. The demands of news reporting meant that she was following recipes like a cook when what she wanted was the freedom to create like a chef.

Her dad would have been proud of her. His name - McCarthy - would appear over her article. Showered, dressed, and still munching toast, she made her way down to her car. Her phone buzzed in her bag. She waited until she was in the car before she answered.

'Hello, it's your mum,' the familiar voice announced.

'Hello, Mum.' Anne waited for a response.

'What are you doing?'

Anne tried to keep the annoyance out of her voice. 'I'm on my way to work.'

There was a pause.

'Are you coming over Sunday? Your sister will be bringing her fiancé.'

'I'll try, Mum, but I'll have to see what I've got on.'

'What you've got on, on a Sunday? Don't tell me they have you working at weekends?'

She could visualise her mum, cleaning the kitchen as she held the phone to her ear.

'Yeah, Mum, we are on a rota. The paper has to come out Monday.'

'Call me, and tell me if you'll be bringing someone, okay?'

'Mum, if I come, it'll be on my own. Look, sorry, I'm driving, I'll call you later. Byeee.'

Anne ended the call. Her mum was completely random with the phone; the calls could come early morning or late at night. Anne guessed it was a kind of surveillance strategy. Her mum listening for who or what was in the background. There was usually very little point to the calls or very little for her mum to discover.

It was 9.30 am before Anthony arrived in the office. Anne sprang into action, timing to perfection her delivery of a fresh coffee to his desk, just as he settled into his careworn and squeaky swivel chair.

'To what do I owe the honour?' he asked.

'Nothing. Can't a subordinate show appreciation of her betters?'

'Mmm, okay, leave it here. I'll look over it when I get a chance.' He lifted the cup and breathed in the rich aroma of coffee.

Anne left her copy and retreated to her desk. She sent her

quotes on the Orange march to her colleague in features; if they appeared in the weekend edition, they might be attributed in a shared byline, although she knew it was more likely to be tagged as "city desk." Anne returned to the task of inputting subscribers into the database.

A short while later, Anthony appeared behind her. 'Not bad, not bad at all…just one available W missing.'

'Really?' Anne scanned the copy.

'We don't know the "why." That's beyond our scope at this time, but as for the "who?"' Anthony raised a single eyebrow.

'No one knows who the remains belong to yet,' Anne said.

'That may well be true, but what other "who" is available to us?' Anthony sat in an empty chair opposite Anne.

Anne thought for a second. 'The builder, the developer.'

'Exactly.'

'I've got the name in my notes. Give me a minute.'

'Okay, well done. It's a workable piece.' As he stood, Anthony said, 'Shame we don't know how he died.'

Anne was flicking through her notebook and looked up. 'A blow to the head.'

'Really?'

Anne's stomach churned a little. 'Yeah.'

Had she done something wrong? She started biting her lip in anticipation.

Anthony sat back down. 'You mean the police told you?'

'Yeah, a DS Cooper.' Her voice was weak and unsure. 'Death by blunt force trauma to the skull.'

'Then why isn't it in your piece?'

The question hit her like a blow to the stomach. 'Because it was off the record?' It was halfway between a statement and a question, her voice rising at the end.

'No, no, that won't do. "Off the record" means we don't attribute quotes, but it doesn't mean we bury the story, for Christ's sake.'

As she listened, she was shrinking. The stomach-churning grew. 'But I kind of promised him.'

'Now you know why reporters don't have many friends. You're gonna have to un-promise him. You have to decide if you want to be popular or be a journalist because you can't be both. If you haven't got what it takes, do us all a favour and find another hobby.' He reached down and took the copy from her.

Anne turned back toward her desk. She put her head between her hands and exhaled. The churning in her stomach had stopped, only to be replaced by a hollowed-out emptiness.

Chapter Eleven

Vinny

Vinny arrived home knackered. It wasn't so much the work - he could do it with his eyes closed. He did, however, resent the brain space all those shoe names took in his head.

The bike ride from town was only a couple of miles, but it was all uphill. The cycle and not sleeping well left him feeling drained. He was lucky to have a flat in "The Georgian" quarter, as the area was becoming known in the brochures of property developers and estate agents. Its historic name of Toxteth was associated in the mind of many with poverty, the riots of '81, and struggle. So, the name was eased out in the same way the locals were. Housing associations had replaced the council, and properties were sold off or left to fall into disrepair before being boarded up, ready for demolition.

Vinny's flat was in a Georgian house; at least this part of the brochures was true. Three storeys high, with wide bay windows, high ceilings, solid brick architecture adorned with decorative plaster carvings. These houses were once the homes of the merchants, doctors, and lawyers - the professional and moneyed men of Liverpool.

Local historians and activists had begun to unearth a darker side to Liverpool. Many of the city's most majestic civic buildings were built on the proceeds of the slave trade. The men who gave generously to celebrate civic pride were memorialised in its famous street names: Bold Street, Rodney Street, Blackburne Place, and even one of the most famous street names in Liverpool - Penny Lane, was for years thought to honour a slave trader James Penny. Beatles fans may have given a sigh of relief when the connection was disproved, but Vinny realised that slavery was in the bones of the city; he loved history because it explained the present, not the past.

Vinny felt the houses were now returning to their roots. Those owned by housing associations were sold off to developers, speculators, the new urban wealthy. His house had been converted into six flats, two on each floor, by a Housing Association in the early '80s, and was now ripe for redevelopment.

He dragged his bike up the stairs. He had found to his cost that chaining bikes outside was no use.

He had to work out his problem in writing his proposal for university. He knew he could do the research into how the city had changed since the end of the war, but what was he trying to show? Liverpool was in competition for the title European Capital of Culture. There was something about the campaign that annoyed him, but he couldn't work out what it was. It wasn't that Liverpool would get lots of money if they won - money for theatre and film, concerts and festivals - all of that was great. A part of it was knowing that little of that money would find its way to the poorer areas of Garston and Speke. Something didn't feel right with the slogan, 'A World in One City.'

Settled on the sofa, he found his anxiety was building. The walls were closing in, and his head ached; he couldn't focus, he couldn't play music, he couldn't read. He had his notebook open in front of him, and he alternated between staring at that and his computer screen. He had hung a noticeboard on his wall with pins and notes and a string between them like a scene from a murder inquiry without a victim.

Irish, Scouse, English

Ireland, Famine, mid–1800s mass emigration, 300,000 to Liverpool

Post–Second–World–War immigration

National Struggle

Wolf Tone, 1798

The Rising, 1916

The Troubles, 1968 – 1998

Hobsbawm, Anderson imagined Communities Nationalism

Prevention Terrorism Act

Catholic – Protestant

Trade Union Struggles

60s Football Music

The Beatles

But it wasn't helping.

He knew all the metaphors for depression: a dark cloud, fog, a black dog, weight to be carried. But his own came in sea and oceanscapes: raging seas and storm-tossed chaos, or the immobility and torpor of being becalmed, unable to move forward. These extremes, it seemed, were ever-present. He was always somewhere between the two. Right now, he was slipping under the surface, unable to grasp a clear idea from the swirling waters around him.

His intercom buzzed. He knew it would be Anne. He thought about letting it ring out but decided to accept the distraction. He answered the intercom. 'Hey.'

'It's me,' she announced.

He pressed the buzzer. Anne's steps echoed in the stairwell. He opened the front door just as she reached it. She walked straight through.

'Hi. Last night was crazy. Are you okay?'

He followed her into the living room. 'Yeah, I'm fine, but it was a bit too close for comfort. You know what I mean? I can't be doing with getting charged with shit now. I've got to get serious with this Uni stuff.'

'I know, I know. I mean how did we end up in that?' She threw her bag down and collapsed on the sofa. 'Any tea?'

'Yeah,' Vinny went to the kitchen.

He switched the kettle on and arranged the cups. He shouted through to the living room, 'You and your guy Michael. That's how we ended up in that mess.'

He popped his head round the kitchen door in time to hear Anne's reply.

'I guess so. But please, he's not "my guy."'

'Yeah, ok, but you should be more careful. There are dangerous people out there.'

'Oh, you don't say.'

Vinny could tell from her voice that she was rolling her eyes. She had a confidence that could take her anywhere. He popped his head back in the room. 'This isn't funny. For fuck's sake, I was arrested last night.'

'I really am sorry about that.'

He went back to sorting out the tea. 'Hold on a minute.'

When he came back into the room, he placed her tea on the coffee table. 'Okay, so he's not your guy, but he's the reason we were there.'

'Yeah, true. But that fight could have happened anywhere.'

'I don't think so.'

'What do you mean?'

'Michael was out of order. Who does that? Kicking someone in the face like it was nothing? You want to watch out. When you stir shit up, you never know what comes up with it.'

'Yeah, well, I think last night was a one-off. Actually, I was calling to see if you wanted to come back down with me?' Anne asked.

'You are kidding, aren't you?'

'Well, I wasn't, but I guess I've got my answer,' Anne said.

'Is everything okay?' Vinny sensed there was something else. 'Why are you going back there today?'

Anne shifted in her seat. 'Apart from pissing off my sub-editor? It's fine. But I need to find out more. So anyway, you're not coming with me?'

'Nah, I can't, even if I wanted to.'

'Are you working?'

'No, no hours today. I've got to do a presentation later.'

'What for?'

'Uni. We have to present our ideas, a kind of early doors peer review of what we intend to do research on.'

'Sounds serious,' said Anne.

'Yeah, I guess. It's not like a pass or fail thing. I just don't want to look stupid.'

'Come on, you'll be fine. You're the smartest miserable man I know.'

'And you're the prettiest cub reporter I know.'

There was a beat, and his words hung in the air without reaction.

Shit, I meant the most annoying. Anyway,' he rushed on, 'I think I know what I want to do, but presenting it academically is a different thing. Jesus, I'm fucked. I think they're all gonna realise what a fraud I am.'

Anne sat in silence for a few seconds, then resumed, 'You're not a fraud. Come on. This professor, she thought it was a good enough idea. She must've done. Otherwise, she wouldn't have accepted you.'

'Yeah, you're right,' Vinny said. 'I just have to sort myself out.'

'Can I ask?'

'Ask what?'

'Well, this Uni stuff, are you all right with it, really?'

He knew the question came from a place of concern. Vinny replied, 'Yeah, don't worry, it's just nerves. I have to get used to the idea that this is who I am.'

'I'm not sure if we get ever used to that. My dad was from Barbados. I don't really know anything about the place, so I've got that, no doubt... but I'm Scouse. I'm from Liverpool. I'm black, there's no issue. My problem isn't who I am, but what I am,' Anne said.

'What you are?' Vinny asked.

'A journalist? A writer? Or a pretentious wannabe.'

Before Vinny could respond, she added, 'I know what you're going to say..."you're all three".'

'This Scouse thing annoys me. It's not just an accent. People are giving it cultural or historical values, some kind of regional specialism. "I'm not English - I'm Scouse." It's weird. Have you seen the slogan? "The World in One City,"' Vinny asked.

'Yeah, I have. I like it. You know, kind of celebrating all cultures.'

'I get that, but the more I read, the more it just seems false. This place was built on slavery. No one wanted the Irish here; they had campaigns to send them home. Do you know after the Second World War, Liverpool deported 1,300 Chinese sailors?'

'No, I didn't,' Anne said.

'Neither did I 'til I started reading for this. Three hundred of them had families. They worked all through the war. Then, after it was over, the police just picked them up, put them on ships, sent them packing - kids never saw their fathers again.'

'Really?' she asked.

'Yeah, really, then they'll put a fucking plaque somewhere and say, "Ok, history is history, it's time we moved on." Let's celebrate how multicultural we are. The whole thing pisses me off.'

'Are you sure you're not being paranoid?'

'Okay, look, a simple thing, right. We passed the Orange parade in town, happens every year, right?'

'Yeah, I would think so,' said Anne.

'I've been doing some research. From the 1970s right through to the '90s there was no St Patrick's day parade in Liverpool. They have them all over the world, except here, arguably one of the most Irish places outside Ireland. There used to be St Patrick's day parades in the north end before the First World War, but even then, there was always trouble. The few they have tried to organise recently have been attacked and pushed off the streets. Hundreds of police, with dogs and horses, even a bloody helicopter, to stop people getting beaten up.'

'Ok, yeah, I kind of see what you mean,' Anne said.

Anne looked lost in thought for a minute. 'But you're English. You always say you're English.'

'I am because I was born here, what else could I be?' Vinny reacted instinctively.

'Irish? Just like part of me is Barbadian, Bajan.'

'It's not so simple.'

'Why?' Anne asked.

'I don't know. Okay, so I know my dad was Irish, but I was brought up Catholic, not Irish. Everything was about the church. This whole thing is doing my head in.'

'You started this, the whole University project. I'm sure you will work it out.' Anne collected her things. 'Look, sorry to rush off, but I better get going.' She drained her tea. 'Thanks for the cuppa, and really, you will be fine. Just tell them what you've just told me.' She reached down and gave his hand a squeeze.

'Yeah, you go and chase your skeletons in cupboards,' said Vinny.

'There's no need for that. You do have a knack for pissing people off. You do know that? Anyway, I'll see you later.'

It seemed like every time Anne moved toward Vinny, he couldn't help but push her away.

Chapter Twelve

Anne

Anne was prepared for a difficult reception going back to The Dealers. The end of the bar was empty, there were a few people further down, a combination of pensioners popping in after a walk to the shops, and "nurses" - people who "nursed" half a pint for an hour. Like most of Vinny's terms, once heard and pictured, they were hard to get rid of. She was amazed at how many ways he could put people down.

She sat on a bar stool, put her bag on the bar, and waited. Before long, the barmaid came through from the other side. Somewhere in her late fifties, she had clearly been an attractive woman in her day, although the edges and lines of that attractiveness were fading and "heading south," another of Vinny's remarks she resented.

'Hello again,' Anne said.

'Hi, what can I do for you?' The voice was a little sharp, the look disdainful. The woman moved away, wiping the bar down.

'I came to apologise,' Anne declared.

'For what?'

'The thing last night.' Anne was trying to look as straight and honest as she could, her hands open on the bar as she spoke. 'Look, I know you are probably busy, but I would be happy to buy you a coffee or a drink, anything you would like. I really am sorry. You were so welcoming. I felt terrible the way things ended. I hope the police didn't cause you any trouble?'

The woman stretched her out her hand. 'Molly. We didn't get to meet properly last time.'

Anne reached forward. 'Anne, Anne McCarthy. Pleased to meet you, Molly. I really am sorry - '

Molly interrupted her. 'Don't worry yourself, love. This place has seen far worse over the years.'

'Thanks, do you want a drink?' Anne asked.

'What are you having, love? This is my job.'

Anne replied, 'I'll have a coffee if you would like to join me.'

Molly took a quick look around the bar. 'Just let me check the other side.'

Anne started to take off her coat. 'Sure.'

She relaxed a little. It was only her second time in this pub, but she was beginning to understand its attraction. There were four customers: an elderly man and woman sat either side of a small round table, and further along, two guys sat on a long leather seat that backed onto the wall. Each sat at separate small round tables. Despite the space between them, nods and words were exchanged, sometimes thrown out indistinctly as if into the ether, but caught and responded to by the next customer along. This was a world away from the bars and cafés of The Ropewalks or Liverpool One. These people would be politely but firmly shooed and rushed along to make space for younger, wealthier customers. Here, they could wear their tracksuits or slippers. Drag their shopping carts through the bar. Let the dog lie at their feet.

Molly made her way back in with a tray, with two coffees, sugar, and milk.

'Thanks.' Anne nodded.

Molly put the tray on the bar. 'Help yourself.'

'It's a nice place you have here.' Anne motioned toward the bar.

'Give over, love. You don't have to go that far,' Molly said, smiling.

'No, I mean it. It's warm, clean, comfortable - it's nice,' she insisted.

'Looks a bit like a daycare centre right now, but we have our moments. Saturday nights are still a bit special. We try and get an act in, nothing too big, just a local singer, and Sunday afternoons the place still has a good turnout.'

'Have you been here long?'

'Me an' my old fella have had this place going on forty years, but before this, we had the Cock and Trumpet on King Street.'

'Under the bridge?' Anne asked.

'Yeah, that's right. Why the questions?' Molly asked in return.

Anne slipped her hand in her coat pocket and produced a card. 'I'm with *The Chronicle*.'

Molly picked her glasses up from beside the till and scrutinised the card.

'I just want to be straight,' Anne said.

Molly put the card down. 'I'm not sure how I can help you.'

Anne explained, 'I did want to come and apologise, first and foremost. I felt bad about what happened -'

'And?' Molly interrupted.

'And, I was sure you would be the perfect person to give me an idea of what Garston is like.'

'Well, you're not wrong there. There isn't much that has gone on or goes on that stays secret round here. Is that what you were doing with Michael? And Paddy Connolly's boy?' Molly asked.

'Yeah.' As Anne responded, she looked quizzically at Molly. 'Paddy Connolly's son? You mean Vinny, the guy I was with?'

'Yeah,' Molly replied.

'I knew him as soon as I saw him. Bit taller now, and hairier.' She laughed. 'He could do with a haircut and a shave. Is he your man, then?'

'Vinny? God no. Don't get me wrong, I love him, but not like that.'

Molly's smile remained in place.

'You said Paddy Connolly? Did you know his dad?' Anne was shocked but tried not to show it.

'Yeah, he was one of the lads, you know, one of the men round here. In the old days, he used to go about with the Powers, Jack and Charlie. There were a few of them. The Wicklow Boys.'

Anne took a gulp of her coffee. This was weird. As far as she knew, Vinny didn't know his father.

'I guess you were asking about the bones that were dug up?' Molly said.

It was Anne's turn to smile. 'I think you are right, there's not much that gets past you.'

'Well, makes sense, you being from *The Chronicle* and all.'

'So, any ideas?'

'You mean who it is?' Molly waved away the idea. 'No, no love, different times then. From what I heard, you're going back to the '50s, '60s.'

'Yeah, from what we know. Can I ask what you mean by, "It was different times then?"'

Molly took a sip of her own coffee. Anne could see she was debating how much to say, and how much not to say.

'Okay…How about The Wicklow Boys?'

Molly's eyes closed briefly. Her head shook a little, and a look of doubt crossed her face.

'It was just a name we called them. They would go about together. At one point, they used the Palatine, but then later, they would be in here on Saturday nights. Jack had the Palatine for a while. Later he had a building company, shops, and garages, all kinds, really. Old Mike used to knock around with them. He was big with Jack and Charlie, the brothers. Your fella's dad for a while, too, before he disappeared.'

'Disappeared?' Anne asked.

'Well, we didn't see him no more, but it wasn't unusual in

them days. People would come over from Ireland or go back there. Men moved around the country for work, on the railways, the roads. My dad was away weeks on end painting electricity pylons, if you can believe it. But then we had the trouble in the docks, everywhere really. It was a strange time.'

'It's funny. You know when we hear of the '50s and '60s nowadays, it always seems like the good old days, when kids played together in the street, and everyone could leave their doors unlocked. You know what I mean?' Anne said.

Molly smiled. 'Yeah, and that's all true, it was like that. Kids in and out of each other's houses, all that stuff. You have to remember, love, a lot of these families were related. You would get a single man come over during the war. They needed men to work because so many were off fighting. Then they would start families, and cousins and brothers would come over...'

'But there was more going on?' Anne suggested.

'Isn't there always, love?'

One of the older men from the end of the bar made his way over. 'Here, Molly, love, can I have another of these and one for Liam down there?'

'Right you are,' Molly replied, and deftly pulled two pint glasses from under the bar.

Anne sat in thought. When Molly returned, she was ready. 'Okay, so we have got men coming backwards and forwards from Ireland, we have people going away to work, and we have the Wicklow Boys...'

'Sounds right,' said Molly.

'And the docks stuff?' Anne asked.

'Ok, you've got me there.' Molly raised her hands as if in defence. 'I didn't understand it then and don't now, not the union stuff.'

'Fair enough. One final question, if you don't mind.'

'Sure, go ahead.'

'The Wicklow boys, were they into anything illegal?' Anne

asked.

Molly looked serious. 'Honestly, love, I don't know. I'm not sure you should be asking questions like that. Not round here. They hung around together, backed each other up, that kind of thing. If there were some bother with the Orange lot, then you know they would look out for each other.'

'You mean Protestants?'

'Protestants, but not really your normal people. You see, we always knew who was who. Sometimes, there was one side of the street Catholic and the other Protestant, and we usually didn't go the other side of Window Lane. We just stayed out of it down near King Street. That was our end, if you know what I mean. It was a close community, but we had our different churches and chapels. We had Holy Trinity, and they had Banks Road School. People just rubbed along. But we knew who to avoid, knew who was in the lodge, and worse. No doubt they knew who to avoid on our side as well, and, apart from the 12th of July, kids and women just got on with things.'

'And the men?' asked Anne.

'That was a different story, but you should ask Mike about that.'

'Were the Wicklow boys political?'

'It depends. Sometimes just existing is political, but I don't think you mean that, do you?'

'To be honest, I'm not sure what I mean.' Anne smiled, then asked, 'Existing as Irish?'

Molly nodded. 'Especially in the '70s.'

Anne drained her coffee. 'Molly, it has been really useful. If you don't mind, I might come back at some point. Thank you.'

'No problem, love,' Molly said, as she began to clear away the coffee things.

Anne slipped an arm in her coat and said, 'How much do I owe you for the coffees?'

'Three pound,' Molly replied.

Anne dug in her purse for the coins.

A voice from deeper inside the bar rang out. 'Billy Harrington.'

Anne turned from the bar. She was off her stool now and took a few steps toward the back of the room. 'Sorry…' she announced to no one in particular, not knowing who had actually spoken, and finished putting on her coat.

'Billy Harrington, that's the guy you want. I couldn't help hearing you talking.' It was one of the guys sitting on the leather bench seat that ran along the wall.

'You must have good ears,' Anne joked.

'Oh aye, not the only thing still working, eh, Jim?' He laughed to his drinking partner, sitting at the next table.

'Give over, you would be so bloody lucky,' Jim replied, looking disgusted.

'Anyway, if you want to know what went on back in the day, he's your man.'

'Oh, right, and do you know where I can find him?'

'He doesn't come up here much, once in a blue moon nowadays. He lives in those houses on the right as you go into Speke, opposite the Metal Box Factory, the edge of the Dymchurch estate. You'll see the houses at an angle behind the bus stop, number eight, I think he is.'

'Thanks very much.' Anne was turning to go when the man said, 'If you can't find him there, try the Noah's. That's his watering hole these days.'

'The Noah's?'

'Noah's Ark, love. Pub in the Parade, or what used to be the Parade in Speke. Opposite the police station.'

'Oh right, thanks,' Anne repeated and turned toward the bar.

'Good name for it, too,' Jim replied.

'Why's that?' Anne asked.

'The animals go in two-by-two.'

Both men laughed.

'Don't mind him, love, he's pulling your leg.'

'Okay. Well, thanks again.' Anne turned and walked back to the bar.

Molly was tidying round the bar.

'Thanks again, Molly. It was good to chat with you.'

'No problem, love.'

Anne headed for the door. 'Bye.'

Chapter Thirteen

Vinny

The seminar room was full. There was a U-shaped arrangement of table and chairs for participants and an extra row of chairs for observers. Dr Sheehan was at the head of the U, and the open end was where presenters would give their talks.

Vinny was feeling blank, not just unable to think, but not really feeling, as if his sensations, along with his intellect, had gone out for the day. He had scribbled notes and references on his notepad in front of him. He stared at the page, trying to scan the notes, but nothing was registering. He could see the words, but they were just words on a page. There was no reality behind them, no connected thoughts, narrative, or plan - or if there was one, it had deserted him.

He started cautiously and nervously. His voice had a quaver, a tremor he could feel in his throat. He wasn't sure where it came from and tried to shake it.

'Good morning. Firstly, I would like to thank Dr Sheehan for this opportunity to present my research proposal.' He took a breath and continued. 'The starting point of my proposal is to fill a gap in the knowledge we have about our society.'

As he spoke, he began to feel better. 'The story of Irish immigration into Liverpool between the mid-19th to mid-20th century has been told extensively. There is a serious body of work, some provided by our own Dr Sheehan. So, the first part of this project is to investigate and document the experience of Irish immigrants to Liverpool from the end of the Second World War up to the turn of the 21st Century. I want to look at the experience of migration to the UK from Ireland post World War Two, particularly in Liverpool around the Garston and Speke area. Attracted by the post war rebuilding projects and the economic expansion opened up in the '50s and '60s, migrants continued to arrive and settle in Liverpool.

'The project will aim to find out the extent of this migration, what they did for work, and how they integrated socially and politically. The later period of the 1960s and '70s were a time of increasing militarisation of the situation in Northern Ireland and saw the introduction of the Prevention of Terrorism Act in the UK. This was combined with a growing level of trade union struggle in the UK through the '70s and '80s.'

At last, he was able to relax a little. 'This will be done through archival research, contemporary print sources, and, where possible, through oral history. There are a number of elements: How many came? Why did they come? And what did they do when they arrived? A part of this research will be to look at the physical data, census, employment, and electoral records. When I have it, it will tell its own story. Further to this, there are a number of areas I would like to investigate...'

As the words tumbled out, Vinny grew into himself.

Chapter Fourteen

Anne

DS David Cooper was waiting as Anne pulled up outside the Noah's Ark. The building stood alone, a detached pub fronted by a car park. The walls and door were graffitied, so Anne guessed it wasn't exactly a gastropub. DS Cooper stood near the door in trainers, jeans, and a brown leather bomber jacket. Anne was pleased to see him. His brown hair was thick, and although short at the back and sides, the fringe regularly dropped to cover his eyes, making him toss his head to throw his hair back. Anne couldn't help noticing it, along with his broad but slim frame.

As Anne got out of her car, DS Cooper walked towards her, smiling. 'Hey, can't keep away?'

'Something like that. Thanks for meeting me.'

'My pleasure. Are you sure you want to go in here?'

'Yeah, of course.'

DS Cooper raised his eyebrows. 'Okay, well, I'm glad you called me first.'

'Yeah, about that. Do you mind, if the guy I'm looking for is here, making a tactical retreat?'

DS Cooper laughed. 'Afraid I will cramp your style?'

'Sorry.'

'It's fine. At least I get the chance to have a drink with you.' He hesitated then said, 'Come on.'

DS Cooper entered the pub first. There was a small foyer, and, three feet in, another set of doors that opened directly into the pub. In this antechamber to the bar, the military rattle of drums provided the backdrop to Eminem's melodic voice.

Anne looked at him as he nodded to the music. 'Do you know that?'

'Of course, don't you?'

'Not my thing,' she said.

'Okay, listen.' He opened the door into the bar. '"Toy Soldiers", Eminem.'

Anne was slightly embarrassed by the DS moving to the beat as they approached the bar.

The main room was quite large, spanning the full run of the building. She could see clear across to the windows on the other side, and the bar in the middle came out in a semi-circle, so whatever part of the pub a person was in, they could be seen from behind the bar.

The walls were fitted with curved bench seats and small stools surrounding the tables on the other side of the bench seats. The seats were covered with what looked like red leather. The curtained windows let in the late afternoon light.

As soon as they entered, Anne noticed all eyes turned to them. A few of the tables were circled by three or four drinkers, and some lone individuals were at others. The drinkers were mainly male. At a quick glance, Anne saw two women of the ten or twelve people dotted around the bar.

DS Cooper walked to the bar with Anne close behind him. A young woman came forward to serve them. He ordered a pint for himself and an orange juice for Anne.

'They're still looking at you,' Anne whispered.

'Yeah, don't worry. They know who I am. It means you won't get any trouble. They know I'm just over the road.'

Anne suddenly realised the little dance he had done on the way in was a sign of ownership, dominance. He could do what he wanted. He was beyond their judgment. It made her uneasy.

DS Cooper stood while Anne arranged herself on one of the taller stools near the bar. 'Is there normally trouble here?' she asked.

He shrugged. 'More than in the past. It used to be Alan Rudkin's pub.'

'Who?'

'You've never heard of him?'

'No.'

'He was a boxer. Not only a boxer, one of the best British bantamweights ever. British and European Champion. Even fought for the World title three times. I met him in here a few times.'

'Not exactly my sport,' Anne said.

'Lovely fella. Had this pub for years. Very softly spoken. When he had it, people knew to behave. Anyway, who is it you're looking for?'

'A guy called Billy Harrington.'

'Do you want me to ask around?'

'No, not yet. Have your drink. I wanted to ask you something else.'

'Yeah? Go for it.'

'Can you do research? You know, on people from round here? Criminal records, that kind of thing?'

DS Cooper shrugged. 'Depends who it is and what it's for.'

'I have an idea. I hope I'm wrong, but I need to find out some information on Paddy Connolly, well, Patrick, and anything you have on the Powers.'

'Okay, explain,' he said.

'You know the guy who was with me last time?'

DS Cooper nodded, and Anne continued. 'Paddy Connolly is his dad.'

'And why do you want me to check him out?'

'I think it's possible that the skeleton was him.'

He raised his eyebrows. 'Wow, you don't hang about, do you? Of course, I can check, but what makes you think it's him?'

'Let's just say *sources*.'

'Proper journalist now, are we?'

Anne felt a bit embarrassed. She wasn't sure if he was mocking her or not. 'Well…on that, I should warn you, my editor might change the copy I submitted this morning.'

'Change how?' he asked.

'I'm not sure yet. He's the editor, he gets to decide.' She wasn't ready to jeopardize the relationship with the truth. 'On Patrick Connolly, I know he was in the Garston area from the '50s to some point in the '70s when he disappeared.'

'Okay, I can try. But it's a bit of a long shot. The best thing is if you let me know as soon as you find anything that looks dodgy.'

'Yeah sure, but I think there's something more. Can you see what you have under the name Power, Jack or Charlie? They were all a part of a group known as "The Wicklow boys,"' Anne said.

'And this Michael, the guy you told me about last time. Is that why you were with him?'

'Well, it wasn't then, but I've found out a bit more, which means I would like to speak to him again.'

'Okay, yeah, I can do some checking. All above board in pursuit of a genuine enquiry. There is something you could do, too.' DS Cooper raised his eyebrows in a way that looked almost comedic to Anne.

'What?'

'Well, in order to try and establish identity, you could get your mate to give us a DNA sample.'

'Oh yeah. How stupid am I? I didn't even think of that. Kind of the ABC of crime-solving these days,' Anne said.

'Well, it's another long shot, so let me see what I can dig up first.' DS Cooper downed his pint. 'Ready?'

'Yeah.'

'Excuse me,' he called the server over. 'Billy Harrington, do you know him?'

She nodded towards a lone figure at a table near the window.

'Thanks,' DS Cooper said.

He put his pint on the bar and turned to leave. 'It's all yours.' He made the sign of a phone with his hand. 'If you need anything, I'm over the road.'

'Thanks,' Anne mouthed.

She ordered a second juice and steeled herself. Anne crossed the bar to the lone figure. 'Hi, are you Billy?'

'Yes, I am, love,' Billy Harrington said.

'Do you mind if I join you?'

'Well, that all depends on what you want.' Billy leaned back on the bench seat, increasing the space between them.

'Just to talk, if you don't mind,' Anne said, aware, and sure he was too, that other eyes in the bar were watching them.

'Go on, then, sit down.'

Billy seemed to relax a little. 'How can I help you?'

'I'm from *The Chronicle*.' Anne handed him one of her business cards.

Billy placed the card on the table in front of him.

'I'm looking for some information about Garston and the docks.'

'Why are you asking?'

'It's kind of background. You know, just trying to get a feel of how things were.'

'Well, it depends what you want to know. Not sure my memory is up to much these days.'

Anne got the impression he was pleased to have company.

'There are two things to start with. If you don't mind telling me what comes to mind. Okay, so, the two things are "trouble on the docks" and the "Wicklow boys."'

'Wow, you get straight to the point, don't you?' He sounded suspicious but intrigued.

'What do you mean?' Anne thought she had messed up by being so direct.

When she leaned forward, she could smell the alcohol on him.

'Okay, when are you talking about?'

Relieved, she asked, 'How about you give me a run-down, then I'll ask if I need more?'

'Well, I can only tell you about what I knew. I started on the docks as a young lad, must've been the '50s - about '53 or '54. It was a busy time down there. At one point, all the bananas in the country were coming through Garston. Fyffes had their own fleet of ships serving the port.

'Let me tell you, kids in Garston never went short of a banana.' He smiled at the memory. 'You had coal and finished goods going out. The trains would rock up right next to the boats and coal unloaded into the holds. Fellas would come out as black as the guys on the banana boats, no offence,' he added.

'None taken,' said Anne.

'The place was crawling with people. Not like now, everything in containers. Back then, everything was loose: barrels, bales, sacks, logs, mountains of stuff had to be shifted onto and off the ships.' Billy paused to drink, opening his mouth wide.

Anne caught sight of his false teeth slipping a little before clicking back in place.

'So, it was busy?' she offered.

'Like you wouldn't believe.'

'And there was trouble?' Anne took the opportunity to move things on.

'Again, that depends what you mean. There was always arguments. Things would flare up, but they were sorted out man-to-man if you know what I mean. In the old days, before the union, things were worse, everyone had to look out for themselves, but by the time I got my start, things were pretty solid.'

'Solid, you mean, union-wise?'

'Yeah, you know, a busy port, ships, and material needed moving quick. That gave the men a lot of power, so things went along pretty smooth, mostly. You had the Blue Union that caused some bother for a few years.'

'What was that about?'

'The first union down there was the Transport and General. They had a white union card, and they kind of had things sewn up. Everyone had to have a union card. When the Blue Union came along, they were real fighters, more militant like. There was trouble for a few years, '54 and '55. I think we were out more. Thousands left the T&G and went with the Blue Union. There was an organiser in Garston. They had a group in Birkenhead that produced a paper, newsletter thing, *The Clarion...Portworker Clarion*, something like that. You might want to check that out.'

Anne had her notebook out and made a show of writing it down.

'You mentioned an organiser? Who would that be, do you have a name, where he lives now?'

'Yeah, Bob Pennington. He was well-known round here then. Used to speak at the meetings and such. Not from here, but came in to organise. Bit of a character. You know, you heard rumours about him. He was a miner, or he was part of the mutiny in the army at the end of the war, all kinds of stuff. A genuine guy, though, but like all of them, he could talk the hind leg off a donkey.'

'Do you know where he is now?'

'No idea, love. Like I said, he wasn't from round here. Those political types moved on, you know, never settled. Not with a family, things like that. Guess they were used to it,' said Billy.

'And the Wicklow Boys?' asked Anne.

'Well, funny you mention that...' he seemed to be enjoying himself.

'Why?'

'They were not too friendly with the union men, especially Pennington. I think they had a few run-ins. That was the talk, anyway.'

'Why would that be?'

'The docks, love. All kinds of things came in and out, not all of it was supposed to be going in or out, if you know what I mean.'

'Not sure I do,' she said.

'Come on, a few boxes going missing, and maybe a few things going the other way that shouldn't have been. You've got to remember they were all Paddies, as well.'

Anne raised an eyebrow.

'It was the '50s and '60s, so not as bad as later. In the '70s it was worse, obviously. But don't think it didn't exist before then.'

'What didn't exist?' she asked, not following his logic and shaking her head.

Billy's voice took on a harsher tone. 'The fucking IRA, what do you think? Remember, we all knew about the attacks on the pictures. You don't forget that kind of thing, and these Paddies were in and out. We had ships from Wicklow, Arklow, Dún Laoghaire, like it was the 82c bus to Speke. That's how often they were in.' He sat back.

Anne was processing the information. She asked, 'What pictures? You said attacks on the pictures.'

'You haven't done your homework, have you, love?' Billy said. 'It was before my time, but we all heard about it - the IRA gassing pictures. Cinemas, not just one, mind you, but quite a few of them. The Gaumont, the one in Woolton, all over. Well, all over Liverpool. Can you believe that? But they did.'

'No, I had no idea. That sounds crazy,' Anne admitted.

'Yeah, so you know, we kept separate. Even when people worked together, we knew who was who.' He nodded to add emphasis.

'And who were you?' Anne asked.

'What?' Billy's eyes narrowed, and he gave her an uncomprehending look.

'Well, what side were you on?'

'I'm a Protestant and loyal to the British Crown,' he replied, as if she were stupid.

'Are you saying the Wicklow boys might have had connections to the IRA?'

'I'm not saying anything, love.' He took another drink. 'I think we have finished here, don't you?'

'I didn't mean anything. I didn't want to upset you.'

'You haven't, love, but there's a line. I don't know you from Adam.'

'It's just background,' she said.

'I'm not being funny, but you've got your background. You came in here with a copper. I don't know who you are.'

'Okay, fair enough. How can I convince you that you can trust me?'

'You can't. But a couple of pints wouldn't go amiss.'

'Yeah. No problem.' Anne dug around in her bag, pulled her wallet out, and left a ten-pound note on the table.

She stood to leave and extended her hand. 'Anyway. Thanks for your time, and for the chat.'

Billy shook her hand and picked up the tenner.

'If you don't mind, I might come back at some point, not sure when,' she added.

'No problem. I'm not hard to find. In here most days, when I can afford it.'

A minute later, Anne was outside. She tried DS Cooper, but there was no answer. She texted him and sat on the low wall that enclosed the pub car park.

Dropping her phone in her bag, she pulled out her notebook and began writing.

'All done?'

She looked up to see DS Cooper standing in front of her.

'Yeah, I think so. Thanks for your help.'

'No problem. So, no earth-shattering discoveries, then?'

'Well, not yet anyway, but interesting, though,' Anne said.

'Interesting how?' DS Cooper asked.

'I'm not sure yet.' Anne closed her notebook and paused, looking up at him.

'Go on, then.'

'Go on, what?'

DS Cooper was smiling. 'You have something you want to ask.'

'Well, yeah, actually.'

'Go for it,' he said.

'A couple of things - another name, if you can check it out for me?'

'Who?'

'Bob Pennington, around at least in the '50s, on the docks in Garston, a union guy. He wasn't from Liverpool, but around at the time.'

'Okay, it's a long time ago, but I'll see.'

'One more thing, not sure if you can help with this. Billy Harrington, I got the feeling he knows more than he's letting on, maybe something to do with Protestants?'

'You mean like the Orange Order?'

'Yeah, maybe... it was just a feeling.'

DS Cooper looked lost in thought for a moment. 'You're not going to give up on this, are you?'

'Should I?' Anne asked. She half closed her notebook.

'No, I'm not saying that, but there are those who would file the report and just wait 'til they heard from us.' He shrugged. 'You know, for an easy life.'

'That's not me, though.' She wondered where this was going.

'No, I can tell. Actually, there is someone. I'll have to make a few calls.'

'That would be great. I'd really appreciate it.' She dug around in her bag for her car keys.

'How much?' DS Cooper asked.

'How much what?'

'How far does your appreciation go? Stretch to meeting me for a drink?'

Anne smiled and looked around. 'Yeah, I think so, but just so you know, I would've said yes anyway.'

'That is good to know. I will get back to you. You know your list of people is growing longer,' he said.

'I know. It seems like the more people I talk to, the more loose ends turn up.'

'Welcome to the world of investigation.'

'Okay, Sherlock. Well, you just follow my clues.'

'Will do, Watson, and I'll call you about that drink. Is Woolton okay for you?'

'Yeah, sure, why not. One last thing, though. How do you take a DNA sample?'

'Your friend would have to come here. It's got to be done under controlled conditions.'

'Okay, I will get back to you.'

'Great. I better get back in there.'

'Yeah, me too. Thanks again.'

She watched him cross the road and enter the police station. *Is it professional to socialise with police officers?* she wondered. He didn't seem bothered by it. She couldn't help feeling this was part of the journalist's world, mixing with detectives and having informal drinks. She turned back to her notebook.

A black Mercedes turned into the car park. She was aware of it because it looked too nice and new for a pub customer. Behind her, she heard the engine die and an alarm beep.

She carried on writing. As she closed her notebook, a hand reached round and snatched it away. She turned quickly without getting up.

'Hey, that's mine.' Her reaction was instinctive. No time for fear, just surprise.

A man backed away from her, holding the notebook up. He was in his thirties, wearing a white tee-shirt and jeans. She could see he was well-built beneath his t-shirt. Her fear grew. She swung her legs over the wall and took hesitant steps toward the pub. She looked over her shoulder in the hope of activity from the police station, but there was nothing

'Look, there's nothing in there. It's worthless to you. Can I have it back?'

'Come and get it.' He grinned.

She tried to sound strong. 'The police are just over the road.'

It didn't work. He was near the door of the pub, still moving.

'Okay, look - I will buy it back off you, how much?' She was frightened but hopeful. *Surely he wants money - what else can he be after?* She edged towards him.

He lowered the hand holding the notebook. Anne sensed victory. She turned her eyes toward her bag and was shocked to feel his grip around her throat. He swung her round, so her head banged against the wall of the pub. Her panic grew as his grip tightened.

His face moved into hers; she could smell his breath, see the individual hairs in his sparse moustache, his pock-marked skin and dark eyes. Behind him, she could see the police station.

His right hand around her neck, his left hand moved toward her breast. Panic and disgust combined when she felt him squeeze, massage her breast. She felt warmth spreading between her legs as her bladder released.

'Stop asking questions, you fuckin' bitch, or next time, I will really hurt you.' He released his grip around her throat.

Anne slumped down the wall as he walked to his car. Again, the beep, the engine starting, and the black car slid out of the car park.

She scrambled in her bag, hands shaking, and typed into the

notes in her phone: *LV 5421.* Picking herself up, she staggered to her car, fumbling for the key. Anne opened the door, threw her bag in, and collapsed into the seat. She closed and locked the door. She thought of phoning DS Cooper, but she was shaking. She looked down and saw a wet patch between her legs. 'Bastard.'

She wanted to get away from there.

On the drive home, Anne's mind was racing. She just wanted to get to the shower. She had two names and one phrase going round and round her brain - Paddy Connolly, Bob Pennington - *stop asking questions.*

Chapter Fifteen

Vinny

'Hello again.'

'Hello.' It took Vinny a couple of seconds to recognise the woman outside Uni. She joined him, walking towards the entrance.

'Did you read the flyer?'

He struggled to hear the question through the noise of the traffic. 'Er, yeah. About cleaners, right?'

He remembered the bright eyes and the smile. He guessed she was Somalian.

'That's right. We're trying to get the Uni to employ us. Not the contractors.'

'Why?' It seemed an obvious question to Vinny, although the simplicity of the question must've confused her, given the look on her face.

'We have temporary contracts, with no holidays, no overtime payment.'

'Look, I understand you would like better conditions. But if you don't work for the University, surely it has nothing to do with them?'

'They should employ us directly, not use subcontractors.'

'I can see why you would want that, but why should the University agree to it?' he asked.

She was defiant. 'Because it would be fairer. Don't you think they should?' she asked. Her smile was gone, and deep lines were furrowing her brow.

'Maybe, but I don't think that is going to do anything.' He pointed at the petition.

'Will you sign it?' She handed him the petition on a clipboard with a pen attached by a piece of string.

He read the opening statement and handed it back. 'No. Look, I sympathise and all that, but this is not going to achieve anything. It doesn't matter how many signatures you get; it won't change anything.'

'So, we shouldn't try?'

'I'm not saying that. I'm saying this isn't the answer.' He pointed at the clipboard. 'You have to change who you are. You seem intelligent, dynamic. You should be inside, getting qualified, not out here with this.'

He walked off, leaving her bemused on the pavement behind him. Inside, he rapped on Dr Sheehan's door and swung it open. 'Hi,' he said as he entered.

'Vincent, good to see you again,' said Dr Sheehan.

'Actually, it's Vinny.'

'Okay, Vinny, can you just give me a minute?'

'Oh, yeah, sure. Shall I wait outside?'

'Yes, thanks.' She turned back to her computer screen.

He waited in the corridor. Five minutes later, the door opened, and Dr Sheehan stood there, hand outstretched to welcome him in. It wasn't until he was seated that he noticed the crucifix again. From his seat, he was looking directly into the agonised face. The eyes of Christ were open, but he thought he remembered them closed. They were light blue, and the blue contrasted with the bloodshot redness that clung around the edges.

'Thanks for coming.'

'I appreciate the chance to speak to you. Is it about the presentation?' he asked.

'Yes, partly. It is also to see where we go from here, establish a framework, and maybe put down some markers for progress. How does that sound to you?'

'Yeah, fine. I wanted to get your perspective on a couple of things.' Vinny pulled his notebook from his bag and let it rest open on his knees. 'I would like to look at the numbers of Irish immigrants after the war. There have been a few studies, mainly around London and Birmingham, but I think it's possible to extrapolate from those. Maybe back them up with census results from Liverpool. The figure I have seen is around 300,000 in the '50s and '60s, across the UK. But I need to establish this. Also, take a look at employment patterns, housing, and social inclusion.'

The eyes of Christ were still on him.

'Fine, and what are you looking to establish?' she asked.

'Well, the facts first, then I can evaluate potential conclusions from that. Just in terms of scale and effects,' he said.

'And then?' Dr Sheehan began writing as he spoke.

'I want to look at the question of how identity is forged. This will involve a reading of Benedict Anderson and Hobsbawm. So "imagined communities" in relation to Liverpool.'

'Can I ask what you want to achieve?' She stopped writing and lifted her head.

He thought this was a weird question. 'Well, you've got all these Irish people arriving here, mainly in the '50s and early '60s. They get jobs, some start families. They are Irish but living in England. How do they see themselves? Then just a few years later you get the development of this whole Scouse thing for people who live in Liverpool. Does that include the Irish? People from the Caribbean? The Chinese? Again, how do they see themselves? Then on top of this, you've got the military situation developing in Northern Ireland in the late sixties. It seems like a very dynamic time, with profound changes.'

He paused for a second.

'I am beginning to think the idea that Scouse as an inclusive identity that covers everyone in Liverpool is a myth. Celebrating Scouse now is supposed to mean we recognise the city is made up of all these influences from all over the world as a port city.'

'And you don't think it is?' Dr Sheehan put her pen down and linked her hands in front of her on the desk.

Vinny's eyes shot back to the crucifix, those points of blue, surrounded by whitish pink and edged in blood red.

'I think the people are here, the cultures, but most of the time, those cultures and people were not welcomed. Not by everyone, anyway. Maybe it would be a start to be honest about that.'

'So, this is about honesty and identity?'

'In part, yeah.' Vinny was thinking on his feet. 'I think it's false to celebrate the Irish influence on Liverpool, or the Caribbean or African, or Chinese influence, and say the city has always been a "melting pot" without first recognising that this city, its leaders and a lot of its population, have done everything possible to stop it.'

'You sound angry.'

'Yeah, maybe I am,' Vinny said.

Dr Sheehan opened her hands. 'Okay, that's no bad thing, but you should use the emotion as a motivator, not allow it to determine your results.'

'Okay, fine, but is it the same? Being English? Irish? Scouse? Does it make any difference?'

'They are good questions. Where do you go to clarify them?' she asked.

'Anderson on imagined communities, Hobsbawm on nations?'

'That's all good. I think, though, that you have to be careful not to mix the personal and the historical. You don't want to risk your objectivity.' She paused, then made it clear the interview was over. 'I will expect a finished proposal by the end of the month. Let me stress, this is not optional. If you want any chance of a bursary or financial support, you will have to show you can commit to deadlines.'

The pressure was on.

Vinny slid his notebook back into his bag, stood and walked to the door. He turned and looked at the crucifix. From his angle, with Christ's head bowed, the eyes looked closed.

'Is there something else?' Dr Sheehan asked.

'Yeah, I was just checking.'

Dr Sheehan followed his sightline to the crucifix. '*Elohim*.'

'Sorry?'

'*Elohim* in Hebrew is the name of God.'

'The name of God?' Vinny looked confused.

'"Very truly, I tell you, before Abraham was, I am. *Elohim* - I am." John chapter eight, verse fifty-eight. "I am. The only identity we have."'

'I guess so,' Vinny answered.

As Vinny walked along the corridor, he wasn't sure what had just happened, but something had. *I am, I am, I am, Elohim.*

1965

Chapter Sixteen

Paddy

The knocker on the door rattled against its brass plate. In trousers and vest, Michael opened up.

'Up and at 'em, eh, Mike?' Paddy walked through the hallway into the living room. 'All clear, then?'

'Yeah, she's gone.'

Paddy avoided arriving too early. Michael's girlfriend Shirley didn't hide her hostility when their paths crossed. She was on the production line at Thompson and Capper, known locally as Mothaks because among their chemical products were mothballs.

'Don't know what she's got against me.'

'No, of course not, lad. Pure as the driven snow, aren't you?'

Walking over to the stereogram, Paddy turned the knob on the radio to increase the volume. He sang along to "My Girl" by the Temptations as he sashayed across the room.

Michael, a piece of toast between his teeth, lowered the volume on the radio. 'Give it a rest, will ya.'

'Any of that going spare?' Paddy nodded toward the toast.

'In the kitchen, put a couple of slices under the grill.'

Paddy walked through to the kitchen. The door to the yard was ajar, showing the stone flagging that covered the small space. While he was sorting out the toast, he called through to Michael. 'What've we got on?'

'We'll go to the yard, make sure the lads got out okay, then we've a job to do.'

'All good.'

Paddy made his toast while Michael finished dressing - nothing too smart, he never knew what the day would bring. Trousers, shirt and cardigan - semi-casual - and, of course, proper shoes, not dress shoes, mind, but no boots. Black slip-on shoes, bit of spit and polish, just the job.

'You and Shirl at the dance this Saturday?' Paddy asked.

'At the baths? Yeah, should think so,' Michael said. 'You taking anyone?'

'Not sure yet. Maybe Kathleen, or Rita,' Paddy replied.

'They're sisters, aren't they?'

'Yeah.'

'You're playing with fire there, mate,' Michael said.

Paddy laughed. 'Yeah, I know. Maybe I'll ask that Lynne from the café. She's a cracker.'

'Don't know her.'

'Yeah, you do,' Paddy replied. 'Blonde, all the bits in the right places. Works in the café in the Village.'

'All right, Casanova, let's get a move on, eh?' Michael led the way out the front door.

Stepping out into the bright morning sunshine, Paddy went round to the driver's side. The sky-blue Mark 1 Cortina, with its angled edges, looked sharp and smooth. Paddy felt like the toast of Garston, driving it round. It was Jack's car, but Paddy did most of the driving.

The short hop to the yard took a couple of minutes, but as he was turning the ignition and the motor kicked into life, he turned on the radio. The gravelly voice of Johnny Cash singing *It Ain't Me Babe* soon filled the vehicle.

Most of the guys were out on jobs. Jack rented the yard but owned the building company. They started with Charlie doing odd jobs; through a combination of hard work and influence, they had built it to a respectable size. Charlie was in charge, but nowadays, he mainly did the pricing and money collection. Their work was mostly subcontracting for bigger firms employed by the council, clearing bomb sites and slum demolition.

Charlie was a good tradesman, an all-round builder. His one flaw was a short temper, a temper that meant employee relations were not his strong suit. That side of things was delegated to Michael and Paddy, with a real foreman in the yard to supervise jobs and materials. Paddy was a strong and intimidating presence when needed. Paddy and Charlie had started on the tools and were now part of the small team around Jack.

After checking in the yard to make sure the various gangs were out and working, Michael turned to Paddy. 'Does she need juice?'

'What for?'

'What do you think for? We've got a drive.'

'Nah, she's full. I did it on my way to your place this morning. How far we going?' Paddy loved getting the chance to take the car a bit further.

'Out past Runcorn.'

'Yeah, that's no trouble.' Michael checked his watch.

'Have we got time for a bite before we head out?' Paddy asked.

'You've not long had toast,' Michael complained.

'A growing boy here, need my nutrition.'

'Yeah, go on, then. We're all right for time. Where do you want to go?'

A few minutes later, Paddy parked opposite the baths in the village. Michael said, 'Bloody hell, Paddy.'

'Come on, I'm buying.'

'Fucking right you are if I'm helping you get your leg over.'

Paddy, grinning, led the way toward the café. On the pavement outside, in among the passing shoppers, two men were handing out leaflets and collecting signatures. Paddy edged his way through.

'Do you want to take one of these?'

'Do I know you?' Michael asked.

'It's a meeting in support of the seamen's demand for a forty-hour week,' he said, ignoring Michael's question.

Paddy pushed open the half-glazed wooden door to the café, then turned round to see where Michael was.

'Aren't you Tommy? Tommy Healey?' Michael asked.

'Yeah, I am.' Tommy didn't look impressed. 'The meeting's tonight. There are speakers from the Seamen's and Docker's unions.'

'Not for me, thanks,' Michael said.

Paddy was holding open the café door.

'I guess you're not in a union,' Tommy said.

'You guess right. Nothing to do with me.'

Tommy moved aside to let him pass. 'Don't be so sure. We all need solidarity.'

Michael waved Paddy on, but Paddy ignored him and stayed by the door.

'What do you mean?' asked Michael.

'We all depend on other people. We have to stick together. For working people like us, that means unions,' Tommy replied.

'Not in my line, it doesn't.'

'Yeah, well. Like they say in the song: "The times they are a-changin."'

'Shit song, too,' Michael responded, and followed Paddy into the café.

The dozen café tables had patterned plastic tablecloths. Each table had four chairs, most of them empty. A couple of elderly women were enjoying tea and cigarettes, and a young mother sat with her son, the child drinking lemonade through a straw. The radio was playing The Beatles' "Ticket to Ride" in the background.

Michael chose a table while Paddy went up to the counter. Looking up from her order pad, Lynne gave a broad smile when she saw Paddy. 'Well, look who it is,' she said.

Paddy made his best attempt at a Bogart voice. 'Yeah, out of all the cafés and all the bars, imagine meeting you here.'

'Yeah, very strange since I'm here ten hours a day. Who'd've guessed it,' she said.

'Good to see you, though, and looking great as usual.' Paddy smiled.

'Why, thank you, sir, and how can I help you today?' Lynne did a little curtsy.

'Today, we will have two full breakfasts and two mugs of tea.'

Looking more serious, Lynne asked, 'What do you want with that?'

'The works.'

'Righto, have a seat. I'll bring your teas over.'

'That's for today, but there is something else you can do for me,' Paddy added.

'Ye - ss,' Lynne said hesitantly, as she arranged the mugs, 'and what would that be?'

'Saturday night, are you going to the dance at the baths?'

'I don't know yet. I'll have to check my diary.' She looked directly at him.

'Okay, well, have a think, I'll be over there.'

'Here, take these with you.' She poured the tea from a huge pot behind the counter. 'I'll just take your order through.' She turned and went into the kitchen.

Paddy watched as she walked through, then turned and took the tea to Michael.

'How'd you get on?' Michael asked.

'Still working on it. Do you recognise her?'

'Yeah, I've seen her around. You know she's a proddy, don't you?'

'Doesn't bother me what she is.'

'Well, I hope the breakfast is worth it.'

'Me as well.'

'What's the thing in Runcorn then?' Paddy asked as the door to the café opened.

Lynne had come back out from the kitchen and was tidying around the counter. A tall, dark-haired young man in work clothes entered and headed straight for her.

'Is it ready?' he snapped at Lynne.

'Hold on,' she replied.

'Come on, girl. Get a grip.'

Paddy looked at Michael. 'What's his game?'

'None of yours,' Michael said quietly.

Lynne disappeared back into the kitchen. Seconds later she came out carrying two breakfast plates, heading toward Paddy and Michael.

The man at the counter wasn't happy. 'For fuck's sake.'

Paddy couldn't help himself. He stood. 'Why don't you just take it easy, mate.'

Lynne reached the table. 'Paddy, leave it. Here, have your food.'

She put the plates down.

'And why don't you mind your business…Paddy,' the man added with a sneer.

'Leave it, will you,' Lynne snapped at him, walking back to the counter.

'He's me brother, take no notice,' she directed at Paddy as she did a half-turn.

Michael was up and standing in front of Paddy. 'Not now, we've got work to do.'

Lynne went straight back into the kitchen and returned with a plastic sandwich box, handing it to her brother.

'Yeah, you listen to your mate,' her brother said, taking the box. Then he added, 'And stick to your own kind.'

This time, it was Michael who spoke. 'Fuck off out of here

before I let him loose.'

Lynne pushed her brother out the door.

'Come on, sit down, let's eat,' Michael instructed Paddy.

Lynne returned to their table. 'I'm really sorry about that.'

Paddy didn't look at her. 'Forget about it,' he said.

'He's always like that,' she apologised.

'Forget about it,' Paddy said again, a little harsher.

Lynne went back to the counter, a little deflated.

'I'll see that fucker again,' Paddy declared.

'No doubt,' said Michael.

Chapter Seventeen

Michael

It wasn't often they left Liverpool, so Michael was enjoying the drive out along the new Ford Road. It was a simple route - out of Garston, over the bridge, past the tennies and the airport, along Speke Road. Airport to the right and factories on the left.

When the airport finished, the prefabs were on the right, made out of lightweight materials and asbestos roofing. Used for airmen during the war, it had been extended and expanded, so they now housed families waiting for permanent homes on the Speke estate. Michael knew this was how normal people lived and worked, shuttling between the estates and factories.

After Evans Medical on the left, they were on the Ford Road itself, a straight, fast road. It wasn't listed as a motorway but felt like it. Soon, the sprawling Ford Halewood factory site would take up their view on the left. Ford Halewood was actually between Halewood and Speke and was virtually the last thing in Liverpool. The road ahead led out through the chemical factories of stinking Widnes and into Cheshire. Michael also knew the road ahead in life would not end well, if he didn't change something.

Michael turned the radio volume up when The Righteous Brothers' *You've Lost that Loving Feeling* started. 'Love this song. Perfect for a slow dance at the end of the night.'

The Mersey Estuary opened out into the Irish Sea, travelling upriver; Garston was the last navigable point for shipping. At low tide beyond this, the river almost disappeared into a series of channels between the sand and mud banks. Silted up over many years, it was useless for trade and had been replaced in the late 1800s by the Liverpool-Manchester ship canal that ran beside it. Both waterways ran out under the Runcorn Bridge, an imposing steel structure that spanned the Mersey and provided a crossing from industrial Lancashire to the more rural Cheshire. The river had got its name from the Anglo-Saxon mæres, '*of a boundary*,' and ēa, '*a river*.'

Rumbling over the bridge in bright sunlight, Michael began to give directions. 'Take the next left, we're going toward the town.'

'Righto.' Paddy followed the curve of the exit down.

'Ok, keep going. There should be a pub coming up in a few minutes.'

The road turned back on itself after leaving the bridge, and they were now on the edge of old Runcorn. To the south and east, a whole new town had been built. Row upon row of low-level flats, designed as an overspill for Liverpool, had expanded rapidly over the past ten years. Modern housing developments were springing up around the new "Shopping City," an indoor mall in US-mode.

'There, that's it. Pull in.'

Paddy turned into the car park and parked at the farthest corner away from the road.

'So, what's going on, then?' Paddy asked.

'We're meeting someone.'

'Out here?'

'Yeah, out here.' Michael didn't bother adding anything.

After thirty minutes, Paddy was getting impatient. 'Can't we go in?'

They had been waiting in the car park and were now outside the car, smoking.

'We're sticking out like a sore thumb here,' Paddy said.

'You can't drink anyway. You're driving.'

'I can have one,' Paddy asserted.

Michael raised his hands. 'Just the one.'

The pub was modern, obviously hoping to cash in on the growing population. Its newness also meant it was light, clean and fresh, unlike most of the pubs they knew in Garston. Michael got the drinks and led them to a table with a view of the car park.

'What about Lynne, then?' Michael asked when they were seated.

'Nah, not after that. Can't be arsed. Anyway, she supports the wrong team, doesn't she?'

'I thought you didn't care what she was. Catholic or Protestant.'

'I don't. I don't mind a Protestant, but I'll be fucked if I'm going out with a Liverpool supporter. She had a scarf with her bag and coat behind the counter.' He widened his eyes in exasperation. 'Come on, with the likes of Peter Farrell and Tommy Eglington, got to be a blue, haven't you?'

Michael laughed. 'You're not right in the head.'

'Speaking of dolls, what d'ya reckon to Teresa?' asked Paddy.

'Jack's woman? Are you stupid? He'd cut your hands off,' Michael said.

'I'm not gonna do anything.'

'Jesus, don't even think it.' Michael looked a little more serious. 'Paddy, you need to settle down before you get yourself killed. I'm not kidding.'

'Yeah, I will, when the time is right.'

'I don't just mean with women...although that would be a start. You're always one step away from chaos.'

'What about you, then? Ready for nappies and all that?'

'Could be worse. You've seen our Jim's little fella Paul - cute little thing, he is.'

'Leave that for the mugs - that's not us.' Paddy took a long drink.

'That's the problem.'

'You worry too much,' Paddy laughed, putting his glass down.

'No, you worry me.' Michael looked out the window. 'You're up and down like a prozzie's knickers.'

'Sounds like fun.' Paddy smiled.

'Yeah, maybe.'

'Okay, well, looks like the time is right now. Here they are.'

'Where?'

'There, the blue Rover pulling in, that's them. C'mon, let's go.'

As they walked across the car park, the Rover came alongside. Michael nodded to the driver and pointed to their car and followed. The Rover parked next to Jack's car. The two men got out. The older of the two, tall and slim, held out his hand, while the other opened the boot. 'Michael, long time no see.'

Michael shook it. 'How are ya?'

'Good, and yerself?'

'Grand.' Michael nodded to the second man.

Paddy stood a little to the side, watching but taking no part.

'Open the boot, Paddy,' Michael directed.

Paddy walked to the rear of the vehicle. The other three followed and stood in a close group. Michael indicated to Paddy, and he and the third man reached inside the Rover's boot and lifted out a heavy green metal box. It was three feet long and a foot wide and deep, with a small handle at each end. Paddy had to lean in to lift it since it was heavy.

They swiftly lowered it into the Cortina, and the boots were closed. Michael shook hands again, and that was it. Everyone climbed back into their cars. Paddy waited while the other car reversed, straightened, then left the car park.

'I guess I shouldn't ask,' Paddy said, as he drove back over the Runcorn bridge.

'Yeah, you're right, you shouldn't.'

'Some fucking weight in that, though.'

Michael didn't respond. 'Now it's my turn,' he said, turning up Val Doonican on the radio. 'Got to love this fella.'

Pulling a face, Paddy changed the subject. 'Okay, so where are we taking it anyway? You can at least tell me that.'

'It's going through the dock, so we just have to keep it overnight 'til it's collected in the morning.'

Paddy was quiet for a while as they drove, then asked, 'Where's it going? Through the docks, I mean. Where will it end up?'

'Honest to God, I don't know.'

They drove on in silence, listening to the radio. The day had dragged on, and by the time they were back in Liverpool, it was early evening. The brightness was just dimming with the lowering sun.

As they approached the traffic lights at the crossroads of Speke Boulevard and Speke Hall Road, about five hundred yards ahead, the lights were red, traffic queued, so Paddy put his foot on the brake. The light changed to amber, then green. The traffic started moving, and Paddy raised his foot off the brake and lightly pushed down on the accelerator. They were gliding through the lights.

Paddy saw it first and shouted, 'Look!…Fuck!'

Michael leant forward, straining to see through the windscreen. 'Shit!'

The sky flashed red and white. A roar hit their ears as a Cambrian Airways Viscount Vickers Airliner boomed above them to the right. Filling the sky, the plane barrelled through the air. Its wings flipped 360 degrees as it bore down on the road. It passed feet above them. The car vibrated with the intensity of the sound. Propellers screamed, and the plane's metal skin screeched as it twisted and turned - then the crash, the boom and flash of a blast as the plane flew straight into the roof of the Thompson and Capper factory.

Paddy was just through the lights and swerved left, so the car mounted the kerb. He braked hard to stop.

'Jesus, Mary, and Joseph!' Michael crossed himself.

Cars stopped in every direction. Motorists got out of vehicles. Paddy and Michael also climbed out of the car. Smoke was pouring from the wound in the side of the factory roof. The cockpit and half the plane were buried inside; the plane was upside down.

'I saw the fucking pilot.' Paddy repeated, 'I saw him, upside down.'

'What do we do? What should we do?' Michael asked.

Paddy opened the car door to get in. 'Get the fuck out of here. That's what we should do. This place will be crawling with police any minute now.'

Michael sat on the grass verge.

Paddy shouted at him, 'Mike, come on, we've got to go, let's get out of here.'

Louder this time, he shouted again. 'Mike, move!'

Michael got up. 'Oh, Fuck. Shirley!' His legs were weak, and his stomach turned over. He checked his watch, 6:28 pm. 'She should have finished. She should be home.' A rush of adrenaline coursed through his veins.

The sounds now were of fire, crashing, smashing, a roaring sound like wind through a tunnel, growing in intensity and depth. A fire alarm was getting nearer.

'Ok, come on, go!' Michael was now pushing Paddy. 'Come on, get a fucking move on, will ya.'

'I am. Calm down. You said yerself. She'll be well home by now.'

They pulled back out into the road as two fire engines raced towards them full speed, on the other side of the dual carriageway. Michael heard the sirens as screams.

'What if she was doing overtime? Come on. Move it,' said Michael.

The drive was only five minutes, but Michael felt every second, every traffic light an eternity. As they passed the airport terminal, Michael lowered his window and gagged. He was convulsing, but nothing was coming up.

They turned left after the airport into Horrocks Avenue. A minute later, they were in Banks Road.

Michael wiped his mouth on his sleeve. People were on the street. Groups of women stood arms folded. Kids were running and playing, sensing the excitement in the air. Michael looked round through the back window. He could see the black column of smoke rising, swirling then spreading, drifting in the early evening sky.

Paddy screeched round the corner into Window Lane. More and more people were coming out. Paddy pulled up at the kerb, and Michael leapt out, knocking furiously at the door while trying to get his key into the lock

'For fuck's sake.' His key kept slipping.

The door was pulled open, and he nearly fell inside. His key stuck in the lock and stayed there.

'What the hell's wrong with you?' Shirley stepped back and let him tumble into the hallway.

'Jesus Christ.' He reached out and pulled her close.

He hugged her tight before letting his arms fall. 'I need a fucking drink,' he said.

Paddy walked straight through the open door.

Shirley called after them, 'Will someone tell me what the hell is going on?'

She followed them through to the kitchen. Paddy opened cupboard doors until he found a half bottle of Johnny Walker. He put three glasses on the table and poured.

'Here, get that down ya,' Paddy said to Shirley, then threw his own down his throat. 'Your place has only gone and blown up.'

'Don't be stupid. What are you on about?' Shirley snapped back.

'He's not kidding,' Michael added. 'A plane has just gone into Mothaks, straight into the roof. Didn't you hear the bang?'

'I didn't hear nothing. Really?' she asked. But the question was redundant as soon as it came out of her mouth. She could see in Michael's face that it was the truth.

'Yeah, really. The thing nearly had us, I'm not kidding. I could see the fucking pilot, upside down he was,' Paddy said.

'Oh, my God.' Shirley ran and switched the radio on. She played with the dial until she found Radio Merseyside. The radio was playing Sinatra's "My Way," so she turned the volume down again.

She turned to Michael. 'Shouldn't you go to the police? Tell them what you saw?'

'What for?' he asked.

'You're a witness, say what happened.'

'They know what happened. A fuckin' plane flew into the factory.'

'Yeah, I don't think there's much use,' said Paddy.

Sinatra finished, and a sombre male voice took over. Shirley rushed back to the radio and turned the volume back up.

'We have to interrupt this programme with some devastating news. We are receiving reports of a terrible crash. In the past hour, a plane has crashed into the Thompson and Capper factory at the corner of Speke Hall Road and Speke Boulevard.'

The three were now listening intently as the report continued.

'The plane was scheduled to land at the Liverpool passenger terminal. At this time, we don't know why it was unable to do so. We are in touch with Merseyside Police and Fire Brigade, who are dealing with the emergency. We have been told that the Fire Brigade are suppressing the ongoing fire. We have no information on casualties at this moment, although we have been told that the plane, a Cambrian Airlines Vickers Viscount, was not carrying passengers. I repeat, the information we currently have is that the plane was not carrying passengers.

We can further report that the day shift at Thompson and Capper had finished. We have no information at this stage about casualties from within the building.'

There was a pause.

'Rest assured, we will bring you more information as soon as we have it.'

The radio returned to instrumental music. Michael picked up the bottle, and all three walked into the living room. Michael and Paddy took opposite armchairs while Shirley sat on the sofa. The bottle was in the middle of the coffee table, and each topped up as required.

'I was only there an hour ago,' said Shirley.

'Who would be in there at this time?' asked Michael.

'Maybe a couple of supervisors, but we haven't had overtime. We haven't had any for two weeks now. We've been going mad about it.' Shirley stopped, and her eyes widened. 'Oh, my God, an hour earlier there would have been three hundred of us.'

She crossed herself, filled her glass again. 'I feel weak.' She took a drink. 'Jesus Christ… Did you actually see it?' she asked.

'He wasn't kidding, Shirl. The thing nearly scraped the top of the car,' said Michael.

'Oh my God. We've both been saved.' Shirley crossed herself. 'You're at mass on Sunday.'

Michael rolled his eyes.

'Don't you roll your eyes at me. You get a sign, you get given a chance, you are going to mass if I have to drag you there myself. And another thing, there's no sex in this house until there is a ring is on my finger - we'll see Father McDonagh on Sunday. If they read the banns, there's no reason we can't be married in a month. My God, what an escape.'

Paddy laughed. 'For you maybe, but what about Michael here? Church on Sunday and shackled in a month? No escape there.'

Shirley turned to Paddy. 'And you, running round like a dog

on heat. Out.'

'What?'

'You heard me, sunshine. Get yourself out of my house.'

Paddy looked at Michael. Michael shrugged. As he was going out the door, Paddy shouted over his shoulder, 'I'll see ya in The Dealers.'

★★★

The news spread rapidly. Radio Merseyside did on-the-spot reporting with updates every thirty minutes. By the time they reached The Dealers that evening, everyone knew that two workers, as well as the pilot and co-pilot, had been killed.

Chapter Eighteen

Shirley

The walk under the bridge and up through the village took longer than usual. Shirley didn't mind as she stopped to speak to people about the crash. The Dealers' juke box seemed louder than usual. She could hear the music from outside. Entering the long bar, Michael led the way. Shirley followed. She liked his broad back and rested her hand against it as they edged their way towards the bottom of the pub, near the dartboard. They normally sat between the dartboard and the rest of the bar. Theirs was the last table, farthest away from the door.

Jack's wife, Teresa, was at the table with Jim's wife, Peggy. Jack was talking to Paddy and Charlie.

Teresa waved to Shirley. 'Shirl, love, here, we've kept you a place.'

Teresa's jet-black hair was bunched, gathered, and sprayed into a beehive. It shook as a whole unit whenever she moved her head, which she did every time she spoke. She was an attractive woman, with fine, clear features on a symmetrical face. The effect of her make-up was to sharpen the angles and highlight the symmetry, producing a faintly skeletal effect.

Jack and Teresa had two children. They had made their move out of life under the bridge by leaving their terrace in Shakespeare Street for a three-bedroom end-of-terrace house in Speke, with front and back gardens. Shirley liked her, although Teresa never missed an opportunity to show off. But Shirley had something to be proud of tonight, although she was keeping it quiet for now.

Jim's wife Peggy was a modest woman, a practising Catholic who still liked a drink. Jim, Michael's brother, was a genuine guy with no interest other than working until he got pensioned off and seeing his son Paul happy and healthy - not unreasonable ambitions.

'Have you heard?' Teresa didn't wait until Shirley had sat down.

'That's not the half of it.' Shirley was settling herself, but looked back up at Michael. 'Lager 'n' lime. No, tell you what, after today, get me a Babycham as well.' Turning to Teresa, she said, 'I need something extra after today.'

'I know, awful, isn't it,' said Shirley. 'But d'you know Michael was nearly hit by the same plane?'

'I believe so. Paddy here was telling us all about it.' Teresa threw Paddy a smile and raised her glass.

Shirley also threw Paddy a look. *Doesn't he just always ruin everything?*

The men were at the bar. Michael was being served, and Shirley could see him recounting the near miss.

'Where was Jack today?' Shirley asked.

'I don't know. He was gone all afternoon.'

'Weren't you worried?'

'You know, I never even thought about it,' Teresa said.

'It's got me shaken. I don't mind admitting it,' said Shirley.

'Well, yeah, you work there. An hour earlier, it could have been you.'

'Not just me, all of us. Doesn't bear thinking about.' Shirley paused before adding, 'It's more than that, though, what with Michael being so close, just makes me think.'

Michael delivered Shirley's drink and was about to return to the bar.

'Close shave, then,' Teresa said.

'You're not kidding,' Michael replied.

'Dodged a bullet for sure there.' Paddy was behind him. 'That's the way it goes, innit, you dodge one, the next one gets you.'

'That's no way to talk, Paddy!' Even though she was admonishing him, Teresa smiled.

'What's going on here then, a meeting?' Jack joined them.

'No, I was just saying, Michael dodged one bullet then caught another,' Paddy repeated.

'How do you mean?' asked Jack.

'He missed the plane but got caught by Shirl's follow up. Didn't you say you were getting married?' Paddy threw the words like a barb at Shirley.

She screwed her face at him. *Bastard.*

Michael looked round at Paddy. 'That's right, mate, as soon as we can sort it out.' Michael turned to look at Shirley. 'Isn't that right, love?'

Shirley was beaming with pride as she held his gaze. 'Yeah, that's right. Come here, you big...' the words trailed off as she pulled Michael in for a kiss.

Michael accepted it, leaning in over the table, then made a show of saying, 'Gerroff, woman, you haven't got me yet.'

A roar of laughter and clapping erupted, as glasses were raised.

Jim made his way from the bar. 'Congratulations.'

Michael shook his hand.

Jack shouted to behind the bar, 'Give us a bottle of champagne, Molly - '

Paddy interrupted. 'You'll be lucky.'

Molly shouted from behind the bar, 'Paddy Connolly, you wouldn't know a bottle of champagne if someone was hitting you over the head with it.'

Jack responded, 'Wet, sweet, and bubbly, and she'll do.'

'Just how I like my women.' Paddy added.

★★★

Laughs, flirtatious giggles, and shrieks filled the warm night air. Garston was on the move. Somewhere between eleven and midnight, the pubs emptied. St Mary's Road became a stream of celebrants, moving down toward the village. Fish-and-chip shops made a roaring trade as punters tried to soak up the alcohol. The tradition well-established, the girls would walk on under the bridge, while the guys queued for the food.

'We want those chips warm when you get them home, so don't be hangin' round talkin' all night.' Shirley nudged Michael.

Shirley and Peggy walked arm-in-arm under the bridge.

On cold winter nights you could hear the foghorns of ships as they negotiated the narrow channels of the Mersey. On summer nights, the river was quiet, but sparkled with the lights of the oil terminal across the river at Ellesmere Port. Michael was feeling good.

Men and women were coming down the hill from the direction of Garston Hospital. Michael recognised Lynne's brother among the group. He walked in silence beside Paddy and Jim. He saw them enter the chip shop, four of them, but they were further back in the queue. He avoided eye contact. When he did glance in their direction, he knew they were looking at him and Paddy. He sensed the trouble ahead.

'So, you're actually gonna do it, then?' Paddy asked.

'I'd be a fool not to. I know when I've met my match.'

'Same with me and Peggy,' Jim said.

'Like a pair of old women.' Paddy laughed.

Jim responded to him, 'You'd be better an' all, finding yerself a nice girl.'

'I do every weekend, Jim. Then I find another one the next week,' said Paddy.

'Get out of it. You'd be lucky to get a kiss behind the bike shed. All this bravado, it's all a show,' said Jim.

Michael laughed.

'You wish! Both of you lads are proper tied now, collars round your neck, and if you're lucky you might get a long leash.'

'Ah, give over,' said Michael.

The shop was full of the sound of orders being filled, shouted, and discussed.

'Fish 'n' chips twice, chips 'n' gravy, and a couple of fish cakes and chips.' Jim gave their order over the counter.

The warmth of the evening increased inside the shop by the proximity to the boiling fat. Paddy took his jacket off to roll up his shirt sleeves.

'Like a dog in heat…' The voice came from behind them in the queue.

Paddy and Michael looked around.

'Does one of yous fellas have something to say?' Paddy shouted back at them.

Michael put a restraining hand on Paddy's chest.

Jim took the completed order, wrapped in paper. He held the whole bundle in his arms. 'Come on, guys.' He tried to hustle them out.

Jim led the way out of the shop; Paddy and Michael were behind him. As they passed the group, one of them flicked a hand out, trying to knock the food from Jim's grasp. Jim clutched it tighter and made it out of the shop.

Lynne's brother was with three friends.

Michael was behind Paddy as Paddy squared up to him. 'Okay, bollocks, you've been wanting this all day.'

'Piss off, Paddy. No one's impressed with you here,' he answered.

'Know me name, do ya? Ya long streak of piss. Well let's see, d' ya wanna get outside and get to know me better, do ya?' Paddy's brogue deepened and sharpened as he built himself up.

Paddy was leaving him nowhere to turn. It would be hard to refuse such a public challenge. Paddy left the chippy, and Michael followed him out.

'Are you right?' Paddy asked Michael.

'I am. If any of those others try to get in, they'll have me to deal with.'

'Come on guys, let's go. It's not worth it,' Jim said.

'We're staying,' Michael said.

Michael took Paddy's jacket. Paddy limbered up outside the chippy, stretching his arms.

'Come on, where are they?' Paddy was getting impatient.

'They're getting served now,' Michael said, looking into the shop. 'Now, Paddy, you give the fella a slap, but nothing too much. Are you listening to me?'

'Stop worrying,' Paddy said. 'Really, what the fuck is going on with you?'

Michael had been here before and knew that when unleashed, Paddy had a side as dark as coal.

'Here they come,' said Jim, taking a step back.

Lynne's brother was at the back of the group as they left the chippy. Paddy pushed the others aside and confronted him. 'Come on then, bollocks, let's 'ave ya.'

He took a swing at Paddy. Paddy put up his left arm to block it and sent a right fist straight through the middle. The punch connected hard and well, sending the man staggering backward. Paddy shook his right hand, and though still hurting, he swung another, this time a hook that caught the guy in the side of the head. Lynne's brother toppled over sideways.

Michael, arms outspread, still holding Paddy's jacket, stood between Paddy and the other men, warning, 'Don't do it, let them sort it out.' Turning to Paddy, he shouted, 'That's it, he's done. Come on, let's go.'

Michael reached over and pulled Paddy by the arm away from the figure on the ground. 'Come on, that's it,' he repeated.

Paddy allowed himself to be pulled, and they moved away slowly.

'He had that fucking coming,' Paddy said, nursing his fist.

'No question,' Michael said. 'You did well, leaving him on the ground.'

They started walking round to the bridge. Jim let out a cry, and there was a crash. A Coca Cola bottle bounced off Jim's head and smashed against the wall. Jim stumbled and dropped the food. Michael and Paddy turned in time to see the three other men charge. They stepped forward in front of Jim, who was doubled over, holding his head, then moved to meet the oncoming rush.

Michael turned sideways quickly enough to avoid a kick that came flying at him. He swung his left forearm out and caught the guy in the throat. Paddy was grappling with his attacker, trying to land punches as they dragged and pushed each other. Michael moved on; the third attacker was clearly having second thoughts and started to back off. Michael lunged forward at him. This was enough to make him turn and back off.

He then spun round in time to see Paddy, forcing his opponent down by the neck. He was bent over him. Michael pulled the guy, who was holding his throat out of his way and pushed him back toward the village.

Jim shouted, 'No, Paddy!'

Michael saw Paddy holding the guy by the throat with his left hand and holding a knife to his face with his right. Michael sprinted over and let a kick fly. The kick smashed into Paddy's right hand, sending the knife flying.

Paddy straightened and turned to face Michael. 'What the fuck?'

'Enough!' Michael shouted. 'Come on, we're going. Now.'

Jim was holding his head as he walked. Michael grabbed Paddy and pulled him along the street.

'Let's get out of here. Pick that fucking knife up. Come on.'

'Have you still got the chips?' Paddy asked Jim.

They moved quickly through Church St, then along Banks Road.

Some time between putting his head on the pillow and waking up the next morning, Michael decided he wouldn't work for Jack again. He was finished.

Chapter Nineteen

Paddy

He'd enjoyed the day. The plane coming down. He could see the pilot shitting himself. Eyes wide open. Paddy guessed the pilot wanted to see death coming. *Well, he saw me*. He'd swear it. Their eyes had met for just a flicker of a second. Can't be many people who could say that.

He didn't like Michael not telling him stuff. It wasn't right, and his missus, Shirley, had a right face on her. *Crack a smile, for God's sake. Fuck them, fuck them all*, he thought.

When he left Michael's, he looked for a phone box and dropped his penny. He knew the number, had it memorised. Jack and Teresa lived in Speke, in a nice house with a garden. Teresa was fit. One of the kids answered.

'Hey, is yer mum or dad there?'

'Hello.' It was Teresa.

'Hello, babe, how's it going?'

He heard her chase the kid away. 'What the hell are you doing?' she said.

'Is he there?' He already knew he wasn't, or she would've made an excuse and put the phone down.

'No, he's out.'

'Ha, I knew it.'

'You're a bastard, do you know that?'

She liked effing and blinding with him. He didn't think Jack let her do it. He didn't mind. He thought it got her going.

'Where is he, then?'

'You probably know better than me,' she said.

'I'll pick you up in ten.'

'Jesus, Paddy.'

'On the corner. Don't leave me hanging around,' Paddy said.

He imagined Teresa putting the phone down, and he knew it was on. She was a right goer, Teresa. He thought the danger made it better for her. You always hear how some women like it. Well, it didn't put her off, that's for sure.

Teresa was there when he pulled round the corner. She looked good. Her skirt was above the knees. He liked that, made life easier.

'Come onto fuck, get in,' he said.

'You're moaning at me. After you phoning the house?' She climbed in and slammed the door.

'Easy.'

'Don't tell me, "easy." Whose bloody car is it?'

He took her to Oggie - Oglet shore - a mile from the estate, down a tiny road that passed the end of the airport runway. You could see it used to be farmers' fields, the ones the airport wasn't using as runways. But at the end of the tiny road, you got to the bank of the Mersey. Down a steep hill was the river's edge. Up at the top, he pulled the car into the bushes. The best fucking spot for miles around.

Before they got there, she was on it. Rubbing it before getting it out. She knew what she was doing. So good, he had to stop her, or there'd be nothing left. They got out of the car, she leaned over the bonnet, and that skirt was a good choice. It was only a quickie but *pure right class*, he thought.

On the way back, she ran into the Parade, got some bread and milk from the shop. They were back in less than half an hour. He was feeling good. The day was getting better, and he had the prospect of a few jars in the night. They turned into the street, and who was stood at the end of her path except her man himself. Jack.

'Oh shit,' she said.

He didn't want her nerves affecting him. 'Shut it, leave it to me.'

When they pulled up, he ran round and opened her door, like she was a lady.

'Where the fuck have you been? I've told you before not to leave the kids,' Jack said.

'I just saw her on the street on the way back from the shops. I thought I'd give her a lift, get her home quicker,' Paddy said.

Jack looked at him, then her. 'Go on, get inside, woman. You did right, Paddy.' He shook his head. 'How was the day for you, boys?'

'All good, got the parcel and everything.'

'That's good. Have you dropped it off?' he asked.

'Yeah, all sorted, Jack. I was on my way to tell you meself.'

'Good. Get yerself home then, and we'll see you tonight.'

Back in the car, Paddy had to laugh, and thought, *I'd better sort that fucking parcel out after all. Parcel my arse. It was rifles.*

That evening in the pub, Teresa had been giving him the eye. But he knew he had to be careful, can't rub a fella's nose in it. Not someone like Jack, anyway. Michael and Jim were around too, so it was easier for Paddy to just mix in. He was pretty sure no one else could see the looks Teresa was giving him.

Paddy didn't understand Michael and Jim. Strange things, brothers - he had no idea what his own were like now. Probably working on someone's farm. That wouldn't be a bad life if you could put up with the muck and shit of it. Jim was a shithouse, but we've always known that. Weird how the same blood was in both brothers, yet they came out so different. He didn't know why they let Jim hang round with them. Yeah, he did, he was family. Family and fuckin' Wicklow, that's what mattered to Jack. Paddy knew he would never be either.

Michael took his medicine, getting hitched to Shirley. Paddy thought maybe he should start looking for a regular bird. That would make sense, having a house, someone regular. Even Lynne, just to piss her brother off. She was fit enough. He wouldn't mind having a regular bash at that.

They'd ended up in a scrap on the way home. Paddy would've done the fella, except for Michael. He sorted Lynne's brother outside the chippy, no problem. Then three of them thought they would have a go when they were under the bridge.

Fair play to Michael, he could handle himself. *I was just gonna mark the guy*. Michael was getting a bit weird.

Cracker of a day all round.

2004

Chapter Twenty

Anne

Anne's laptop was playing "Laundry Services" by Shakira. She loved the Latin-based rhythms, the upbeat mood. Her hips were moving as she pulled on her jeans. Anne wore dresses for special occasions; skirts were okay for work, but she felt most comfortable in jeans, tops, and jumpers. She'd always been told she looked good in jeans.

She had agreed to meet DS Cooper in Woolton for a drink and knew it wasn't just the story. There was something else going on for both of them. She wasn't sure how far it would or could go. *But no need to decide that now.* She did put a spare pair of panties, toothbrush and body spray in her handbag, and finally picked up a condom and threw that in too.

The bowl of condoms in her bathroom was more a statement of intent than a practical resource. They'd been given out free when she was at Uni. She wondered for a minute if they had "use by" dates, but somehow, checking would be just a little too close to actually planning something, rather than just being prepared. The only nods in the direction of this being part-date in her choice of clothes were the flat black shoes instead of trainers, and a lighter, silky black bomber jacket instead of her usual heavier leather one. She was dressed, prepped, and ready to go. Her hair, which was normally tied and pinned up, was out of its confines, and she liked the bounce and feel of it.

She didn't have an Afro. Her hair was more loosely curled. She loved that Afros were becoming fashionable again and seriously wished she had her dad's hair. Anne tied a burgundy scarf around her head, so she had a band of colour breaking the lush black of her hair.

Anne didn't usually wear much make-up. She didn't think it suited her skin, which was a deep, natural olive. She lightly brushed her cheekbones and wore light eyeshadow. Everything was simple and toned down. She chose a gloss lipstick in a similar colour to her head scarf. It was the one showy bit of her look.

She wasn't sure what she thought about Dave. *Should I call him Dave?* He was attractive enough in a straight kind of way, a sort of slightly more exciting version of a professor. He seemed smart enough, and, she supposed, a bit more streetwise.

She hadn't had many boyfriends.

There had been a guy at Uni, and they'd been on and off for over two years, but somehow, it never got beyond the stage of nights out and sleeping together. The progression she saw in other couples - visits to families, joint holidays, even engagement and marriage in one case - didn't happen in her relationship. She accepted this at the time but since wondered if it was her fault. Did she limit her relationships to companionship without reliance? Why were sex and friendship different things?

Before she opened the front door to leave, she stopped, breathed deeply, filled her lungs with oxygen then exhaled, hoping that the escaping air carried her nerves with it.

It was a twenty-minute drive. Anne was meeting Dave at The Baby Elephant. She knew the pub from driving through Woolton. You couldn't miss it because a painted statue of an elephant stood in an alcove above the main door. She had never been inside.

Lateness was a precaution to make sure he was already there.

Anne looked around the room. It was a good place to meet. It wasn't too crowded, and there was a mix of men and women, couples, and small groups. Music was playing, but at such a low level, it was difficult to work out what it was under the hubbub of voices in chatter. She couldn't see Dave, and for a moment, she wondered if she would have to wait on her own.

As she moved further in, she saw him and was relieved, her smile genuine. He looked good, and she felt a little surprised to catch herself thinking they would make a nice-looking couple. Dave had a drink waiting for her.

'Hey.' She waved.

He waved back as she made her way through the room. She put her bag on the seat next to her and gratefully accepted the drink.

She raised it to eye level and made a show of examining it.

Dave's eyes narrowed. 'You are kidding? You think I would spike it?'

'A girl can't be too careful these days.' She smiled and added, 'Thanks.'

'You're welcome,' he returned, a little too formally.

'Mmm, that's nice, what is it?'

'I took a chance. Spritzer: white wine and soda.'

'Good choice,' she said, putting the glass down. 'How are you?'

'Yeah, good. Have you been in here before?'

'No, first time out in Woolton. Seems nice, though.'

'You know this is where John and Paul met?'

'John and Paul, who?' Anne took a sip from her drink.

'The Beatles.'

'What, in this pub?' she asked, looking around.

'No, St Peter's just up the road. Eleanor Rigby's grave is there, too.'

'Oh, right - no, I didn't know that.' There was a pause before she changed the subject. 'Did you find anything?'

'Down to business, eh?'

'Yeah, sorry, no offence. But I'm pretty keen to find out what's happening.'

'Well, yeah, since you ask.' He pulled out a copy of the local paper from under his jacket. He had circled the piece on page two.

HUMAN REMAINS FOUND IN GARSTON

Chronicle News Desk. Anne McCarthy

Human remains have been found buried on a building site by contractors carrying out excavation work. Police were called to the site at about 9:00 GMT on Monday, 3rd July, after the discovery in Garston, Liverpool 19.

Bones from 'an adult male' were discovered buried in what is now a Brandon development project of private housing. The area was formerly occupied by council housing.

The bones, believed to be from one individual, were found in a small area of the site which had been undergoing excavation work for the past month, Merseyside Police said.

Experts have confirmed the bones are human and are now working to establish their age, in a process which could take several days.

Further excavation after the discovery did not uncover any further remains, police added. The force said it had not yet opened a criminal investigation, but inquiries remained ongoing. Detective Sergeant David Cooper of Merseyside Police said, 'Officers will review whether further action needs to be taken in due course.'

Meanwhile, eyewitness reports of the excavation suggest foul play.

'Foul play?' Dave asked.

'Yeah. It could have been a lot more.' Anne defended herself.

'It doesn't say the police think this.'

'Why say it at all?'

She felt he was pushing a little.

'Because it's true, whether you say it or not. The builders on the site saw the bones, they knew it wasn't normal.'

Dave lifted the drink to his lips. 'Okay, but I think we should be more careful. I could get into real shit if anyone knew I helped you.'

'Well, don't go crazy but - ' Anne wasn't sure, but knew that she should tell him.

'What do you mean?'

'Outside the Noah's Ark after you left - ' but she couldn't tell him the worst bit.

'Yeah?' he interrupted. 'Come on…'

'Okay. Let me finish.' She took a drink. 'Someone had a go at me.'

'What do you mean, had a go? For fuck's sake. I was over the road.' Dave looked frustrated.

'I know. It all happened so quickly.'

'What happened?'

'A guy grabbed me, and he took my notebook.' She looked down at the table, avoiding his gaze.

'Anne.' He reached out to her.

She leaned back and raised her hands. 'I'm fine, honestly.'

'Did he hurt you?'

'Well, he nearly choked me.' She wasn't going to tell him any more than that.

'For God's sake, why didn't you call me?'

'I texted you when I got out of the pub.'

'I mean after, or during it,' asked the DS.

'I couldn't. I just wanted to get home.'

Dave took a long drink of his pint. 'What did he say?'

'He said I should stop asking questions.'

'This is serious. Did he say anything else? Any idea who sent him?'

'No, that's all he said, "Stop asking questions."'

'Do you have any idea who could have sent him?'

'Actually, I do. An idea. I've got no proof. No evidence. But I did get his number plate.'

'You got his car registration?' Dave looked shocked. 'Why didn't you tell me that straight away. You should've come over the station, and we could have looked for him right away!'

'Yeah, sent out an APB, like in the movies?'

'This isn't funny.'

'Does it look like I'm laughing? I wanted to get out of there. I wanted to get home.'

'Okay, okay,' he said.

Anne felt his frustration passing. She placed her hand on his. 'I appreciate your help, really.'

The lines of his face softened.

'To be honest, it's harder than I thought,' she said.

'What is?' he asked.

Anne withdrew her hand as she spoke. 'All of it, really. You know, you have all these ideas, what the job will be like. And when it comes down to it, it's just me, being nosey and asking questions, not sure who or what to believe. There's no investigation, nothing. I haven't even told my editor I was there, 'cos I think he'll go crazy.'

'Your article was well-written, though, and at least you spelled my name right.' Dave smiled.

'Thanks.'

Dave leaned back. 'Okay. How about this? You give me the car reg. I'll check it out. If you find anything, or anything else happens, you let me know. From now on, we share the information. Just don't tell anyone where it comes from. How does that sound?'

'Works for me.' Anne took a long drink of her wine; she felt back in control. 'Look, I know we could talk about your dog and your car, but I'm really curious to see if you found anything else.'

Dave smiled as he teased her, 'Well, I don't have a dog - my car is pretty special though, E 3 Series, satellite navigation, electronic brake-force distribution, four-wheel drive - '

'Sounds great,' Anne interrupted.

'Oh yeah.' Dave smiled. 'On the information side, there is a bit of a breakthrough: the window has narrowed. We are looking at early or mid-1970s.'

'That's a real development.'

'Yeah, it came back today. But on the names, we had a few Patrick Connollys, but nothing for the time and location of your Paddy Connolly, same with Bob Pennington. No charges, no convictions. That doesn't mean a lot. There could have been lots going on, just nothing on file. But you should be careful with Michael. We know he and his mates were up to no good.'

'In what way?'

'They were on our radar.'

'Nothing on file? Isn't that what you said?'

'Yeah, but there are reports on the situation in the area, and these are circulated to people who work on the ground. Some with names, some without...'

Anne followed Dave's gaze as two men entered the bar.

'Hold on a second, I just need a word with someone,' he said.

Dave got up and moved quickly through the bar. Anne watched keenly as he approached the two young men. The discussion was brief, followed by a handshake.

Anne was torn. The anticipation from earlier had morphed on contact with reality into relief about the article. Dave clearly fancied her. Maybe it was time for her to relax a little. Replace the negative with something positive.

He returned to his seat. 'Something for later.' He opened his palm to show two small circular yellow pills. 'Are you okay with this?'

'Wow, you're taking a risk, aren't you?'

'Nah, it's fine.' He slipped the pills into his pocket.

'You know those guys, then?' Anne nodded toward the two young men.

'Yeah, we know all the dealers: Speke, Garston, Halewood. Of course we know. We're not stupid.'

'Did you pay for them?' Anne was hoping he couldn't see her shock.

'Freebies.' He smiled.

'And you just let them deal in here, do nothing.'

'Doing something can be worse than doing nothing.'

Anne pulled a face. 'How does that work, then?'

'Now, we know who is doing what - cocaine, weed, heroin - generally we know where it's coming from, who's bringing it in, who's distributing it. As long as everyone behaves, then they get on with it.'

'So, in other words, you allow it?'

'Not officially,' Dave said. 'Can I trust you?' he asked. 'About the paper and all that?'

'Of course, we're having a drink, aren't we?' Anne wasn't sure if he was trying to impress her, this was all bullshit, or this behavior was completely normal for him.

'Yeah, but you never know.'

Anne pulled out her bag and opened it in front of him, her hand rummaging through the contents. 'Look, no recorder.'

She saw the condom and spare panties and closed the bag quickly, hoping Dave hadn't noticed.

'Anyway, the truth is, if we close the supply down, the shit hits the fan. With H and crack, you've got junkies going crazy looking for gear, shooting up any shit. You've got kids thinking this is their chance to get in the game, start fighting it out to become the next boss. Bodies start dropping everywhere: users, dealers, civilians caught in the crossfire. That's when we get it in the neck, from politicians and your lot in the papers and media.'

Dave took a break to drink and then continued. 'We make sure people behave, don't break the rules. Occasionally, we will pull in a big distributor or importer, but we know within days someone else will have stepped up, so things start all over again. This way, we know who's doing what. They know, we know, anyone gets out of hand, they give us the nod. Or if we need to find anyone…It's always been like this, always will be.'

'So, you just watch it all happen?' It was wrong, and she should know better, but something was exciting about his lack of care.

'No,' Dave said. 'We have our hands full catching the scallies, rounding up the arseholes kicking shit out of each other. Then you've got the rapists and paedos. I could go on. So, don't worry, we've got our hands full.'

'Yeah, I guess you do.'

'It might not sound like much, but this is way better than uniform. I hated being in uniform. It was like having a big sign on your back - like the kids in school - "kick me" or "spit here."'

Anne changed the subject. 'So, what you were telling me earlier is that you've heard rumours. About Michael?'

'More than rumours. Intelligence. Michael was connected to a couple of serious people.'

'The Powers?'

'Yeah.'

'So, what does your intelligence tell you they were doing?'

'You name it. Stealing off the docks like most thieves, but more organised. They started paying people to turn a blind eye, and from there, sponsoring other people to do it for them, setting up distribution networks. The usual combination of muscle and greed.'

'How about the body? The missing person, I mean? '

'We had a few names, people disappeared over the past twenty, thirty years, from south
Liverpool. Narrowing it down to the '70s is easier.'

'So, who's gone missing?'

'Mostly teenagers, runaways, so they're out. A few older guys. My guess is they left for domestic reasons. So, the best option we have now is that we try and match DNA. If a father disappeared, we can take a DNA sample from his kids and see if there is a match. We will have a DNA sample from the remains in the next couple of days so we can start that process. But neither of your names were reported missing,' Dave said.

'Which means either no one cared, or the people at the time knew where they went, even if no one remembers that now,' said Anne.

'Yeah, probably. There's an old saying, "No body, no crime." Not strictly true, but not far wrong. If the body never turns up, you've got no evidence, no timeline.' Dave brought his hands together, fingertips touching, then flicked them open. 'Puff, vanishes into thin air.'

'So, burying the body in a backyard in Garston is one way of getting rid of it.'

'Seems so.'

Anne was a little disappointed.

'Hey, I tried.'

'No, it's not your fault, and thanks.' She reached out and put her hand on his, just long enough for them to enjoy the touch before withdrawing it. 'Just so you know, I'm not sure where to go with this.'

'You mean us or the story?'

She felt the heat rise to her face. 'Both,' she replied.

'I don't know if it will help, but I did make a couple of calls, and there is someone we can talk to.'

Anne brightened up a little. Was he doing this to help find the identity or because he liked her? Maybe it was all the same. 'That sounds interesting. Who?'

'Ex-Special Branch, was around in the '70s, knows this area.'

'How do you know him?'

'We get briefings on intelligence collection. He used to do them, still does some as a kind of consultant.'

'Normal police and intelligence, do those terms go together?'

'Yeah, even us lowly "plod." You'd be surprised.'

'Yeah, maybe I would.'

'Okay, so when do I get to meet him?' asked Anne.

'He's retired now, so as long as he's not on the golf course. Let me know when you are free, and I'll check in with him,' Dave said.

'Sounds good.'

'And on the other subject, time for another?'

'Yeah, but let me get it. Working girl, I can pay my way.' Anne had decided to enjoy herself.

'Nice to hear.' Dave finished his pint. 'You won't get any complaints from me, but why don't we move on? If you're ready? There's a couple of wine bars we can go to. Vibe's a bit better.'

★★★

The next morning, Anne woke first. The light was just breaking through the curtains. It was quiet except for the odd car passing in the street below, and Dave's laboured breathing next to her. She was wearing one of his t-shirts. He was naked. She lay back in no rush to move. Images or memories, she wasn't sure, floated uncertainly through her brain. Dancing, drinks, the kiss…

Her phone rang, and she scrambled for her bag. As she turned it off, she recognised the number. Her mum again.

Chapter Twenty-One

Anne

Anne rang the intercom to Vinny's flat and listened to the distant ringing before a change of tone and crackling, which meant he had pressed the button at his end.

'It's me,' she spoke into the machine.

There was a sharp buzz and a click, and when she pushed the door, it swung open. Her steps rang out on the stairs. *Must be a nightmare for people in the lower flats*, she thought.

On the second landing, she pushed open Vinny's unlocked door. He was placing a cup of tea on the coffee table.

'That was quick,' she nodded toward the tea.

'Yeah, well, guess I know you by now.'

'Not working?' Anne asked.

'No. They cancelled my shift.'

'I don't know how you manage it.' Anne surveyed the room.

'It's a pain in the arse. I'm supposed to do two five-hour shifts a week, but I never know what days it will be.'

The room was full of furniture, or it was more like the furniture filled the room. There was a patterned velveteen-covered sofa against the wall, a coffee table in front of it, and two armchairs side by side. Squeezed in at the end of the sofa, there was just room for a TV on a little table. A CD player sat among books on a shelf above the TV.

Anne picked her way between the furniture and sat on the

sofa. Vinny sat next to her. His laptop was open on the table, playing a Van Morrison album.

'How are things?' he asked. The question was casual, but they both recognised the undertone.

'Yeah, good.' She wasn't sure whether to tell him about the night before, mainly because she wasn't sure about it herself.

'You look well,' Vinny said.

'You look tired.' It seemed odd to say this when she was the one who had been up half the night.

'Not sleeping too good. What've you been up to?' asked Vinny.

'Nothing much. Well, the whole Garston thing, obviously.' Anne took a drink of her tea.

'Yeah, obviously. Does any of that include the copper?' He looked at her, head tilted.

'You know it does.' Anne felt no shame. It just wasn't his right to know anything.

'Really?'

'Yeah, you know he's helping me, and his name is Dave, by the way.'

'Right. Dave,' he said.

Anne was feeling a little piqued. 'Come on, Vinny, it's no big deal.'

'I dunno. I think there's something you're not telling me, maybe?'

'So, how did it go?' she asked. 'The report?'

'Oh, I see, changing the subject?' He raised his eyebrows.

'No, come on...' She appealed. She didn't want this conversation.

'Wait,' Vinny stared at her. 'There is something. There's something going on?'

Anne remained quiet and pointedly picked up a book and flicked through its pages.

'Okay. Fine, if you don't want to talk about it.'

She put the book down before returning to her question. 'So, how was the report thing?' She was running out of patience.

'Okay, yeah, not so bad. The comments were all, you know, constructive. The presentation was a bit boring, but the questions opened it up a bit.'

'They asked you questions?' Her interest was growing.

'No, I asked them,' Vinny said, his tone a bit warmer.

'How did that work, then?'

'I liked it. I thought it was really good.'

'Go on, then, what questions?'

'Okay, I'll do it with you, all right?' He appeared animated now.

'Yeah, whatever.'

'Okay, well, after I did the presentation, and they were asking me stuff, I said, "You know the best way I can show you what I mean is by showing you what is missing. Not what exists, but what doesn't exist."'

'That sounds crazy,' Anne said.

'I know, they looked confused too. Okay, here goes. What city received the largest influx of Irish immigrants in England after the Famine?'

'Liverpool,' Anne replied confidently.

'Correct.' Vinny nodded. 'Nearly 300,000 in the few decades after the 1840s. What city had both an Irish Nationalist MP and a Unionist MP until around 1920?'

'Liverpool?' said Anne, a little more tentatively.

'Correct. What English city is affectionately referred to as the capital of Ireland?'

'Liverpool, again. Okay, I can see where you are going with this.'

'Then I did the thing about St Patrick's Day.'

'And it went down well?'

'Yeah, it was fine because what is missing is Irish culture in Liverpool. No parades, celebrations, we had parish stuff to do with the churches. We saw the priest every week. We had separate Catholic and Protestant schools. We celebrated church holidays: Lent, Easter, Palm Sunday, Ascension Day. I could go on, Catholic, all of it. But not the Irish stuff. It's weird that I'm only realising this now for the first time.'

'Realising that the Irish was missing?' Anne asked.

'Yeah. Unless it was Orange, then it was out there in public. What is it they say? "You can't miss what you never had." But it's not true. I didn't know I was missing it. But now, it's like "how did I not miss it?" Maybe some families had it, kind of privately. But I'm sure most were like mine - everything under the carpet, everything kept quiet, in case you upset somebody. Irishness was transformed into Catholicism. At least while I was growing up.'

'Yeah, okay, I get it.' It sounded sharper than Anne meant.

'What?' Vinny asked. 'Am I boring you?'

'No, it's not that, but we have been through this stuff before. It's not exactly a new conversation.' Anne regretted the words as soon as they left her mouth.

'Well, excuse me - '

Anne interrupted him. 'It has to mean something. All this talk of yours, the history, the facts. What difference does it make? The thing that annoys me is you never do anything about it.'

'We have to know where we come from,' Vinny declared.

'Yeah, you're right. I didn't mean anything by it.' Anne backed off. 'Anyway, I have some questions for you. Is that all right?' She knew how to engage him.

'Yeah, go on.'

'Who would I speak to if I wanted more info about someone who worked on the docks in Garston, or for the union, anyway.'

'The union. I guess the Transport and General,' Vinny answered.

'But it's not the same union. It's what they called the "Blue Union."'

'You could try the CASA.'

'The bar? Café?'

'Yeah, except it's not just a bar. The place was opened by dockers who were sacked during the strike in '98 or '99, I think it was. They run the place. There's usually a few of them in there, but they would know who to ask, anyway.'

'Okay, thanks. I'll give it a try. I have a couple more questions, if it's okay?'

'Sure, fire away.'

'It's about your dad,' Anne said nervously.

Vinny looked confused. 'What about him?'

'How well did you know him?'

'Not very well. He left when I was really young.' He paused a moment. 'Why are you asking this?'

'Your dad was Irish, wasn't he?' Anne pressed.

'Yeah, you know that, though. What's going on?' Vinny asked.

'Nothing, I just wanted to find out a bit more about him,' Anne lied.

'There's nothing to say. He left, walked out, left my mum and me.' The echo of his dad leaving. Was that why he couldn't see his son Charlie?

'When did he leave? And you never heard from him?'

'No, I didn't, and I don't know why we are having this conversation.' Vinny shifted in his seat. Part of his fear was the present and not the past.

'When did he leave?' Anne asked again.

'When I was, I don't know, four or five.' Vinny's answers were hesitant.

'That would be the mid-seventies?'

Vinny finished his tea and stood. 'You know what?'

'What?'

'We are not having this conversation,' he said firmly.

He started walking toward the kitchen.

'I didn't mean to upset you,' Anne apologised.

'I'm not upset. But I don't know why you're asking me about

him, and I don't want to talk about it. About him.' He stopped by the door to the kitchen. 'It's none of your business. I don't know what you think you're doing, but it's not working, okay?' He was defensive, with anger creeping into his voice.

'Okay, calm down, I'm sorry.'

'I am calm. I just…He left. Walked out. That's all I know, okay?' The anger had peaked, and his words became short and clipped.

'Did you ever try and find him?'

He returned to his seat. 'How? I was a kid. One day he was there, then, boom, nothing. No word, no messages, no phone calls. I guess I was so young it didn't really have an impact on me.'

'But you remember him?'

'Just a few things.' He was talking as if it were physically tiring, the words heavy and hard to use. 'Like scenes in my head, not even sure if they are real. I remember the smell of smoke. He smoked Woodbines, you know, those disgusting old things. No filter, just tobacco. Seeing him get dressed, collar, tie, smart shoes. He would polish his shoes with the stuff from the tin, use two brushes, one to put it on, the other to buff it up. I think he liked to look good.'

There was a pause. 'I'm doing it, aren't I?'

He placed his empty mug on the table. 'You won't talk about the copper, but you've got me talking about my dad.'

Anne said softly, 'Only if you want to.'

'You know I don't want to. Don't bullshit me. When have I ever spoken about him?' Vinny's voice became sharper.

'You haven't.' Anne realised she had pushed too far.

'Exactly. Because there is nothing to say. Nothing. He wasn't there, wasn't around. There is literally nothing to say.'

'But it has an impact on you. The absence, the, I don't know…' Anne paused. 'Emptiness?'

'No, no. What the fuck are you up to? You do know I've got

a son?'

'Look, don't get angry. I just thought that maybe, this college stuff, the research - '

Vinny interrupted her. 'What? You think it's about him? My dad?'

'Well…What are you looking for?'

'No, it's not. I want to understand the dynamic within the community. I'm starting to see how our identity was pushed into Catholicism. There are lots of questions.'

'Is it also about you?' She knew this was painful for Vinny.

'No…Well, yeah, in the sense that I have these questions. I'm from that community. In the sense it's me that is thinking about it, but no. It's not all about me. Jesus, Anne, where the hell did all this come from?'

'It just seems like something you need to deal with.' Anne knew she needed to continue.

'I have dealt with it. He fucked off, we moved on, that's it.'

'You know I have been talking to Michael.'

'Not him again. I told you he was full of shit.' There was anger in his voice now.

'Well, not just him. Molly, the landlady at The Dealers. Did you know your dad and Michael were mates, knocked around together?' Anne said.

'No, how would I know that?' Vinny said.

'Well, apparently they were.'

'What was all that shit in the pub, then? Why didn't he say something?'

'I don't think he knew then who you were, but he definitely knew your dad.'

Vinny's anger had turned into curiosity. 'And…so what? What difference does that make? Does he know what happened? Why my dad left?' The lines of Vinny's face hardened. 'Nah, I'm not interested. This is bollocks.'

There was a heavy silence until Anne broke it softly. 'It might be a chance for you to resolve some of these issues.'

Vinny was quieter. Anne could see his frustration, as if it were difficult to get the words out, difficult for him to give voice or sound to his thoughts. She reached out and put her hand over his. He didn't move. His features and expression had changed, his face sagged.

'What issues?' he said in a barely audible whisper.

When she spoke again, she just said, 'Vinny.' It was an appeal.

Vinny breathed deeply. 'Fuck, I don't know. I mean, I don't know why this is getting to me.'

Anne could see his emotions were jumping all over the place. He was struggling. His eyes began to tear up, but he was holding himself back.

'He just fucking disappeared.' His voice was breaking, silent tears running down his face.

He sat still, his only movement a hand to wipe his face. 'Just fucking gone, no word, even me mam never fuckin' mentioned him. Like he didn't exist, never existed, ever…can you believe that?' The words came in rushed groups. 'No explanation, no discussion. I used to tell other kids he died in the war. How fucking stupid was I?' He was on the edge, but still holding himself back. 'The war was years before. It was impossible for him to have died then. I used to tell teachers, or anyone - how fucking stupid must I have looked?'

Anne gave his hand a squeeze. 'It wasn't stupid. You did what you had to.'

'Yeah, well, fuck him. I didn't need him then, and I don't now. He didn't give a shit about me. How could he leave if he cared?' Vinny wiped his face again, and in doing so, appeared to be trying to wipe away the emotion.

Anne could see him physically pushing the pain away.

'Look, I feel terrible doing this, but I have to. What if your dad had no choice, if he didn't leave you, but was taken?'

'What? What the fuck are you on about? Taken, taken by

who?'

'There is no easy way to say this, and I am probably 100% wrong...'

'But... go on, spit it out.' He pulled his hand away.

'Would you give me, or rather the police, a DNA sample?'

'DNA? What the fuck! What for?'

Anne sat still.

The anger had returned, but this time, it was the disappointment in his voice that hurt Anne the most. 'Oh no, I get it. For fuck's sake, you and that stupid old twat, that stupid Michael have been dreaming up some story. What - you want the front page, do you? Reporter uncovers mystery of hidden body. Or was it the copper? Your new fucking boyfriend?'

'No, it's not like that.' She wasn't physically afraid, but her feeling of guilt grew with his sense of betrayal.

His tone had changed. He seemed charged, full of energy and life.

He stood and began to pace. 'Yes, it is. You want to say it's my dad that was in that fuckin' hole? You and that bastard making up shit. The copper gets promotion. You get the story, and what does the old fella get, eh? A few quid for interviews? A few pints for going along with it? He probably never even knew my dad. This is bollocks. Come on, I've had enough.'

Anne was pleading. 'Vinny, calm down.'

She had seen him cross, even irate, but never like this. She was frightened that she had hurt him, and she shared his pain.

'No, don't fucking tell me to calm down. Come on, I've had enough.' He picked up her mug and walked toward the door. He opened the living room door.

'What? You want me to leave?' Her face flushed. She was shocked. She could feel the blood pumping through her temple.

'Bingo. Got it in one.' Vinny wouldn't look at her.

'Vinny, come on...' She struggled to stop her voice from breaking at this rejection.

Anne collected her stuff.

'Make sure you close the front door on your way out. And one more thing, you don't have to tell me. I can smell the fucker on you.'

The door slammed behind her.

***

Fuck, that hadn't gone well. Anne made her way down the staircase, unsure of what to do next. She didn't want to think about Vinny and herself now. She knew something was going on, but she guessed it always had been.

She liked the idea of having male friends - no sexual tension, no flirtation, just mates, and yeah, definitely some feeling, just not in that way. She knew she was kind of unapproachable. She kept people at a distance - and yet, she thought, here I am, just back from shagging a copper.

The drive home took just a few minutes, and she tried not to think about her friend, how hurt and complicated he was. She headed along Princes Avenue, through the gates, then round the park. The tree-lined road with the park on one side and the large Victorian semis on the other felt like somewhere else: not minutes from the city centre, but suburban, peaceful; the light breaking through the overhanging trees dappled the windscreen with shadows. Light and shadow.

She was tired and needed a bath - not a shower today but a bath, a good old soak and the chance to think. She couldn't get Vinny out of her mind. She was desperate. He was so upset. In her desperation, she also realised how much they meant to each other. Light and shadow.

Chapter Twenty-Two

Anne

Anne heard the car horn beeping. *What a dick*, she thought. She threw her phone and purse into her bag. She was sitting on the edge of her bed while she did up the laces on her trainers. The horn beeped again. *For fuck's sake*. Grabbing her bag, she left the room, allowing the door to close behind her as she raced down the steps three at a time.

Dave was in the driveway. He had turned the car around and was facing the street.

'Hey.'

'Hey,' Anne responded. 'Where's the fire?'

'Ah, you know,' Dave said.

'Yeah, right.' Anne climbed in beside him. 'Are you gonna get your light and siren going too?'

'Who knows, maybe if you want a bit of excitement. Do you like it? BMW E 3 Series, sat-nav, electronic brake-force distribution, four-wheel drive.'

This was the second time she'd heard this. 'I'm impressed,' she lied.

The truth was, since falling out with Vinny, something had changed. Something had been reset inside her. He was complicated, damaged - maybe she wanted to fix him. She was finding it hard to remember what she had seen in Dave, beyond the obviously cute floppy hair.

He leaned across to kiss her.

Anne withdrew. 'Nah, let's keep focused, eh? Remind me, who are we seeing today?'

Dave pulled back and switched to business mode. 'Inspector Barlow, ex-head of Special Branch in Merseyside.'

'Sounds important.'

'Yeah, I guess he is.'

'Why is he willing to speak to me?'

'Maybe he wants to help. Anyway, some news, not great, but news. The car you saw in Speke, outside the Noah's Ark…'

'Yeah…'

'Nothing, I'm afraid. Looks like it was stolen a couple of weeks ago.'

'So, no clues there?'

'Fraid not. Okay, let's hit the road.' As he said this, Dave put the car into gear and edged out onto Aigburth Drive.

He looked around. 'You like it round here?'

The area was just off Lark Lane. The large Victorian house contained six flats and faced Sefton Park. The park was two-hundred-and-fifty acres of green spaces and water features, designed in a series of ovals and concentric circles. Generations of kids from all over Liverpool had travelled to the boating lake and palm house. Many had discovered an elemental rule to life in the city. Whatever the attraction, straying from your own area always carried the danger of conflict and violence. From a young age, the lesson learned through bloody noses and bruised egos was "stick to your own."

'Yeah, what's not to like, the park on the doorstep, especially in summer. Close enough to town, good pubs on Lark Lane. How about you?' she asked.

'I haven't been down here much, to be honest. Looks nice, though.'

'Where are you from?' Anne realised she knew very little about him.

'Originally? Woolton.'

'You haven't strayed far, then.' Anne smiled, trying to lighten the mood.

'I guess not, no reason to. I mean I have travelled, don't get me wrong, but nah, I'm okay here.'

'By here, you mean Liverpool?'

'Yeah, why not?'

'A proud Scouser?'

'Yeah, guess I am.'

'How about crime, poverty, racism. How about those?'

'And what, Manchester or London are better?'

'No,' Anne responded defensively.

'Look at what we've got: football, music, the Mersey. Town's been done up, Capital of Culture coming. Have you been round town recently? The place is buzzing. Students, tourists everywhere. I think the place is on the up,' Dave said.

'I suppose so,' Anne admitted.

'You don't see yourself as a Scouser, then?'

'No, it's not that. I mean, I was born here.' Anne had never tried to define who she was.

'Is it because you're half-caste?'

'What?' Anne turned in her seat to face him.

'You know, half and half, like.'

'Did you really just say that?'

'What? I didn't mean anything.'

'Half-caste. Jesus. I guess you missed the diversity training day.'

His face flushed, and he looked straight ahead. 'Okay, sorry, mixed-race. Is that better? Look it doesn't bother me. I don't have a problem with anyone. Shit, this isn't going well, is it?' He turned to face Anne.

'Don't panic. Do you think I would be with you now if I thought you were racist? But you shouldn't use "half-caste". I'm a full person, not *half* anything.' She was disappointed that she needed to explain.

'Yeah, okay, sorry. I didn't mean anything.'

Silence filled the car.

'Are we ok?' he asked.

'Yeah, but...' Anne turned towards him, started to explain.

'The famous "but." Look, it's okay, I can take a hint. One night of magic. Then back to reality.'

Anne smiled. 'Something like that. Like you said, no offence.'

'None taken. Just friends - Watson and Sherlock. Although I must admit, I do have my doubts there.'

Anne's smile broadened. The silence seemed suddenly much lighter.

They had come through Dingle with its tightly packed terraced houses leading down to the docks and the river. Dave chose to go down Parliament Street onto what was the old dock road.

Anne's phone buzzed. She slipped it out of her jacket pocket. 'It's work.'

She apologised. Dave waved his hand.

'Hey, yeah...Yeah, of course...I'll do it first thing.' She was looking out the window as she spoke. They were passing the Albert Dock complex, a network of luxury flats, bars, cafés, and tourist attractions, all housed in the huge brick warehouses that used to be the busiest docks in England. 'Okay, see you tomorrow.' Anne swiped the phone.

They passed the Pier Head. On their right was Water Street, which led to the old shipping and commercial centre of the city. On their left was The Liver Building, topped by the famous Liver Birds, the symbol of Liverpool Football Club and the city itself.

She could see Dave enjoyed driving. He was weaving in and out of the traffic. Between the town centre and the modern container docks at Seaforth, they could see the mountains of rusting scrap metal that were now one of the largest exports from Liverpool.

'Have you been out this way?' Dave asked as they were leaving the docks and city behind and entering Crosby.

'No, don't think I have. No reason to before.'

'It's nice. There's something I want to show you after we see Inspector Barlow. If you're up for it? Just as friends.'

'Yeah, sure. Didn't you say he's retired?'

'He is, but it's kind of protocol to call him by his rank.'

'Oh, right, okay, good to know.'

A few minutes later, they were driving through a set of gate posts and pulling into a curved drive. The gates were open, and the house was set back off the road. It was a large, detached house, brown brick with two large bay windows on either side of the door, the bays extending up to the first floor. *Not ostentatious or showy*, thought Anne, *but not without means, either*. The car crunched to a halt on the gravel driveway. They had driven past the front door and parked in an area just to the side. Dave was quick to get out and open Anne's door.

'M'lady,' Dave quipped.

Anne gave him a forced smile.

They walked side by side to the large front door. Dave rang the bell and stood back. 'Here we go.'

A minute later, a thin, grey-haired man opened the door. 'Good afternoon. Ron Barlow,' he announced, taking control of the exchange.

Dave and Anne responded, shaking the offered hand.

'Come in, please.' He stepped back, allowing them to pass him and enter the hallway.

The house was well-kept. A polished wooden floor in the hallway led to stairs on the left-hand wall and a balcony around the first-floor hallway at the top of the stairs.

'This way, if you don't mind.' He showed them to a door on the right. 'We'll use the lounge - a little bit more comfortable than the office.'

A figure appeared beyond the stairwell. 'Tea, anyone?'

'Mrs Barlow there,' the inspector clarified. 'Yes, thanks,' he added.

'That would be lovely, thank you,' Anne confirmed.

The inspector held open the white door to the lounge, a large room fronted by the net curtained bay window. There were two sofas and two armchairs arranged around a large wooden coffee table. The grey leather furniture was soft and comfortable.

'Please.' His hand extended toward the sofa.

Anne and Dave sat, and the inspector took an armchair opposite and across the table from them.

'Thanks for seeing me, Inspector,' Anne began.

'Well, the sergeant here tells me you are in need of assistance and that he would like to help, and having now met you, I can see why he would.' Barlow smiled at Dave.

His face is trim, Anne thought. For someone his age, he had kept his muscle tone, no drooping neck or jowls. His movements were clipped and direct. If anything, she was surprised by his eloquence and smooth delivery, expecting something more military.

'Well, as I think you know, the first requirement is for us to agree that anything I say, anything I divulge, is strictly background and unattributable,' Ron Barlow said.

'Of course,' said Anne.

At that moment, Mrs Barlow entered the room with a tray of tea things. She set them on the table and retreated. *This is not your first time in this role*, thought Anne.

'Okay, with that minor caveat out of the way, how can I help you?'

'I'm kind of new to this. I know from Dave, Sergeant Cooper, that you were involved in the Special Branch in Garston?'

'Liverpool, really. Garston was part of our field, but we were a divisional outfit operating across the city and wider sometimes, depending on requirements, but yes, south Liverpool would have been a place we had our eyes on.'

'For any reason in particular?'

'Well, as I remember, there were a couple of serious operators active in the area, serious teams of thieves. Of course, we kept an eye on them, but then again, the '70s were a somewhat turbulent period, politically speaking. What with the insurgency in Northern Ireland, and major political upheavals on the mainland itself, it's fair to say we were fully engaged.'

'Did the SDS operate in Liverpool?'

The inspector turned to Dave. 'I see your friend has been doing her homework.'

Turning back to Anne, he said, 'The Special Demonstration Squad was primarily a Met operation, not really our thing…'

'This is the undercover unit,' Dave said.

Barlow ignored him. '…from the late '60s, really got going early to mid-seventies. Long-term infiltration was its bread and butter - politicos, anarchists, republicans. Quite effective. Produced real results, not always popular, or welcomed, of course, but then effective policing rarely is.'

'You mentioned political groups. Would that cover unions?' Anne was poised with pen in hand but took few notes.

'Seamless.' The word appeared to spring from nowhere and relate to nothing. It hung in the air until he said, 'Thing is, sometimes, it's hard to know where a political group ends and a trade union begins. These things are so integrated.' As he spoke, he raised his hands and intertwined his long thin fingers to emphasise the point.

'But, forgive me, aren't unions legal?' Anne asked.

'Mmmm, I would say rather that unions are like people. Every one of us is legal, and yet everyone has the capacity to do something illegal. Our responsibility was, and is, to protect society from illegal acts. Not only in the execution, but pre-emptively in the planning and organising. Specifically, we were tasked with the political, terroristic, subversive, and the conspiratorial.'

'Okay, I think I understand. Can I ask specifically about a couple of issues?'

Spreading his hands in a show of openness, he replied, 'I'm here to help.'

Dave leaned forward. 'Tea? Shall I pour?'

'Thanks.' Anne nodded to him.

'Milk, no sugar,' the inspector instructed.

'Inspector, I have two questions about issues, general areas of interest, and then maybe if it's okay, a couple about people. Maybe I could run some names past you?'

'Milk and sugar?' Dave asked, rattling the cups around.

'Milk and one,' Anne responded brusquely.

The inspector accepted his tea from Dave, who spread coasters around the table.

'The areas I'm interested in are firstly Ireland; were there contacts or relations between communities in Liverpool or Garston and Ireland? Is there anything specific you know about, and then - '

'Okay, well, let me interrupt you there. Whatever the second question is, the first one is enough to keep us here all afternoon.'

'Yeah, I kind of figured that,' Anne offered, 'but I was hoping for things about Garston in particular.'

'Sure, and I will answer, but if I may paint a picture. I think people today have convenient amnesia about the events of that period. 1968 saw the resurgence and reformation of the IRA after the civil rights marches in the six counties. We had intense urban warfare on the streets of Northern Ireland. British soldiers were dying at the rate of one a week in the mid-'70s. The IRA had unleashed holy terror on the streets of the mainland with bombs in pubs in Birmingham and Guildford.' He paused for a second. 'No offence, I wouldn't expect either of you to understand. No doubt, this would all be decades before you were even born. The Horse and Groom and The Seven Stars in Guildford, The Kings Arms in Woolwich, the

Mulberry Bush and The Tavern in The Town in Birmingham, these names roll off my tongue today because dozens were killed, hundreds wounded.'

He paused again.

'The pub bombings in 1974 were our 9/11, and as a state we took the required measures to protect ourselves and to seek out and destroy our enemies. I think the nearest we can imagine is that the IRA were the Al Qaeda of their day. If you swap Irish for Muslim, you wouldn't be going far wrong.' He smiled.

Anne spoke calmly. 'That certainly puts things in perspective. Thank you. Can I ask, so within Liverpool, were you looking for IRA sympathisers?'

'That's a tough one. As a unit we were certainly part of a national strategy of vigilance. You had the military boys who were front-facing in terms of ASUs, but certainly we were aware of and ready to respond to any indications of - '

'Excuse me,' Anne asked. 'Did you say ASUs?'

'Active Service Units. IRA gangs operating on UK soil. People like the Balcombe Street gang had been terrorising London throughout '74 and '75 - bombings, shootings, you name it.'

'Okay, I see. Sorry for interrupting.'

'No, by all means, best not to set me off, though, not on this subject.'

'Okay. Well then, if it's okay, Garston?'

Dave interjected, 'That's why we had the PTA?'

Anne looked at Dave.

He clarified, 'Prevention of Terrorism Act 1974.'

'The Sergeant here is correct. Our most useful tool, it allowed us to detain anyone we suspected of supporting or aiding a proscribed organisation. In casual parlance, we could "lift" anyone we liked for forty-eight hours, up to a week if we really wanted.'

'And did you?'

'Of course, although to be honest, in many situations, the

threat is more powerful than the act. After we lifted one or two, the message got out.' Barlow shifted the discussion. 'But if I can be allowed a turn to ask a question?'

Anne raised the teacup to her lips. 'Of course.'

'Then I would ask, what is it is you have found?'

Placing the cup back in its saucer, Anne explained. 'I have an idea who the skeleton is, but I'm not sure. Mainly I want to check out what else was going on at the time so that I don't miss something obvious.'

'Interesting, and who, if I may ask, do you think it is?'

Anne looked at Dave, who was nodding. Even in Barlow's roundabout style, this seemed pretty direct. 'Possibly someone called Bob Pennington, or maybe Paddy Connolly. Pennington was a union organiser and Connolly, probably a low-level criminal.' She felt a little disloyal describing Vinny's dad like that.

'And who do you have down as the culprit?'

'Maybe the Powers. They seemed to run the criminal side of things locally, but I'm not sure they were capable of murder.'

Anne wanted to change the dynamic of the conversation and get information from him. So far, he hadn't revealed much. 'But if you don't mind. What can you tell me about Garston? You have been talking a lot about Ireland. Were the IRA active there?'

'Yes, well, right. It's a funny thing, not well known, and certainly nothing we would ever publicise. Despite the large and well-embedded community of Irish nationals and their offspring throughout Liverpool, we never really had direct coordination, not on the nationalist side, anyway.'

Anne looked a little confused. 'Not Catholic, you mean?'

'Yes, although you can't pin it down to that. "Catholic" - it's one of the common misconceptions about nationalists. You could on the Loyalist side. 100% of activists were Protestant, but Republicans had a wider pool to fish in, as we say. There was more crossover between Irish, Catholic, socialist, communist, or radical. Generally, a much more political bunch.'

'So, you were watching radicals as well as Irish people?'

'Both, actually. You could say we were aware of contacts between certain groups and individuals - criminal elements here in Liverpool and figures in Ireland. These were more family and community ties. Garston has always had a connection with Wicklow. We knew of people who travelled back and forth, but from our point of view, it was never seen as a real threat. Not that they weren't up to some shady business, just not business we would get our snouts into.'

'For example?'

'Even in the '70s, we were a relatively new unit. By the time I was on the job, stories had grown, no doubt mountains out of molehills or kiss of the old Blarney stone. In Garston, we were aware of a family organization - the Powers, a pair of brothers – the same guys you mentioned. There were stories about bodies disappearing into the Irish Sea, but to be honest, we never saw them as anything more than local hoodlums. Strange as it might seem, our information was that it was among Protestant extremists that there was the most communication, contact, and actual collusion with elements in the north. If I remember correctly, there were a couple of individuals from the Garston area who progressed from the Orange Lodge into the more serious and murky regions of loyalism. Not quite paramilitary engagement, but certainly flirtation. There were people who travelled to the north to take part in their celebrations and commemorations, which usually ended in planned and organised community strife. Yes, I think I can be certain that level of sectarianism was part of the local scene.'

'So, maybe we are looking in the wrong place?' Dave asked.

Anne wasn't sure what to make of this. 'You mean actual Protestant para-militaries?'

'I'm not sure I would go that far, but no question there were people who saw themselves in that light. I'm not sure how much more I can say about that.'

'Okay, thanks, I understand. Can I ask about the other area I am interested in?'

'By all means.'

'It's kind of in two parts. The first is trade union activity, and did you follow it? The second is undercover activity. Did you have anyone operating in the area undercover?'

'I can answer both questions, the first in the affirmative, the second I would have to say it depends when. We had some people in and out for a few months, maybe. As the Special Branch, we were the first line of civilian defence. As a nation, we were under attack, in Ireland and here. The early to mid-seventies saw the growth of not just the official trade unions, but much more militant and radical splinter groups, in a way that we haven't seen since. The alphabet soup of initials, revolutionary this, international that, communist, socialist, you name it. We had them all, and although they were never more than thirty, forty, maximum fifty-thousand people nationally, the effect of these people should not be underestimated. They were not like today. These were more like missionaries, obsessives, people who ate, slept, and drank radical politics. And they had an audience - the sea in which they swam. You can do your own history on this. Miners' strikes brought down the Heath government. I can remember sitting round with candles during the three-day week. Can you believe it? Two days a week there would be no electricity. Transport, the car industry, docks, it took until Thatcher came in to sort them out. We followed it all. Unlike the Met, we didn't put operatives under deep cover. We didn't need to. We could get all we needed through attending meetings and demos, gathering information, but by far, our most valuable assets were informers.'

Anne was struggling to keep up. 'Locals, you mean?'

'By and large, yes. There were various organisations we could use for information. The Economic League was fairly useful for identifying radicals, quite good at keeping them out, too.'

'Economic League, that's new to me.'

'They kept lists: communists, union militants. Companies could check new recruits against their list.'

'And stop people getting jobs?' Dave asked.

'Blacklisting,' Anne clarified.

'Certainly, these people were enemies.'

'And the informers, why did they do it?' asked Anne.

'Some were ex-army, some were union members, but these were real patriots who wanted to defeat the radicals as much as we did.'

'Can I ask about an individual?'

'Certainly, I'm not sure I will be able to shed any light, though.'

'Okay, the guy I mentioned earlier, Bob Pennington, on the docks at Garston. I'm not sure if he actually worked there, but he was definitely active in organising something called the "Blue Union."'

'He sounds like someone we would have taken an interest in, but without reference to the files, I couldn't be sure.'

Anne was frustrated; he was too evasive, she wanted to get out before she said something she would regret. Whoever this guy Barlow was, she didn't like him or the cloak and dagger world he occupied.

Anne began to stand. 'I really appreciate your time, Inspector, but I'm afraid I have a prior engagement.'

'Deadline and all that stuff, is it?'

'Yeah, exactly.' Anne lied for the second time that afternoon.

'Nice to meet you, Anne.' He held her hand just a little too long. 'If I can, I would just say, my advice is to leave it alone. Let DS Cooper here and Merseyside Police do their job.'

They moved toward the front door, and Mrs Barlow magically reappeared to open the door.

'If I could just have a word with the Sergeant here.' Barlow indicated toward Dave.

'Of course, I'll be at the car. Thank you for your time.'

Leaving the house, feet crunching the gravel, Anne was deep in thought. She waited by the car. Something didn't seem right, but she didn't know what it was.

Dave came out a minute later.

'All good?' Anne asked.

'Yeah, sure.'

She climbed in the passenger seat. 'What did he want?'

'Oh, nothing.' He waited before starting the engine. 'Where to?'

'I'm not sure. Is there anywhere we can get a coffee? I just need to process some of that.'

Dave turned the ignition. 'Yeah, I know just the place.'

Dave drove slowly through the well-kept and clearly prosperous streets. Detached houses set back from the road were the norm; Anne thought the gated entrances, high walls, and privet hedges no doubt served as protection against the straying natives of Liverpool. She couldn't help thinking, *Am I one of those straying natives? Trespassing on Barlow's lawn?*

A couple of minutes later, Dave pulled into a car park next to a children's playground.

'This is it?' Anne felt doubtful.

'Yeah, but hold on with that judgment.'

'You got it,' Anne said.

Dave paid for the parking, and they walked side by side through the park.

'Is it worth asking?' she held her hands outstretched.

'Not yet.'

They were crossing a well-kept grassy area that led to a path, which ran alongside a stretch of water bounded by rock clusters. It was an artificial arrangement. Piles of rocks were used to border the waterway, and, she assumed, to stop the erosion or draining of the lake. Despite her misgivings about where they were going, she walked alongside Dave, their steps and pace soon falling into a rhythm. The slight breeze and clear air were refreshing. She could see the ground rise as they walked, and they were soon climbing a half-grass and half-sand ridge. As they neared the top of the ridge, the grass fell away, almost completely, leaving tufts of taller, rougher grasses sticking out from the sand. The going was tough through the sand. Dave held out his trailing hand, Anne grasped it, and he helped pull her up to the top.

'Wow.' Anne looked over a series of dunes to the wide beach of the Mersey estuary. The tide was out, so she could see an expanse of what must have been a least half a kilometre before the first channels of gleaming water cut through the soft yellow sands.

'Was it worth it?' Dave was looking pleased with himself and hadn't yet released Anne's hand.

'Yeah.'

The sand and water merged into a huge sky that ran the range of light blues and soft greys. The breeze sharpened as they crested the dune. It was now pulling at Anne's hair and jacket, but it felt good, somehow liberating. Dave's hand still held hers, and for the moment, she was fine. She relaxed and held his in return.

'Wait, there's more.'

They slipped and scrambled down the dune, and it was hard not to laugh. They walked to the embankment railing and found the concrete steps down onto the beach. At the bottom step, Anne sat and began removing her trainers. 'Come on, we might as well get the full effect.'

Dave sat beside her and followed suit. She placed her trainers besides the steps and tucked her socks into the tops.

'You're not leaving them here, are you?'

'Yeah, why not?'

'They're decent trainers, and my boots cost over a hundred

quid.'

Anne was beginning to realise that the gulf between them was as wide as the estuary in front of them.

'If someone is that desperate, to be honest, I don't begrudge them,' she said.

Dave held his hands up in submission. 'Okay, but if they are gone when we get back, the coffees are on you.'

'Deal,' she said.

They had unclasped their hands while they took off their shoes, and Anne kept enough distance as they walked barefoot out toward the river, to avoid holding hands again.

'Do you want to talk about it?' Dave asked.

'No, not yet. Let's just enjoy this.'

'No problem.'

They were walking out toward the channels of water, and Anne became aware of a figure standing still in the distance. It wasn't until they approached closer that she realised it was a statue embedded in the sand. 'Wait, what is that?' Her face lit up with recognition. 'Ahh, I know, I've heard about these.'

'The statues,' said Dave.

'Yeah, Anthony Gormley. You know, I've been meaning to come and see these for ages. It's so cool to be here.'

Anne walked around the red and rusting metal figure, one of a hundred along three kilometres of beach. They stretched one kilometre out to sea and were submerged and revealed with the ebb and flow of the tide. The statue, legs together and arms at its side, was taller than her. It had no facial features or detail, as if the tidal waters had removed them in its incessant motion, leaving rounded soft edges and curves. She touched the cast figure and felt the surface rust and the red powder stain on her finger.

Dave was wandering a little further afield.

Stepping back from the statue, Anne stood behind it and looked from its point of view at the incoming tidal waters.

What could he see? What was he looking for? Was he waiting for something, someone? Someone who would arrive, or was he looking back, to where he had come from? This figure, this scene, suddenly felt so real to her. Halfway between the land and the sea, halfway between the city and the world outside, but belonging completely to neither. Not knowing which was real, which was true, to which he belonged. An overwhelming sense of sadness gripped her. What had he lost that made him stand out here? A tear grew and rolled down her cheek. Wiping it away, she understood for the first time, that what she and Vinny were doing was the same thing.

'Hey.' Dave was watching her. 'Are you ok?'

'Yeah, can we go get that coffee now?'

'Sure.'

She leaned toward him and kissed him gently on the cheek.

'Now, I'm definitely glad I brought you,' Dave joked.

She smiled a little sadly. She knew it was a goodbye kiss.

1975

Chapter Twenty-Three

Michael

Michael pulled his donkey jacket over his blue cotton overalls and slipped the clip around his trouser leg. He maneuvered his bike out of the hallway and closed the front door. He had twenty-five minutes to get to the factory. The timescale was tight, but he enjoyed it, whatever the weather. In the cold, it was invigorating and challenging, cutting through the sharp air, the wind lashing his face. When it rained, he splashed through the puddles with his head out to feel the raindrops on his skin. In warm weather, he pushed himself even harder to break out into a sweat.

Tonight was cold and damp, perfect for cycling. He rode along the boulevard and passed the airport entrance. He stopped at the traffic lights on Speke Hall Road and mounted the pavement. He was about to turn left when he caught a glimpse of a familiar face, Paddy Connolly, in his car, waiting at the lights. Michael thought about waving, but Paddy was staring straight ahead. He wouldn't have noticed him. Putting his head down, Michael continued on his way to work.

Michael swung his bike left through the gates of Speke No2 Standard Triumph body plant. Six years earlier, in 1969, when it opened, it was one of the most modern car production plants in Europe. It would take ten minutes to get from the bike shed through the plant to his clocking-in station. He used the bike shed near the press shop. Fewer people went through this area because of the pounding noise as the presses stamped shaped panels and bonnets from steel sheets. All around him, men were moving to the rhythm of the huge presses, pulling out the pressed metal sheets and sliding in new ones before the press slammed down again. It felt like the air itself was being pounded and crushed. This continuous motion would last the length of the shift, every machine in the shop fed by the constant movement of people and metal. As Michael walked through the press shop, all the twenty-plus presses were working. He pushed through the flexible plastic curtain into the assembly area.

Every workstation was in the process of changing over. After clocking in, men lined up, ready to relieve their shift partner, everything organised so production was maintained, and the flow of silver-grey metal being shaped, bent, fitted, and joined together continued.

Michael took his card from the rack, punched it through the clock, and re-slotted it in the rack on the other side. He continued on to a row of lockers where his colleagues were locking away personal belongings before moving onto the line.

'All right, Mike?' Tommy said, as he put his coat and cap away.

Tommy's locker was the only one with a Transport and General Workers Union poster on it. The others were a combination of Liverpool and Everton articles from the football papers or page three of The Sun. Tommy's poster showed a clean, fresh-faced man in blue overalls giving the thumbs-up. The text ran in lines next to him, each one ending in a ticked box.

Wage Representation ✔
Health and Safety Representation ✔
Legal Representation ✔
Injury and Death Benefits ✔
Join the Team ✔

'Not bad, how about you?' Michael answered.

'Did you get any kip?'

'Yeah, you know, same as usual. How about you?'

Tommy pulled a face. 'Fucking council or someone was digging up the road.'

'Fuck.'

'Yeah, tell me about it. Anyway, see you later.' Tommy slapped Michael on the shoulder and headed off to his place on the line.

Michael checked the clock. One minute to ten: just enough time to put his sandwiches, flask and newspaper away and get to his workstation.

Blaaaaaaah. The klaxon sounded, and he stepped up. His workstation was part of a short line with steel guide rails between him and his oppo. He nodded to Ted. They would face each other for the next ten hours of the shift, and usually spoke no more than a couple of sentences.

Ted was a nice guy. He liked this job because it was indoors, unlike building sites or the docks. Michael knew what it was like to be out in all weathers. When he'd first left Jack Power without a trade, he was consigned to the physically arduous tasks of the labourer: mixing and hauling cement, bricks, timber. Everything that needed moving up, down, or around half-built muddy sites. As he entered his fifties, this was stable, warm, regular, but soul-destroying work.

A Faustian pact meant hours spent inside the factory were traded for the financial ability to live outside. Except Faust had chosen to enter his deal with the devil. Michael and his workmates had no choice or control. It was work or the steady decline of poverty.

On permanent nights, he had little contact with the world during a normal week. For some workers, this was a bonus - a garden, a dog, football, and a few pints were all they needed. They had largely given up on life as participants. They became providers and spectators; paying with their own lives became their main contribution to family life. Every night Michael worked opposite Ted, he could see his own future - and hated it. But the factory didn't care if you hated, resented, or simply endured - it demanded its price.

The spot-welding gun hung next to him. The counter-balanced weight meant he could handle and move the gun around the chassis that would come sliding down the rails. The steel panels fell into the jig, which closed to hold it in place. They had two minutes to swing the huge gun around the chassis, lining up the elements to apply electrically-generated heat to weld the parts together. When the trigger was pulled, the two arms of the gun closed, and the resulting electrical charge melted the metal forming the weld. Michael and Ted began to swing the guns around the chassis with just enough time to complete the thirteen welds before the jig popped open and the panel slid onto the next station.

A ten-hour shift from 10:00 pm until 8:00 am would be broken by a forty-minute break to eat sandwiches halfway through. A ten-minute tea break was allowed in the first part of the shift, and then the same during the second half. If the toilet was required in between these times, although it was frowned on, it was allowed. Workers would raise their hand as they worked, trying to catch the attention of the foreman. The chargehand would then assign the floater to replace them for the few minutes allowed to get to the bathroom and back.

As soon as he took his place at the workstation, Michael tried to empty his mind, allowing his body to act out the motions required. He needed to be alert enough to find the locations for the weld and manipulate the gun, but he knew he could do it in a state of semi- or near-consciousness by concentrating on his physical movements, building a rhythm so that every movement was part of a choreographed sequence. *Step up. Raise the gun. Lower and twist. Fire. Swing up. Fire. Up again. Fire. Twist round arch. Fire. Move up. Fire. Move up.*

Fire. Round right and down. Fire.

The whole sequence repeated hour after hour. Conversation broke the rhythm, bringing him back to real-time, real space, so it was avoided. Here, the clock dominated everything. He didn't want to be here. He wanted to be in a place where time didn't exist, just the movement.

'Right, Mike.'

The chargehand tapped Michael on the shoulder. He had ten minutes: a minute to get to his locker and get his flask and paper, thirty seconds to get to the closed-in rest area. The rest area was open at one end. It was half-glazed and had a roof. These areas were dotted around the walls of the main production area, cutting the time necessary for workers to get to and from the line. He sat at the large wooden trestle table, and soon, Tommy joined him.

'How's it going?' Michael asked.

'I'll get through. I'll sleep in the morning, though.' Tommy opened his lunch box and pulled out a sandwich. 'We've got a meeting next week. There should be a couple of guys from Fords, Evans Medical, and the rail guys. We're hoping for quite a few. Think you can make it?'

Michael sympathised but wasn't interested. 'I support the union and stuff, not sure if I need to go to meetings, though.'

'Got to make things happen, mate. Can't sit round, hoping things get better.'

'Yeah, okay, fair enough, but still.'

'Your choice, Mike, I'm not trying to push you. Just want to make sure you know that things are happening.'

'Yeah, I know, no problem.'

Tommy changed the subject. 'How's things?'

'What do you mean?'

'You know, here. The job.'

'Shite. What can I say?' Michael half-laughed.

'You regret it?'

'Leaving the other bollocks behind? Nah, I needed to.'

'You know, I always knew there was something about you.'

'Come on, get out of it.' Michael wasn't interested.

'No, I'm not kidding. Even back then, there was something different.'

'Give me a break, Tommy,' Michael said.

'A social conscience. You knew where you were from, and recognised what we were fighting for,' Tommy said.

'Don't kid yourself. I've been around more than enough shit.'

'Do you remember the first time we met?' asked Tommy.

'No, probably not. I've seen you around long enough.' Michael's indifference grew into annoyance.

'It was outside the docks. You were part of Jack Power's gang, warning Bob Pennington off.'

'Was I?' Michael looked uninterested.

'You know his legs were broken a couple of weeks later?'

'Tommy, you're okay, but stop this.'

'I'm just saying - ' Tommy didn't get the chance to finish.

Michael interrupted him. 'Well, don't. What the fuck do you think would happen to the likes of me, in meetings and fucking speeches?' Michael was out of his seat and on his way back to the line.

He took his position and place in the dance and was soon back in the flow of things. The constant movement was only stopped once the chassis had been pushed forward to the next station. Returning to accept the new one, there could be as many as ten or fifteen seconds as they waited for the previous station to finish their welds and send a new chassis into their jig. These halts in movement became his focus, pushing Ted opposite him to move faster and lengthen the stops. They had identical welds to make in mirror image, and Ted naturally followed where Michael led. If he slowed down, so did Ted. Now he had sped up, so Ted did too. Without a word spoken, they were synchronised.

Tommy had annoyed him. *What was the point of bringing that shit up?* They both knew the score, knew what had happened. Michael supported him in the union because if they didn't look after themselves, no other fucker would. He didn't need the history or the arguments. He knew the miners were right, Heath was wrong. He knew Labour were better than Conservatives. He knew Britain shouldn't be in Ireland, but he also knew Tommy had been born and bred in Garston, not Wicklow.

The days after the Birmingham pub bombings, the atmosphere in the plant was electric. Newspaper headlines against the IRA had been posted on lockers and noticeboards. National Front posters with the slogan 'Hang the IRA' and a dangling noose began appearing around the plant. There were rumours that workers in the Birmingham Solihull plant had walked off the line and joined a demonstration against the IRA. New laws meant people could be arrested and detained without charge. It was illegal to support or collect money for the IRA. This meant any public discussion of Ireland was seen as traitorous. The words "rebel," "traitor," and "communist" were spat out in pub, factory, and street.

Ted met his pace, and so they moved together. *Step up. Raise the gun. Lower and twist. Fire. Swing up. Fire. Up again. Fire. Twist round arch. Fire. Move up. Fire. Move up. Fire. Round right and down. Fire.*

On and on the gun swung in perpetual motion. The night wore on with no change in sound, light, or temperature. The conditioned atmosphere of the plant stood outside of time, weather, and physical reaction to the world outside. In this way, it was hoped the brain would be tricked, the body clock fooled to accept that swinging the gun at 3:00 am was as natural an activity as cutting a hedge or mowing a lawn on a Saturday morning.

Michael, in his mind, was in Wicklow on the hill above town, looking out from the ruins of the Black Castle over the Irish sea, looking out to where the journey across sea would lead. The sharp cold wind slapped his face, sending his hair flying. He was about to leave for England.

The chargehand stepped up behind Ted. Ted and Michael finished the welds together and pulled the guns up and out. The jig sprang open. The chargehand checked his watch. 'Go on then, ten minutes.'

Then, taking Ted's place, he helped push the chassis on to the next station. They stood waiting for the jig to be reloaded.

Ted returned. The chargehand checked his watch then stepped down and away. Ted was looking at Michael. 'Ready?' he asked.

Michael shrugged, the chassis landed, the jig closed, and they swung their guns in and down. Michael could see Tommy walking along the line behind Ted. He carried on past them but was looking at Michael.

'Where's he off to?' Michael asked.

Ted turned and looked at Tommy briefly before concentrating again on the welds. He didn't reply.

Michael finished and pulled his gun out, their sequence broken. Ted was struggling to finish. He fired his last weld just as the jig opened and the chassis rose, lifting his gun with it. The movement trapped the gun and knocked Ted off balance. He staggered back a step, grabbing the handrail for support. Michael was ready to slide the chassis out of the jig but stopped. Ted's hand on the guide rail would have been sliced by the chassis.

'What're you doing?' shouted Michael.

The next chassis was heading toward the jig.

'Whoa, hey, hold up.' The chargehand was behind Michael, shouting at the workers in the station before them.

'Hold up, hold up!'

He pushed Michael aside. 'You, in the office.'

The line had stopped; workers down the line were straining to look at the chargehand and Michael. 'You heard me, in the office.'

'What for?' Michael was confused.

'Don't stand there jabbering. Get off the line. You're wanted in the office.'

'Fuck this.' Michael backed away, turned, and stepped down.

The chargehand shouted to the men on the line. 'Right, let's get this thing moving.'

As Michael walked towards the foreman's office, Ted and the chargehand sent the chassis on its way, restoring momentum. It would take a couple of minutes for the wrinkles in the flow of production to be evened out. Michael walked along the line. People were watching him.

Tommy was already inside the office. Like the eating area, it was closed in and half-glazed, allowing visibility both in and out from all sides. Tommy turned and saw Michael approaching. He met him at the door. 'Mike…' he began.

'What are you doing here?'

Tommy moved aside. 'They called me in as your steward.'

The foreman cut them off. 'Healey, Byrne, come on.'

Tommy nodded, and Michael passed him and entered the office. Tommy closed the door. The foreman was behind his desk. Instead of the blue overalls worn by workers, he wore what looked like a blue doctor's coat, a line of pens in his chest pocket, over a shirt and tie.

'Sit, please, Michael.' The politeness and tone were unusual.

'What's up?' Michael was trying to think if he had done anything wrong.

'Are you going to sit?' the foreman asked again.

'Nah, I'm good.'

'Sit down, Mike,' Tommy pressed.

Michael sat on the straight-back chair facing the foreman's

desk, Tommy alongside him.

'What's this about, if it was the stoppage...'

'It's not that,' Tommy said.

'We've had a phone call,' the foreman began. 'Michael, I'm afraid I have some disturbing news for you.'

'What? Who from?'

'Merseyside Police,' the foreman said.

'What? What the fuck?'

'Listen, Michael, please.' The foreman was trying to remain calm, but instead, he was speaking in slow motion.

'All right, get on with it.'

'I'm afraid I have some bad news for you.'

Michael was angry now. 'Will you spit it out.'

'Mike, calm down, mate,' said Tommy.

'Your brother's son, Paul - '

Before the foreman could finish, Michael was up out of his chair. 'Oh, fuck, fuck no...'

The foreman was clearly struggling with the words he had to say. 'I'm afraid he's dead.'

Michael was pacing around the room. Both Tommy and the foreman were on their feet. Tears were rolling down Michael's face, but his expression hadn't changed from the anger that formed before the news. There was no softening, no break, just tears on a rigid face.

'What happened? Stupid fucking question. Who called? You said the police. What's this got to do with them?' Michael asked.

Tommy said, 'I think they are just helping the army contact relatives. Look, I'm sorry, mate. Anything we can do?'

'They wouldn't say anything else, I'm afraid.' the foreman added. 'You can take the rest of the shift as personal leave.'

'The rest of the shift, my arse. He's got at least three days bereavement due.'

'Tommy,' the foreman appealed. 'You know that's immediate

family.'

Michael was wiping his face on his sleeve.

'I'm taking him home,' Tommy announced.

'Now, hang on a minute.' The foreman started rising from his chair.

'Come on, Mike, let's get your stuff, I'll drop you home.'

The foreman was standing behind his desk. 'Tommy, I don't know if I can allow that.'

'You want to try and stop me? Come on, Mike, we're out of here.' Tommy opened the door.

Michael was still wiping his face as they left the office. They walked back along the line. All faces were turned toward them. The foreman had rounded his desk and was catching them up.

He shouted behind them, 'Healey, I'm telling you, you don't have permission to leave this site.' The foreman's voice was strident now, his arm extended as he pointed at Tommy.

Tommy stopped halfway along the line. Men started dismounting from workstations. The chassis were still. It was clear that the news had spread. Workers began congregating around the three figures.

The chargehand appeared. 'What's going on? Who stopped the line?'

Tommy turned to the growing number of workers. 'I guess you've heard the news. I'm taking Mike here, home.'

'If you do, it will mean disciplinary action.' The foreman shouted.

'This line isn't moving again until I get permission to leave,' Tommy said.

The chargehand was barking orders. 'Back to work, come on, no one said you could stop.'

No one responded or even acknowledged his ever-shriller commands.

'Come on. Let's go.'

The foreman knew if his line was stopped much longer, the

knock-on effect would soon be noticed by the feeder lines and the lines waiting for his chassis. 'You come right back after you drop him. And make sure you clock out.'

Tommy turned to the group again. 'You all heard that. He just gave me permission.'

The men started turning and heading back to their stations.

'Let's go,' Tommy said.

The foreman turned and headed back to his office. Michael took no notice. His tears had stopped, his face was still, but his shoulders hung lower. His eyes were glazed as Tommy led him away.

Leaving the false daylight of the factory was always a shock to the system. The two worlds collided. Suddenly the chill in the air, the darkness, and the silence of night brought on a sense of dislocation. The yellow sodium lights of the car park distorted colour on this moonless night. There was no escape from the knowledge that the world around them was sleeping. Tommy drove slowly and carefully through the empty streets.

'Shit, it's fucked. I wonder what happened?' Tommy wondered aloud before asking, 'How long has he been over there?'

'Three or four months,' Michael replied.

'It's fucked up. Why is a kid from Liverpool over there in Ireland? It's not natural,' Tommy said.

'Natural, yeah, like slinging car bodies around at 3 o'clock in the morning is natural?'

'You know what I mean.'

'You mean, that he's Irish, his dad is Irish, his grandparents were Irish? Is that what you mean?'

'I don't know, Mike. It fucks me up. We work our arses off, and we still get the shitty end of the stick.'

'You're the politician, mate, you tell me.'

There was a pause. Both watched the streetlights pass as they drove along an empty Speke Boulevard. Michael was the first to break the silence. 'He was a nice kid when he was younger.

Then, I don't know, something switched somewhere. It drove our Jim nuts. They tried to stop him joining up, but he was determined, didn't want anything else. He wouldn't listen to anyone. Joined the army at sixteen, boy soldier, dead by nineteen. Good fuckin' choice, son.'

They turned into Banks Road, and Tommy asked, 'Where do you want me to take you?'

'Home.'

'You don't want to go to Jim's?'

'No, not now. I'll go in the morning. No doubt they'll be in pieces. They don't need an audience for that.'

'No problem.'

Tommy turned off Banks Road, and a minute later, they were pulling into the kerb at Michael's house. As they turned the corner, Michael could see his living room light was on, the only lit window in the street.

'Let me know if you need anything,' Tommy said.

'Are you not coming in?'

'I don't want to get in the way.'

'Come on. I don't know about you, but I could do with a drink. Unless you have to get back to the factory?'

'Fuck them. It'll be fine, facility time. We negotiated time off for union duties. I can claim it.'

'Okay, come on, then.'

Michael opened the front door slowly and quietly. He turned, putting his finger to his lips. Tommy waited; the door was ajar a few inches. Michael went over to Shirley, who was asleep in an armchair next to the gas fire that was on very low. 'Shirl, come on, girl.' He shook her gently by the shoulder.

Rousing herself, she pulled her housecoat around her. 'Michael.' She stood and put her arms around him. 'It's so terrible.'

'I know, love.' He held her. The hug was close and warm. 'They phoned me at work. They didn't say what happened.'

She was now crying quietly. 'I don't know. No one is saying anything, the poor lad.'

'Come on, let's get you to bed, love. We'll find out what's happening in the morning. We can't do anything now. I've got Tommy from work here. He brought me home.'

'Oh, look at the state of me.' She pulled back from Michael. 'Well, don't leave the man standing outside. Where's your manners?'

Michael opened the door. 'Come in.'

Tommy entered hesitantly. 'Sorry for your loss, Mrs Connolly.'

'Thank you,' she said. 'Come on in, sit down. You'll excuse me.'

'Of course, thank you.'

'Michael, get the man a drink, and no doubt you'll be having one too.'

'You know, I think I will.'

'Okay, well. Goodnight, Tommy.'

Shirley reached for Michael's hand and quickly squeezed then released it as she left the room.

'Goodnight.' Tommy sat in the armchair opposite the one Shirley had just left.

Michael followed his wife upstairs.

Tommy relaxed a little into his chair. The room was warm and cosy. A TV stood on four legs in the corner, a sofa on the side wall was opposite the fireplace. A single photo stood framed on the mantelpiece, a black-and-white photo of Michael and Shirley on their wedding day. Tommy recognised the doorway of Holy Trinity, less than half a mile away, a doorway he had been forced to enter every Sunday morning until he was too old and too big to be coerced.

Every Sunday, there would be three morning masses: nine, ten and eleven o'clock. All the Catholic kids were sent, although fewer of their parents made the short walk from the terraced streets across Banks Road through that brick arched doorway. He was sent up to the age of fourteen, although for the last couple of years, they would go down the shore, or to the playground instead. They caught mass-goers on the way home to find out which priest had done the service, so they could answer correctly to the inevitable questions when they got home. 'Who said the mass?' The answer, Father Montgomery, or Cunningham as appropriate, would be readily accepted. 'Okay, well, go and play 'til your dinner's ready,' was the normal response.

Michael came down a minute later. 'She's done in.'

He disappeared into the kitchen and returned with two glasses and a half bottle of whiskey.

'Just looking at your photograph there,' Tommy said.

Michael sat in the chair opposite Tommy and pulled a small table over between them. He started pouring the drinks. 'She's a good woman. God knows she's put up with enough from me.'

'No kids?' Tommy asked.

'No, didn't happen for us.'

'I'm sorry.'

'Well, to be honest, she did get pregnant twice but wasn't to be. It hit her hard, and now this. She took to her nieces and nephews all the more.'

'Yeah, sure,' Tommy said and raised his glass to his lips.

Michael raised his glass. 'Paul, you fuckin' idiot, we told you not to do it.'

He wiped a hand over his face. 'I'll have to go round there in the morning. Jesus, what a mess.'

'If there's anything…'

'No, you're all right. What can anyone do?'

'Well, I'll go in the office tomorrow. You'll get your three days.'

'Okay, thanks for that.'

'I suppose you'll help Jim organize the funeral.'

'Yeah, but Christ, I wonder if he'll want the army there? You know, military guard and all that stuff?'

'I would guess it's normal if a serving soldier dies,' Tommy said.

'Yeah, probably. Be strange, though.'

'Is Jim political?'

'Our Jim? No, not at all. Never spoke a word to me. He was gutted Paul joined up, but that was just, you know, the danger of it. No, Jim's your straight-up fella. Was at work as soon as he came over here. He had the chance to join me and the lads, but he wanted none of it. Worked in the tannery for a while, then eventually he got into Evans Medical, been there a good few years now. Salt of the earth and all that - honest, hard-working, did everything a good immigrant should do - and where did it get him?'

'That wasn't for you, though?' Tommy asked.

'No, I was a young lad, wasn't I. Thought I knew it all. Nothing could frighten me. A fella back in Wicklow put me on to Jack when he knew I was coming over.'

'What made you break with him?'

'With the Powers?'

'Yeah.'

'I don't know. When you're young and stupid, drive round in cars, cash in your pocket, it's all good.'

'But?' Tommy asked.

'Yeah, well, Jack's a canny fella, you know, would keep a lot up here.' He tapped the side of his head as he spoke. 'He'd have you doing things. You just didn't know how deep things were. Some things were right there: smack some fella round for money he owed, put the frighteners on someone else. All in a day's work. But there were things, let's just say, didn't smell right. Not for me, anyway.'

He took a drink and savoured the feeling as it went down. 'You know, at one time, he would have things going in and out the docks like nobody's business, give the police a nod and a wink. First job I did for him was that, taking a big old crate down through the docks.'

'Smuggling?'

'Like I said, we didn't know what was in 'em, and so your mind starts working on it, like.

'Here…' Michael poured another drink.

'Thanks. Is that why you warned Bob off?'

'Yeah, the strike was getting in the way, and you guys getting organised meant it was harder to get things through.'

'He was a good bloke, Bob.'

'No doubt, mate, but we did what we were told.'

'Even if meant hurting other working people?' Tommy asked.

'Hurting anyone who needed hurting. Sorry to disappoint you, but I don't know what you expect,' Michael said.

'Nah, I know, it just gets to me. We're too busy fighting each other to change anything.'

'Fighting each other isn't the half of it. Look at Paul over there. Who's he fighting if not his own kind?' Michael paused. 'All respect to you, mate, keeping your hands clean, the union, campaigns, all that stuff.'

'And how about you?'

'What do you mean?'

'You've supported the union.'

'Yeah, that's in work. But if you expect me to put myself on the line, you've got to be kidding. With my history, who I am? I'd have to be an idiot.'

'So, the shit just goes on?'

'Yeah, of course it does. If you and your mates want a revolution, go for it.' Michael drained his glass and, smiling, added, 'I tell you what. When you get your barricades up, give me a shout.'

Tommy smiled back. 'Okay, will do.'

'One more?'

'I'm not gonna be able to drive.'

'It's up to you. You can walk home from here, or I'll bring you a blanket. You can kip in the chair.'

'Yeah, okay, go on then.'

Tommy woke first. His head was aching. At some point, Michael must have staggered upstairs because he was alone in the living room. His mouth and throat felt like sandpaper. The room was stuffy and warm. The gas fire was still on, pumping out its dry heat, and the curtains were closed, so the fire was spreading an orange half-light through the room.

He liked Mike, even admired him in a strange way - admired his ability to close off areas of doubt, to do what he needed to, let someone else do the worrying. He shook his head trying to clear it, but the movement brought stabs of pain.

'Shit.'

He got to his feet and made his way into the kitchen and filled a mug from beside the sink with water from the tap. The cold water refreshed him, eased his throat, and he went back through the living room towards the front door. He thought for a second about leaving a note, but decided against it, and, opening the front door, he was hit by the sharp sunlight. He half-closed his eyes and raised his hand for shade, before he heard the voice.

'Must've been a late one, eh?'

Stepping out of the house with his head lowered and eyes covered, Tommy walked straight into the broad chest of a tall, besuited man.

'Watch out there.' He felt a hand grab his shoulder and pull him sideways.

'Hey,' he half-complained, staggering to his left.

'Clear the way,' the big man said.

There were two of them, both well-built and both looking out of place so well-dressed so early in the day.

'Is Michael in as bad a state as you, then?'

'Er, I don't know. He's not up yet,' Tommy replied.

As soon as his eyes focused, he knew who he was looking at. Jack and his brother Charlie were well known in the area, and Tommy had been aware of him as long as he could remember.

'Been filling his head with your shite, have you?'

'Sorry?' Tommy was confused.

'We know who you are,' said Charlie.

It was Charlie who had pulled him aside, leaving the doorway open for Jack. The door was still ajar, and Jack moved forward to enter.

'He's not up yet.'

'Don't you worry, he soon will be.' Jack laughed. 'Now go on, fuck off.'

Charlie pushed him further from the door. Tommy fumbled for his car keys.

'Yeah, take that heap of shite with you,' Charlie added, kicking the tyre of his Triumph Herald.

Tommy watched them through his rear-view mirror, they entered the house as he pulled away from the kerb.

'He was a good bloke, Bob.'

'No doubt, mate, but we did what we were told.'

'Even if meant hurting other working people?' Tommy asked.

'Hurting anyone who needed hurting. Sorry to disappoint you, but I don't know what you expect,' Michael said.

'Nah, I know, it just gets to me. We're too busy fighting each other to change anything.'

'Fighting each other isn't the half of it. Look at Paul over there. Who's he fighting if not his own kind?' Michael paused. 'All respect to you, mate, keeping your hands clean, the union, campaigns, all that stuff.'

'And how about you?'

'What do you mean?'

'You've supported the union.'

'Yeah, that's in work. But if you expect me to put myself on the line, you've got to be kidding. With my history, who I am?

I'd have to be an idiot.'

'So, the shit just goes on?'

'Yeah, of course it does. If you and your mates want a revolution, go for it.' Michael drained his glass and, smiling, added, 'I tell you what. When you get your barricades up, give me a shout.'

Tommy smiled back. 'Okay, will do.'

'One more?'

'I'm not gonna be able to drive.'

'It's up to you. You can walk home from here, or I'll bring you a blanket. You can kip in the chair.'

'Yeah, okay, go on then.

Chapter Twenty-Four

Paddy

'He's a right little bastard, takes after his dad.'

Paddy was proud of little Vinny, named after St Vincent De Paul, patron saint of the poor, or so his missus told him. Carol was all right, great with the kid. It didn't bother her that she was up at all times with him when he was a little 'un. Not so much now that the little fella was almost running around. Vinny loved it when Paddy grabbed him, swinging him round. Always wanted more.

They had Vinny's christening in St Christopher's. Paddy wasn't into all the church stuff. He would go to weddings and christenings but not much else. Eventually, he got a flat in Speke. One of the maisonettes near the Parade. It was okay, handy for the shops. Jack had moved on. Of course, he would. When Paddy and Carol moved to Speke, Jack moved out, typical. He went somewhere near Southport, a big house.

Carol got the phone when it rang and called to him, 'Paddy.'

'Hey, up.'

It was Jack. 'Got a job for you,' he said.

'Yeah, sure, what's on?'

'Boutique in Allerton, you know it?'

'Yeah, Janet's or something, isn't it?'

'Janice, but anyway, she's not listening. Behind on the rent. Nothing heavy, just needs doing.'

'Sure, what've you got in mind?'

Half an hour later, Paddy was in the Cortina, driving up Menlove Avenue. The first thing he noticed was that there were trees on each side of the road. Not skinny new things, but big and old, branches and leaves spread out over the road. That would be their next move, a place with trees. Parks for the little man to play football in. This was the way to go.

The boys with the van were waiting for him when he pulled up.

'Okay, listen, all nice and friendly. No effing and blinding. We're just here to do a job.'

'Gotcha, Paddy.'

'You know what, even better. Say nothing, not a word,' Paddy said.

Paddy went in first, the boys close behind. She was a looker for her age, proper made up like it was a Saturday night, and here they were, Monday morning.

'Janice, isn't it?' Paddy smiled.

The boys had started already, grabbing handfuls of clothes off the racks.

'Hey, wait, what's going…'

'Calm down, love.' Paddy took control. 'I believe you're behind with the rent.'

'Wait, you can't do that. Leave that alone.'

Paddy stood in the gap between her counter and the rest of the shop, so she was stuck. Her arms were flailing around as the boys took the stuff out to the van and piled it in the back.

'Now, listen, Janice. Your stuff will be fine. We're just looking after it 'til the rent is paid. It's Monday now. You've got 'til Friday to come up with what's owed.'

'You can't do this. This is not right.' She went through a door behind her.

The lads carried on emptying the shop. She came down with her fella.

'What's going on here? You have no right to do this,' her fella said.

Paddy was in the same place, so her fella would have to get through him to get into the shop area, and they both knew that wasn't happening.

'I'm calling the police.' Janice was getting a bit excited. She picked up the phone.

Paddy swapped a look with her fella, and he got the message straight away. Paddy was experienced with these things. It's not the pain that drives people to do things, but fear; the fear of pain is a powerful tool, and, used properly, it meant he could cut down on the physical stuff. Unless he enjoyed it, and Paddy never had. He could take it or leave it.

Her fella wasn't daft. He took the phone out of her hand. 'Jan…Okay, look, we'll get the money.'

'Friday.' Paddy looked him in the eye.

'Yeah, okay, I understand.'

'You call me when you have what you owe, and your dresses are back, shop open again.'

It was a bit awkward because Paddy had to wait a couple of minutes while the guys finished off. He could've left, but Paddy knew management is about making sure things are done properly. All it needed was one of them to say something stupid, one of the boys to react, and before you know it, bigger problems. Turns out, the guy was an Everton fan as well. So, they had a chat while the guys finished up.

'One dress each.' That's what Paddy told the boys they could take.

He got Carol a flowery thing. Eight to ten she was, so he picked a ten. After the baby and all, she carried a bit extra. Bloody long thing, though. 'Maxi.' He didn't like them, like wearing bloody curtains, but it was the style, so she was happy.

It took Paddy until early afternoon to sort this out. He made sure the guys stored the stuff somewhere that wasn't going to ruin it. He knew management was about details, not just the big picture. People forgot that. Jack forgot it sometimes, too - not just getting something done, but how it was done.

Paddy had learned a lot from Mike over the years. Michael probably wouldn't know it. He wasn't in the game anymore. Good luck to him. Paddy didn't believe in fate and that kind of thing. He just knew when he was in the right place. It wouldn't be Vinny's place. Things would be different for him. No Christian brothers to try and break him. He wouldn't be in the fields. He would have the things he needed. And Vinny was smart. It amazed Paddy sometimes. He didn't just mean baby smart. He could see him looking, and he knew, *knew* Paddy was doing everything he could for him.

When it all came down to it, the little fella was what Paddy would leave behind in this world. This was who he was meant to be.

2004

Chapter Twenty-Five

Vinny

Vinny picked up his phone, expecting Anne. It wasn't her.

'Hey, Vinny. Can you come in today?'

'Hi, Robbie. I wasn't expecting to. I'm doing some work on my Uni thing.'

'Yeah, sorry about that, but Lucy has let us down. We need to get some cover for lunchtime.'

'I'm not scheduled, though.'

'I know, but we really need it, mate.'

'Can you find someone else? I'm kind of in the middle of something.' Vinny was hoping his annoyance couldn't be heard.

'Sorry, mate, we need you down here.'

Vinny thought about telling him where to go, but he knew if he did, he would lose his regular hours, and that was the only thing paying the rent.

'So, eleven, okay?' Robbie asked.

'Should be. I'll try.'

'Great, see you at eleven. You're booked in now. So not a good idea to be late. You've got a clean tee, right?'

Vinny wondered if it was part of his training to be able to threaten and warn in a voice that sounded like giving good news.

'Yeah, sure,' Vinny lied.

'See you later,' Robbie said.

The line went dead.

Fuck.

The cycle ride down to town avoided bus fares. The trip back up the hill kept him lean, no gym membership or equipment needed. The shop on Bold Street was supposed to be trendy. Vinny guessed it might have been interesting about ten years ago, but the industrial warehouse, the exposed brick look, had definitely had its day. Robbie, however, was a man of the moment - corporate, ambitious, positive, friendly, and a piece of shit. He ran the store with all the fake enthusiasm of a crumbling fairground ride. *Roll up, roll up, for the terrifying adventure of a lifetime.* Standing before faded, painted ghosts and smiling skeletons of a clapped-out ghost train. Except in Robbie's case, he was selling an image, the kind of "cool" that is manufactured by child labour in Vietnam and China. Branded leisure footwear, not trainers for running, or playing basketball. These were products for the style-active rather than the body-active.

Vinny had to stop at the lights next to St Luke's. The external walls of the gothic revival church were still standing. The roof and interior had been destroyed by German Bombers in the blitz of 1941.

He freewheeled down Bold Street, chained the bike to a lamppost and entered the shop. The music was always slightly too loud, slightly too upbeat.

'Hey, Vinny, you up for this?' Robbie asked.

'Yeah, mate, all good.'

Carly, the other part-timer, was serving a customer.

'Okay. Can you empty the bins, then do some tidying on the stock room? As soon as it gets busy down here, I'll give you a call.'

'Yeah, sure. Whatever.'

'Here, take your radio.'

Robbie raised the radio to his lips and called, 'Vinny, radio check. Can you hear me?'

Vinny's radio crackled in his hand. He raised it to his face, depressed the speak button, and, looking straight in Robbie's eyes, answered, 'Vinny here, who's calling?'

Carly was smiling as she processed her customer's card behind the counter.

Robbie depressed his button. 'It's Robbie - '

'What do you want, Robbie?' Vinny interrupted without using the radio.

'Radio check,' Robbie continued.

'Radio working loud and clear,' Vinny said, again without lifting the radio.

The stockroom was floor-to-ceiling shoe boxes, arranged by brand, style, colour, and size. Vinny checked they were on the right shelf and in the right order. His radio buzzed.

'DC Manteca, grey 11.'

He grabbed the right box and made his way downstairs and handed it over to Carly. Shoppers were looking around the shelves.

Robbie indicated for Vinny to stay on the shop floor. The shop was getting busier. Between 11.30 and 2.30 were the busiest periods on weekdays. Robbie opened the shop alone and closed the shop alone. Staff were only required when there was a chance of sales. Zero-hour contracts meant the company wasn't obliged to give Vinny any hours during the week, but he had to make himself available for work should he be required. For Vinny, this meant not committing to another employer.

Most people had two contracts on the go, negotiating the hours between them. It was the only way to survive. Instead of earning a regular wage over an eight-hour day, the company could now call you in for the two busy hours of likely sales, then send you home again. It also meant managers like Robbie were super popular among the female student staff as they competed for hours. Vinny needed his university project to work, but to start teaching, he needed a postgrad degree. What he needed was to sort his head out.

'Hi, can I help you?' The customer was at the older end of the range, but that was not unusual, maybe thirty-five.

It was common for upwards of forty-year-old guys to come in for the latest Vans or DC's. Skateboarders might die, but they never age, apparently.

The customer didn't make eye contact or engage, which was fair enough. So, Vinny backed off. The customer didn't look like a skateboarder. He wore blue jeans and a smartish t-shirt, more your Nike and Adidas, or black going out shoes. The customer looked around as if checking out the shop and moved back over towards Vinny. He was tall and well-built, with dark, close-cropped hair. *He has an almost imbecilic look*, Vinny thought.

'Hi, do you need any help?'

'No, but you might,' the guy answered.

'Sorry?' It took Vinny a second to switch into gear.

The shop was busy; both Robbie and Carly were serving people. It looked like Carly was busy with two sets of customers at once. *Earning her bonus.*

The stocky guy moved in. 'Tell your girlfriend to fuckin' drop it. Stop asking questions. This is her last warning.'

Vinny moved back towards the counter then edged behind it. *Okay, this is weird.* The guy was big. He looked like he could handle himself - and Vinny couldn't.

The guy followed him and leaned into the counter. Vinny was beginning to panic. His stomach was doing somersaults, and he felt weak.

'Did she tell you? I had a nice piece of her tit?' As the guy said this, Vinny pressed the broadcast button on the staff microphone on the counter.

It automatically cut out the music. So, the words 'Did she tell you? I had a nice piece of her tit?' boomed out loud and clear across the shop. Vinny kept the broadcast button depressed. The guy stood back in shock. Everyone in the shop was staring.

'This man has just admitted sexually assaulting a friend of mine,' Vinny said over the loudspeaker. 'And is trying to threaten and intimidate me.'

The man backed away.

Robbie came marching over. 'Excuse me, we have a respect policy in this company, and if you can't treat my colleague with R- E- S- P- E- C- T, you will leave, or I will call the police.' He pointed toward the door and raised his voice. 'Immediately!'

The guy swore at Vinny but left the shop, barging into Carly on his way out. Robbie stood, chest out, and puffed up. Vinny gave him a high-five. Carly applauded, and some of the customers joined in.

Vinny declared. 'I can't believe you spelled out the R-E-S-P-E-C-T.'

Robbie smiled. 'Come on now, back to work. These customers won't serve themselves.'

A little while later, Vinny called Anne. 'Hey, we need to meet.'
'Yeah, sure.'

He could hear the surprise in her voice.

'How about Cafe Tabac, the top of Bold Street? I should finish at half two, can we do it just after that?' Vinny asked.

'Yeah, see you there.'

Chapter Twenty-Six

Anne

'Hey.' Anne approached the table.

It was a small modern café that served a range of coffees and teas. Although called Cafe Tabac, no doubt from French influence, it always had the feel of an upmarket diner for Vinny.

'Hi.' Vinny had a pot of tea and cups ready.

Anne sat down heavily.

'Rough day?' Vinny was aware he had thrown Anne out the last time they met.

'Nothing special, you know. Normal work stuff.' Anne clutched her bag in her lap and kept her coat on.

'Yeah, I think I do.'

'What's going on with you?'

'I just had a visitor at work. He told me to tell you to stop what you're doing. Let me see, the actual quote was, "Tell your girlfriend to fuckin' drop it."'

'Shit. Who was it?' Anne put her bag down.

'Big guy, short black hair, about thirty-five.' He wasn't sure describing him would help.

'Let me guess, shitty moustache?'

'Yeah, now you mention it. Yeah, he did. You know him?'

'That's the guy. The one who took my notebook.'

'What do you mean "took your notebook?"' He couldn't help sounding shocked.

'The other day, outside the Noah's Ark in Speke.' Anne was looking down at the table.

'Bastard.' It was all Vinny could think to say. He was both angry and offended. He started pouring the tea. 'We have to think about this.'

Anne got out her replacement notebook. 'I think this is getting a bit too much. It's getting out of control.'

She looked directly at him. The eye contact was enough to show whatever issue they had was now over.

Vinny heard the quaver in her voice. 'We can work it out…let me think. Here.' He passed her tea over.

'Thanks.'

'Look, the guy in the shop… Sorry about this… said something about grabbing your breast.' Vinny didn't like saying it, but he knew they had to face this thing together.

Anne flushed, 'Yeah, he had one hand round my throat, and yeah, well…he did.'

'Fuck. Why didn't you tell me?' It was an appeal made out of frustration, not a reprimand.

'I was going to, but then we fell out. Remember?'

'Yeah, sorry about that.' He was embarrassed thinking about how he had acted.

'No, maybe you're right. This all about me trying to prove myself. I should stick to the retirement parties.'

'Without you, we wouldn't have any idea what's going on. Whoever is in that hole, and however they got there, no one else gives a shit. Don't put yourself down. We can both try and find out what's going on. From now on, we do this together. Okay?'

'I don't know. It's just kind of blowing up, all kinds of stuff I don't even understand.'

'Drink your tea.' He pushed her cup closer to her. 'It'll make you feel better.'

Anne laughed. 'Everything seems better after a cup of tea.'

'Don't mock it. There's a lot of truth in that. The sugar gives you an energy boost and the liquid - '

'All right, I believe you, Dr Connolly,' Anne mocked.

They were both smiling.

'Okay, let's look at this. How did this guy know you were in the Noah's Ark? Could people have overheard you talking?'

'I guess so. The barmaid maybe, but I sat away from the bar with the guy, Billy.'

'Could other customers have heard you?'

'No, we sat on our own,' Anne replied.

'Who else knew you were there?'

'Dave. DS Cooper, but you don't think….?' she trailed off.

'Who knows that we are connected? I mean, how did this guy in the shop know who I am? Was it in your notebook?'

'No, why would it be?'

'Okay. So, Dave again. He knows how close we are.'

Anne gave a half-smile. 'You really think so?'

Vinny took a drink of tea. 'I don't know, but it's possible.'

'Why would he help me? If he wanted all this to go away? What's it got to do with him, anyway? Why would he care one way or the other?'

'How has he helped you?' Vinny asked.

'I don't know…he took me to see this inspector guy.'

'What inspector?'

'A guy out in Crosby. Barlow, I think his name was. Big posh house, was in the Special Branch, all about informers, politics, and the IRA.'

'Did he help? Did you get any useful information from him?'

'Not really, general background stuff.'

'So why did Dave take you there?'

'To be helpful,' Anne suggested.

'Maybe, but what if Dave hasn't been trying to help you? What else could he have been doing?' Vinny asked.

'Trying to find out what I knew?' Anne said, her eyes widening as she clapped a hand over her mouth.

'That Barlow guy was asking me who I thought it was,' Anne explained.

'Did you tell him?' Vinny asked.

'No. How could I? I don't know who it was. I mentioned the Powers, but that was all.'

'Okay, I think you should be careful about what you tell DS Cooper, at least for now.'

Anne was out of her seat and round to Vinny's side of the table. She reached down to give him a hug, and it was one of the most awkward, yet one of the nicest hugs Vinny had ever received. She was standing, and he was sitting.

'Okay, okay, so what do we do now?'

Anne sat back down. 'I'm going to find out what happened. As much as I can, anyway.'

'It won't be easy. We might not find out who it was or what happened. It was over thirty years ago.'

'I know, but at least I want to be able to say I tried. I gave it my best shot. But it's not just about me…'

The silence hung between them until Vinny said, 'Yeah. I agree with you. We give it our best shot. Even if it means I have to deal with some shit too.'

'Okay, I've got something to do,' Anne announced.

'What?' Vinny looked concerned.

'Remember you told me about The Casa? Well, I'm going there now.'

'Do you want me to come with you?' Vinny started to stand.

'No, look, I appreciate the thought. But if I stop now, I'll never be able to do this job.'

He sat back down. 'We are supposed to be doing things together?'

'We are, but I still have to operate. I am a reporter. You need to have faith in me.'

'I do, more faith in you than anyone else I know.'

Anne laughed. 'So…what's one more pub? It feels like I'm spending my life in them. Can we catch up later?'

'Yeah, sure, but bring some chocolate,' Vinny said.

'What's that? The price of admission?'

'Maybe,' he said.

***

Getting into her car, Anne knew where she was going. Two minutes later, she was parking near the Catholic Cathedral, or "Paddy's Wigwam" as it was known locally. Catholic priests collected money from working-class families, many in poverty themselves, to build this large, modern, circular, tent-like structure. Begun and completed within five years in the 1960s, it was built next to the site of an old workhouse. Anne liked this part of town. Nowadays there were lots of Chinese faces and voices. The University was doing well out of China's booming economy. She knew from *The Chronicle*'s reporting that it had a campus in China.

Anne walked past the Everyman Theatre along Hope Street, the Catholic cathedral behind her and the neo-gothic Anglican cathedral dominating the view at the other end of the street. On her left, the tall and narrow brick terraces covered three floors, with stone steps leading up to glossy black front doors. The brass fittings glinted in the sunlight and gave an air of elegance, spoiled only by the noise and fumes of the traffic rushing by.

The Casa was at the end of the terrace, slightly wider than the other buildings, a red star proudly displayed over the entrance. She climbed the steps and walked through what would have been the old entrance hallway. To her left, running the length of the room, was the bar. It was still early afternoon, so the place was quite empty. On her right were two openings, separated by a supporting column, leading into a seating area. She could see a corridor ahead, which led to the toilets and function room. She let her eyes wander over the walls: memorabilia of past trade union and political struggles, posters celebrating striking dockers, miners, and a large framed commemorative embroidery of Spanish Civil War volunteers.

Two men were standing at the end of the bar where it curved into the wall. One had a newspaper open before him, the other engrossed in the television high above the bar, which was silently showing a race meeting.

'Hi, what can I get you?' The guy behind the bar was in his twenties, with a smiling face and friendly demeanor.

'White wine, I think,' Anne said.

He reached into a glass-fronted chiller cabinet and produced a bottle. She noticed the sleeve of tattoos that covered his arm.

'Actually, sorry, could I make that a spritzer?' Remembering she had to drive, Anne decided one would be okay.

'Sure thing.' The barman deftly swapped the wine glass for a straight one.

Anne looked around the walls again. This time she saw advertisements and posters for current events. There was also a plaque explaining that the bar had been set up by sacked Liverpool Dockers as a non-profit organisation to support community activities.

Her drink was delivered, and as she handed over her money, she commented, 'Not the usual pub decor.'

He smiled. 'No. Your first time here?'

'Yeah, a friend recommended it.' Anne handed over her card.

He looked at the card. 'Oh, okay, Anne. Anne from *The Chronicle*,' he read. 'It's nice to meet you, Anne. I'm Adam.'

They shook hands over the bar.

'Actually, maybe you can help me, Adam.'

'If I can, what do you need?'

'Well, it might be difficult, but I'm trying to find out about a docker, from Garston. I was told someone here might be able to help.'

'You should speak to our secretary or someone from the committee. Who is it you are looking for?'

'A man called Bob, Bob Pennington.'

'I can give you a number, if you'd like, for Joe, the secretary, or if you come in on Sunday afternoon, you'll probably catch him.'

'Yeah, that would be great, thanks very much.'

'Who is it you're asking about?' The guy reading his newspaper had folded it over on the bar.

He raised his reading glasses, but instead of lifting them over his head, they somehow managed to perch on his forehead. 'Sorry, couldn't help hearing,' he offered.

Anne turned towards him, waiting for his glasses to drop back down over his eyes, but they didn't. 'No problem. Bob Pennington. He was an organiser for the Blue Union in Liverpool or Garston, at least.'

'Yeah. I knew Bob.'

'Really?' Anne was surprised. 'You actually knew him?'

'Yeah.' He laughed. 'What's up? It looks like you've just seen a ghost.'

Anne smiled. 'It feels like it, actually, but never mind. You don't look old enough.'

'Ha, thanks, but you don't need the bullshit.'

'No, I meant it. From what I know he was in Garston in the 1950s.'

'Yeah, that would be about right.'

'Well, can I ask how you knew him?'

'I knew him quite well for a few years, back in the day.'

The guy wasn't exactly offering information. She didn't know if it was his speaking style or he was actually wary.

Anne probed, 'So it was after he had been involved in Garston?'

'Yeah, long after. By the time I knew him, he was in his late fifties, maybe even early sixties. I don't know, just going off how he looked to me.'

'Sorry, but how did you know him, and when was this?' she asked.

Anne took the few steps that separated them and offered her hand.

'Anne McCarthy, *The-*'

He interrupted her. '*Chronicle*, yeah, I heard.'

He unfolded his paper and began scanning the pages, leaving her hand dangling, and she dropped it to her side.

'So, you were saying…'

'Yeah, well, I knew him. What's your story about, exactly?'

She could feel the suspicion. 'It's not even a story, to be honest. I've been hearing about this Blue and White Union stuff, and his name has come up a couple of times as someone who was a part of that. I thought I would like to interview him,' Anne said.

'Yeah, well, sorry, but *The Chronicle?*' the man asked.

'We've all got to start somewhere.' She shrugged.

'True enough. I just don't want to say anything that might be out of place, especially not to a reporter.'

'Fair point.' Anne was disappointed but hadn't given up just yet.

'Are you local?' he asked.

'Yeah, you could say that. Grew up in Asbridge Street.'

'The Granby?' he tried to clarify.

'Yeah.'

'You should have said. What was your name again?' His demeanor changed as soon as he heard this.

'McCarthy.'

He put his paper down. 'That rings a bell. Who do I know, McCarthy?'

'Not sure. My dad was Robert, people knew him as Bobby.'

He asked along the bar, 'Who was Bobby McCarthy?'

The other drinker smiled. 'You know, don't you?'

Anne looked at the other drinker quizzically.

His smile broadened. 'You're losing it, do you know that?' He tapped the side of his head.

'Ignore him, he doesn't know what day of the week it is.' The first guy responded.

'Bobby Mac!' the second guy laughed.

'Bobby. Aah, I know Bobby, Bobby Mac, yeah.' The first guy's face lit up with recognition. 'Black guy, worked on the railway.'

'Yeah, that's the one.' Anne smiled.

'Good guy, your dad. Used to know him back in the day. Did quite a bit of Anti-Apartheid stuff. Died a few years back. Sorry to hear that. Yeah, he was sound, your dad.'

Anne was smiling broadly now. 'Thanks.'

'Bobby Mac used to drink in the Alex.'

'Yeah, that would be him.'

'I'm Paul.' The first guy offered his hand. 'And the baldy one over there is Jimmy.'

Anne took it and shook it warmly.

'Is your mam still around?' Paul asked.

'Yeah, she's going strong, getting on a bit now.'

'Yeah, she would be,' he said.

'Aren't we all,' Jimmy, the second guy, said.

'Ignore him. No one listens to him. They only let him in because nowhere else will have him. Jimmy, the slaphead.'

Jimmy shot back, 'I'm not the one that was barred from the Blackburne.'

'Don't talk to me about that hole. Georgian Quarter my arse. A load of bollocks. Microbreweries and fuckin' cocktails. They're driving out the locals.'

'You're barred from the Cracke,' Jimmy added.

'Oh, shut up. Have you got nothing sensible to say? That's the old fart that runs the place. Talk about thin-skinned, you could see right through him, and when you did, all you saw was pound coins. Sell his soul for a couple of quid, that one.'

'The Cambridge, you were barred there.'

'Don't start me on that place. Full of pseudo-academics. Wouldn't know an original thought if it came and bit them in the arse.' Paul turned away from Jimmy and addressed Anne. 'He was a full-timer for the IMG when I knew him.'

'IMG?' Anne gave him a quizzical look.

'Yeah, the International Marxist Group. He worked at the national centre in Upper Street, Islington, down in London.'

'Trotskyites,' Jimmy chimed in.

'The slaphead there is an old Stalinist,' said Paul.

Anne looked toward Adam.

'It's like "who's your favourite: The Beatles or The Rolling Stones" for communists,' Adam said, shrugging.

'Well, if your cultural and historical world is governed by pop music, then yeah, that would be right, but for others, the progress of humanity is measured in the struggles of the working class and the oppressed. Marx, Lenin, Fidel, Thomas Sankara, Maurice Bishop,' said Paul.

'Okay, well, I got Marx and Lenin, does that get me any points?' Anne said.

'Tell you what. Your dad knew Sankara and Bishop, Burkina Faso, and Grenadian revolutions strangled at birth. Look them up sometime.'

'I will,' said Anne.

'You should. Your dad would be proud. We've got to know our history.'

'Okay, so what were you saying about Bob Pennington?'

'Oh, right, yeah, a good bloke. To be honest, even when I knew him, I didn't really know his history in Garston. It was only later I learned he was actually hired by the Blue Union as an organiser.'

'When did you know him?'

'It would be the seventies, around the mid-to-late seventies.'

'You sure about the dates?'

'Yeah, we ran the Socialist Unity campaign in '79. He wasn't up here then and had been gone a while.'

'Is he still alive?' Anne asked.

'No, he died way back, well at least ten years ago now.'

'Are you sure about that?'

'Yeah, not a very nice story.'

'How's that?'

'From what I heard, he ended up on a park bench in Brighton. Had a drinking problem, and well, I think you can guess the rest.'

'So, he ended up on his own?' Anne asked.

'It sounds like, yeah. When I knew him, he had been national organiser for the IMG. I got on well with him, but to be honest, even then, you could see he was losing things a bit,' said Paul.

'How do you mean?'

'I was down in London one time, can't remember what for, some meeting or other, and I thought I would look him up. His address was in Brixton. I went there, no answer. This was before mobile phones.'

'Before television, too, if you were young,' said Jimmy.

'Ignore him, he'll be going for his afternoon nap soon. Anyway, then I found Bob in a pub. He was quite surprised to see me, but what was funny was he loved how I found him.'

'You knew his local,' Anne guessed.

'No, I went to his flat, and he wasn't there, so I asked someone in the street where the nearest bookies was. Found that, then went into the pub nearest the bookies. There he was, pint on the table, racing pages in front of him. He got a good laugh out of that, but it kind of showed where he was at.'

Anne felt quite affected. She didn't know why, but somehow, even though she had never known Bob Pennington, a picture had been developing. It might have been romantic or unrealistic, but she had begun to think of Pennington like Etienne, the heroic character from Emile Zola's *Germinal*, a miner who led his colleagues out on strike in the 1860s. She remembered Etienne's passion and fire for the miners he lived and worked with. All she knew was that this Bob had come to Liverpool as an activist and organiser, he had worked among the dockers, and by all accounts, he was respected and built the union in Garston. That he died alone on a park bench in Brighton left her feeling deflated.

'Thanks for the information.' She drained her drink. 'You are sure about this?' she checked.

'Yeah, he was a good bloke, though,' Paul replied.

'Okay, thanks. Can I buy you a drink?'

'You don't have to do that. I'm happy to have helped Bobby Mac's daughter. Say hello to your mum. She'll remember me.'

'I will. And I want to buy you a drink.'

'Fair enough, more than your dad ever did.' Paul laughed.

Anne laughed with him.

'I'll have another of these.' He raised his glass to Adam. 'Just joking, he did get his round in.'

'Thanks, love, a rum and coke for me,' Jimmy added.

'She wasn't offering you.'

'It's okay.' Anne nodded to Adam.

Jimmy said, 'Make it a double.'

Adam looked at Anne.

'A single.'

'Can't take you anywhere,' Paul grimaced. 'Just goes to show you can take the man out of Speke, but you can't take Speke out of the man.'

'Bollocks, you old fart,' Jimmy responded.

Anne finished what was left in her glass and handed a ten-pound note to the barman. 'Thanks, Adam.'

'You're welcome, come back soon, eh?'

'Yeah, now I know where you are, I might just do that. Where's your ladies'?'

He pointed along the corridor opposite the entrance.

'Thanks again.'

A few minutes later, as she was leaving, she waved to Paul, who stood alone at the bar. Anne met Jimmy smoking on the steps just outside the doorway. She stopped for a second. 'Was that true about my dad?'

'Yeah, we both knew your dad. He helped us on pickets, leafleting, and stuff.'

'You know what? I never knew that.'

'He was a good man. Ignore us. We like to have a joke, but all that aside, your dad was okay.'

'Bit of a character in there, isn't he,' Anne said, nodding back towards the bar.

'Yeah, but the old bastard is the sharpest person I've met, and that's no joke.'

'I can believe it.' Anne carried on down the steps.

'Bye, then.'

Driving home, Anne wondered about her father. She was lucky she had known him, unlike Vinny, and yet she had known him as a daughter knows a father. The mixture of love and fear, respect and resentment, pride and disappointment. It's part of who we are, she realised; as we grew, our understanding of those around us changed. She had met a part of her father for the first time as an adult. A man engaged with the world, not just his daughter.

Anne turned off the radio. The constant jingles for Radio City were annoying her. She fumbled in the side pocket of the door, pulling out CDs: Sinead O Connor, Adele, Joss Stone. She laughed at the recognition of female angst, love, and betrayal. *Is there nothing else worthy of music?*

Still rummaging, she found Freak Power's "Drive Thru Booty" and smiled. This was a relic of her student days - the mix of acid jazz and funk was perfect for her. She slid it into the drive and was immediately lifted by upbeat rhythms.

She car-danced the rest of the drive home.

Chapter Twenty-Seven

Anne

Dave's car was parked outside. Anne saw it before she saw him. She steeled herself. Turning off the music, she pulled in next to him. They got out at the same time.

'Hi.' Dave's car beeped, and the indicators flashed as he locked it.

She turned her key to lock her door. 'I wasn't expecting you.'

'Yeah, I know, but I've got a bit of news I thought you might want.'

Anne felt compelled to be polite but was very wary. 'Ok.' She did not trust him at all now.

'Any chance of a coffee or something?' Dave asked.

'I don't really have a lot of time.' Anne tried to put him off.

'Won't be long. I'd rather not talk out here, if you know what I mean?'

'Okay. Five minutes,' Anne agreed.

'Sounds great.' Dave smiled.

'Come on in then, but just a coffee, don't get any ideas. Right?' She wanted to be clear.

'Just coffee.' Dave spread his hands wide in a gesture of innocence.

As they reached her flat door, she thought about asking him to wait while she tidied, but she decided against it. He followed her in. The flat had one room with a kitchen area. Anne pulled her duvet over the bed, covering her pyjamas where she'd thrown them in the morning.

'Have a seat, I'll sort the coffee out. It's instant, okay.' It wasn't a question.

'Yeah, whatever you've got.'

Dave flicked his fringe of hair back in place as he sat in one of the two armchairs. From the corner of her eye, she saw him look through the bookcase next to him. He picked up a title *The History of Madness* and flicked through its pages, before returning it and selecting another: *Germinal.* 'Heavy stuff.'

Anne turned. 'Mainly Uni reading. I guess I've fallen out of the habit recently.'

She poured the boiling water from the kettle into two mugs and placed them on a small table between the armchairs. They sat facing each other.

'So…news?' she asked.

'Oh yeah, the place the bones were found. We've traced back ownership, and at one stage, it was a builders' yard. That would be between the early sixties and up to the late seventies. It was done up then and turned into residential housing. There were at least a couple of flats before being knocked down for this new development.'

'Okay, that's interesting. Do you know who the builder was?'

'We're still checking that. I thought you might know?'

Was he trying to find out what she knew? 'No, not come across anything.'

'How about this Connolly fella?' Dave asked. 'Have you spoken to him?'

Anne was definitely suspicious now. She felt a chill as she realised that Vinny might be right. Ever since they met, Dave had been using her. 'Not since that disaster of a night in Garston.'

'Yeah, okay.'

'My editor is getting on my back about this stuff.' Anne

handed Dave the sugar.

'Nah, I'm good, got to look after this.' He indicated his body. 'Temple and all that.'

'Yeah, right.' Anne couldn't keep the sarcasm out of her voice as she spooned two heaps into her own drink.

'Are you losing interest?' he asked.

Anne was shocked for a second, thinking he hadn't got the message, before she realised he was talking about the case.

'Well, I've kind of run out of road, nowhere else to go.'

Anne stood and went back to the kitchen to get the milk. As she opened the fridge, Dave appeared behind her. He put his hands on her waist. Anne recoiled from the physical contact. She turned with the milk in hand, and gently squeezed past him. He followed her across to the chairs.

'Sit.' She pointed to the armchair, and Dave flopped down.

'Well, from the questions you were asking the inspector, seems to me you either think the body is Paddy Connolly or Bob Pennington?'

'Paddy Connolly…Bob Pennington…or literally anybody else, not exactly a theory. Anyway, I know it's not Bob Pennington.' She shook her head.

'How?'

'I've just come from a place in town where I met with a guy who knew him. He said he knew him in the late seventies. Apparently, he died a few years ago, down in Brighton, I think he said.' She thought it was safe to tell him this.

'Well, that's progress, crossing him off the list.'

'List? Two people isn't exactly a list. Have you got anywhere on your missing persons?'

'Not really. The names we did find have been filtered for sex and age. Now we have to try and find them. Most are not in Garston or even Liverpool. I'm afraid the wheels turn quite slowly. Did you ask your mate about the DNA test?' he asked.

'Yeah, I did. He didn't really take it well.'

'Why not? It could rule him out. He could find out if the body is related to him.'

'I think he's going through some other stuff right now. I don't know, or maybe he's afraid it could really be his dad.'

'He should man up, get on with it.'

'Man up?'

'You know, just deal with it.'

Anne didn't respond.

'I can check out the Pennington thing, if you want? Find out how he died?'

Anne had really had enough of him now. 'I was told on a park bench, ended up an alky. Shame, really.'

'Why? You heard the inspector. These guys were communists, trying to bring down the government and all that. Serves him right.'

'You don't really believe that, do you?'

'What do you mean?'

'Serves him right.' This was a pointless discussion, and she knew it. She just couldn't let it pass.

'Yeah, of course I do. I don't know what you're worrying about him for,' said Dave.

'I'm not worrying about him. He's dead. But I can respect what he tried to do,' Anne said.

'Respect what? Trouble-making at the docks?'

The look of disdain etched her face, but she said nothing.

'Not my thing. I don't get the whole politics thing,' he said in frustration.

'Yeah, well, middle-class boy from Woolton, why would you?'

'What's that supposed to mean?'

'Just that you probably haven't had to deal with the sharp end of things.'

'Oh, I get it. Because I'm from a nice area, I can't understand anything?'

'Basically, yeah. Do you think the guys who are out there

hustling would be doing it if they had your experience?'

'Funnily enough, I do. Some people are just bad. Scallies - we meet them all the time.'

'You mean your mates, the ones you got the pills off?'

Dave responded, 'What? You're Cinderella now, are you? I don't remember that the other night.'

Anne didn't appreciate being reminded of her behaviour. 'Okay, well, thanks for bringing the news.' She picked up his coffee cup.

'Oh, invitation over?' He looked disappointed.

'Yeah, I'm tired. I need to catch up on stuff for the paper. This Garston thing is over.'

'Shall I call you, maybe another drink? I don't mind going somewhere else. It doesn't have to be in Woolton.'

'I don't think so.'

Dave stood to leave. 'Well, I guess that's it, then?'

Anne moved to open the door. 'I guess it is.'

The door closed behind him.

She was relieved he was gone. She didn't want to think about Dave, but it was becoming clear her choice in partners had not always been great. She cleared away the coffee things.

So, if it's not Pennington, the chance that it was Paddy Connolly has just increased. She knew this could make things difficult with Vinny.

The next day at work, Anne put her bag on her desk and flopped into her chair.

'Wow, we are honoured. Ms McCarthy, I believe.' Anthony appeared at her side.

'Hey.' She placed her bag on the floor and turned on her computer. 'Thank you.'

'For?' he asked, taking the chair opposite her.

She swivelled round to face him. 'The article. You only changed the last line. You didn't say the info came from the police.'

'You are good, Anne. No doubt someday you will be very good, but until that day, my job is to make sure you walk the fine line between the truth as we know it, and the truth as we can show it.'

This is why she liked him. Who else could deliver a line like that?

'I have been following the Garston story,' Anne declared.

'I know you have, because otherwise, I would have to ask where the hell you have been over the past few days. The school award ceremonies, the retirement parties, and the discovery of celebrity vegetables continue apace. What's more, other, no less talented cubs have had no escape.'

'I know, and I'm here now.' Anne felt guilty.

'Okay, well, before we get to your next earth-shattering assignment, why don't you tell me what you've got?'

'What have I got? I've got an unidentified skeleton from thirty years ago. I've got an old man, Michael, who at the moment is making me feel like a fool because everywhere I turn, he seems to be connected to it. I've got a copper who I don't trust, to say the least. I've also got a friend who, because of me, now thinks the skeleton might be his father. And I have got some kind of Irish trade union struggle, dispute, that I can't even begin to understand.' As the words came out, her weariness increased. 'So, you tell me what I've got?'

Anthony swivelled from side to side. 'You have a job, and you have a story. What you don't have are facts and an article. Best not to confuse the two. You also have a new assignment. Mrs Hardcastle has spent fifty years of her life devoted to educating the urchins of our fair city. Do you think you could spend fifty minutes of yours celebrating that?' He handed her a card with the details.

'Photographer?' she asked.

'Phil - '

'I know,' she interrupted. 'The cot.'

' - Is on his way as we speak.' Anthony finished his sentence. Anne picked up her bag and turned her computer off.

'Do the job you are paid for, not the job you would like. Leave Garston alone,' Anthony said, 'Before things get messy.'

Before, Anne thought.

Chapter Twenty-Eight

Anne

Vinny buzzed Anne in. When she reached the landing, she found the flat door open. Vinny was reading.

'Anything good?' Anne asked.

'Uni stuff. How are you?'

'Good. Just had two hundred kids swarming round me at their headmistress' retirement ceremony.'

'Sounds like fun.' Vinny put his book down. 'Did you bring the chocolate?'

'You know, I've finished that thing with Dave.'

'I wouldn't expect any less,' said Vinny, hiding his delight.

'Aside from all this other stuff, I guess I just realised who he was.'

'A copper, you mean?'

'That's not fair. He seemed like a decent enough bloke. Well, that's what I thought. Anyway, it wasn't really a thing.'

'Can we get back to the important stuff? Did you bring my chocolate?'

'Yeah, bloody blackmail.'

'If you want to get back in my good books, there is a price to pay.'

'Who says I want to get back in?'

'I do,' he said, standing. 'Now, where's my choccy?'

Anne reached into her bag, pulled her hand out, but held it

behind her back.

Vinny moved forward and tried to reach around her. They were both laughing. Anne struggled to keep the chocolate hidden. Vinny had both his arms stretching round her, his head next to hers. He could feel her hair against his face. Anne was using her body to push him away. They fell back on the sofa. Anne's hands were still behind her with Vinny's weight pressed against her. His face was so close to hers, and then it happened. At first tentative and nervous, as if their lips just brushed against each other, but then eager and urgent - somehow, they were kissing.

Anne freed her arms and wrapped them around Vinny. Between kisses, she asked, 'Do you want your chocolate?'

'Fuck the chocolate,' he said.

★★★

Anne lay next to Vinny. For the second time in a few days, she was in bed with a man, although now, she knew this was the right place to be. Vinny was sleeping, his slim frame naked beneath the quilt. His upper body exposed, she liked his athleticism. It was somehow more raw and real than toned flesh and muscles. His short dark hair was tousled and unkempt. She let her fingers move along his arm, softly and gently so as not to wake him, but enough to feel his smooth, warm skin. He was sleeping on his side, back facing her. She could see his spine and followed the bumps with her eyes. *Everything*, she thought, *seems right*.

She was about to reach out and follow this range of hills with her finger when he shifted and turned onto his back. Half-awake, his arm reached out for her. She moved within his reach, getting close so that his arm drew her in. He snored softly, and she closed her eyes, then measured her relaxation to its sonorous rhythm and drifted off to sleep.

Chapter Twenty-Nine

Vinny

Vinny felt the darkness. It wasn't the absence of light. It was heavy, pressing on all sides. His arm was being pulled to the ground. Looking down, he saw the hammer head dripping with blood, each drip pulling his arm and body down lower and lower. The hammer touched the growing pool of blood and began to sink into it, disappearing inch by inch. Still his arm was pulled down until it, too, touched the growing mass of red. The warmth and energy pulled his hand in deeper. His arm was disappearing. He was being dragged down, further and further down.

'Are you okay? Vinny…Vinny, wake up.'

Vinny heard the voice. Its warmth, concern, light, broke through the darkness.

'Vinny!'

Vinny shook his head and raised his hands to wipe his face clear of sweat.

'Are you okay?' Anne's eyes narrowed in concern.

'Yeah,' he reassured her.

'What is it?' Her hand rested lightly on his arm.

Opening his eyes, he saw Anne was staring at him.

'You were sweating, mumbling. A nightmare?'

'It's fine, I'm fine.'

Anne sat back a little. 'It's not the first time, is it?'

'What do you mean?' He roused himself and sat up, leaning against the headboard.

'These dreams or nightmares.' She brushed his hair away from his eyes. 'How often do you have them?'

'I don't know. Every few days, once a week, it's hard to tell. I guess more often, recently.'

'And what is it? I mean, what do you dream about?'

'It's weird. I don't know. Sometimes it's just…darkness and fear, you know? I'm scared of something but don't know what. Other times, it's worse: violence, blood, screams. Not me, someone else.'

'Someone else doing the violence?'

'I don't know, maybe it's me.'

'Do you know what's causing it?'

'No, wish I did.' Vinny was honest, but also knew the dreams were happening more often now. He didn't know if it was the discussion about his father or the stress of the University project, but something was happening.

'How long have you been having them?'

'On and off for years, I guess.' He couldn't remember when they started, but he knew they were intensifying.

'That's weird.' Anne reached out to stroke his hair again.

He pulled his head away. It was an instinctive reaction. Not to Anne, but to the physicality of concern.

'Don't be like that,' Anne admonished.

'Like what?' Vinny asked, confused.

'Pulling away.'

'All right. Sorry, come here.' He reached out and pulled her in.

Anne spoke softly into his neck, her lips brushing his skin. 'It's just worrying, you know? There must be something behind it.'

'I know. I wish I knew what it was.'

She sat upright. 'I'll have to get my Sigmund Freud out.'

'No, please, for fuck's sake, you'll be telling me I killed my dad so I can shag my mum.'

She hit him playfully. 'That's definitely not funny, and a caricature, not fair on Freud.'

'Perfectly fair from what I've seen.'

'But why did you say your "dad"?' Her expression was an exaggerated quizzical look.

'Because that's all old Ziggy-bloody-Freud talks about.' He paused for a second, recognising her joke. 'Oh, okay, I get it.'

He climbed out of bed. 'I'll have a shower, then I'll make some tea.'

'Sounds great.'

He let the water pour over him, and, leaning against the wall, he enjoyed the sensation. The dreams, once rare, were returning with unnerving regularity. Every one of them was different, but the same.

A few minutes later, he placed her tea and toast on the bedside cabinet. 'Are you ok?' he asked.

'Fine, and you?'

'Yeah, more than fine,' he smiled.

'We need to talk.'

'About us?' he asked.

'No, everything else. I think we're okay.'

'Yeah, me too, and yeah, I know what you mean. I'm sorry about the other day.'

'It's okay, I understand. Come here.' She held her arms out.

Vinny moved in and they shared a warm embrace. He pulled back a little.

'I was just getting stressed, with the Uni stuff, and yeah, this thing about the body and everything. It has made me think more about my dad and the dreams. Not just my dad, but me being a dad, too.'

'I know. I know. I'm sorry. I must have seemed heartless, the whole DNA thing, and having told you about Dave. It was stupid of me. Not just stupid - insensitive.'

'Well, I don't think the timing was great, but actually, you are right.'

'Right about what?'

'The DNA thing. Go on, eat your toast.' He lifted the toast for her to take a bite. 'I mean, if there is any chance it could be my dad, I have to find out. It would be crazy not to.' He paused before saying, 'We have to be careful around that copper, though. I don't know what his game is, and I don't trust him. There's something not right.'

'It doesn't say a lot for my judgment of character,' Anne said.

'You can't blame yourself. Anyway, we don't know anything for sure yet. And you're with me now, aren't you? Pretty good judgment, if you ask me.' He moved forward to kiss her gently. 'But back to reality. What do I have to do for this DNA thing?'

'I don't know. I guess I'll have to call Dave.'

'That should be a nice phone call.'

'Yeah, right.'

'Okay, you call him, but I think we should do something else as well.'

'What?'

'Go and see my mum and Michael.'

'You want me there?' Anne asked.

'Yes, I want you there. This is your story.'

'No, don't say that,' Anne replied.

'I mean it, forget what I said last time. I was angry at you, at my dad for leaving, at my mum for not telling me anything, angry at everyone,' said Vinny.

'And now?' asked Anne.

'I don't know, but I think we should find out what we can. Whatever happens, it's your story. *Death of a Mudman.*'

'Sounds good to me.' She hesitated before asking, 'But what if it is your dad?'

'We'll cross that bridge when we get to it. Talking about bridges, maybe *Under the Bridge* would be better.'

'Yeah, maybe,' Anne answered.

Chapter Thirty

Michael

'We will do the test thing, go to see Michael, and then your mum - that okay with you?' Anne asked as she drove.

Vinny turned the radio on, and the opening chords of 'Something' by George Harrison came through. He slapped his hands on his knees to the opening drum salvo, then played air guitar to the piercing notes that followed. He improvised to the music, '*Something in the way she drives, attracts me like no other lover.*'

Anne loved it but didn't want to lose focus. 'Are you sure about this?' she asked.

'About the way you drive? Yeah, absolutely.'

'Come on, silly, you know what I mean. Going to do the test?'

'Not what I would choose to be doing, but, yeah, I need to find out, need to face it. Have you called him?' Vinny asked.

'Yesterday.'

'How was he?' The edge in Vinny's voice was clear.

'All right. Polite, official,' she explained.

'Does he know about us?'

The 'us' was without question now. They had both settled into a rhythm as unconscious as it was smooth.

'I think he's guessed.'

'You didn't tell him?'

'I don't think so, not directly.' She was hesitant.

They were passing Penny Lane and would soon hit Menlove Avenue.

'Do you like it here?' Vinny was looking out of the window.

'Allerton?'

'No, Liverpool.'

'I don't know. I like where I live. I like my job, especially now I'm getting to do a bit more. Why are you asking?' Anne asked.

'Sometimes it just feels like there is so much history here. I can't look at anything without seeing what's behind it. I don't know, the ghosts of the past,' Vinny said.

She pointed out the window. 'Okay, so what's out there?'

'Calderstones Park,' he answered.

'Secret history?' she probed.

'I was being serious, it's not a game.

'Okay, but…it can be a game too.'

'An old manor, now a park, obviously. Full of American trees.'

'American trees?'

'Yeah, the place was sold to the council by a family called the McIvers. The family were partners in the Cunard shipping line. They traded with America, owned the Lusitania.'

'I've heard of that.'

'Sunk by a U-boat in 1915, hundreds died, the crew was mainly from Liverpool.'

'Why is it a problem…you knowing this stuff, I mean?'

'Like I said, ghosts. You were right. This Uni stuff is partly about my dad. Not consciously or anything. But working out who he was is part of me. I guess that's why I'm doing this Irish in Liverpool project…'

Anne slapped her forehead. 'D'oh!'

'Yeah, I know. Ok, ok. I guess you saw it coming way before I did. It's something I have to deal with, knowing where I come from. And the more research I do, the harder it is to turn a blind eye to things.'

'In history, you mean?' Anne asked.

'Not just history. Time kind of leaks, the past into the present.' Vinny ruminated. 'Somehow, since the Beatles, everything is supposed to be all happy Scousers together. Look here - music and football. What more could you want?'

'You mean like bread and circuses? What the Roman rulers used to keep the people happy?' Anne said.

He smiled. 'You're not as daft as you look, are you?'

'Heeey.' She took a hand off the wheel to hit him.

'No, I mean it. I never thought of that, "bread and circuses."'

'So instead of gladiators, we have Goodison and Anfield?' she suggested.

'Something like that.'

She wondered aloud. 'And the bread?'

'Good question.'

'Maybe property?' She answered her own question.

'Yeah, that would work. As long as prices are good.'

'Exactly, so when house prices are going up, people think they are safe. As soon as prices drop, then the bread is taken away,' Anne said.

'And people realise how close they are to the edge. Even the circus can go wrong.' He paused. 'Think about the biggest thing to hit Liverpool, maybe even to politicise the city.'

'The Militant, the whole Derek Hatton thing?'

'No, something deeper and longer-lasting.'

'The Hillsborough tragedy?'

'Yeah, but even calling it a tragedy, as if it was some God-given event, like a hurricane or tsunami.'

'But it was an accident,' she declared.

'Born of contempt and disregard. The whole cover-up and whitewash, same as the riots in Toxteth. You know, most people won't buy *The Sun* because of the way they blamed the victims.'

'Yeah, course, I know that.' Anne gave him a look.

'But the *Daily Mail* or the *Star* are okay?' he asked. 'They do exactly the same to other groups of victims: refugees and asylum seekers.'

'Yeah, but it's not so easy to draw the links,' said Anne.

'The authorities, the police, treating normal people as if they are some dangerous species that needs controlling, corralling, pushed here and there as required. At Hillsborough, or in Liverpool Eight. Somehow, we are not as human as they are, without the same feelings. As if we don't know humiliation and contempt, we can't feel it.'

Anne started singing, 'I feel it in my fingers, I feel it in my...'

'Fuck. I guess I asked for that,' Vinny said.

She was half-laughing and half-singing now.

'Okay, point taken,' he said.

'Sorry, but we need to lighten things. It feels like we are turning into a mutual depression society. But...another thing I don't get...'

'Go on.' Vinny smiled.

'We're coming into Speke now, right?'

'Yeah.'

They were turning from Speke Boulevard into Western Avenue.

'What's wrong with it?' Anne asked.

'What do you mean?'

'It's got a terrible reputation. But why?'

'See there?' He was pointing right out of the window.

She looked quickly and saw a normal mid-terrace council house.

'Paul McCartney lived there. His mum was a midwife.'

'Really?'

'Yeah.'

They turned left into Central Avenue.

'And a bit further up, a road on the left, was where George Harrison lived.'

'I never knew that either,' she said.

'Not many people do. You never hear of Speke when people

260

talk about The Beatles. There are no Beatle buses or Magical Mystery tours here.'

'Why? But hang on, I didn't finish. What I don't get is that the houses are nice. Why does the place have such a bad name?'

'The thing about Speke is isolation - and deprivation. These two things continue to eat away at any chance people here had,' Vinny explained.

'We're here,' Anne announced.

'Yeah, I can see.' Vinny wasn't happy.

Anne pulled up at the kerb opposite Speke Police Station.

Vinny shuffled his feet awkwardly as they entered the building.

Anne took control of things. 'Good morning, we're here to see Sergeant Cooper.'

'Is he expecting you?' the officer behind the counter asked.

'Yeah, Anne McCarthy.'

'Okay, hold on a second.' The officer disappeared into a back room.

Vinny was reading the posters. Anne joined him. 'That could be you.' She pointed to a sketch on a poster, identifying a man wanted for sexual assault.

'Thanks very much.'

'Well, maybe I'm being a bit harsh. He does have a strong jawline.' She nudged him gently.

'Really?' Vinny put his hand to his jaw to assess the shape.

A door to their left opened with a click. Dave stood in the opening to the interview room.

'Come in, please, Anne.' He held out his hand.

Anne shook it formally. 'Sergeant Cooper.'

'I think you can call me Dave.'

Anne flushed a little at this reference to their familiarity.

'Mr Vincent Connolly?' Dave offered his hand.

'Yeah.'

They shook hands.

'Please.' Dave indicated for them to sit.

On the table between them was a sealed plastic package.

'Can I see some I.D.?' asked Dave.

'Yeah, sure.' Vinny pulled out his passport and student card.

Dave handed back the card and began writing the details from the passport on a form.

'Can you confirm why you are volunteering this DNA sampling?' Dave asked.

'Because of the remains found in Garston. I want to make sure that it's not my father.'

'Okay, that's fine. If you can just fill in this form here, and then sign at the bottom for me.'

Vinny started reading the form.

Anne was also looking down at the sheet of paper.

Dave stood and opened the door to the inside of the police station, and a WPC appeared out of an office on the main corridor. Dave addressed Vinny. 'This is PC Johnstone. She will conduct the test and witness your signature.'

PC Johnstone entered the small room, brushing past Dave as she did so. Dave was looking at Anne and smiling. He raised his hand and let it brush the small of PC Johnstone's back as she passed. Anne stared back without smiling. Vinny noticed the tension.

'Okay, Jane?'

Jane was slim, with dark hair wound up in a bun. She had pale skin and was wearing a matt red lipstick. 'Yeah, all good.'

Ten minutes later, they were back in the car.

'What a shit.' Anne started the car.

'What do you mean?' Vinny asked.

'All that Jane this and Jane that, you know what that was about?' She pulled out into the road.

'You mean the woman copper?' Vinny guessed what had upset Anne.

'Yeah.'

'I think I can guess,' he said.

'He's either shagging her, or he wants me to think he's shagging her. It was so obvious.' Anne moved up through the gears.

'Does it bother you?'

'That he's shagging her? No.'

'It sounds like something does.'

'Yeah, what bothers me is him showing me. Or trying to prove something. It's such a male thing to do.'

'Okay, well anyway, I'm glad that's over.'

'Yeah, me too,' Anne said.

'I meant the test.'

'Yeah, I know. Sorry, he just wound me up.'

'Yeah, I can tell.'

'He's just a shit.'

'Okay, can we forget him now?' Vinny asked.

'Yeah, I'm sorry.'

They drove in silence for a while.

'So, the thing with Speke.' Anne picked up the conversation from earlier.

'Yeah, go on,' he said.

'But am I going to regret asking?'

'Probably,' he answered.

'Okay, no pain, no gain, as they say.'

'I will try to make it as painless as possible. At first, it was an artificial community, one that never completely gelled. In our road, we had a next-door neighbour from the Dingle. Further down, we had people from Scotty Road, and we had come through Garston. It was a strange mix. There were Catholics and Protestants next door to each other, but the main thing was there was no history to connect us to the place, each other, or anything around us,' said Vinny.

'No community?' Anne asked.

'Kind of. I can only speak for myself, but there were different communities. One, the people you went to school with, either Catholic or Protestant. The other, the people you lived next door to, and they were separate. We knew that, without even mentioning it,' he said.

'But you had decent houses, schools, jobs,' she said.

'For a while, yeah, but over twenty thousand people lived here. If you think two parents and, on average, three or four kids, and to be honest, half of these were Catholics, so the average was more like five or six.'

'Okay, so loads of kids. You start to get to know the neighbours, build a community,' Anne reasoned.

'Up to the mid-seventies. Then the jobs started to disappear: Dunlops and Standard Triumph within about a year, Ford and Evans laid people off, and these were the big names that people took notice of. Loads of smaller companies also disappeared.'

'So, unemployment?' she asked.

'Yeah. But more.'

'How do you mean?'

'It wasn't just unemployment. In Dunlops and Standard, some tried to stop the redundancies and lost. So, you had defeat. Some people took the redundancy money the first chance they got, so defeat and bitterness.'

'And you think this what turned people against each other?' she asked.

'Then the drugs - heroin, smack. All these kids who were teenagers and older now, most unemployed, some started robbing, and dealing.'

'Robbing from who?' Anne asked.

'That was the problem. There is nothing else for miles around, two miles to Garston, two miles to Halewood. They started robbing each other. The estate sort of turned in on itself, began eating itself,' Vinny said.

'Fuck, I can see what you mean,' Anne said.

'Every house had gas meters, electricity meters, and some

telly meters. It was like hitting the jackpot on a slot machine, pockets full of fifty pence pieces,' Vinny said.

'It sounds like you are talking from experience?'

'Don't go there.' Vinny said, half-joking. 'But no, not really. I knew a lot of kids who did. And to be fair, a lot joined the army or moved out. Those who were left had no choice but to try and carry on.'

'Sounds like an interesting story,' Anne said.

'Is everything a story?' he asked.

'I don't know. I guess so. Isn't that what we are doing now?'

'Like Bob Pennington's story?' he asked. 'That whole thing affected you, didn't it?'

'Yeah, it did. It's like what you were saying about Speke. This guy arrived in Garston and was part of trying to build that idea of community, not through schools, or churches, but through…'

'The unions?' Vinny volunteered.

'Yeah, maybe, or wider, the people, workers.'

'You told me he died on a park bench,' Vinny said.

'Yeah, a true hero's death, eh?'

'Same as any other death.' He paused before saying, 'Alone.'

'Jesus, we reeeeally have to stop this.'

'Stop, what?'

'It's depressing.'

'Should've asked your copper friend for another pill.' Vinny was smiling.

'I'm starting to regret telling you that,' Anne said.

Chapter Thirty-One

Anne

Anne rang the doorbell, and they waited. The house was a mid-terrace, with its front opening directly onto the street. The paintwork was old and peeling in places.

'Michael knows we're coming, right?' Vinny was back under the bridge for the first time in years.

The narrow-terraced streets were being replaced piecemeal. New developments seemed to be springing up everywhere. It left a weird mix of whole streets boarded for demolition, and half-built semis with driveways and gardens.

'Yeah, of course.'

'Hi,' Anne said when the door opened slightly.

'Yeah?' A thin sliver of Michael's face was visible between the door and the frame.

'It's me, Anne. I rang you.'

'Did you?' Michael opened the door a little wider. The TV was on in the background, its blue light flashing in the darkened room.

'Yeah. You said it was okay to come by.'

Michael hesitated before responding. 'Oh, okay.' He opened the door wider. 'You'd better come in, then.'

'You've met Vinny. Do you mind if he joins us?'

'I guess it's okay. I wasn't expecting you. I mean, just now.'

Michael turned off the old box TV and opened the curtains.

'Can't see the thing on the TV with these open.'

The room suddenly filled with floating specks of dust as the light streamed in.

'Come in, sit down.' Michael began removing the chip papers and polystyrene containers on the coffee table.

Anne and Vinny settled on the sofa. Vinny pulled a newspaper from underneath him and laid it beside the sofa.

Michael moved an armchair away from the TV to face them. 'Do you want a tea?'

'No, I'm fine, thanks,' Vinny answered.

There wasn't so much a smell as a thickness to the air in the room.

'Same for me. Michael, I think you knew Vinny's dad. Paddy Connolly.'

'Paddy Connolly, yeah, of course.' He smiled. 'Well, what do you know. I don't know why I didn't see it before. Maybe I had an idea, but it was so far back it just didn't occur to me.'

As if explaining it to himself, he continued. 'I think you said you were English as well. That might have thrown me.' Michael reached across with an extended hand. 'Nice to meet you again. I saw you when you were a kid as well.'

'Really?' asked Vinny.

'Oh yeah, you wouldn't remember, of course. You were a nipper.' He held his hand a couple of feet off the ground. 'About so high. You know your dad was very proud of you, always talking about how clever you were, *he can do this, he can do that.*' Michael smiled. 'Parents, eh?'

Vinny was quiet. Anne reached over and touched his hand.

Michael turned to Anne, 'So what can I do for you?'

'I just have a couple of questions; thought you might be able to help?'

'Yeah, sure, if I can.'

'The building site now, it used to be part of Raglan Street?'

'Yeah, I think so. The thing is, they have knocked the old streets down and are replacing them with these new developments. You know, building everything in circles, so it's hard to tell what was what.'

'Yeah, I can see that, but do you remember that street?' Anne knew what she was after.

'Yeah, I guess so. Like I say, it would be hard now to say where exactly things were.'

'Did you know a builders' yard in Raglan Street?'

Michael didn't answer right away. He appeared deep in thought for a minute.

Anne watched Vinny as his eyes scanned the room. She followed his gaze to the TV. On top of the TV, there was a black and white photo in a metal frame. It wasn't large, maybe four inches by six. There were three men in the photo. The central figure was a younger Michael. His face and features were sharper. The lighting, and maybe the monochrome colouring made him look stern as he stared at the camera. It was taken outdoors, and there were houses in the background. The two other men were smiling. Anne wondered if one of them was Vinny's dad.

Michael's answer brought her attention back. 'Yeah, there was a builders' yard. Jack Power's place for a while. I think they turned it into flats later, so it would have been before that.'

Michael had passed this first test of honesty for Anne.

'It was a builders' yard up to the mid-to-late seventies?' Anne asked.

'Yeah, that would be right. Before that, it was a bombsite. That's why they turned it into a yard. Just kind of cleared the ground, put up a couple of sheds.'

'You knew Jack Power?' Anne asked.

Michael nodded. 'Yeah,' he said, a little more hesitantly.

'Worked with him?'

'For a while.'

'Can I ask what you did?'

Michael was quiet for a minute. 'If you're asking, you probably know. He had the building firm, a couple of pubs.'

'He was into some other stuff too?'

'Like I said, I'm guessing you know.' Michael shifted in his chair.

'With my dad?' Vinny asked.

'Yeah,' Michael answered.

'You knew him well?'

Michael leaned over and pulled the photo from off the TV. 'That's your dad on the right, me in the middle, and our Jim on the left.' He handed the photo to Vinny. 'I'm surprised you didn't recognise him.'

'Me mam's not big on photos. What was the occasion?' Vinny asked.

'Whoa…it would have been, I dunno, '63, or '64. You know what it was? Harold Wilson beating Heath.'

'Were you that political?' asked Anne.

'Not really, but after the miners and all that, a lot of people were happy to get rid of the Conservatives. Maybe it was just an excuse for a few pints, but I seem to remember it had to do with Wilson,' said Michael.

Anne looked at the photograph. The man was smiling with his whole face, including his eyes. His short dark hair was pointed at the front like an early but not so prominent DA that rockers wore. He was young, handsome, and looked full of life.

Anne said, 'The body was found in that old builders' yard, or where it used to be…'

'Could be.' Michael shrugged.

'Any idea how it got there?' she asked.

'No. Genuinely, no, no idea.'

Anne didn't know if her face made it obvious she wasn't convinced. But Michael continued. 'If you are asking me did we do some dodgy things, the answer is yes. But you have to remember, I stopped all that in the early seventies.'

'My dad carried on?' Vinny said.

'Yeah, your father worked with the Powers 'til he went, did a bunk, or whatever.'

'You know where I've just been?' Vinny asked.

'No, but I'm sure you're gonna tell me.'

'Speke Police Station, to do a DNA test.'

'What for?' Michael looked surprised.

'To see if the body that was found was my dad.'

Michael sat back in his chair. 'No. No, that wouldn't happen. It couldn't happen.'

'Why not?' asked Anne.

Michael stood and began pacing around the small room.

'It just wouldn't happen, not to one of our own. Paddy was one of us.'

Is he trying to convince himself? Anne wasn't sure. 'One of who? The Wicklow Boys?'

'If you like. We were all "the boys." Dingle boys were always coming down to Garston to cause mayhem. It was a common thing. A group of lads were called "the boys." It was just us, the Powers, me, Paddy. There were all in all about eight of us. A few more around the edges. Maybe you got younger ones coming up, you know, adding to it, but it was a pretty tight group, family, really,' said Michael.

'All from Wicklow?' Anne asked.

'Yeah, mainly Wicklow, but not always. Your da, for example, was from Tipp, a bit a country boy.'

'Tipperary?' Vinny asked.

'But you were known as The Wicklow Boys?' asked Anne.

'By some.' Michael stopped pacing and nodded. 'It was mainly the Orange lot called us that. They had their boys, but they knew that we wouldn't take any of their shit.'

'Why are you so sure it's not my dad? He disappeared right around the same time,' Vinny said.

'I saw your dad.' Michael stood and looked at Vinny. 'Before he went. You know the last time I saw him was our Paul's funeral. We were having a drink in The Fox.'

'Do you know the date?' Anne asked.

'I do, tenth of October 1975.'

'How do you know it exactly?' she pressed.

Michael stopped pacing and sat down heavily in the armchair. His life and energy sapped. 'It was the date of Paul's funeral, and the day before my own birthday, so since 1975 I have never been able to celebrate it. As that time of year comes round, all I remember are those few days. Anyway, who wants to celebrate getting older, eh? Look, I don't know about either of you, but I could do with a drink. Will you have one?'

'I can't,' Anne said. 'Driving.'

'Vincent?'

'Yeah, go on. You know what, I think I will.' He looked toward Anne, who shrugged.

Michael stood and took a step toward a sideboard that ran the length of the wall beside the TV. He flipped down a shelf to reveal a drinks compartment. Inside the cupboard, there was another framed picture. Black and white, a man and woman holding each other outside a church. He wore a flower in his lapel; she held a small bouquet.

'Is that you?' Anne asked, nodding toward the photo.

Michael picked it up for a second. 'Yeah, me and Shirl. Got married round the corner, Holy Trinity. Whiskey?' Michael asked.

'Fine,' said Vinny.

'She looks pretty, your wife.'

'She was. Not with us anymore. Cancer got her over fifteen years now, a young woman really, too young for that.'

'I'm sorry,' Anne said.

'Yeah,' Vinny agreed.

Michael put the photo down and closed the cupboard.

'I might get myself a glass of water if it's ok?' Anne asked.

'Of course, love. You'll find a glass next to the sink. Can you bring in the jug too?'

'Sure.' Anne left for the kitchen.

She ran the tap to rinse a glass and filled the jug next to the sink. She started towards the living room but stopped when she heard Michael.

'Do you trust this woman, son?'

Anne was surprised Michael was asking the question. She felt weird waiting for the answer, but when it came, she let out her breath.

'Yeah, yeah, I do,' she heard Vinny answer.

'Are you together?'

There was a moment's silence, then Vinny answered, 'Yeah, we are.'

She felt the warmth in Vinny's voice.

'Because some of this stuff is a bit dodgy, with your da an all. She is still a reporter.'

'Yeah, but I trust her.'

Anne returned with her glass and the jug of water.

'Okay,' Michael said as he poured the drinks.

Anne put the jug and glass on the table and said. 'You were saying you saw Paddy at the funeral?'

'Yeah, like I said.' Michael poured a splash of water into both whiskeys.

'That was the last time you saw him?' Anne asked.

'Yeah, we hadn't been so friendly in the few years before that, but we went back, knew each other.' He passed a drink to Vinny.

'How was he?'

'Not right, if you ask me.'

'How do you mean?' Vinny asked, before taking a sip of his drink.

'Your da was a nice fella. He could be hard and didn't take no shit, but he was always smiling. You know: a happy guy, liked life, loved the women, liked a drink. Your da was one of those who would be dancing, flirting, singing. He could be tough, but he wasn't a bully.'

'And at the funeral?'

'It wasn't the funeral. It was the pub after, and it was nice of him to show. But he wasn't right, I could see that. He was different.'

'How?' Vinny asked.

'Okay, well, let's just say, he seemed more upset than anyone there.'

'What do you mean? It was a funeral. Wasn't everyone upset?' asked Vinny.

'He cried when we met. I mean *tears*. This wasn't your da, whatever, or whoever he was crying for, it wasn't Paul. He hardly knew him. Something was going on with your dad that day.'

'Do you know what it was?' Vinny appeared to have taken over the questioning.

'No, I didn't then, and don't now.'

'Were the Powers there?'

'Yeah, he was with them, but to be honest, he didn't seem happy about it.' Michael took a drink, and the pause allowed Anne to resume.

'So, just humour me here.' She looked across to Vinny. 'If Paddy had a falling out with the Powers, why couldn't it be Paddy that was killed?'

'Okay, if you're asking me, I don't know.' Michael raised his hand. 'But it wouldn't fit, if you want my guess. Paddy, yeah, fell out with them, and skipped back to Ireland. We have the docks down the road. If he wanted to get away, he could.'

'Did you kill people?' Vinny asked.

'What? Where did that come from?' Michael looked shocked.

'I just want to cut through the shit. It's not enough to say, we did some "dodgy stuff." What does that mean?'

Michael drained his glass and refilled his and Vinny's. 'I wouldn't take that from anyone else, but this is your da we're talking about. So, I guess I owe you something. Did I kill anyone?' He answered his own question. 'No. Were people beaten, broken, tortured? Yes. I'm not justifying it. I got out of that shit. What your dad did after I left, I don't know. That's the truth - ' Vinny interrupted him. 'This is bollocks.' He stood. 'Come on, let's go. We're not going to get the truth here.'

'Wait,' Anne said.

Vinny glared at her but sat back down.

'Do you know who the body is?' Anne asked.

'God's truth? No, I don't,' Michael replied.

'Did you know an Inspector Barlow?' Vinny asked.

'Sergeant Barlow, you mean? He was on the docks when I first arrived.'

Anne looked directly at Vinny to indicate she understood the significance of this.

'When was that?' Vinny's eyes widened.

'That would be '55. First job I did for Jack Power. Later, I would see him around Garston. He never really bothered us, though. What's he got to do with this?'

'Are you sure?' Anne asked.

'Yeah, he was in Jack Power's pocket. Jack paid him off.'

'How do you know that?' Vinny asked.

'He told me if I had any trouble with coppers at the docks to ask for Sergeant Barlow.'

'What were you taking through the docks?' Vinny asked.

'To be honest, I never opened a parcel and saw,' Michael said.

'But you have your guesses?' asked Anne.

'You're not printing any of this, are you?' Michael asked Anne.

'No, you have my word. My editor wouldn't touch it with a barge pole.'

'It was mainly knock-off gear. Jack had people in Wicklow who would pay a good price: booze, ciggies, radios, stuff like that.'

'Anything else?'

'I can't prove this, and I will deny it if anyone asks. But one time at least, rifles, guns.'

'Okay, one last question,' said Anne. 'There were rumours that bodies were sent out to sea.'

'I think once, that I know of.'

'That's pretty heavy.' Vinny shook his head.

Anne and Michael both stood.

'I'm sorry, lad. Your da was like all of us, some bad, some good. For what's worth, I always liked him.'

Anne offered her hand to Michael. 'Thanks for seeing us.'

'No problem.'

Vinny had opened the front door and was stepping out through it without acknowledging Michael.

Anne looked at Michael. He shrugged. 'Don't worry, love. He's a good lad.'

She followed Vinny out, closing the door behind her.

Anne got in the car. Vinny did too. As she turned the ignition, he reached over and turned the radio on.

'Have you had enough?' she asked.

'A bit, yeah, you?'

'The idea was to go and see your mum now. You still want to do that?'

'I think we have to,' Vinny said.

'So, Barlow, Inspector, Sergeant, whatever, was working for Jack Power,' Anne said.

'I wouldn't bet on it,' said Vinny.

'But you heard Michael.'

'Think about where the power ended up, however it started out. It's much more likely that by the end, Jack Power was working for Barlow.'

'Shit. I knew there was a reason I liked you,' Anne said.

'Okay, let's go do it,' Vinny said firmly.

Michael heard the car start, the engine engage, and the low

rumble as it moved off, the sound disappearing to leave silence. He crossed the room to the cupboard, took his wedding photo out, placed it on the table, and poured himself another drink.

Whiskey, photographs, and silence.

Chapter Thirty-Two

Anne

Vinny rapped the gleaming brass knocker on the varnished door. Anne was feeling nervous.

'Don't you have a key?' She asked.

'Why would I? I don't live here,' Vinny said.

'I've got a key to my mum's.'

'Well, maybe she trusts you.'

Anne heard the locks being turned then the door opened slightly.

'It's me, Mam,' Vinny half-shouted.

The security chain was released, and the door opened fully. 'Come in, lad. What are you doing here?'

Vinny led the way in. Anne followed behind. They walked through a carpeted hallway, where a cushioned seat and a phone table with a mirror above it were the only furniture. The stairs immediately to the right of the front door ran up to the bedrooms. They walked along the hallway toward the kitchen.

Entering the kitchen, Anne saw Mrs Connolly for the first time. She was neat and trim. A beige jumper topped a navy skirt, and she had navy slippers on her feet. A thin gold chain with a simple cross was visible around her neck.

'Mam, this is Anne, a friend of mine.'

'Nice to meet you,' Anne said.

'Hello. How is Helen and that little boy?'

'Not now, mum.' Vinny said.

She turned to Anne. 'You do know he has a son?'

'Yeah, I do,' Anne replied uncomfortably.

'You'd think a grandmother could see her only grandson.'

'I'll speak to Helen, mum. I promise,' Vinny said.

'I haven't seen him for weeks. How long is it since you've been here?'

'A couple of weeks,' Vinny defended himself.

'Months, more like.' The severe face, sharp features, and deep lines opened in warmth when she smiled. 'But you're here now, that's what matters.'

The room smelled of lemon cleaning fluid. The surfaces were spotless, and the chrome kettle shone.

'It's a nice place,' Anne offered.

'Oh, it's nothing, but at least we've got a decent kitchen. Do you remember the one in Linner Road? Couldn't turn round in that thing,' Mrs Connolly said.

'Yeah, I do,' Vinny answered. Vinny looked slightly on edge, not sure where to sit or stand.

'Well, come on in, sit down, and I'll put the kettle on.'

Anne moved toward the pine table with a bench on either side of it.

'No, not here, love. We'll go in the living room, a bit more comfortable.'

'Vinny, you show Anne the way, and I'll get the tea on. Milk and sugar?' Mrs Connolly busied herself with the tea things.

'Just milk for me,' said Anne.

'Still two for you, is it? He always had a sweet tooth, you know.'

'Yeah, fine. Come on.' Vinny moved back along the hallway.

A door on the right led into the living room. A grey leather sofa and armchair dominated the space, with a polished glass coffee table in front of them. There was no fireplace. A radiator ran the length of the wall opposite the doorway. Above the radiator, a net curtained window looked out into the back garden. The sofa and armchair faced a flat-screen TV mounted on the wall.

Vinny and Anne sat side by side on the sofa. She reached for his hand and gave it a squeeze. He smiled weakly.

The only picture on the wall was a smiling boy in school uniform. Anne stood and moved in front of it. 'Is that you?'

'Yeah, Holy Communion.'

'How old were you?'

'I don't know, maybe seven or eight.'

'You look so cute with your hands joined like that ready for prayer, and your short trousers.'

'Doesn't he just.' Mrs Connolly appeared carrying a tray.

Anne turned sharply. 'Please, let me get that.'

'Thank you, love. He was clever, you know, although what good it does, I'll never know. Are you working?' she asked Anne.

'Mam,' Vinny objected.

'No, it's fine.' Anne smiled. 'Yeah, I'm on *The Chronicle.*'

'Oh really? Now that's what I mean. I don't mind people studying if means getting a job. But Vincent here, he's got certificates coming out of everywhere, and no job to show for it. You can't call working a shoe shop a job. That would be girls' work in my day.'

Mrs Connolly sat back in her armchair. 'So, you have your name in the paper, do you?'

'I've not been there long, but yeah, sometimes.'

'Your mum must be proud of you.' As she said this, Mrs Connolly was looking straight at Vinny.

'She is.'

'Come on, then, love, sit yourself down.'

Anne joined Vinny on the sofa.

Mrs Connolly poured and offered the tea. 'Now what's all this about?' she asked as she poured the last cup. 'Are you engaged? You're not having a little one, are you?'

'No,' Vinny objected. 'Mum, please.'

'Oh, don't get embarrassed, we're all adults now. And where's your family from, then?'

'We were brought up in Toxteth,' Anne replied.

'A bit rough, so I've heard.'

'They say the same about Speke,' Vinny said.

'And they wouldn't be wrong. Go back a few years it was a different story. We never had a chance here. As soon as the jobs went, that was it. Saw grown men lose heart. Now, kids driving motorbikes on that backfield, blowing up cars, you wouldn't believe it. The police are not interested. Not that I'd call them, mind you, but even so.'

'Mum, look, that's partly why I'm here.'

'Oh, Jesus.' Mrs Connolly crossed herself. 'What have you done now?'

'Nothing. Nothing like that.'

'Shall I explain?' Anne offered.

'Yeah, go on, she might listen to you,' Vinny said.

'Who's she?' Vinny's mum snapped at him. 'The cat's mother?'

Vinny pulled a face to Anne. 'Okay, sorry. Yes, can you please explain to my mother.'

Anne said, 'I was reporting on the discovery of human remains in Garston. There was a construction site that uncovered a skeleton.'

'You know, I think I heard about that.'

'Well, as it turns out, it looks like the body was from around the mid-seventies, and as far as the police can tell, it was not death by natural causes, meaning they are viewing it as suspicious. They are trying to identify the victim but are having trouble putting a name to the remains.'

'Well, it wouldn't be the first,' Vinny's mum said.

'What do you mean?' Vinny asked.

'People disappeared. Lots of men came through. Some stayed, some didn't, some went to London or Birmingham. You met someone one day, then never saw them again. How many times we had someone stay on the sofa? Off the boat one day, and then moving on the next.'

Vinny sat forward. 'Okay, well, listen, Mum…I went to the police station do a DNA test.'

'Jesus. What the hell did you do that for?'

'To rule out my dad.'

'What do you mean, rule him out?'

'To find out if it was him. He went missing in the seventies. It could be anyone. How do we know if we don't check?'

'You could've asked me.' Mrs Connolly put her cup back on the tray.

'You're having a laugh, aren't you?' Vinny protested.

Anne reached out for him. He sounded sharp.

'What do you mean?' his mum asked.

Vinny stood. 'I asked you as a kid. Do you remember what you told me?'

'No.' She shifted in her seat. 'It wasn't something you spoke about with children,' Mrs Connolly said.

'Exactly, you didn't tell me anything. Nothing,' Vinny said.

'You were a child. What was I supposed to say?'

'I don't know, the truth, maybe? Did you ever think of that?'

Vinny pushed passed Anne and pointed to the photo. 'See that?'

Anne said softly, 'Sit down, Vinny.'

'Do you see it? Phony, that's what that is. When that photo was taken, every other boy stood with his dad. When it was my turn, there I am, on my own.'

'You weren't the only one. Don't act like it was just you.' There was an edge to his mum's voice, and the hard lines appeared on her face.

'Yeah, but the others knew. Phil Symmond's dad had a heart attack. Matty Caffrey's dad was always away working. What happened to my dad?'

'Well, he didn't end up in that bloody hole, I can tell you that. You should know it does no good stirring up the past.'

Vinny sat back down. 'You know, don't you?'

'Know what?' Mrs Connolly had folded her arms across her chest.

'You know what happened to him. To my dad.' Vinny's accusation was in his tone.

'Of course I know, and so do you.'

'What do you mean, I know?' Vinny looked confused.

'You were there, the night your dad told me.'

1975

Chapter Thirty-Three

Michael

'Ready, love?' Michael asked.

Shirley was fixing her hair in the hallway mirror. 'Yeah, here, let me give you a brush.'

She swept the brush over his suit jacket in strong, confident strokes. 'Got to look right.'

'Come on, no one's interested in that,' he said.

'We put on a show for the lad. It's the least we can do.'

'Yeah, a right fucking show.'

Shirley gripped his arm. 'This is for Jim and Peggy.'

There was a beep outside the door.

'You're right. Okay, come on, let's go. The taxi's here.'

They stepped into a cool bright morning. The taxi sat with its engine running.

Ten minutes later, they turned into Linner Road, Speke. There were few car owners there, but today there were cars parked on both sides of the street, leaving a narrow path for the taxi to negotiate. Michael paid him and held the door open for Shirley. A short pathway led up to the house. A group of black-suited men stood smoking outside. The curtains in all the windows were drawn closed, and the front door was open.

Michael nodded to the men as they approached. Two men moved aside to allow entry through the front door.

'No, it's okay, we'll go round the back.' Michael led Shirley along the side of the house then turned into the back garden and to the back door.

Stepping through into the small kitchen, Michael moved toward the living room door with Shirley behind him. A dull murmur of voices could be heard coming from the living room.

'Here, Michael.' Someone thrust a glass of whiskey into his hand.

He noticed Shirley decline the one offered to her. He drained his in one gulp, and felt the warm glow spread through his upper body. He grasped the door frame and went through. The room was full of people arranged around the edges in small groups. In the centre, almost as long as the room, was the closed casket, the wood and brass reflecting the electric light of the curtained room.

Peggy sat on the sofa with a sister on either side of her. Shirley moved past Michael, edged round the coffin, and made her way to Peggy. She leaned down to put her head next to Peggy's. Peggy's sobs were suppressed, and the muffled sound was caught by a handkerchief pressed to her face. When Shirley's head came back up, tears were falling over her cheeks.

Michael stroked Shirley's back, nodded to Peggy, and asked in a low voice, 'Where is he?'

Peggy pointed upwards. Michael weaved his way through to the hall door and began to climb the stairs. Grabbing the banister, he took the steps two at a time. Nearing the landing, he saw the bathroom door was closed. As he climbed further, he could hear the flat croaking, crying, a hoarse screeching sound. He knew Jim was fighting to keep the sound inside and failing. Michael opened the door slowly. The sounds were forcing their way out of Jim's crumpled body as he sat slumped on the floor.

'Jesus, Jim, come on.'

Jim struggled to his feet, his chest heaving, jaw clamped tight, sound and spittle both squeezing through his lips in waves.

Michael pulled Jim's head into his chest and closed the door behind him.

As soon as he held Jim, a deep 'aaargh' was released, followed by sobs. Among the tears and spittle, Jim's anguish burst out. 'He might've done it himself.'

Michael kept his hold on Jim, tears streaming down his own face. 'Oh fuck,' was the only reply he could manage.

Jim pulled himself away, straightened, and, leaning over the sink, turned on the tap and swilled his face. He stared into the mirror, before lunging his head forward, smashing it with his forehead.

Michael pulled him back; the shards of mirror clattered into the sink and onto the floor. Pulling him round, Michael could see Jim was unscathed. 'Come on, mate, you've got to get through this.'

Michael opened the door and walked out of the bathroom. Jim followed him. Breathing deeply, he stepped past Michael and entered the bedroom. Michael entered behind him. Jim handed Michael a bottle of whiskey he'd picked up from the bedside table. Michael took a swig and passed it back. Jim closed his mouth over the neck of the bottle.

Michael waited while Jim buttoned his white shirt and threaded his tie through his collar; he took Jim's jacket from a hanger behind the door and held it up for his brother, who slipped his arms into the sleeves. Leaving the bedroom, Michael led the way down the stairs, and they entered the living room.

Jim walked to the centre, lay one hand on the coffin, and addressed the room. 'Thank you for coming, make sure you get yourselves a drink.'

He turned and moved from group to group, accepting handshakes and condolences.

Michael made his way out through the kitchen into the rear garden. He felt a slap on his back and turned sharply to see Jack and Charlie Power with Paddy Connolly.

Jack approached him. 'How's your kid doing?'

'Jim will be fine.'

'Rough time for the family,' Jack said.

'It is.'

'Any news on the matter we discussed?'

'No, nothing.'

'Come on now, Michael.'

Michael stepped back. 'I've told you, Jack. It's nothing to do with me.'

He turned and moved back toward the house. Paddy and Charlie were standing in front of the back door. Paddy was further to the side.

Michael nodded to his old friend. Paddy looked away. Michael stepped forward using his shoulder to edge Charlie out of the way. He heard Jack behind him. 'We will be around all day.'

Michael stopped his forward movement. His hand was on the door handle. Instead of opening it, he turned sharply around. 'Don't fucking push it, Jack, not today.'

Back inside, Michael was surprised to see Jim speaking in low tones to a uniformed army officer. Two soldiers in dress uniforms looked uncomfortable standing behind him. Jim shook their hands and nodded as they moved forward with a folded Union Jack flag. A soldier stood on either side of the casket, and between them, they unfolded the flag to cover the casket.

Peggy stood and moved to pull the flag from the coffin. Jim stepped across the room and held her by the shoulders. Peggy tried to push past him, but he held firm. 'Leave it now, love.'

He nodded to the funeral director.

People were spilling out the front door to make way inside as the funeral director and his colleagues moved to transfer the coffin from the house into the hearse. Neighbours stood in silence at the kerbside along the street. The hearse pulled out and crawled forward, followed by the other cars. They made their way slowly up Linner Road turning into Stapleton Avenue on the way to St Christopher's.

Michael, with the immediate family, was in the funeral car following the hearse and was surprised to see children from All Hallows Secondary school lining either side of the road in uniforms. Teachers watched closely as students stood in silence with all the curiosity of youth. They watched the coffin holding Paul, who just five years before would have been among their ranks, pass slowly by. The silence of the street was not replicated inside the car.

'I didn't want the army. It was them that killed him,' Peggy spat out.

'It was his choice. You know it was what he wanted.' It wasn't an argument from Jim, just a statement of fact.

'He was nineteen. You tell me what the hell he was doing over there.'

'I can't. I told him not go,' Jim said.

'You didn't stop him. You should've stopped him.' The pain was spiced with bitterness.

After the funeral, Michael and Shirley entered The Fox. Michael felt strange. Going into a pub in daylight was a new experience recently. The death of his nephew had not hit him. In some strange way, he was removed, his feelings contained. But then he remembered the words, "He might've have done it himself." He hadn't thought about the act itself. For a soldier, no doubt, the opportunities were plentiful. It was the crisis, the pain he must have been feeling, the sense of being trapped, nowhere to go, but out. This pain he understood, and this pain he felt. It wasn't death but the anguish of a life that hurt.

Michael had known and loved his nephew in the way that people love familiar things. He was able to recognise the smile and good looks, share a joke. Watching him grow into a fit young man, he knew Paul could look after himself. He had that swagger and confidence of young men in their prime. He played football, was a mad Everton fan, and he loved being in the army. *What the fuck happened?*

'I'm going to sit with Peggy. Are you okay?' Shirley asked, holding his arm.

'Yeah, I'm fine. You go.'

He had to stop thinking. As each hour passed, the darkness within him was growing. He knew and could feel it. Charlie and Jack were sat in a corner of the bar. Paddy was at the bar on his own, a pint and a short in front of him. He turned and saw Michael approaching.

'Hey.' Michael held his hand out.

Paddy ignored it and reached forward, pulling him into a bear hug. Paddy's hand rested affectionately on the back of his neck. This unexpected human contact, the warmth of the hug, unleashed tears, silent and fast-flowing. He pulled away, wiping his face, recovering his composure.

'Fuck, get me a drink, will ye.' Michael could see Paddy had tears of his own.

'Two Jamesons, and a pint for your man, here.' Paddy coughed and cleared his throat. 'Sad day,' he said to Michael.

'It is.'

'He was a good lad. Makes me think of my own.' Paddy finished off his whiskey as he was handed the two Jamesons.

'Are you okay?' Michael asked.

'Sure, I'm fine. It should be me asking you,' Paddy answered.

'Well, looks like you have made a good start here.' Michael nodded toward the empty glass.

'What can you do, a day like this. How are things besides this mess - you being an honest worker and all that?' Paddy asked.

'What can I say. It drives me nuts. Permanent nights I'm on, did you know that?'

'Yeah, I heard from your Jim. I see him pretty regular. He still comes into the Dealers. Unlike yourself.'

'Yeah, don't get out too much these days, between work and the missus. Jesus, I do sound like an old man, don't I,' Michael said.

'Same for all of us, mate,' Paddy said.

'How's your boy doing? Vincent, isn't it?'

'Oh, he's fine. Grand little fella. Runs rings round me, has me wrapped around his little finger, but what can you do?'

'Nothing, they take over.'

'They do indeed.' Paddy drained his whiskey. 'Another?'

'Are you okay? You're knocking them back.'

'I'm fine. I'm fine.'

'Let me get this.' Michael waved to the barman.

'No. You put your money away, slaving away in that godforsaken place. I'm not letting you spend that hard-earned cash on me.' Paddy paid the barman.

'So, what about you, then? Still working with Jack?'

'For my sins, I am. You know, you did the right thing,' said Paddy.

'Yeah, right, ten hours a night.'

'No, all kidding aside now, you did the right thing. You're a smarter man than me. Always have been.'

'Don't put yourself down,' Michael replied.

'No, I'm not, it's the truth. I shoulda done what you did. Earned some honest money. But never mind that, it's too late for me now.'

'It's never too late. I can ask at work if there are any openings. They're always taking people on.'

'No, it's good of you, Michael. You always were a good man, not made for this shit, the shit we do.' Paddy finished the Jamesons.

'Maybe you should slow down a bit, Paddy.'

'No, I've really gone and fucked it this time. But never mind that now, come on, let's have another,' Paddy said.

'No, I'm fine, Paddy. I've got to be here for our Jim,' Michael said.

'Ok, I'll drink on my own.'

'What's up, mate?'

Before Paddy could answer, they were interrupted.

'Did I hear you trying to poach my best man here?' Jack Power slapped Paddy on the back.

'Just having a laugh,' Paddy replied.

'Didn't seem like a funny conversation to me, but hey, where are my manners?' He held out his hand to Michael. 'Condolences on your nephew. I've passed on my regards to Jim and Peggy.'

Michael shook his hand.

'So, what's Paddy here filling your head with?'

Michael looked at Paddy. Paddy was looking down at the bar.

'Why don't you go and join the guys, let me and Michael here have a conversation.'

Paddy nodded to Michael, picked up his drinks, and moved to the table Jack had left. Michael looked at Jack. 'I think I'm just going to check on Shirley.'

Jack reached out and grabbed Michael's arm. 'We don't want a scene here, Michael. I just want a few words.'

Michael shrugged his arm off and turned back to face him.

'Here, let me get you a drink,' Jack said.

'I'm fine.'

'Barman, two Bushmills. Do you like Bushmills? Always preferred it myself. We need to have a chat.'

'I've told you, there's nothing I can do.'

'Look, I have never bothered you. Left you alone, and the things you know, things you've seen, but I let you go your own way. No skin off my nose. We know a lot about each other is what I'm saying. Do you understand?' Jack asked.

'Yeah, I do,' Michael said.

'So, I have never asked you for anything, despite me putting plenty of money in your pocket over the years. Isn't that true?' Jack asked.

'Yeah, it is,' said Michael.

'Well, now I am asking for something. If you don't want to do it for me, do it for that old mate of yours.'

'You mean Paddy?'

'I need something moving, to get it through the docks. You know what it's like these days - can't do anything without union men. We just need it loading. Once it's on board, we'll handle it. You speak to your mate Tommy, that's all I'm asking.'

Michael didn't answer. He walked across the bar and sat beside Shirley. 'How is she doing?' Michael asked.

'Not great. And your Jim?'

'You know, on the surface he's okay, but I think he's gutted.'

'It's no surprise. Have you heard what people are saying? Shameless, isn't it.'

'No, I think it's true, love. Jim himself said something before we left the house.'

'Oh my god, how awful. Now I know why she's so angry. Those bastards.' Shirley put her hand to her face.

Michael reached out and stroked her arm. 'We don't know what went on, or who knows what happened.'

'Peggy and Jim are saying it was an accident,' Shirley half-whispered.

'Dear God, what are they supposed to say?' asked Michael.

'I don't know how I could live with that kind of pain. God forgive me.' Shirley crossed herself.

'Shhh, love, don't think about it.'

Shirley nodded towards the doorway. 'Here's Jim. You go and see he's okay.'

Jim entered the pub. Alongside him was a uniformed officer, the two soldiers from earlier following them. In their dress uniforms and peaked caps, they couldn't have looked more out of place. Michael walked across to meet them.

Jim introduced them. 'This is my brother Michael, Paul's uncle.'

'Captain Hargreaves, Kings Royal Infantry.'

Michael nodded and shook his hand.

Jim continued. 'These Kingsmen, Ken and John, were Paul's mates.'

'Nice to meet you, lads. I'm sure you could all use a drink. Captain?'

'I will stay for a short one, but with apologies, I really have to get back. I'm sure the lads would appreciate a pint, though,' he replied.

'Of course, we understand.' Michael led them towards the bar. 'A whiskey and two pints?'

Jim nodded to Ken. 'Ken here was telling me about Paul's boxing.'

'Is that right?' Michael asked.

Ken replied in a thick Mancunian accent, 'Yeah, he was a cracker. Got up to regimental level, really quick hands.'

'He loved his sports,' Michael added.

'Football too. He was a right toffee. Even when we were in Hong Kong, every week he would be waiting for his parcel.'

Jim smiled. 'He made me send him the football *Echo* every week.'

'He said you took him the match,' John said.

'Yeah, I did when he was little, but by the time he was fourteen or fifteen, he was going on his own. His mum didn't like it. It could get a bit rough up there, but he loved it - "the boys pen" - wouldn't miss a game. He would be scraping and scrounging the money all week to get the bus fare and ticket money. Even if he didn't have the ticket money, he would try and sneak in after the game had started.'

'He was a good mate.' Ken raised his pint. 'To Paul.'

The others raised their drinks. The Captain finished his whiskey in one draught. 'I should go and say my farewells to Mrs Byrne before I leave.'

'No, best not.' Jim held out his hand.

'Right. Okay, well, once again - '

'Yeah, thank you,' Jim said, cutting him short.

'The lads can stay. They know what time they are due back,' Captain Hargreaves said.

'Come on, let's get a table.' Jim led them to an empty table.

Michael, Ken, and John followed. 'It must be hard for you lads, not knowing anyone here.'

Ken answered, 'It is, but not as bad as you think. We've been together nearly three years now since basic training. We get to know each other and even the families, you know what I mean. Mostly we read our letters out unless we get one from a girl.' He smiled. 'But that doesn't happen often, never home long enough.'

'Can you get the lads another pint?' Jim asked.

Michael stood. 'And how about a chaser?'

'Yeah, why not,' Jim answered for them.

'Where are you from?' Jim asked.

John answered first. 'Preston.'

'Manchester,' said Ken.

Michael headed to the bar. He saw Paddy looking worse for wear at the table with Jack and Charlie. When he returned with a tray of drinks, John was speaking. 'Yeah, I was lucky, took Paul to a couple of games.'

'What's this, then?' asked Michael.

'Just saying we went to the football,' said John.

'How about in Ireland? What did you get up to?' Jim asked.

'Yeah, look, I'm sorry, we're not allowed to talk about that.' It was John who replied.

'No, I just mean, in your free time, like. Must be a bit hard.'

'No, he's right, we can't talk about it,' Ken added.

'Not even what you did when off-duty?' asked Michael.

'Nah, we can't. We were told. We were warned,' said John.

'Warned about what?' Jim asked.

'Official secrets. We can't talk about anything to do with

297

Ireland.'

Jim sat back a second. 'Sure, I understand. Hold on here a minute, lads. I'll introduce you to some of Paul's mates.'

Jim stood and walked to a group of young men on another table. He brought them over and introduced them. But before leaving the table, he said to John, 'Warning. Don't talk about Man United, or these guys will eat you alive.'

Jim nodded to Michael, and they left the table.

'Get a couple of drinks down them,' Jim said to Michael as he led him to the bar. 'We'll have another go later.'

'Are you sure you want to, Jim? You heard what they said,' Michael said.

'I don't care about official secrets. They know something.'

Paddy joined them at the bar. 'Jim, what can I say, mate. Terrible, terrible thing.' Jim nodded. 'If there's anything I can do. I mean anything.'

'Okay, Paddy,' Michael said.

'Anything,' He pulled a wad of notes from his pocket. 'If you need money. Here, here.' He was pressing money in Jim's hand.

Jim slapped his hand away and the notes went flying in the air.

'What the fuck are you doing? He doesn't want your money.'

'I'm sorry, Jim.' He looked at Michael. 'Michael, I'm sorry mate, I didn't mean anything.'

'Go and sit down, will you.' Michael pointed to the table Paddy had left.

Paddy staggered off. Michael watched him flop back into his seat.

'What the hell is wrong with him?' Jim asked.

'I don't know, but something is.'

'You know what, let's get these army lads out of here.'

'What for?' Michael asked.

'They're not going to say anything here, are they? We'll get them back to the house,' Jim said.

'I'm not sure about this,' Michael said.

'I am. Are you going to help me or not?'

The pub door opened, and Tommy walked in, followed by the priest who'd conducted the service.

'Shit, hold on. I'll have to sort out Father Cunningham,' Jim said.

Tommy and the priest walked over, and Jim introduced Michael to the priest. 'I knew James here had a brother, but I don't think I've had the pleasure. What parish are you?'

'Holy Trinity, Father.'

'Oh right, well, you've a good priest there in Father McNamara.'

'That we have,' Michael lied, not liking the priest mentioned.

'Tommy, I need a word. If you'll excuse me, Father.'

Michael led Tommy to the bar, conscious of Jack Power's eyes following him. Jim took the priest to the women around Peggy.

'Thanks for coming,' Michael said.

'No problem. I just wanted to pay my respects,' said Tommy.

Michael ordered himself and Tommy a drink. 'We might have a bit of a situation.'

'What's that?' Tommy asked.

'Jack wants to get something through the docks.'

'What's that got to do with me?'

'Well, he thinks the unions control the dock, and you're a union man, so...'

'Jesus, not exactly the sharpest tool in the box, is he? It might be the same union, but it's a completely different section.'

'I know, I know, and I'm not asking you to do it. I'm just warning you that he sounds pretty desperate.'

'Is that why he was at your house? I met him on the way out.'

'Yeah, he wanted me to try and sort things out for him,' Michael said.

Tommy let the silence hang for a moment then asked, 'Have

you heard the rumour?'

'What about?'

'Well, it's going round that Paul committed suicide. I just thought you should know.'

'Thanks, and it's not just a rumour. It'll get out soon enough anyway.'

'For fuck's sake.' Tommy was visibly affected.

'Are you okay?' Michael asked.

'Yeah, sure. Just angry. Our lives are literally worth nothing. A young man destroyed.'

Michael pushed Tommy's drink toward him. 'Come on, get it down you.'

'Yeah, sorry. I didn't even know Paul.'

'That makes it all the more important you are here.'

'What shall I do about Power?' Tommy asked.

'Nothing. Leave it to me.'

Michael watched as Jim approached the soldiers. He was surprised to see them stand and follow Jim toward the door. Jim nodded to Michael.

'Okay, thanks for coming, mate, but I have to go,' Michael said to Tommy.

'No problem,' Tommy replied.

★★★

'Have a seat, lads.' Jim led them inside.

John and Ken sat on the sofa.

'We really have to be going soon, Mr Byrne,' John apologised.

'No problem, son, like I said. I just want to show you a few of Paul's things. Michael, get the lads a drink.'

Michael went into the kitchen and poured whiskeys. When he returned, Jim had a suitcase open.

'He saved these. There's another stack of them upstairs.' Jim was opening old football papers and placing them on the table.

'Look, football programmes.'

Michael placed two drinks on the table.

'Must be years' worth here. Every match he ever went to, he marked the score on them. Everton v Ipswich 1-nil to Ipswich, that was last year. Here, 1973 Oct 7th Coventry City, 2-1 to Everton. Here, he wrote, "we won!" What else have we got here? Some photos. Look, here's his passing out parade. Here, is that you, Ken? Where was this?' Jim kept flipping through the contents.

'It's okay, Jim, the lads get the picture,' Michael said.

'Do they, though? Do you?' He threw the programmes and photographs down.

John reached out for his drink. Ken stood. 'Look, I'm sorry. This was a bad idea. I think we should go.'

'Go. Go where?' Jim stood in front of Ken.

Michael moved between them and shoved Jim back.

'Don't push it. It's not our fucking fault,' Ken said.

'Let's calm down, can we,' said Michael.

'We couldn't do anything,' John said. Tears were streaming down his face. 'I was there. I saw it.'

Ken sat back down. 'Fuck, John, you don't have to.'

'I know, I know, but I need to,' John said.

Michael stood by the fireplace. Jim pulled a chair over and sat opposite John.

'I was on my bed in the barracks, reading. There are eighteen of us, beds either side of the room. Paul's is almost opposite mine. His is the last bed in the row on that side.' John choked back his tears and wiped his face.

'Have a drink, lad.' Jim handed him his glass.

John took a gulp.

'He'd been in the NAAFI and had had a few pints, but he seemed fine. It was about half eleven. A few guys were in bed, and it was very quiet. The light was on. He came in and walked to his bed; as he passed, I said, "All right, Paul." He just nodded.

He went to his bed and opened his locker, so I couldn't see him anymore. The locker door was blocking the view. Except his feet, I could see his boots.' John went quiet.

Jim encouraged him. 'Come on, finish it.'

'I heard a bang. I jumped out of my skin. I knew it was a gunshot, then I saw Paul's legs, his boots sliding down. They kind of slipped all the way down. I shouted for someone to get the MO. I went over and saw him.' John sobbed. 'I couldn't do anything.'

Ken reached over and grabbed his arm. 'It's okay, mate, we know.'

Jim sat back in his chair, his hands on his head.

'His SLR was next to him, the place stank of gunpowder. There was no magazine in his rifle. He was lying with his head toward the wall, one hand across his chest. His mouth looked cut, and there were black marks on his face, blast marks. He had put the rifle in his mouth. I didn't see the blood at first, there was a hole in the ceiling where the bullet came out. I didn't want to look anymore. I left him to find the CO. He was my mate, my fucking mate.' John's tears came steadily, and the sobs were deep.

Jim stood and left the room. The silence was broken by a huge crash. Everyone jumped. Michael could see genuine fear in the soldiers' eyes.

'Stay here,' Michael commanded.

He rushed into the kitchen. The floor was covered in glass, and Jim was pouring himself another drink.

'I'm okay, I'm okay.'

'You knew?' Michael asked.

'Yeah, but I wanted to hear it from someone who was there. I don't trust those bastard officers.' Jim finished his drink and went back into the living room.

Ken had his arm around John. John's head was in his hands.

Jim asked, 'Why?'

Michael was the first to respond. 'That's not fair. How can you expect these guys to know?'

Jim wasn't ready to give up. His voice carried an appeal. 'You knew we were Irish and Catholic. You must've known?'

'Of course we knew.' It was Ken who replied. 'He got some shit for it at first, but John's right. We were mates. We had each other's back.'

'They know all right,' Jim said to Michael, the desperation beginning to turn to anger. 'They know what they were doing over there, that caused my son to kill himself.'

He wasn't Irish, though... or English, or Scouse. He wasn't enough of anything. He was none of those things, Michael thought, but didn't say. Maybe in being nothing, he was the future.

The soldiers stood. Michael moved across and held Jim by the shoulders. 'Enough. Okay, enough!'

Jim collected himself. 'Yeah, you're right... I'm sorry, lads. No one will hear what you told me tonight.'

He moved forward and offered his hand to Ken. Then he embraced John. John's head rested on his shoulder, and Jim stroked his hair. Michael and Ken looked on, neither Jim nor John moved.

If you are sent to kill people like yourself, why not take the short cut? Michael thought.

Chapter Thirty-Four

Paddy

The call came around six. Paddy was at home, as usual. The settled life wasn't working out too badly for him. The little man had just finished his tea. It was Charlie on the phone, and Paddy had to go and help him with something. Paddy knew that whatever it was, it had to be kept quiet. Charlie normally ran his own side of things and didn't need any help. They would sometimes meet up for a couple of pints and have a chat unless something a bit out of the ordinary came up. Then they would go double-handed when required.

He dressed, ready for most things, in trousers, suit jacket, and shoes. He liked his shoes polished, and the little man had taken to helping him. Carol wasn't so happy as the polish could end up anywhere. But Vinny loved trying to buff the shoes up, get a good shine. His brushing was a bit wobbly, but it was with lots of effort.

Paddy met Charlie at the Kings Arms in King Street. Charlie had drunk a couple by the time Paddy arrived but was still sound.

'What's up, then?' Paddy asked.

'There's someone in the Blue Union Club we need to have a word with,' Charlie said.

'What kind of word?'

'A serious word.'

Paddy knew what that meant. Someone was going to get a few slaps. They couldn't go in the bar before sorting someone out. It was just too public. Not clever. So, "slowly, slowly, catchee monkey," as the saying goes. They waited outside.

They sat in the Cortina, smoking and having a natter. He was curious. It was only natural, but they had a system these days. It came down from Jack. You know what you need to know and don't ask questions. Paddy figured Charlie would tell him if it was important, but it didn't matter - Paddy had his own source of info these days.

A bit later, a man came out. He'd had a few, but he wasn't pissed. He was a fair size, but a young fella, and from the look of him, he was a regular guy - brown cotton jacket, flared trousers, thick black hair. He looked the part of country boy, wandered into town.

'We're on,' Charlie said. 'We'll get him to the yard.'

Luckily, he was walking in the direction of the Cortina and would pass the car. Charlie jumped out and stood by the boot. The man reached the car, and as soon as he passed Charlie, Charlie stepped up behind him and clocked him one to the side of the head. The fella didn't know what had hit him and dropped like a sack of spuds. Charlie opened the door, bent down, and tried to lift him into the car.

The guy kicked and held onto the car door. Paddy had to rush out, go back there, and help out. A few digs later, they got him in, and Charlie jumped in the back almost on top of the guy, holding him down. He was moaning all the while, and Charlie was struggling to hold him. Paddy drove, and they were at the yard a minute later.

Paddy still had no idea what this was about. Charlie threw him the key, and he opened the yard. They dragged the guy into one of the sheds. It was full of building stuff, but he wasn't quiet, so it was either that or risk disturbing the neighbours. They didn't turn the light on, so it was pretty dark, just about light enough for what they needed. He slumped against the back wall of the shed. Charlie landed a few on him.

'You're gonna learn to keep your mouth shut. D'ya hear me?' Charlie emphasized each word with a punch.

'Yeah,' the guy said. His mouth was bloody, and it looked like he'd had enough.

Charlie whacked him again. 'No more lying about Jack.'

Then, out of nowhere, Charlie was falling back and the guy was getting up.

'Give that to your snitch fucking brother,' he said.

He hit Charlie with something, and he shoved Charlie out the way and flew towards Paddy. Whatever he'd hit Charlie with was in his raised hand.

Paddy's hand went to the workbench next to him and picked up the first thing he could find. Charlie was splayed out now, and the guy was swinging round at Paddy. Paddy hit him plumb on the nut with the ball-peen hammer, and the hammer went straight through his skull. Paddy could feel the ball head sinking in, getting stuck. As the guy fell forwards, Paddy let go of the hammer.

It only took a second. He was out, face down on the shed floor.

Charlie picked himself up and came over. Paddy stood there, stunned. This wasn't even his job. Nothing to do with him.

'Turn him over,' Charlie ordered.

'I'm not touching him,' Paddy said.

'You just put a fucking hammer through his head. What do you mean you're not touching him? Get out the way, then.' Charlie turned him over. 'He's dead. Jesus Christ, why did you do that?'

'Because you let the fucker get up. You were on your arse, and he was coming at me. What was I supposed to do?'

'For fuck's sake. We're gonna have to clean this up.'

'You can clean it up. I'm done here.' Paddy wanted to get out.

'You can't go anywhere, you dick, you're covered in his fucking blood.'

Paddy put his hand up to his shirt, which was warm and sticky.

'You're gonna have to stay here. I'm gonna go an' get you some clothes, and I have to tell Jack. Fuck knows what we do with this.'

Paddy threw the car keys to Charlie, and he was off and away. Meanwhile, he was stuck here with God knows who. He sat to wait it out.

Paddy's mind wandered to home. Vinny would probably be going down for the night, laid out in his bed. He knew being a dad was a big thing. For him, anyway. Some fellas, you wouldn't know if they had a gang of kids at home - any chance they got, they were out on the ale. Maybe that was the thing: if you had a gang, each one merged with the others. He didn't know, but having just the one - he knew Vinny was special. He did things with Vinny his dad never did - playing with him, talking to him, simple things.

Simple things that this fucker could ruin. Shit, if this got out, if he got collared for this… But Mr Barlow would help, he was sure of that. Otherwise, fifteen, twenty years? Self defence though, *he was coming at me*. But he couldn't see that working. *We did drag him here. Thank fuck they've stopped hanging, or my neck could definitely be stretched.*

The body was laid out on his back, staring up. The hammer had come out when Charlie turned him over.

Paddy hoped this guy would go upstairs, so he could see his folks if they were already there. If there was a Heaven up there. *You could do me a favour*, Paddy thought, *and let me know.*

Probably too late for him anyway, he thought. He shouldn't have come at him like that. What was he supposed to do? The guy's eyes were open. He didn't look angry or in pain. He looked kind of bored. He had a good thick head of black hair, a bit matted and sticky now. He was a young'un. The more Paddy thought, the more he could see that it was a good thing. It meant he probably didn't have kids. Paddy did what he had to do. But he wouldn't like to think of a little one going without his dad. But then, everyone is someone's kid. Young enough so his folks would still be alive. *Guess we couldn't send you back to them.*

Paddy was getting angry. *Fucker, why had he done that? He could've taken a few more hits, that would have been it. Just promised Charlie what he wanted, then he could have walked out of here. Was it worth dying for? Calling Jack a snitch? You can't go round saying things like that. It could ruin his reputation.* Was Jack talking to Mr Barlow as well? *That didn't make sense.*

Where the fuck was Charlie? Paddy stood and began to undress. He took off his jacket and shirt. He felt his trousers. They were sticky too. He took them off. He sat back down next to the body.

If Jack was a snitch, what if he gave Paddy up for this? What if he was doing it right now? Jesus, all this when he could have been at home watching the telly, the little man in bed. All because Charlie couldn't deliver a slap on his own.

Who were you? Did you have brothers, sisters? What's your name, eh, young'un?

There was just enough light to find the guy's pockets. Paddy found a card, a union card. Name *Mark Riley*, with an address in Preston.

'Well, Mark, this isn't how I wanted my day to end either,' he said to the corpse.

Charlie was back. 'What are you doing?'

'Just saying hello to our friend here.' Paddy caught the clothes Charlie threw at him.

'We've got to wrap him up in a tarp. Jack's gonna try and get him out,' Charlie said.

'Get him out where?' asked Vinny.

'Through the docks,' Charlie said.

'Why did Mark call Jack a snitch?'

'What the fuck are you on about? Mark?' Charlie wasn't looking happy.

'That was his name.'

'Get dressed. I'm taking you home, then we're gonna sort this shit out.'

They wrapped the body up and moved it to the second shed. They put it right at the back, surrounded him with wood and boxes, and Charlie locked the shed.

When Paddy got home, Carol and the little man were asleep together. Vincent had climbed into bed with her. Paddy could have squeezed in too, but didn't want to pass on the connection to Mark. He didn't want Mark to be a part of Vinny's life.

★★★

Paddy didn't go to Paul's funeral. He went to the pub after. He didn't want to see the lad put in the ground. He was dead. He knew that. But seeing him go in the ground was different.

Paddy knew what Jim and Peggy were going through losing their son because he knew he was losing his. *Paul, Mark, Vinny, we were losing them all, they were all going from us.*

Carol said she wouldn't go to Ireland, and he knew why. He couldn't be angry now. It wasn't Mark's fault he'd met the wrong people at the wrong time. It wasn't Paul's fault he'd joined the wrong army at the wrong time. It wasn't Vinny's fault - he just had the wrong dad in the wrong time. Paddy knew his boy was smart and would be strong. He was smarter than his dad, stronger than his dad. He couldn't let Vinny know him, like he knew Vinny. He was giving him the best thing he could. He was letting Vinny live without him.

Leaving him would be the best thing he ever could have done.

2004

Chapter Thirty-Five

Vinny

'What do you mean?' Vinny asked.

Anne could feel the rising tension.

'You weren't supposed to be there, but he must have woke you when he came in. You were sat at the top of the stairs listening. I turned around to see your little head poking through the banisters,' Mrs Connolly said.

'I don't remember. So, what happened?' Vinny asked his mum.

Anne watched him edge forward in his seat.

'It was the night of the funeral. Jim Byrne's son was killed in Ireland. Your dad went to the pub with them. He came back. It wasn't so late. He tried to be quiet, but I was a light sleeper. You were in bed, curled up with me. I thought you were asleep and went to the living room.

'He came in a bit worse for wear, more than usual. The strange thing was his shoes and trousers were all covered in mud. It looked like he had been in the grave with that poor lad. I asked him about his clothes, and he started getting mad, angry. I guess the shouting woke you up.'

Anne glanced at Vinny. He was wringing his hands.

'He never hit me. Your dad had a reputation, but he never laid a hand on me. Your dad wasn't nasty, not mean, not to me anyway, nor you. He was so proud of you.'

'Enough, Mum. I don't want to hear all this again.'

'If you're going to talk like that, this conversation is over,' his mother said.

'I'm sorry, but I want to know what happened that night, what he said.'

'He was upset. He was drunk, talking about Paul dying, but I knew there was something else. He said we should go to Ireland. I told him I wasn't going anywhere.'

'Why would he want us to move?' Vinny asked.

'Are you sure you don't remember anything?' his mother asked.

'No, nothing.'

'The next morning, he was up and out early. I never saw him again. I got word a few months later he had died in a motorcycle accident, somewhere in Ireland. I'm not even sure where.'

'But why did he leave?'

'I only know what he told me. I didn't know if it was true or not. He said him and Charlie Power took some fella back to the builder's yard. They were supposed to work him over, give him a beating, but somehow it went wrong, and the guy died.'

'Jesus Christ.' Vinny was shaking his head.

'After he left. I never heard any more of it. I don't know. It just sort of went away.'

'How, how did it go wrong?' Anne asked.

'I'm only going by what your dad said. He said he hit the fella with a hammer,' Mrs Connolly said, still looking at Vinny.

'Bloody hell.' Vinny was up again and pacing about the room.

'So, why all the mud?' he asked.

'They buried him, the night of the funeral. In the builder's yard. He said they tried to get the body out on a ship. That Jack Power had done it before, but there was some problem on the docks. So, they had to bury him. They buried him the night of the funeral.'

Anne and Vinny shared a knowing look.

'So, he just left? Just disappeared?' asked Vinny.

'Yeah, he would have taken us, but I told him I wasn't leaving Garston. Not for God knows where in Ireland.'

Vinny sat down and put his head in his hands. After a short silence, he asked, 'And who was it?'

'I don't know,' his mother said.

'He didn't say?' asked Vinny.

'He said his name was Mark, but he didn't know who he was, and I believed him. Whoever it was, he wasn't local,' replied Mrs Connolly.

'How do you know that?' Anne asked.

'Well, no one went missing, no one disappeared - '

'Except my dad,' Vinny interrupted.

'Yeah, that is true,' his mum said.

'And all this time I was listening?'

'Yeah, your dad was quite upset when he saw you on the stairs.'

Anne's phone buzzed. 'Do you mind?' she asked Vinny's mum.

'No, you go on, love.'

Anne shrugged to apologise to Vinny. He waved it away. She took the call in the hallway, trying to keep her voice down. She was aware of the silence in the living room. The call was from Anthony, her editor.

'Who was it?' Vinny asked as she re-entered the room.

'My editor.'

'What did he want?'

'Michael has been arrested.'

'What?' Vinny's jaw dropped.

'He's being held in Speke. I've got to go. See what I can find out.'

'I'll come with you.'

'You don't have to.'

'I know I don't.'

'Okay, let's go.'

'So, is that it? I don't see you for weeks, you come here stirring up things that should be left alone, then disappear?'

'Like father, like son,' Vinny said.

His mother stood. 'That's not funny.'

'Tell me about it,' Vinny replied.

They said their goodbyes and got in the car.

Anne and Vinny were quiet on the drive to the police station. Anne parked on the opposite side of the street. 'I'm going to call Dave Cooper.'

'Yeah okay. What do we say about all that?' He was pointing over his shoulder to where they had come from.

'I don't know. Nothing? Your dad is dead, though. We know that now,' Anne said.

'Yeah, in a hole in Ireland instead of Garston. Does that make it better?' Vinny said.

'Different, not better, but let's see what I can find out here.' Anne held up her phone.

'Go for it,' said Vinny.

Anne put the phone on speaker, and Dave answered after a couple of rings.

'Hi, Dave, it's Anne.'

'Hello.' He sounded wary.

'I hear you've made an arrest?'

'Oh, I see.'

'I was wondering if I could ask you some questions?'

'You have the number of the press office.'

'Come on, really?' Anne rolled her eyes at Vinny, who mouthed the word 'Arsehole.'

'Yeah, really, what do you expect?'

'I thought we might be at least civil. You've arrested Michael Byrne?'

'Not arrested. Just in for questioning, and I am being civil.'

'Okay, thanks.' She tried to get on his good side. 'Look, I'm sorry if I wasn't very clear,' she paused for a second, 'about us.'

'No problem. I thought you were very clear,' Dave said.

'If you want to get a coffee sometime, that would be cool. In fact, I'm outside now.'

Vinny mouthed, 'What?'

'I know. I saw you and your boyfriend pull up. I think I'll pass.'

'Just questioning, then?' Anne asked.

'For now, yeah. We know he knows something about the remains. I think you know he does as well. You know it can be a crime to obstruct a police investigation?'

'How long will you be holding him?'

'I think I've said enough.'

'Shall I come in?'

'No. What for? Your guy will be out soon anyway.'

'Really, when?'

The line went dead.

'He's such a prick. What do you think, then? Was he taking the piss, saying Michael would be out soon?' asked Vinny.

'I don't know, but he was also talking about obstruction. Is he worried?' Anne asked. 'Worried we will find something before him?' She paused for a second. 'Maybe he is worried about what we might find. Are we getting this thing back to front?'

'How do you mean?'

'Like, you were saying if he isn't helping, what the hell is he doing? Why is a copper trying to get in the way? Does he know something he doesn't want us to know?' Anne checked her watch. 'Anyway, I think I should check in at the office. Do you want to go in? Get me an orange juice, or a coffee if they do it. We might be waiting a while.' She pointed to the Noah's Ark.

Chapter Thirty-Six

Vinny

Vinny got out of the car. He knew the pub but hadn't been in it for years, and even then, just once or twice. He walked towards the bar. He always felt a little self-conscious going into pubs, especially on estates. You had to own it, do it with confidence. *Let people know that you belonged in pubs like this*, he thought. All eyes would be on you, most only momentarily. Others would linger, looking for signs you didn't really belong. He ordered a lager and an orange juice; coffee would be one of those signs.

It was early evening, the point between the end of the afternoon shift and start of the after-work shift, two different groups of drinkers, each normally held to their own times. In city centre pubs, you had passing trade - people who dropped in for a quick drink with lunch or after shopping. Here, everything was routine, no passing trade, and anything outside the routine stood out.

Anne waltzed in, seemingly oblivious to anyone and everyone who watched her entrance. 'I've got to go into the station,' she announced - a little too loudly for Vinny's comfort. 'I called the office. They want me to go in and see if I can get anything more.'

'Sounds useless.'

'Yeah, I agree, but I've got to try. Are you okay to wait here?'

'Yeah, sure.'

'I'm sure they won't give me anything, so I'll see you in a couple of minutes.'

'Yeah, no problem. Good luck.'

Vinny watched Anne leave, both proud and embarrassed that she didn't give a shit where she was. She was who she was. *I am, Elohim.* The words of Professor Sheehan came back to him. The Hebrew word that Jesus called himself, *Elohim.* Yahweh and Allah were different versions of this. *I am...I am English? Irish? Scouse? The son of a murderer.*

He pulled his notebook out of his rucksack and began making notes. His pint was going down slowly. He had lost interest and no longer cared who else was in the pub. This, more than anything, made him look at home.

Chapter Thirty-Seven

Anne

Anne buzzed and entered the police station. The officer at the desk told her to wait. A minute later, Dave opened the door into the now-familiar side room. 'Hello, Ms McCarthy.'

'Hello.' Her answer was hesitant.

'Can you come this way, please?'

'I'm sorry. Why?'

'We would like to ask you some questions about an ongoing inquiry.' Dave's formal register was clearly meant to intimidate Anne.

'What. Really?' Anne said.

'There is nothing to worry about, Ms McCarthy. Now that you're here, we thought we would take the opportunity to ask some simple questions. It should only take a few minutes. This way, please.'

Anne entered the room. Instead of sitting down at the table as she expected, Dave - or DS Cooper, as she now saw him - opened the other door in the room to the interior of the police station. 'Please, follow me.'

She did but felt increasingly uncomfortable. The corridor was standard office beige, with half-glazed wooden doors, through which she could see computer terminals and office layouts. The end of the corridor led to a chest-high counter, behind which a uniformed officer waited.

'Sarge, do we have a free interview room?'

'Yeah, room two is available,' the sergeant replied, looking Anne over.

'Okay, thanks.'

Another corridor turned at right angles from the counter. DS Cooper led the way. After the Sergeant's desk, everything changed. She was now surrounded by battleship grey. Every door was steel. There were no windows. Some of these were cells. Those not occupied were open, revealing a stainless steel toilet and sink combined, and a steel bed that stuck out from a graffiti-covered wall. As she was passing interview room one, her stomach turned over. The door was ajar, and she saw Michael with his head in his hands, leaning over a table.

Anne's composure and confidence were draining fast.

'Here we are.' Dave indicated the open door to interview room two. 'You've met PC Johnstone.'

The woman police officer sat at a blue-topped table. Against the wall was a set of recording equipment. Dave took the chair next to the PC and indicated Anne to sit opposite him.

'Wait,' Anne protested, her fire rising. 'I'm not sure what's going on here.'

'Just a few questions,' said DS Cooper.

'I don't want any questions. I don't have to…I shouldn't be here. I came here to ask questions, not answer them.'

'Can you confirm you came into this station voluntarily, Ms McCarthy?' asked DS Cooper.

'Yes, but not for this,' Anne said.

'Look, it's Anne, isn't it? Believe me, it's in your interest to sit down and answer a few simple questions. Then you can leave,' PC Johnstone said.

Anne glared at DS Cooper. How could she ever have seen anything in him? She sat down, determined to be out of there as soon as she could.

'Shouldn't I have a lawyer?'

'Do you need one?' he asked.

He nodded to the PC, who turned on the recording device. He was pushing through her resistance.

'Detective Sergeant David Cooper and Police Constable Jane Johnstone interviewing Anne McCarthy, 29th July 2005, 18.30 hundred hours. Anne, you don't mind if I call you Anne?' he asked.

She hated her name in his mouth. 'Ms McCarthy.'

'Okay, Ms McCarthy. I, we, believe you have information regarding the death of an as-yet unknown person in Garston, the remains of whom were discovered recently - '

'Wait, wait,' Anne interrupted him. 'If you think I'm talking about this without a lawyer, you're sadly mistaken.'

Anne thought he was trying to find out what she knew. Trying to force her to tell him.

'You can either answer these questions voluntarily, or we can compel you.'

'Are you going to arrest me?' Anne stood. 'I've done nothing wrong. You know what? I'm finished here. I'm leaving. If you want to arrest me, go right ahead.' She threw the words at him in a challenge. 'Maybe you could ask me about the last person to give me an E?'

'Interview terminated at 18.35,' Dave announced. 'Stop the tape!' he demanded as the PC fumbled with the machine. 'No one is arresting you,' he said.

'Good. Then I can leave.' Anne turned and started to walk back through the corridor.

She looked in the room Michael had been in, but it was empty. When she reached the sergeant's desk, Michael was being released. They walked out of the police station together.

'Fancy a drink?' Anne asked.

'Not this time, love. Maybe it's time I gave this old body a bit of rest,' Michael said.

'Can I give you a lift?' Anne said.

'Yeah, that would be great.'

Ten minutes later, Vinny, Michael, and Anne sat in silence as she drove back along the Boulevard to Garston.

Chapter Thirty-Eight

Vinny

Vinny knew Anne was next to him as he was waking. He didn't remember, he knew. Opening his eyes, he met hers. 'Hiya. Have you been watching me sleep?' he asked.

She reached out to stroke his hair. 'I was worried. You hardly said anything last night.'

'Don't be. I'm fine, really.'

'You slept well?'

'Yeah, really well. No dreams, nothing.'

He shifted to a sitting position, and she followed. 'But it's nice to be worried about. You know, something clicked yesterday.'

'How do you mean?' she asked.

'When I was in the pub on my own, waiting for you. It's stupid. Or maybe it isn't, I don't know.'

'Come on then, spit it out.'

'All right, it was something Dr. Sheehan said. "*Elohim.*" It means "*I am.*"'

Anne looked puzzled. 'I am…What?'

'That's just it - nothing. It's the way Jesus described himself. "*I am*" in Hebrew is *Elohim.*'

'You've lost me. Do you want some toast? I'm gonna do some.'

'No, wait. Listen to this.' Vinny leaned over and pulled his notebook out from his bag and flicked through the pages. '"Very truly, I tell you before Abraham was, I am". It's the

Gospel of John. It was Jesus's way of saying, I am God, 'cos I was here before Abraham and will be around forever.'

Anne gave him a strange look. 'And? You're not religious.'

Vinny was smiling. 'I know, and I'm not. In the next line: they threw rocks at Jesus, so he ran away.'

Anne was smiling now. 'Has someone thrown a rock and hit you in the head?'

'No. The thing is, God doesn't have to explain who he is, or what he is, or why. Try it.' Vinny paused. 'I am. Not I am this or that, just I am, with the emphasis on the I.'

Anne stood next to the bed. 'I.' She paused. 'Am.' Another pause. 'Going to make some toast!'

Vinny threw a pillow at her.

'Okay, look, joking aside, I think we should speak to Michael later.'

'Are you sure that's a good idea?' Vinny asked.

'Yeah, we need to see that we are all on the same page with stuff if the police come back again.'

'Yeah, fair enough. I have to see my supervisor, then there's something important I need to do.'

'Anything I can help with?' Anne asked.

'No, don't worry.' Vinny said, stretching. 'Listen, after we've met Michael, we might need to go somewhere else, okay?'

'Where?' Anne asked.

'I'll tell you later. Just make sure you've got some petrol in the car. There's something I need to find out first. Can we meet down at the Albert Dock?'

'Yeah, I guess so, but why there?'

'I will be in the Maritime Museum.'

'Okay, but you do know you're sounding really weird?'

'Just trust me.'

After Anne left for work, Vinny grabbed a pair of shorts and chose a simple white t-shirt. His Adidas trainers were looking a bit worn, but he thought they would last out the summer. He carried his bike down the stairs, double-locked the house door, and launched himself along the pavement.

The streets were busy, but Vinny relaxed and enjoyed the warm air as he dodged and weaved his way through the traffic. In no rush, he decided to go through the University campus. The pavements were harder to negotiate when he left the road. Chairs and tables were out, and groups of students sat around the main campus square. He passed the coaches bringing tourists to the cathedral and walked his bike across the lights at the busy Brownlow Hill intersection.

'Hey, we have to stop meeting like this.' Her smile was infectious. 'Do you remember?'

'Yeah, of course I do. Give me a second.' Vinny locked his bike. Straightening up, he asked, 'Justice for cleaners, right? Still going on, then?'

The smile faded as she answered, 'Yeah, right, and yeah, it is. Will you sign our petition?'

Vinny reached for the clipboard. 'Will this actually help?' he asked.

'To be honest, probably not. But it's not really about the signatures. We will try and present it to the Uni and get some publicity. It reminds people we exist.'

'What do you mean?'

'We are invisible, or might as well be. Unseen, unknown, here one day, gone the next. No one cares if we are paid the right money, get overtime, or sick pay. We could disappear, and no one would know or care what happened to us. That's why we have the union.'

Vinny signed the petition. 'Good luck!'

He started toward the steps of the building but abruptly stopped moving forward and slipped his backpack off. 'You're right, we are invisible. All of us that work, do normal jobs, we never feel important enough - our identity has been trashed and de-humanised - we spend our lives trying to be something else - identifying as something else, as if human is not enough. Sorry,' he apologized. 'Not sure where that came from.'

She smiled broadly. 'No problem.'

Vinny entered the building.

★★★

'Hi, Vinny, how are you?' Dr Sheehan asked.

'I'm okay, thanks,' Vinny said.

'Any insights, or developments with your project?'

'I'm not sure…maybe.'

'Please, I'm all ears.'

'Can I ask a question first?' Vinny said.

'Of course,' Dr Sheehan said.

'The crucifix…' His eyes turned toward the figure.

'Yes.'

'It's unusual. I don't know…there's something about it. I guess most figures of Christ you see on the cross show the crown of thorns and the wound in his side, but there is also an acceptance, maybe forgiveness. Your Christ is different - he looks hurt but angry, mad as hell.'

'It was my father's. One of the few things I have of his. I've never thought about it that way, but maybe you are right.'

'Are you religious?' Vinny asked.

'No, I'm not. I was brought up Catholic, of course, but nowadays…no, not religious. Maybe some sentimental attachment to the traditions, but that's about it. My dad brought the cross from Ireland. I don't have much of his.'

'Something you said last time stuck with me. In my project, I was kind of debating the identities of Irish, English, Scouse. You know, which was the dominant one and why. I know the explanations that all of these identities are constructed to hold us in, tie us into someone else's vision and plan. Do you mind?' He nodded toward his bag.

'Of course not,' she said.

He reached down to pull out his notebook. 'I think, as a society, there is a constant shift in the story being told. An identity is being created, and as long as the identity doesn't challenge the story of power - who has it and why - then the story is allowed and encouraged - '

Dr Sheehan interrupted, 'Okay, I'm following, but how would you explain this to your mum?'

'Not a good example,' Vinny replied.

'Okay, to a mate in the pub.'

'Maybe not everything can be explained in black and white terms,' Vinny said.

'Yes, a reasonable point, but every complex idea benefits by the attempt to explain it simply. It especially benefits the person doing the explaining.'

Vinny knew she was right.

'Okay, let me try again. Stories or histories are created, and we are surrounded by them as we grow. We get these stories from everything around us - papers, TV, even parents, and school. Eventually, we choose the story we identify with. But we are only ever told the part of the story they want us to hear. We get attached to "our" story. We believe it is a part of us, literally part of us. *We* feel it in our bones. *We* won the Second World War. *We* won the World Cup in 1966. *We* built an Empire. But ask the same person, did you make money from slavery? They would say, of course not. I wasn't even alive then! Did you support the white government in South Africa? *No*, nothing to do with me! How about the bombing of Iraq? *No*, that was Tony Blair!'

'Okay, you present it well, but these are not really new ideas.'

'I think Scouse is one of those stories. It allows us to feel special, like a comfort blanket. It's not us that invaded Iraq or cut benefits, or whatever it is. It was London, the government - '

'Can I ask?' Dr Sheehan interrupted.

'Sure,' Vinny said.

'Are you a Scouser?'

'Yes, I am, I am also English and Irish, but none of those stories are me. Because those stories I also choose to forget. It's not just what we are encouraged to identify with, but what we choose to forget. Because our storytellers choose to forget something, doesn't mean it didn't happen. If *we* won the Second World War and that is part of our identity, *we* also committed atrocities in Africa and exploited peasants in India. You can't have one without the other. You know the whole nostalgia thing, The Beatles, the '60s. I asked someone recently, do you want your country back? Meaning an earlier age. You know what he said?'

'No, go on, enlighten me.'

'He said, "no, it was shit for us then. I don't want to go back. I want to make it better."' Vinny paused for a moment. 'You know, I have been thinking a lot about *Elohim - I am* - and it kind of pulled me in. We all want to know who and what we are, where we come from. But the key is working out who *we* are. That was the thing for me, moving from "I am" to "we are."'

'Okay, and who are *we*?' asked Dr Sheehan.

'In terms of my project, I think there has been and there still is a confusion of identities. With Irish immigrants and their descendants choosing a combination of all three: English, Irish, Scouse. I was somehow trying to choose between these. I didn't need to because *we* can be any colour, any nationality. *We* are the factory workers, the seamen, the dockers, or in today's world, the Uber drivers, the call centre operatives, the zero-hour employees, the cleaners.'

'At the risk of sounding disparaging, this sounds very 20th Century collectivist,' said Dr Sheehan.

'I know, but if there is one thing this project has taught me, individual solutions can only ever work for individuals. While for the rest, things get worse and worse. What you call collectivism brought decent wages, council houses, health services. So, it's not "I am", it is "we are." "I am" leads us to define ourselves against other people. "We are" means we have to find what we have in common, and that's what we have to get back to, and it's not nationality - English or Irish, or a regional variation of it like Scouse or Geordie. Are you familiar with Matthew 25:35-40?' Vinny asked.

'Isn't that the quotation about charity?' Dr Sheehan asked.

'Yeah.' Vinny paraphrased, 'For I was hungry, sick, naked, in prison, and you did nothing. Can I read it?' he asked.

'Of course, if it helps.'

Vinny opened his notebook and began reading. '*Then the righteous will answer Him, saying, "Lord, when did we see You hungry and feed You, or thirsty and give You drink? When did we see You a stranger and take You in, or naked and clothe You? Or when did we see You sick, or in prison, and come to You?" And the King will answer and say to them, "Assuredly, I say to you, inasmuch as you did it to one of the least of these My brethren, you did it to Me."* It's not about charity, more like solidarity, or as you put it, 20th Century collectivism.'

'So, what are you saying?

'That nationality is not the important thing, and that it is breaking down anyway. "Britain", the construction that began in 1707, is collapsing around us. There were no "good old days." It was shit then, and it's shit now for most people. The ones who talk about the great past weren't working in the mines or on the docks.'

'Vinny, I think you have done some good work, and the research part of the project is going well. I think your problem is drawing out the consequences or implications. What does this mean?'

'Yeah, I think you're right, but before we know where we are going, we have to know where we came from and how we got here. My past explains me. I didn't know who I was, who or what to identify with,' Vinny said.

'And you do now?' asked Dr Sheehan.

'Yeah, I think so. This project has answered a lot of questions for me.'

'Then I am happy and look forward to seeing the results in your work.'

Vinny stood to leave. On his way out, he asked, 'Do you mind?' He nodded toward the crucifix.

Looking surprised, Dr Sheehan said, 'No, of course.'

Vinny walked across the room and patted the head of the Christ figure before leaving. A look of confusion crossed Dr Sheehan's face.

Chapter Thirty-Nine

Vinny

Anne: *We're in Pumphouse.*
Vinny: *Ok b there in 10*

He mounted his bike and coasted down the hill.

Vinny chained his bike to railings by the dock. He entered the old engine house for the Albert Dock, now transformed into a buzzing pub. The whole Albert Dock complex was high-end apartments and tourist attractions. *It is a pretty amazing structure*, Vinny thought. The brick-built warehouses were huge on a scale that's hard to comprehend until standing in front of them. Years before, tens of thousands of men moved, lifted, and shovelled where tourists now wandered and where history was sold.

He entered the pub and saw Michael and Anne. They looked okay together, like grandfather and granddaughter, a family outing. Michael could be sharing grandfatherly stories about the old days while she could be humoring an eccentric but beloved relative.

'Hey,' Vinny said, approaching the table.

Michael stood and offered his hand. 'Hello again.'

Vinny shook it. He felt no anger toward Michael now. The last few days had drained so many emotions that he felt oddly calm, settled.

'How was your meeting?' Anne asked.

Vinny and Michael both sat down.

'Good, useful.'

'Anne here has been telling me about your project. It sounds very interesting,' Michael said.

'Thanks, yeah, I hope it will be when it's finished.' Vinny looked at Anne.

'Have you been here before?' Vinny asked.

'No, but a smashing place, it is. We had a walk round before you came. All kinds of things. A lot of cheesy tat, all this Beatles and union jack stuff, but you've got to sell the tourists something, I suppose. It seems a long way from Speke and Garston, but nice to see,' Michael said.

'Why did you want to meet here?' Anne asked.

'I've been in the Maritime Museum, doing some research.'

'About...?' Anne said expectantly.

'A lot of shipping records are now held here. Have you spoken about last night?' Vinny asked, changing the subject.

'Not much. I told Michael what your mum said, but I wanted to wait for you.'

'Well, where do we start?' asked Vinny.

'Do you want to tell Vinny what the police said to you?' Anne prompted Michael.

'They knew about the yard being Jack Power's. They were asking me what we did in the old days, who I knew, and if I knew your dad. They were asking me about you two and what I had told you. It was a bit strange, all right. They were asking what I knew, not what I did, or what your dad or the Powers did. They had information, seemed to know what was what.'

'I think they have known more than us all along,' Anne added.

'Anyway, they had nothing on me because there's nothing they can have.'

'I saw you as I went in.' Anne said.

'Of course you did. They wanted you to see me. I reckon that young copper thought he could scare you. They had nothing on me. I think his plan was to put the frighteners on you. Somehow, he knew that I had talked to you. He couldn't get anything out of me, so he tried to put enough fear in you that you would tell him something.'

'More fool him,' Anne said.

'You've got a good one there, son,' Michael said.

'I know.' Vinny smiled. 'I think I've been a bit hard on you.'

'Don't worry. The kind of news you've had lately, I couldn't blame you. But it does explain why your dad was so messed up. You know, now that I think about it, it was why Jack Power was panicking.'

'Why?' asked Anne.

'They were trying to get me to help them get a crate through the docks, wanted me to speak to a mate of mine, Tommy.'

'Did you?' asked Vinny.

'No. They had no chance with Tommy. He would have told them where to go. Bullies like Jack shit themselves when they are brought into the open. They wouldn't dare go after Tommy. He had the car workers and dockers behind him.'

'So, they buried the body in the yard because they couldn't get it out through the docks,' said Anne.

'Looks that way. The night of the funeral. So, it wasn't just rumours. Jack Power really did send bodies out to sea,' Vinny said.

'Who knows? Jack wasn't daft enough to tell anyone what he was doing,' Michael said.

'Where are they now?' asked Anne. 'Jack and Charlie Power?'

'Charlie died a while back, and as for Jack, you'd be advised to leave that to the police. Although with both Paddy and Charlie gone, I can't see what they could do.'

'I think you're right. Okay, so the big question. Who is the skeleton?' asked Anne.

'Don't think you'll ever know that. He wasn't missed at the time, so I can't see anyone finding out now. No doubt there was a mother somewhere with a sore heart, but she's probably found him again now.' Michael crossed himself.

'I wouldn't be so sure. That, we'll never know,' Vinny said.

'You know something,' said Anne.

'We've got one more thing to do,' said Vinny.

Anne gave Vinny a questioning look.

Vinny handed over an address.

'Ormskirk? Who or what is in Ormskirk?'

'Come on, I'll explain it on the way. Will you be okay to get home?'

'Sure. I'll have walk along the river to Otterspool. It'll be good to see the Cazzie again. Cast Iron shore,' he added for Anne's sake.

★★★

Anne and Vinny drove north from Liverpool for about thirty minutes. The small Lancashire market town was a world away from the estates and terraced streets of the working-class areas of Liverpool.

'Nice if you can afford it,' said Anne.

'We should be close.' Vinny checked the street map. 'The next left, here.'

Anne slowed down to take the corner. She was nervous. 'Do you know what you're doing?' she asked.

'Yeah, I've got most of it worked out. We'll be fine. Straight on, it should be about halfway down,' Vinny said. 'Okay, we are here,' he announced.

Anne looked to her right to see the entrance to a large detached house. She parked in the street, and they approached the house. A carved wooden sign bore the name "The Haven."

'Not today,' Vinny said, tapping it as they walked past.

'As long as you know what you're doing,' said Anne.

'Not everything that is faced can be changed, but nothing can be changed if it is not faced.'

'Did you just make that up?' asked Anne.

'No, I wish. It's James Baldwin.'

'Well, James whoever-he-is has a point. Come on, let's do it.'

'You don't know James Baldwin?' Vinny asked.

'Later, eh? Can we sort this out? Are you not worried, though?' Ever since they left Liverpool, Anne had been torn between nervous excitement and dread.

'Nah, I think I've spent enough time doing that,' Vinny answered.

There were two cars in the drive, a black Mercedes LV 5421 and a white BMW 5 series SUV.

'That's the car,' Anne said, pointing to the Mercedes. 'The guy who grabbed me outside the pub.' Anne was starting to feel afraid. 'Vinny, shouldn't we come back with the police?'

'Didn't Dave tell you that car was stolen?' Vinny asked.

'Yeah, he did. The bastard. He must have known all along.'

'I don't think the police will be much help here. We both need to do this. I need to do this.'

They stepped up into the porch and stood before the shiny black front door. Anne breathed deeply, reached to the side, and pressed the brass doorbell. They heard the chimes ring inside.

'I hope you are right about this,' Anne said.

They heard the door lock turning.

'Well, look at who we've got here, Tweedledum and Tweedledee.'

The man who opened the door was the same one who'd warned both Anne and Vinny off. His surprise was soon replaced by a large smile.

There was a shout from inside. 'Who is it?'

'It's your favourite amateur detectives, Dad.'

'Bring them in here.'

The door opened onto a wide atrium, rooms off to either side and a central staircase - the top of which was a balcony extending either side of the staircase. Light bounced off the polished hardwood floor. The doors and frames leading to side rooms were white, which added to the feeling of light and space. They followed him through the hallway into a room towards the back.

Jack Power didn't get up. He sat slouched in a white leather armchair. His white hair, combed over to the side, sat atop a still strikingly strong-featured face, even if it was supported by a fleshy double chin. He was holding his phone and made them wait until he finished texting and placed it on the table in front of him. 'Come in, sit down. I believe you have been asking questions about me?'

He forced himself upright, shifting his body weight, and leaned forward. 'I think you have both met my son, James?'

'That arsehole sexually assaulted me,' said Anne.

'Come on now, a bit of tit? Hardly crime of the century,' said James.

'You're disgusting. Is that the only way you can get any?'

'And what's your boyfriend here got to say?' Jack asked.

'Plenty,' said Vinny.

He sat down and motioned for Anne to do the same. James sat in the second armchair opposite them. Anne noticed and enjoyed the sight of her footprints on the white carpet.

'I've been thinking a lot about you,' Vinny said.

'A lot of people do. I seem to have that effect on people.' He turned to his son. 'James, get our guests a drink.'

'I don't want anything from you,' Anne said.

'Oh, shut it, love,' Jack said sharply. 'If you don't want anything, what the fuck are you doing here?'

James went to a freestanding bar in the corner of the room.

'Yeah, do as you're told, sonny boy,' Anne said.

'Shut your mouth, b-'

'James.' Jack's bark was enough to silence James.

Anne smiled broadly.

'We've come mainly to let you know we are not scared. But also that we know who and what you are,' said Vinny.

'Okay, Mr Connolly. You want to get down to brass tacks, do you?'

James handed a Bushmills to his father and sat back down, nursing his own.

'The body in Garston,' Vinny said.

'Some fucking skeleton from thirty years ago that no one cares about?'

'You cared enough to try and stop us asking questions, using your lackey here to try and warn us off.'

'You were going round Garston asking questions about stuff that's none of your business. What did you expect?'

'You were a petty thief and a bully,' said Vinny.

'You wanna be careful, lad,' said Jack, taking a shot of his whiskey.

'Nah, I don't think so. Thanks to Anne's investigation, we know you robbed from the docks, got people to rob for you, and used the money and a bit of intimidation to get a couple of pubs, a garage, and a building firm. Your brother Charlie was actually a builder as well as a bully. At least he had some skill, unlike you. The only talent you ever had was stealing and intimidation.'

'Dad, let me…'

It took just a look from Jack to silence James this time.

'Carry on, smart-arse, let's see what you know.'

Anne was sitting back excited but also a little afraid.

'I know you hated the union,'cos like all bullies, you don't like working people sticking together. People like you leech and prey on them. So, you threatened and bullied Bob Pennington. I don't know if you were responsible for breaking his legs or not. I wouldn't put it past you. Actually, it doesn't really matter, because you would have done it if you could.'

'What the fuck is up with you?' shouted Jack. 'You think you know all about me? You little shit.' Jack started getting up. James jumped from his chair.

'I'm not done yet. Sit down! Or everything I say to you now will be all over the Internet and *The Chronicle* by tomorrow. Everything I'm saying, everything Anne has discovered, has been written down and will be delivered as a statement, to *The Chronicle*, to Merseyside Police, and published on the Internet if you try to touch a hair of either me or Anne. Now sit down, I haven't finished.'

Anne couldn't believe how Vinny was controlling them.

'You ordered the beating of Mark Riley, a twenty-two-year-old boy from Preston, a beating that went wrong. When you couldn't get his body out through the docks, you had him buried in your builders' yard.'

'Who?' Jack asked.

'What, you don't even remember his name? Come on, Jack, think back. What was it? Did he owe you money? Did he offend you? Or maybe somehow he knew you were a snitch?'

'Fuck you,' Jack snapped.

'You think you are so clever. Who killed him, hey? Who killed that kid?' Jack's voice grew louder.

'My dad,' said Vinny.

Jack looked shocked. He took another drink and slouched back in his chair.

'Yeah, I know it was my dad. You know what, Jim boy? I think I will have a drink. Water.'

'Fuck you,' James said.

'Get him a fucking drink,' said Jack.

'Water with a twist of lemon for me,' Anne said, smiling.

The air buzzed with tension. Jack sat in frustration, and James left the room looking bemused.

'As I was saying, not only do people like you prey on workers, you also give them false hope. Maybe that's what I hate you more for. People who have nothing and are not prepared to accept it. All it takes is someone like you, waving a few quid and a nice car in front of them, and they think they've got it made.

Think they can escape. Think they are one step above everyone else, not like all the other losers in the factories and docks.'

James brought the water. Vinny took a long drink.

'All right, bollocks, enough of the speeches. Your dad did it. You know it. I know it. So, what now? No one can prove a fucking thing.'

'Some people don't need proof,' Vinny said.

Anne had thought she knew all the information, but she was learning it wasn't just facts, but how you understood them. Vinny was showing how they fitted together.

'What's that supposed to mean?' Jack asked.

'How did shit for brains here know Anne was in the Noah's Ark? How did he know me and Anne were friends? How did he know where I worked? I'll tell you how. DS Dave the copper from Speke.'

'This is stupid. You're making stuff up now.' Jack tried to laugh.

It didn't convince anyone in the room; even his son was looking at him sideways.

Vinny continued. 'You were paying off Sergeant Barlow in 1965. Money in his back pocket to get stuff through the docks for you. Though things never stay the same, do they, Jack? And when you sup with the devil, don't they say you need a long spoon? Sergeant Barlow moved up through the ranks. By the mid-'70s, he was in all his power and glory, running informers, fighting the war in Ireland, using every trick in the book to get an advantage over people trying to get British troops out of Ireland. The same people you were selling guns to.'

Anne was less afraid. Jack was sweating. James was glued to what Vinny was saying.

'In the 1970s you were working for Inspector Barlow of Special Branch. The power had shifted. You weren't paying him. He was letting you carry on your thieving and intimidation as long as you were giving him information on your contacts in Ireland.'

'Were you working for the police?' James asked his father.

'Shut the fuck up,' Jack shouted. 'You little cunt.' Jack overturned the table in front of him and struggled to get up.

His age and weight were working against him.

'Sit down, fat man. You might have been a big man once, but I think you've just been handed your arse on a plate,' said Anne.

'Informing on the IRA? There are some people with long memories, eh, Jack?'

Anne stood. Vinny followed. 'If you, your halfwit son, or anyone comes anywhere near us, everything I have said will be made public, and you can take your chances. In Garston, in Wicklow, anywhere you go, people will know you are a snitch and a grass.'

Vinny and Anne heard a slow handclap coming from behind them.

'Very good, Mr Connolly. We could have used someone with your impressive analytical skills.'

Anne spun round and saw Inspector Barlow entering the room.

'Sit, please,' Barlow said.

Jack slumped back in his seat. Barlow walked over to the bar and poured himself a drink. 'What a situation we have. I think things could best be described as checkmate. Don't you?'

He looked toward Vinny although he didn't wait for an answer. 'Mr Power here is at the limit of his particular skillset. A skillset that I must add has been oxidising for some time.'

'What?' Jack Power asked.

'You're getting rusty,' Anne answered.

'Indeed, Ms McCarthy. Whereas *my* skillset, well, you wouldn't believe how, in the period of Mr Power's decline, our grasp on information has multiplied tenfold. The technology these days is unbelievable,' said Barlow.

'You knew all along, didn't you? You knew everything - who the body was, who killed him,' said Anne.

'It was and is my job to know things, but really, I am impressed. I never thought you would get this far.'

'So, you and DS Cooper were working together? You were just trying to find out what I knew? But why? What was the point? You could have just told me when I visited you. This would have been all over. I don't get it. And how did you know we were here?' Anne asked.

'Ireland,' Vinny said.

Barlow began the slow handclap again.

'You didn't give a shit about this arsehole ripping people in Garston off. Your interest was getting information on Ireland. You turned a blind eye to gun smuggling, and probably much more, just to get information in the war against the IRA. You set DS Cooper up to watch Anne. You probably ordered the dipshit here to try and scare us off. And the fat man here texted you when we arrived.'

'He did, Mr Connolly.'

'Your problem is that if anyone knew that the Special Branch, a part of the British state, knew about gun-running, not just knew, but helped, that it would be a problem. You used him,' Vinny said, pointing at Jack Power. 'You used my dad. You used everyone in your war against the IRA.'

'Very good, Mr Connolly, and do you know what else?'

'What?' asked Vinny.

'You or your little partner here won't say a word about it to anyone. Not on the Internet, not on wikishit, nothing. Do you understand?' Barlow's voice was clear and cold.

'I could –'

Barlow interrupted Anne. 'Your arse would be bounced out of *The Chronicle* so quickly you wouldn't know what hit you. You could forget ever working in journalism again. Do you understand? You would be lucky to get a job in McDonald's. Do you know what a "D" notice is, Ms McCarthy?' Barlow threatened.

'Yeah, it's an instruction by the government to the press not to report something because it would harm National Security,' Anne said.

'A recommendation,' corrected Barlow. 'A recommendation that carries the full weight of the intelligence services in the UK. Mr Connolly, at the start of a promising academic career I believe. Your father would have been so proud.'

'What?' Vinny asked.

'Your father, a good but somewhat unruly man.'

'You knew him?' Vinny asked.

'Let's say we had an arrangement.'

'You bastards…' Jack spluttered.

'Jack, c'mon now, all the time we have worked together, do you think I would ever rely on you? Just you? You know, it's quite satisfying. It's like lifting a curtain, letting the little people see the view out of the window for once. That view could be Belfast, Garston or Baghdad. Well, for this moment, enjoy the view. Because when I leave today, the curtain falls back into place, and you go back to your insignificant little lives. Do you understand me? Do you all understand me? This thing finishes here, today.' Barlow strode toward the door. 'Jack, you have the name, but make no mistake, we have the reality. Good day, Ms McCarthy and gentlemen.'

'What does that mean?' asked Anne.

'Power,' replied Vinny.

Jack slumped back in his seat. 'Get these fuckers out.' He wasn't looking at Vinny or Anne.

Vinny led the way out of the room. He opened the front door and took a large breath of fresh air. Anne was right behind him, and James was following. Vinny stepped outside. Anne turned and aimed a kick at James's groin. It landed. He doubled up. 'If you want more, come back when you can grow a moustache, arsehole.'

Anne leapt out of the door before James could recover. 'Come on, come on.' She dragged Vinny down the driveway.

'I can't believe you did that,' said Vinny.

***

Driving back to Liverpool, Anne asked, 'What do we do now?'

'I think Barlow is right. It's finished,' said Vinny.

'You think your dad was working for him?'

'It would make sense. It would explain why he disappeared. Maybe he was told to.'

'Okay, I think I get everything. You worked out the inspector was the same copper Michael had met in the docks all those years ago. But the body, how did you find out who he was?'

'My dad told my mum the guy was called Mark. Every ship that comes into Garston docks is logged when it arrives and when it leaves. All publicly available information. If a seaman doesn't go back to the ship he arrived on, jumps ship, that is recorded in the ship's log. There is also a disciplinary charge against the sailor, which is also recorded. So, there are actually two ways of finding out. These records are all available online in The Maritime Museum's archive.'

'So, that's why we were down at the Albert Dock.'

'We knew the date of the murder because it happened the day before Paul's funeral. So, I had to find what ships docked in Garston, and if any sailors jumped ship on that date. As it turned out, one did. Mark Riley. He left the ship that day and never returned.'

'Fuck me. You are good.'

'I know, and I will when we get home.'

Anne smiled. 'So, it really is all finished?'

Her phoned buzzed. She answered it. 'Hi, Mum. Get your best china out, I'm bringing my boyfriend over on Sunday.' Then she hung up.

'Hope that's okay?' Anne asked.

'Why not? You know my parents.'

'This Mark Riley? How do we deal with the police? Or his family?' Anne asked.

'I will tell them what I've found. Let them contact surviving family members, if any, to do a DNA analysis. Let the family bury him. But they are never going to get Jack on it, even if they wanted to. My guess is he has enough shit on Barlow for them both to want to keep it quiet.'

'You were great in there, by the way,' said Anne.

'You weren't so bad yourself - and that kick!' said Vinny with admiration in his voice.

'Yeah...' She smiled. 'I must admit I enjoyed that. Do you really think it's over? They won't come after us?'

'Power would shit himself if word got out that he had been an informer for years. He won't risk that. I think that's the last we'll see of him or his creepy son.'

'But the D notice means I can't write about it,' said Anne.

'Not in *The Chronicle*, anyway.'

'What do you mean?' Anne asked.

'Well, there's nothing stopping you writing a novel, changing the names.'

'*Under the Bridge*,' said Anne smiling. 'And how are you feeling?' She looked across at him.

'Mmm, it's hard to describe...wind in my sails, powering through the water.'

'Sounds good,' Anne said.

'It is. You know what, though? I think I want to go to Ireland. I need to kind of connect the parts, do you know what I mean?'

'I think so.' Anne raised a hand to smooth down his spiky hair.

'Find out what happened to my dad, or where he came from, and sort things out with Helen, so I get to see my son.'

'Mind if I come along?' asked Anne.

'Course not, as long as you don't write about it.'

'No promises,' Anne laughed.

Acknowledgements

The Liverpool Mystery Series are part family sagas, part historical novels, and of course mysteries, that cover the period from 1920s Wicklow to Liverpool in 2020.

The four novels can be read as stand-alone thrillers, but in reading all of them we get more out of each one. The first book *Under The Bridge* although set in Garston, Liverpool, has its roots in Wicklow, Ireland. It was writing the second novel, *The Morning After*, that I realised this was a series all along. I am currently writing *Fire Next Time* and *The Wicklow Boys* will follow. You can read the novels in any order, like our lives they are a moment in time, connected to what happens before and after. All the characters and events are fictional and do not relate to persons living or dead.

I would like to acknowledge the work of Bill Hunter, Sean Matgamna, and Bob Pennington all of which influenced the Garston dock scenes. For students of Liverpool History the foremost source must be various works of John Belchem. 'Scouse' by Tony Crowley is interesting and informative, for more local social history the two books by Mike Axworthy are also worth a read, and thanks to Laurence Westgaph for his work in revealing the links between Liverpool and slavery.

I am grateful to Leila Kirkconnel for advice and reading, Paul for constant criticism, and Ronan for starting me off. My thanks also go to Shari Damewood who offered early unpaid editorial help, Northodox Press for taking a chance, and Clare Coombes for charting the next steps.

Thank you for reading, *Under the Bridge*, if you enjoyed the novel please recommend it your friends and family. If you want to contact me, you can do so at Jack.byrne.writer@gmail.com and if you want to subscribe to my mailing list please visit jackbyrne.home.blog Look out for the next book in the series and we can continue our journey together.

I am always happy to hear people's stories, who knows 'yours' might be the next one I write

Jack Byrne

NORTHODOX PRESS

HOME OF NORTHERN VOICES

 FACEBOOK.COM/NORTHODOXPRESS

 TWITER.COM/NORTHODOXPRESS

 INSTAGRAM.COM/NORTHODOXPRESS

 NORTHODOX.CO.UK

SUBMISSIONS
ARE OPEN!

WRITER &
DEBUT AUTHOR   [ ]

NOVELS &
SHORT FICTION   [ ]

FROM OR LIVING   [ ]
IN THE NORTH

Printed in Great Britain
by Amazon